DESIRE

Scandalous world of the elite.

Overnight Inheritance
Rachel Bailey

Falling For The Enemy
Katherine Garbera

MILLS & BOON

OVERNIGHT INHERITANCE
© 2023 by Rachel Robinson
Philippine Copyright 2023
Australian Copyright 2023
New Zealand Copyright 2023

First Published 2023
First Australian Paperback Edition 2023
ISBN 978 1 867 29536 5

FALLING FOR THE ENEMY
© 2023 by Katherine Garbera
Philippine Copyright 2023
Australian Copyright 2023
New Zealand Copyright 2023

First Published 2023
First Australian Paperback Edition 2023
ISBN 978 1 867 29536 5

Published by
Harlequin Mills & Boon
An imprint of Harlequin Enterprises (Australia) Pty Limited
(ABN 47 001 180 918), a subsidiary of HarperCollins
Publishers Australia Pty Limited
(ABN 36 009 913 517)
Level 19, 201 Elizabeth Street
SYDNEY NSW 2000 AUSTRALIA

MIX
Paper | Supporting
responsible forestry
FSC® C001695
www.fsc.org

Cover art used by arrangement with Harlequin Books S.A.. All rights reserved.

Printed and bound in Australia by McPherson's Printing Group

Overnight Inheritance
Rachel Bailey

MILLS & BOON

Rachel Bailey lives on the Sunshine Coast, Australia, with her partner and dogs, each of whom are essential to her books: the dogs supervise the writing process (by napping on or under the desk) and her partner supplies the chocolate. She loves to hear from readers, and you can visit her at rachelbailey.com or on Facebook.

Visit the Author Profile page
at millsandboon.com.au for more titles.

You can also find Rachel Bailey on Facebook,
along with other Harlequin Desire authors,
at Facebook.com/HarlequinDesireAuthors!

Dear Reader,

If you've read *The Lost Heir* (Heath and Freya's book), you'll already know that Mae Dunstan's life was turned upside down with the revelation that she's inherited a fortune. (If you haven't read it, don't worry—it's all explained in this book from Mae's perspective.) And things are about to get even more complicated for Mae now that Sebastian Newport is on the scene.

I'm so happy to share Mae and Sebastian's book with you. There are cameos from a range of characters from *The Lost Heir*, such as Heath, Freya, Sarah and Lauren. In fact, this family has been one of my favourites to write and I'm a little sad that they won't be hanging out in my head anymore!

This is also my last Harlequin Desire book, and it's a bittersweet moment for me. Harlequin Desire has been my writing home since 2008 and it's hard to imagine not writing for the line anymore. But I'm glad that my last Desire story is Mae and Sebastian's. I hope you enjoy reading it as much as I enjoyed writing it for you.

Happy reading,

Rachel

DEDICATION

For Vassiliki Veros,
friend and fellow romance novel obsessive.

Here's to many more late-night chats
about books and all good things!

ACKNOWLEDGMENTS

Thank you to my editor, John Jacobson,
who has been amazing to work with on
these two books. You are an absolute gem!
And a huge thank-you to Barbara DeLeo and
Amanda Ashby, who are always ready with virtual
pom-poms and ideas that start with "what if..."

ONE

MAE DUNSTAN—OR MAE RUTHERFORD, as everyone at the party was calling her—stood at the soaring doors to the patio of her aunt Sarah's house in the Hamptons and sighed. Behind her was a glittering party in her honor, filled with the rich, the famous, and the beautiful, and all Mae wanted to do was escape.

In front of her was the velvety night sky and the promise of a few minutes of priceless solitude.

Before she could think better of it, or be called back, she stepped over the threshold. Each step into the backyard brought a decrease in noise and light, and, enveloped by the warm summer air, her entire body relaxed a little.

Since arriving in the US three weeks ago, her life had been a whirlwind, with people pulling her in all directions. Of course, it had been bound to happen once people found out she was a lost heir to a billion-dollar fortune, and now everyone seemed to want a piece of her, whether details, due to their morbid curiosity, or money. The fortune hunters were the worst. Men who were attempting to charm their way into her bank account by way of her DMs and then her bed.

She stepped farther into the manicured garden decorated with fairy lights and took a breath. It didn't help much. She'd barely been able to breathe since arriving from Australia. No, before then. Since her brother Heath had told her that the father they'd been hiding from for her entire life was dead and that they were now both billionaires. She still wasn't one hundred percent sure that it wasn't a mistake and someone would arrive soon to make them hand the money back. At least then her life would return to normal—the elementary school teaching job that she'd had to take leave from, the lifestyle of a small Australian town—instead of the circus it had become.

A patch of darkness along the tall, thick hedge that separated her aunt Sarah's house from the closest neighbor beckoned her with promises of peace, so she headed for its sanctuary. Once encased in the shroud of darkness, she wrapped her arms around herself and looked up at the stars that shone in the moonless sky. The angles of the constellations were different to those she'd grown up with in the southern hemisphere, but being able to see a sky full of twinkling stars was one of the few familiar things she still had.

"Party a bust, is it?"

She jumped several inches off the ground and swung around. No one was there, but leaves were rustling on the other side of the hedge.

She peered through but the foliage was too thick to see much. "Are you seriously lurking out in the bushes?"

"I could ask you the same question." The deep voice sounded amused.

She casually shrugged a shoulder, then realized he couldn't see the action. "I just needed to get some air."

"You're a fair distance from the party. I, however, am strolling along a pathway in my own yard. So tell me—" he lowered his voice "—why are you hiding from what sounds like an impressive event?"

This man was a stranger, and she was hardly going to spill the secrets of her heart to someone she couldn't even see. Even though part of her wanted to. The only person she really knew in the entire country was her brother, and Heath was wrapped up in his new fiancée, Freya. If she told him she wanted to talk, then of course he'd be there for her, but he'd spent his whole life looking out for her, working with their mother to keep them all safe, and now that he'd found happiness with Freya, Mae couldn't bear to taint that with her doubts and fears.

"I am enjoying the party. I'm just taking a moment to admire the night sky right now."

"Liar," he said softly.

Mae frowned at the hedge that separated them. "You don't know me."

"True." There was a pause and she heard the clink of ice cubes in a glass. "Which proves my point. You're talking to someone you've never met and can't even see instead of being inside at that party you say you're enjoying."

Annoyingly, he was right. "You're not there either."

"Wasn't invited," he said wryly. "Besides, I only arrived about half an hour ago."

"Arrived?" Despite herself, her curiosity was piqued. Since she'd landed on American soil, almost every conversation had been about her.

It was a relief to talk about someone else, especially someone not connected to her situation.

"From New York. I have an apartment there where I live most of the time. I'm here for the weekend." The ice cubes clinked again. "Now you know my secrets, tell me why you're out here instead of in there with the who's who of the Hamptons' social scene back in the house."

She closed her eyes for a long moment. Maybe she should. It would be a relief to say it aloud, and didn't people say that it was easier to tell your truths to a stranger...?

"I don't fit in," she said in a rush. "These people, I don't understand them." Mortified, she covered her mouth with a hand, but he didn't reply, so she dropped her hand so she could clarify. "Don't get me wrong, they all seem lovely, but I can't seem to connect with anyone."

"Ah, there's your problem. A party in the Hamptons isn't a place where you make soul-deep connections. Everyone has their guard up. Did you meet anyone famous?"

"Several." She'd been stunned into either silence or babbling several times when she'd been introduced to people she recognized from movie screens or music videos.

"Part of their mind was on whether you had a phone and were going to sell photos of them, or repeat something they said to the gossip columns, so they had their guard up. And if you met someone rich, they were waiting for the pitch."

"The pitch?" she said, drawing the word out as if that would make its meaning clear.

"How you were going to ask them for money." His tone was neutral, matter of fact. "Maybe an investment, or a donation to charity, or straight up handout."

Her mother had always told them that money didn't buy happiness. Sure, having enough for the rent and food was vital for everyone, but after that, money made things worse instead of better. "That's an awful way to live."

He coughed out a laugh. "Better than the alternative, though. Besides, you get used to it."

Mae noted that he included himself in that group, which made sense. "Which type are you? Waiting to be betrayed or waiting for requests for cash?"

Sebastian Newport's face heated at the comparison of him to the Rutherford family and their friends.

"I'm nothing like them," he said with more intensity than he had intended.

"Strange," she said in her cute Australian accent. "You have a house in the Hamptons that you're using for a weekend and an apartment in New York as well. I dare say that it's unlikely you're on the poverty line. So this conversation is either about you waiting for me to prey on you, or..."

"Or?" he prompted through a tight jaw when she didn't continue.

"Or I'm the one who should be wary of you."

"You think I arranged this meeting to prey on you?" He'd been pacing in his own backyard, trying to wind down after the rush to get out of the city and then settle his infant son, Alfie. Once Alfie was asleep, Sebastian had poured himself a generous scotch and, baby monitor in hand, walked outside. Weekends always involved a fight with himself—he hated being so far from work, and his instincts shouted that he needed to be available, weekend or not, but he'd promised his late wife that he'd find more of a work-life balance for Alfie's sake. And deathbed promises were hard to break. So, during the week, his son was primarily cared for by a live-in nanny, while Sebastian devoted himself to long days at the office, and on weekends, it was just the two of them, here, at their holiday home. The last thing he'd been thinking about when he walked out here was meeting a woman through the shrubbery.

"Maybe you didn't set this meeting up, but your own theory means that everything at parties is transactional or avoiding it becoming transactional."

He chuckled. "Touché. But you forget. I'm not at your party."

"Which puts this conversation outside your theory."

Sebastian sank his free hand deep into his trouser pocket. "It's almost outside reality."

"Sounds about right," she said, her tone dry. "My whole life is practically outside reality at the moment."

He hesitated. She might think this was an anonymous encounter, but he'd guessed her identity from her first few words. The lost heirs of the Bellavista fortune, Heath and Mae Rutherford, were all anyone in their world was talking about, and he'd heard his neighbor Sarah was hosting a party for Mae tonight. Add her Australian accent to the equation, and her confusion about how this circle of society worked, and there was no one else this could be but Mae Rutherford.

He was low-key uncomfortable that their encounter in the darkness was anonymous only on one side, but he was enjoying talking to her and wasn't sure she'd continue if she knew who he was. Her aunt and brother must not have warned her that the other major stakeholder in the company they'd inherited owned the house next door, or she'd have been wary. Hell, she'd probably have ignored him from the start. But he meant her no harm. In fact, talking to her was the most fun he'd had with another adult in a long time. She was like a breath of fresh air, and he sorely needed one of those right now.

"Why weren't you invited?" she asked. "Didn't Sarah know you'd be here for the weekend?"

He sipped his drink before replying, "There's some history." That was true, even if it was an understatement. "We generally avoid each other now. But I hear she throws excellent parties."

"It's great, but...this is going to sound stupid."

"Go on," he said, trying to sound encouraging.

"I really don't know how to enjoy myself in there. With all those people."

He remembered being in the same position when he'd started attending society parties as a teenager, and he was hit with a wave of sympathy. She'd likely hate him when she found out who he was, and there was nothing he could do about that. Until that happened, though, one thing he could do for Mae Rutherford was share the insight he'd gained as a teen.

"All those people are showing you a facade," he said. "They've worked out how they want other people and the world to see them and they've slipped that mask on before arriving. All you need to do is work out what mask you want to wear. What face do you want to show them?"

"What if I don't know the answer?" The words emerging from the hedge between them were tentative. Vulnerable.

"Maybe start with working out what you want, and go from there." He rolled his shoulders, feeling the weekday stress beginning to recede.

"You mean what I want out of *life*? That's a pretty broad question."

"True." He watched the blinking lights of a plane crossing the night sky, giving her a moment to process her thoughts. "Do you know the answer?"

"Not really," she admitted on a sigh.

He couldn't imagine not knowing something as basic as your life's direction. He'd had his entire life planned out when he was still in elementary school. Mind you, curveballs, such as his wife dying just over three years into their marriage, had made him start to wonder if he was really in charge of his own destiny after all. For now, though, he was focused on Mae.

"I'm going to suggest that you have some resources behind you if you're at one of Sarah Rutherford's parties and you have possible contacts in the other guests. What do you want from that?"

A twig snapped in the shrubs, in roughly the same place her voice was coming from. "Why do I have to want something from it?" she asked, sounding a little annoyed.

"Everyone wants something." He knew that from experience. "What's the voice in your heart whispering? Fame? Power? Influence?"

She was silent for so long that he began to wonder if she'd left. Then she said, softly, "To make the world a better place."

He almost snorted in disbelief but thankfully

caught it in time on the off chance she was serious. Did people like that really exist? People filled with hope and goodness?

"There's a lot of things that aren't great in the world," he said, probing. "What, specifically, would you like to make better?"

"I'd like to help children. And mothers who are trying to protect them."

The simple sentiment hit him hard in the solar plexus, and he practically staggered with the weight of it. Everyone knew that her father, Joseph Rutherford, had been a terrible human being, and many suspected that his wife had run to protect their little boy, Heath. Heath had reappeared on the scene a few months ago, and it was later revealed that he was a package deal with Mae. Their father hadn't known of her existence, which meant her mother had to have escaped once she knew she was pregnant. Sebastian's own father—and Joseph Rutherford's business partner—wasn't someone he thought of fondly, but he'd been an angel compared to Joseph. Mae's mother had probably done the right thing by running far, far away, and, as a parent himself, he respected her choice.

"That's," he began but had to stop and clear his throat. "That's a good idea. If it's what you want to do, then slip on the mask of someone who can get it done and head back inside."

He heard a long intake of breath and could imagine her straightening her spine and getting her game face on.

"Thank you. I'm ready." There was a crunch of leaves, as if she'd taken a step. "Nice to meet you, shadow man."

He waited until her steps faded, then whispered, "Likewise, Mae."

Mae felt taller, surer. She'd left the party less than half an hour earlier, wanting to be as far from the people and their world as she could. One conversation with the stranger next door and she felt different, and was reentering the party with a sense of purpose. She began to talk to the people she met about their passions and what charity work they did, feeling her way and looking for clues of what she could do with these new connections.

She wasn't staying in the US forever—she'd spent most of her life in Australia and thought of it as home—but while she was here, she could do something to help women who were in a similar position to the one her mother had found herself in when she realized she was preg-nant with her.

Aunt Sarah approached from the champagne bar, the skirt of her turquoise dress swirling around her knees. "You seem different than the last time I saw you." She smiled, and her kind eyes crinkled at the corners. "Less like a startled bird."

Mae chuckled. She really did like Sarah. "I just had an interesting conversation with your neighbor."

Sarah stilled. "Which neighbor?"

"The one over the hedge there," she said, pointing.

Her aunt swore under her breath and Mae was momentarily surprised. She'd obviously only seen Sarah on her best behavior in the few weeks she'd known her. Then she regis-tered that Sarah's expression was stormy too. Shadow Man had said there was some history between them and that they avoided each other when they could.

Mae lifted her hands, palms out, placating. "I'm not sure what the problem is between you, but he was really lovely to me tonight. Gave me some good advice too."

Her aunt's eyes narrowed. "I'll just bet he did."

"Okay, what am I missing?" This seemed like an overreaction for neighbors who didn't see eye to eye.

Sarah glanced around, then beckoned her to follow until they reached a secluded corner on the other side of the kitchen. "I was planning on letting you settle in a bit longer before plunging you into meetings with the lawyers and accountants to explain your inheritance to you. But for now, how much has Heath told you about what your father left in trust?"

"We haven't had much time to talk in detail yet. Just that after our father died, most of his wealth was left for Heath, and you've been the executor, overseeing it in the meantime. And that once you and Freya found him and proved his identity with the DNA tests, he split the money fifty-fifty with me."

"That's the story of the money," Sarah said, inclining her head in acknowledgement, "but do you know anything about the composition of the estate?"

Mae thought about conversations she'd had with Heath and came up empty-handed. She really should have asked more questions. "Not really."

"Okay, here's a quick overview. You've both

inherited a portfolio that contains cash, bonds, and investments. But the main component is stock in a property development company that my father, your grandfather, and his business partner started—Rutherford and Newport. That company passed to their sons—your father, Joseph Rutherford, as well as Christopher Newport. They ran it together for many years, despite disliking each other intensely. They both tried to buy the other out several times, but neither would sell. When your father died and we couldn't find Heath and didn't know about you, Christopher thought he'd won. But I refused to sell the stock and, instead, employed a team to work in the company, to keep the business going and keep the seat warm for Heath, and now for you too."

Mae gave Sarah a spontaneous hug. "I can't believe you kept the faith all that time that you'd find him."

"I never gave up hope." Sarah reached out and cupped Mae's cheek. "And then finding you was such a special bonus."

The touch, the boundless love, reminded her of her mother's love for her, and she found herself smiling. "So what does all this have to do with your neighbor?"

Sarah flicked a glance at the window that faced her neighbor's property, appearing lost in thought for a long moment. "That man is Christopher's son, Sebastian Newport. Christopher is in the process of retiring, and Sebastian has stepped up to take over most of Christopher's duties. So the man who 'gave you good advice' has a vested interest in any decision you make."

Mae's heart stuttered and her stomach sank before she remembered something crucial. "I didn't tell him who I was. I could have been any guest at the party."

"Mae," Sarah said kindly. "How many guests here tonight do you suppose have an Australian accent? And don't doubt that he has a thick dossier on his desk covering every detail about your life that his investigators have been able to glean so far. He would have known exactly who you were."

Mae's chest filled with heat and anger. "Sonofabitch."

"Yeah," Sarah said and handed her a glass of champagne.

TWO

SEBASTIAN NEWPORT LEANED back against the marble kitchen counter as he threw back his second coffee of the morning and prayed it kicked in before his son woke. Thankfully, Alfie had always been a good sleeper, unlike Sebastian.

Of course, it hadn't helped that he'd stayed awake for hours last night, replaying the conversation with Mae Rutherford in his head. He'd tried hard to marry the image of her from the photos in his dossier with the captivating voice he'd heard through the shrubbery but hadn't been able to quite make it click. Last night, she'd been wary and uncertain in a new world. The pictures—private investigator photos in which she hadn't been looking at the camera— had shown a smiling, confident woman. And he couldn't help but want to know more.

The faint tune of his front doorbell sounded,

and he instinctively stiffened in case it woke Alfie. He'd changed the shrill buzzing to a gentle classical-music-inspired sound, and had set the volume to low, but he still waited a beat, listening to the baby monitor, just in case. When there were no stirring sounds from the nursery upstairs, he slid the monitor into his pocket, shoved off the counter, and headed for the front door.

With one hand wrapped around his coffee mug, he unlocked the door with the other and swung it open to reveal the woman he'd just been thinking about. He blinked, wondering if it really was her or he was being too quick to judge. But the long, dark, wavy hair, piercing gray eyes, and dimples gave her away. And the clincher was how much she looked like her aunt. This was Mae Rutherford.

She wasn't smiling, happy and bright, like in the photos. She wasn't smiling at all. Her almond-shaped eyes gave the impression of gathered storm clouds, ready to break and rain down mayhem.

"Do you know who I am?" she asked, before he could say anything.

"Hello, Mae."

"How do you know?" A frown dug across her forehead.

"As I'm sure you've guessed, I recognize you from photos. Though I have to say, they don't do you justice." The photos were, well, flat. This woman before him was so full of emotion and intensity that it was spilling out around her, as if he'd be able to feel it if he reached his hand out to the air near her face or arms. And damn if he didn't want to try...

"When did you first know it was me?"

Ah. "I guessed it was you last night, if that's what you're asking."

She tipped her head to the side, so her hair swung across her shoulder. "Did you know the whole time?"

"Pretty much. Your accent is rare here, so I put two and two together."

She folded her arms tightly under her breasts. "Why didn't you tell me? Why let me think our talk was anonymous?"

He shifted his weight to his other foot. He'd asked himself the same question while lying in bed last night. "I was relatively sure you would have walked away, and I was enjoying our chat."

She didn't speak for a moment, just held his gaze with sparking eyes, nodding slowly. "So,

the advice you gave me last night. It's starting to seem that it was more like manipulation
than advice."

He winced. That was a fair conclusion, and
one he would have drawn himself had their
roles been reversed. And yet...

"It might seem that way to you now, but I
treated our conversation last night in the spirit
of two strangers meeting through shrubbery. I
gave you the same advice I would have given
anyone in that situation."

"You'll excuse my incredulity."

The stirrings of a smile pulled at his lips,
but he managed to keep it from forming. "If
it helps, it's not the same advice I'd give this
morning, to your face."

She narrowed her eyes. "I know I'm going to
regret this, but, what's your advice this morning?"

"Sell to me."

"Sell to you?"

"Sell me your family's half of Bellavista Holdings. We both know you're out of your depth,
so sell it to me and walk away with a very large
bag of cash."

"Did you just call me dumb?"

"Absolutely not. I wouldn't know anything

about teaching school, but it's something you trained to do. I've been training my whole life for *this*. So, sell to me."

"First of all, this is preemptive. Heath and I don't even own it yet. The legalities are still being sorted out. But even so, what makes you think I'd want to sell a company I'd only just inherited? Especially to you, when there's so much history with my family."

"Because I was there, talking to you last night, and you don't want to run a business. But the money you'd make on the sale, well, that could be put to all sorts of good purposes."

"What I do or do not want is—"

Sebastian held up a hand as faint noises came through the baby monitor in his pocket. Not crying, just the sounds of Alfie waking up. The crying would start soon, though.

"Nice meeting you, Mae. I have to go," he said and moved to close the door.

"We are not done," she said.

"True," he said. "We'll continue this another time. Right now, I need to go."

"You do not get to walk away, just because I caught you out—"

Alfie's vocalizations were changing, as if he were working himself up to a cry. "Look, if you're not done, then fine, but I really have to go. You're free to stay or leave, but either way, shut the front door behind you."

He turned and headed for the stairs, taking them two at a time, just as Alfie's wail exploded through the baby monitor.

Mae stood on the threshold and watched Sebastian's retreating back, not really sure what had just happened. She'd been primed for a confrontation—had lain awake most of the night planning for one—and been determined to get some answers. But she hadn't gotten far before he'd…left. And had that been a baby's cry? The sound had been muffled and faint, but it had sounded like a baby.

She frowned as Sebastian disappeared around a corner upstairs. Then she glanced over her shoulder at the border to Sarah's place next door. The sensible thing to do would be to pull the door shut and head back to Sarah's. But then, no one had ever accused her of being sensible.

Besides, Sebastian had invited her in. Sort of.

Feeling a little like she was trespassing, she closed the door and followed him up the stairs. The house had the air of slightly faded opu-

lence, with its heavy wooden furniture, thick
rugs, and expensive drapes, as if the place had
been tastefully decorated many years earlier but
not been updated. Huge portraits in gilt frames
filled the walls, and elaborate light fittings hung
from the center of the rooms on either side of
her. Mae might have been staying with Sarah
for a few weeks already—both here and at her
New York City apartment—but she was still
adjusting to the realization that people really
lived like this.

At the top of the staircase, she turned left—
where Sebastian had disappeared from sight—
but all she found was an empty hall. Pausing,
she heard low murmurs, so she followed the
sound to the first door on the right.

Inside was a nursery, and unlike the other
parts of the house she'd seen, this one was newly
decorated. Fresh mint-green walls, buttercup-
yellow checked drapes, and matching bedding.
It felt bright. Happy. She stepped inside in time
to see Sebastian reach into a crib and lift out a
toddler, maybe eighteen months old, maybe a
bit younger.

Transfixed, she watched as he laid the baby
on a changing table, smiling down at him.
Then, with one square, tan hand on the baby

to keep him safe, he reached with the other to a cabinet above the table for a diaper. The movement showcased his strong, broad shoulders, and she was momentarily distracted. He murmured to the baby as he worked, changing the diaper in economical movements.

He glanced up, seeming to notice her for the first time, and she fought the instinct to shrink back behind the door. The moment seemed too private, too intimate to be observed by a stranger. But Sebastian wasn't angry.

"Meet Alfie," he said and lifted the baby again, holding him to his chest, high enough that their faces were side by side. The intensity of two sets of ocean-blue eyes was startling. Alfie had long lashes and his T-shirt had ridden up to show some adorable, chubby baby belly.

Damn, he didn't play fair. She'd been all worked up and annoyed at him when she'd arrived, and now the wind was totally taken out of her sails. First, when she'd seen him, and his masculine beauty had hit her square in the gut, and, after she had recovered from that, with the realization that his baby was a cherub.

"Hi, Alfie." She waggled her fingers at him. "How old is he?"

"Fourteen months," Sebastian said and tickled his son's belly. "You're getting big, aren't you?" Alfie gurgled in agreement.

"Come on," he said to her. "Alfie is hungry."

"Sure," she said, with no real idea what she was agreeing to.

Sebastian turned for the door, swiping a plush toy elephant from the crib on the way out.

She followed them down to the kitchen and waited while Sebastian settled Alfie into a high chair. This morning was quickly becoming surreal. She'd come over to his place to confront him, maybe yell a bit to get it off her chest, but here she was, standing in a kitchen, watching him with a darling baby.

"I prepped a fruit platter for him earlier, but you're welcome to coffee instead."

"Is his mother still asleep?" she asked, then realized how inappropriate the question was. Did he even have a ring on?

"It's just the two of us," Sebastian said with a shrug that looked practiced. "Isn't it, Alfie?"

"You're divorced?" she asked, unsure why she was pushing the point.

"Widowed." He didn't look up as he slipped a bib over Alfie's head and laid the plate on the high chair's tray.

Her heart clenched tight. "Sorry. I shouldn't have pried."

"It's okay. You're hardly the first person to ask. We get that question a lot," he said, finally looking up. There were those eyes again. Ocean blue and too magnetic for her peace of mind. She needed to focus.

She had a million questions—how did he run Bellavista Holdings when he was a single parent to a baby?—but she didn't know him well enough to ask.

"Okay, I'm ready," he said, squaring his shoulders.

"For what?" she asked warily.

"You said at the door that we weren't done, and I said it would have to wait. You can continue now."

"Oh, right." It seemed wrong to be cranky at a man in front of his infant son, so she said, "You know, I'm still getting my head around our family connection. Sarah told me that your grandfather built this place at the same time my grandfather built the one next door."

He blew out a breath and nodded. "They were best friends. They'd hoped the connections would travel down the generations, but, as you know, it wasn't to be."

"Did you know your grandfather?" She watched Alfie concentrate as he picked up a blueberry and popped it into his rosebud mouth.

"I knew my grandparents well." A smile flitted across his face. "And yours. My own parents didn't like having me underfoot and would send me up here to stay as often as they could."

"I'm sorry—that must have been rough." To have your own parents not want you must be an awful feeling. She might not have had any contact with her father, but that was a completely different thing to growing up with a parent who didn't want you around. Her mother had spent time with her and Heath every chance she got.

"It wasn't so bad." His eyes had a faraway look for a long moment. "I much preferred being here with Nan and Pop. If it had been up to me, I'd have grown up with them."

"Does your father spend time here now?"

"Here?" He handed Alfie a sippy cup. "Never sets foot in the place. Too far from the bright lights and easy convenience of city living. Besides, the house is mine—Pop left it to me—and my father likes to be in places where he rules the roost."

Alfie finished his fruit platter and waved his

arms in the air. Sebastian wiped them over with a damp cloth and then lifted his son out of the chair and held him against his well-muscled chest. Again, she had to remind herself to focus on the issue at hand.

"I have to tell you, Sebastian," she said, leaning back, "you seem to be volunteering a lot of information for a business rival."

He coughed out a laugh. "I'd hardly call it *volunteering*. You're asking a lot of questions. I'm just trying to answer them."

"Unless," she said, undeterred, "this is all calculated. You're trying to give the appearance of transparency, while hiding the real secrets deep."

"Or—" he raised an eyebrow pointedly "—I have nothing to hide."

"That's what you want me to believe."

"Because it's the truth," he said as Alfie patted his cheek—a pale hand against his father's olive skin.

She regarded him for a long moment. "I'm going to work this out, Sebastian Newport. Work *you* out."

He grinned. "You know, I think you meant that as a threat, but I'm strangely looking forward to it."

★ ★ ★

Mae walked down Sebastian's driveway, then back up the path to Sarah's house—no way to cut through between these houses. A thick hedge ran the full length of the border, ensuring that no one accidentally had to see anyone from the other's house. Two houses, built side by side by best friends, now divided by an impenetrable tangle of leafy shrubs—the symbolism was not lost on her.

As the house came into sight, she saw Sarah's driver and all-round right hand, Lauren, depositing a couple of bags into the trunk of her aunt's black Suburban and waved.

Lauren called out, "Heading back to Manhattan in about twenty minutes, Mae," and went back inside.

Heath appeared with a backpack and smiled when he caught sight of her. "You missed breakfast."

"I'll grab something to eat in the car," she said, still distracted by her conversation with Sebastian.

He slid the backpack into the trunk alongside the other bags, then turned and leaned back against it. "Did you take a walk?"

She glanced at the hedge. "Went next door to talk to our neighbor."

"Newport?" Heath was suddenly alert.

Given that she and her brother jointly owned the share in Bellavista Holdings, she should have checked with him first. But facing Sebastian was something she'd had to do alone. "We sort of met last night and I needed to ask him something."

"Get any answers?"

"Not really." She dug her hands in her pockets. "Did you know he has a baby?"

He screwed up his face in thought. "Don't think I did." He surveyed her face and frowned. "Don't you go softening toward him just because he has a kid. It doesn't take morals to pro-create—just look at our own father. It means nothing."

Mae nodded. He was right, but... There was something about the way that Sebastian had smiled at Alfie and cared for him that had raised questions in her mind. Their father might have produced children, but from all accounts, he hadn't been caring to them.

She rolled her shoulders, searching for perspective. "What do you know about Sebastian?"

"Not a lot, personally." He shrugged. "I only

met him a couple of times, and the best thing I can say about him is that he's better than his father."

And they both knew that counted for nothing. "Ethical? Transparent?"

"Well, I trust him about as far as I can throw him, and he's a fairly big man."

She snorted. "So no trust at all. But how many people have we trusted in our lives anyway? Adding Sarah and Freya into our circle of trust in the same year must be a record for us."

He winced and then shoved his fingers through his dark blond hair. "Freya says that I'm hypervigilant, because of our upbringing. She says it's a trauma response."

That made a lot of sense. Some of her earliest memories were about realizing that her responses to things were different than those of other kids. "It kept us safe, though."

"That's exactly what I said to her." He grinned.

The lack of trust was usually something they reserved for other people, but when Heath had found out about their inheritance, and about their father's identity, he'd kept it a secret from her. Mae understood his need to investigate before exposing her to risk, but it still stung. She'd let it go at some point, but she wasn't ready to do that yet.

"So," she said, digging her hands into her pockets, "using your power of hypervigilance, tell me more about your impressions of Sebastian Newport."

"When I went into the office to look around, he tried a pretty basic divide-and-conquer move—tried to get me away from Sarah and Freya to talk alone. I didn't fall for it."

She shifted her weight to the other foot. "Did you find out what he wanted to say to you alone?"

"Oh, yeah," he said, nodding. "To talk me into selling my half of the company to him."

Mae sucked in her bottom lip. It was the same thing he'd asked her. "Were you tempted?"

"To be honest, selling would be the easy option."

"But...?"

"At the time, you didn't know about the inheritance and it wasn't my decision alone, not to mention, it wasn't then—and still isn't—in our names. Besides—" he crossed his arms, seeming less certain now "—it seemed like it was something we should think about."

Mae waited a beat. She knew her brother, and

there was something else, something deeper, here. "Think about what? As Sebastian says, we don't know anything about property development."

"It was something our grandfather built. His life's work."

She rocked back on her heels. That was not the answer she'd been expecting. "We can't keep a huge company out of nostalgia, Heath."

"I get that. But we owe it to ourselves, and everyone whose livelihood depends on the company, to at least think it through first. I realized during my visit to the office that walking in and upending things without a thought to the people it employs, is something our father would have done."

A cold shiver raced across her skin. That one line affected her more than anything else he could have said. "Do you have a plan?"

"It's on my list of things to do," he admitted. "I'm still getting my head around the investments and the whole portfolio."

"Now that I'm here, I can help with that." Through his will, their father had left everything to the only child he'd known about— Heath—but her brother was sharing it with her fifty-fifty, and she needed to step up to the plate.

"That would be great. To start, Freya and Sarah have given me a mountain of reports to read, and we need to visit the businesses we own or have shares in."

"Ugh. Reports? That sounds like homework, and I'm normally the one who gives homework to other people." She was joking and he chuckled, but there was a kernel of truth to her statement. All those business reports were completely outside her wheelhouse.

"There's a charitable trust that looks more your style. Maybe start with that—read up, visit whoever is overseeing it, whatever—to ease your way in. Then dive into the other stuff once you're up to speed."

Mae took a breath and tried not to feel overwhelmed. She looked back up at Sarah's house and scuffed her foot on the gravel drive. "Do you think Sarah would mind if I stayed a few extra days?"

He frowned. "Alone?"

"I just need to catch my breath." The thought of heading back to Manhattan made her head hurt, with the noise and the bustle and the people expecting things of her that she wasn't sure she could deliver. "I could join you in a couple of days."

"I'm sure she'll be fine with it, as long as you're back for Friday night."

A small family dinner to celebrate Heath and Freya's engagement was planned for Friday. Of course, she knew that her idea of a small family dinner and Sarah's would be vastly different, but she was looking forward to raising a glass to her brother and his new love. "I wouldn't miss it. Besides, I was planning on dropping over to see Mum's family one night this week, so I'll come back before Friday."

"That's a good idea. If Lauren can't come back and get you, I'll come out on the bike and pick you up."

He opened his arms and she stepped into a bear hug. Since their mother had passed, Heath was the only person in the world she truly trusted, and she was grateful they were in this together. "Love you," she murmured.

"Love you more," he said.

THREE

LATER THAT AFTERNOON, Sebastian adjusted Alfie on his hip, and knocked on Sarah Rutherford's front door. He hadn't been here since he was a child—back when he'd stay with his grandparents, and they'd bring him over to see their friends. After that generation had all passed, the invisible walls had gone up and any connection between the families had dissolved. In fact, more than that, his father and Joseph Rutherford had become archenemies, and the distance hadn't improved since Joseph's death.

The door opened and Mae stood there, her storm-gray eyes wide, her hair pulled back in a ponytail. The air whooshed out of his lungs. Some people might not call her beautiful—her thin features were a little too severe to meet traditional beauty standards—but what were standards worth with a woman like Mae Dunstan? There was so much vivacious life emanating from her every pore that she glowed. And he couldn't look away.

She didn't speak, perhaps surprised to see him again this soon, and his lungs had stopped working, so he simply stood, drinking her in. Until Alfie squirmed in his arms and broke the spell.

Seb cleared his throat. "I was wondering if we could have a word. Maybe alone."

"That figures," she said, crossing her arms under her breasts. "I heard you like the divide-and-conquer strategy."

"What?" He'd been hoping to avoid a confrontation with the whole family while he had Alfie with him. Babies his age should be protected from tension. "No, I just—"

She waved a hand. "The others left a couple of hours ago."

"You stayed behind without them?" He frowned. She was new in the country, which made it surprising that they had left her out here alone.

She arched one eyebrow. "Wasn't aware I needed your permission."

He readjusted Alfie in his arms. This wasn't going the way he'd hoped. When Mae had left his place earlier, he'd thought they had something of an understanding, but her guard was up again. "Can we start again? I've come to make you an offer."

She nodded, her expression unchanging. "To buy the company from us."

"Not this time. Though that deal is still on the table if you've changed your mind."

"We haven't, but okay, then," she said, her tone challenging. "What's your offer?"

He did his best to look as professional as he could while standing uninvited on the stoop of his family's nemesis, his hair mussed in the breeze, wearing casual clothes, and carrying a baby. "Come into the office and shadow me for a week."

Mae's eyes narrowed. "Shadow you?"

"You can see the company from the inside, and you'll see that I'm not trying to do anything underhanded."

"Is this another version of divide and conquer? Get me on my own and bamboozle me."

Mae Dunstan really was the most skeptical person he'd ever met. He liked that about her. "It just seems like the fastest way to cut through all the suspicion and speculation."

"What would shadowing entail, exactly?"

"You'd sit in on meetings and appointments.

I'll have calls on speaker, and you can read anything I work on." It might be weird and awkward at times, but she and her brother owned half the business, which would make it easy enough to explain her presence.

"If you're hiding something, wouldn't you just plan that only things you're willing for me to see would be on your schedule for that week?"

Alfie began to fuss, so Seb pulled the plush elephant from his pocket and handed it to him. "You're smart," he said to Mae. "You'll work out if I'm trying to defer appointments to the next week or not taking calls from certain people."

Mae watched Alfie for a beat, then looked back to him. "What sort of access to information do I get?"

She was wavering. He gave her the most charming of his smiles. "You can ask me anything, and I promise to share as much information as I have. Also, you can ask the rest of the staff anything and have free access to all files."

In fact, the more she asked, and the more understanding she gained of the business, the faster she'd realize she was out of her depth and agree to sell the company to him. He'd answer every question she had, and then some. Drown her in answers. She expected him to be underhanded, but there was no need to be when the truth would do a better job.

"What do you get out of it?" she asked, her chin tipping up.

He met her gaze squarely and answered sincerely. "I'm hoping you'll find that, not only do I have nothing to hide, but once the veil is ripped away, you'll see that property development isn't the most exciting line of work. I predict that, at the end of the week, you'll be more inclined to sell to me."

She pressed her lips together and a dimple appeared on her cheek. Then she nodded. "Okay, I accept. But just so you know, it's only because I want to see what you're up to."

"You're not very trusting," he said, trying not to grin and failing.

She shrugged. "Family trait. When do you want to do it?"

"Whenever you have time is fine by me."

"This week?" She tucked some strands of flyaway hair that had escaped her ponytail behind her ear.

"Sure." He'd see if his assistant could reschedule his Monday morning to give him some time to bring Mae up to speed, but since that was the only change he'd make to his week, the timing didn't matter much. "When are you headed back?"

She chewed on her bottom lip before replying, "I don't have a firm plan yet. As I said, the others already left."

"You're welcome to travel back with Alfie and me," he said. Alfie usually slept most of the way, and it would be an early start to the plan to overload her with the honest reality of the company. "I'll be driving back tomorrow afternoon."

She regarded him for a long moment, then nodded. "Okay."

"Great." Sebastian let out a long breath. He'd achieved his goal, but part of him wondered if Mae had somehow gained the upper hand.

Mae fiddled with the seat belt in Sebastian's SUV. Alfie had fallen asleep within minutes of leaving, and she and Sebastian had made polite small talk, but her tolerance for chitchat was low, and she'd about reached her limit. Especially since sitting this close to him was making her restless. His woodsy cologne was drifting across the confined space, filling her senses, and every time he checked his mirrors before overtaking a car, or his hand moved to activate his turn signal, he seemed even closer and her skin buzzed.

For the past day and a half, she'd drifted around Sarah's weekend home, thinking about Sebastian and the coming week. With no one there to distract her, she'd thought about him more than she otherwise would have. A couple of video calls to friends back home in Australia had diverted her attention for short periods, but her thoughts always returned to this man beside her. To the fall of his wavy hair over his forehead. The way his lips moved as he talked, shaping themselves around the words, or pulling out into a smile. The warmth that bloomed under her skin every time he fixed those blue, blue eyes on hers.

But an alarm at the back of her brain had been sounding since he'd made his offer. No, before that. It had probably started when she confronted him at his front door and he hadn't reacted as she'd expected.

Don't form a crush on Sebastian Newport.

Her life had been turned upside down—she was in a new country, staying with family she hadn't known existed a few months ago, had inherited more money than she could have imagined, and she had no idea what she was doing. This was the very worst time to develop a crush on anyone, but the person who seemed to be at the center of so much of it? The person Sarah and Heath both told her was the enemy? Yeah, he'd be a stupid person to crush on.

If only her heart didn't beat a little faster every time he was near...

"When does our deal kick in?" she blurted out, needing to stop her thought spiral.

"The shadowing?" He glanced at the rearview mirror, then back to the road. "I get into the office at about eight tomorrow, so whenever you arrive after that."

She was looking forward to that. Heath had already visited the office, and now she wanted a turn to visit it on her own, to look around and form her own opinions. "What about the questions? You said I could ask anything."

"We have a drive ahead of us, and we may as well use that time constructively, so I'm happy to answer questions now, if that's what you're asking."

Now that he'd agreed, she hesitated. There was something she really wanted to ask, but didn't know if it was too personal. Heath always said she pushed too far, but... What the heck. He could always tell her to mind her own business.

"Tell me the story about your wife and Alfie."

He threw her a sharp glance. "I meant ask me anything about the company."

She knew that's what he'd meant, but she was determined to understand what made him tick, and to do that, she needed to see him from all sides. "This is relevant to the company. I'm interested in how a single father to a baby is able to run a company of this size. This question is for context."

He shrugged one shoulder. "Okay, I'll allow it, but only in the spirit of complete transparency."

"Your commitment to the cause is noted," she said with mock seriousness.

As he smiled, his eyes crinkled at the corners, and then his expression changed, becoming nostalgic. "Ashley and I met when we were kids. Her parents knew mine, which meant we crossed paths occasionally, but they lived in Upstate New York, so not enough that we grew up together. By the time we were in our late teens, everyone around us had decided that we should be together. We liked each other and had a lot in common." He shrugged. "It seemed like a good idea at the time, so we started dating, and then I proposed."

"That doesn't sound like a love story for the ages," she said, then bit down on her lip. Insulting the man's marriage probably wasn't the best start to working together for a week.

"It might not have been a great, passionate affair to start with, but we grew to love each other. Ash was a great partner to have by my side, and she was an excellent mother." He glanced at the back seat in his rearview mirror. "For the time they had together."

"How long did they have?" Watching his profile, she saw his jaw tense.

"Almost five months."

"What happened?" she asked, her voice just above a whisper.

"Cancer." He swallowed hard, his Adam's apple moving down in the strong column of his throat. "She had treatment, but it was aggressive and took her fairly quickly."

The tragedy of Alfie losing his mother that young, too young to even form proper memories, made her chest ache. "You've been raising Alfie on your own since then?"

"Pretty much. My mother isn't on the scene,

and I wouldn't let my father near Alfie even if he was interested. Ashley's parents are great, but they're upstate. They try to see him regularly, and we visit them as much as I can manage."

For a couple of minutes, she just watched the road, absorbing it all. Though she was watching him out of the corner of her eye too. She suspected he wouldn't appreciate it if she stared at him, but she'd been raised by a single parent who'd had no support. She knew how big a job it was, and he was running a huge, complex company as well.

"How *do* you manage?" she finally asked.

"I'm lucky," he said with a rueful smile. "I have a live-in nanny who does a lot of the day-to-day care while I'm at work."

That *was* lucky—most single parents couldn't afford a full-time nanny. Though he'd just parented solo all weekend.

"You didn't bring the nanny to the Hamptons?"

He rolled his shoulders back, stretching, then relaxed his grip on the wheel again. "When Ashley," he began, but his voice rasped, so he cleared his throat. "When Ashley knew she wasn't getting better, she made me promise a bunch of things. One of them was that I'd find

some sort of balance between work and parent-
hood, for Alfie's sake. I have the nanny for the
weekdays and I try to get up to the Hamptons
on the weekends where it's just the two of us. I
don't always manage it, but I'm doing my best."

Mae sat back in her seat. That had been a
whole lot more honesty than she'd expected.
"You weren't joking that you'd answer anything."

"I'm an open book." He rubbed a hand
around the back of his neck before putting it
back on the steering wheel. "Actually, that's
not true. Normally, I hate sharing private information."

"So this is all in aid of being able to buy the
company off me?"

"Yes," he said. "No, not only that. There's
something weirdly honest between us. I think
it's from the way we met. It was like we were in
a little bubble, apart from the world that night."

"You knew who I was, though," she pointed
out, still not quite ready to let that go.

"I did, but it still felt…different. You don't
believe me, which is fine, but I was being honest with my advice in that conversation."

She thought about what he'd said back then,
his voice surrounding her in the inky-black

night, and had to admit that he was right. It had felt different to any other conversation she'd had in her life. Chances were that he was conning her to get complete control of the company, but she had to admit one other thing too...

Listening to his deep, smooth voice through the hedge on a moonless night was the real moment she'd started developing a crush on Sebastian Newport.

FOUR

THE NEXT DAY, Mae stepped out of the elevator into the reception area of Bellavista Holdings. She'd left early and walked to get her bearings, but five minutes into the walk, she'd regretted her decision. Not only had the streets been busy, but she had taken a wrong turn and then had to hurry so she wasn't late, and now she was hot and rumpled.

She didn't have any business clothes, so she had borrowed a pantsuit from Sarah, and it was scratchy and a little too loose. The outfit was a long way from the linen and cotton sundresses she wore with open-toed shoes back home in Noosa.

The reception area was large, with a lot of glass and reflective surfaces. It was light, bright, and sterile. From behind a long desk, a guy wearing a headset smiled at her. "Can I help you?"

"My name is Mae, and I'm here to see Sebastian Newport."

He glanced at a screen. "Do you have an appointment?"

"Not really, but he—"

"I'm sure he did," the guy said, heavy on the condescension. "Mr. Newport has a heavy schedule, but if you'd like to take a seat, I'll see what I can do. Or you could call and make an appointment with his personal assistant."

Mae hesitated. "He really will be expecting me. If you could just—"

From her left, a woman came barreling into the reception area, hair in disarray, the bright yellow glasses on top of her head in danger of falling off. "Mae?"

"Yes?"

"I'm Rosario, Mr. Newport's PA. Did you meet Reuben?"

Mae glanced around, feeling more out of her depth by the minute. The guy at the desk raised an eyebrow. "We met briefly. She didn't have an appointment, so I was just about to call you—"

Rosario threw up a hand. "This is Mae *Rutherford*," she said, emphasis on the surname.

Reuben's eyes widened. "Oh, I'm so sorry, Ms. Rutherford. I had no idea. You'd be surprised how many people show up unannounced and ask to see the boss."

"It's fine, really—"

Rosario turned. "This way," she said over her shoulder.

Mae followed her into the elevator for a quick trip up one floor, then down a wide corridor, with offices off each side and people in each one, tapping away at keyboards, or talking into headsets. She was used to school grounds, which were similar, full of movement and noise, but they also had flow. This just felt busy, with everyone in their own spaces, disconnected and isolated.

They reached the end of the hallway and entered a large office.

"This is mine," Rosario said, "and through that door is Mr. Newport's office. You can go in."

"Thanks," Mae said and only hesitated a second before grabbing the door handle. As she entered, she caught sight of Sebastian on his cell, writing something on a notepad, talking faster than she'd heard him in all the conversations they'd had. He was clearly in control of the conversation, though the topic was beyond her, as he used words she didn't recognize in this context, his tone firm yet collegial.

She was glad one of them was in control of themselves. She was having trouble just getting air into her lungs.

When she'd seen him in the Hamptons, he'd been casually put together in shorts and T-shirts. Now, though... Now his suit was charcoal, the cut emphasizing the breadth of his shoulders and his narrow hips. The white business shirt beneath contrasted with the smooth olive of his skin, and the deep blue patterned tie at his neck sat in a perfect Windsor knot. Why did the suit make such a difference? An alarm in her brain told her that if she didn't get a proper lungful of air soon, she'd probably swoon, and that was something she didn't want to do, so she gulped in a breath.

He glanced up and saw her, and a slow smile spread across his face, changing his features from something that might be carved in marble—coolly beautiful—to something warm, appealing. She wanted to reach out her fingertips and touch...

Catching herself again, she straightened. She couldn't be sidetracked by a nice smile. She'd agreed to shadow him for a month so she could find out what was really going on in the company. Naturally, he was going to try and hide things, no matter what he'd promised. He'd made no secret of his goal to convince her to sell to him, so now she just had to see what exactly he was hiding.

She was fairly certain he was going to try to ditch her—perhaps get her to talk to other staff when he had top secret meetings, or ask her to grab coffee when he wanted to open a sensitive file. She'd keep focused and would not be swindled. Spending her days teaching young children had made her good at spotting attempts at distraction. She could dig her heels in if she had to.

She headed to the other side of the room, where a cream chaise sat under a window. The view of Manhattan was expansive. Buzzing and gray-toned, a world away from the ocean's deep blues, the white sand, and the greenery of the national park of her laid-back hometown in Queensland. Heath looked to be putting down roots here, and she couldn't imagine her life without her brother nearby. Could she get used to this view? The pace of life here?

Sebastian wound up his call and she turned as he stepped around his desk. "Mae. You're here."

"Isn't this the time we agreed to?" Had she misjudged how long it had taken to walk here?

"The time is good." He set his cell and pen on his desk. "I wasn't one hundred percent convinced you'd show."

He crossed the room and stuck out his hand. She shook it, feeling the smooth, warm skin of his palm slide across hers and then lock their hands together. Awareness skittered across her skin.

He indicated the chaise, and she perched on the edge, not wanting to get too comfortable. He took a seat at the other end and ran his fingers through his dark, wavy hair.

"I've cleared as much of this morning as I could, but since we only made this plan on the weekend, I haven't had a chance to move a meeting with some lawyers. It's starting—" he checked his watch "—well, about now, but it will be boring as all hell, so Rosario will show you around and introduce you to the staff while I'm there. After that, I have some clear time to take you through a few things."

Mae narrowed her eyes. Was he trying to have a meeting in secret within minutes of her arrival? "This deal is for shadowing you. I'll come to the meeting."

Sebastian regarded her for a minute, then shrugged. "Suit yourself."

Within minutes, Sebastian was ushering her into a large meeting room on another floor. The size of this business and the number of people working at it was impressive. They sat around a long table among a bunch of young, smug and hungry-looking men and women in matching suits—some on the same side as them and some opposite. After jovial handshakes, the meeting was suddenly underway, with all in attendance puffing up as they argued about a subclause in a contract. It was tedious. But worse was the manner in which they were arguing—if this had been her first graders, she would have stopped the meeting and spoken to them about manners, beginning with "Don't speak over the top of other people, and if you're going to ask a question, at least wait for the other person to answer."

After an eternity of listening to them, with an occasional comment from Sebastian, Mae opened her notebook and wrote: *They all need to learn constructive listening. And how to compromise.*

She slid the notebook to Sebastian, who was sitting beside her. Other people in the room were passing notes, so no one even noticed.

Sebastian read the note and smothered a smile before jumping into the conversation again by asking one of the lawyers a pointed question. A minute later, he scrawled something below her comment with his left hand and slid the notebook back, their hands brushing as he did. The light contact set off butterflies in her stomach.

They don't get paid to compromise. They get paid to win.

She watched the arguing back and forth for a few more minutes before adding another line.

This is going around and around in circles. Never been so bored.

With barely a reaction, and while seeming to not lose a moment of the lawyers' conversation, he wrote a reply and then pushed the notebook back to her.

Told you so.

This time it was her turn to squash a smile. And then she sat up straight and made more of an effort to follow the conversation. And not get too distracted by the man beside her.

By lunchtime, Seb was desperate to find his equilibrium. After the meeting with the lawyers, he'd shown Mae an empty office that she could use as her base for the week. It was only a few doors down from his, but it would have given her some territory of her own. She could have taken files in there and had some peace and quiet to read, or had privacy to meet with members of his staff. Instead, she'd banded together with Rosario—when had they become friends?—to find a small, wooden desk and move it into his office.

He stared at it, blinking. Mae had moved the chaise from under the window and put her desk there. In the middle sat a laptop, and neatly aligned to the side was an in tray, and three pens. She and Rosario had talked for a full ten minutes about pens and stationery before she'd made her selections.

From her new swivel office chair, all she had to do was turn her head sideways and she'd see the Manhattan view, but if she looked straight ahead, as she was doing now, she looked at him.

"What's next?" she asked.

His plan had been to order some lunch in and spend time running through his week with Mae. But having her at that desk, so close, making his breath catch every time he caught sight of her… He swallowed hard and tried to ignore the shiver skittering across his skin. The office was too small, too intimate and he suddenly wanted to be someplace busy, where they weren't the only two people in the room.

"Lunch," he said, standing and gathering some pages he needed to show Mae. "There's a place down the street we can go."

"Great. I'm still in sightseeing mode, so any chance to see somewhere new is good with me."

They walked to a nearby upscale restaurant, and Seb firmly told himself that he wasn't choosing it to impress her, since he occasionally had business meetings there. But he knew he was lying to himself. It had nothing to do with the business they—and their families—had together; it was just him showing off for a woman.

"Here it is," he said as they reached the tall doors, which were being opened by a man in full uniform.

Mae's gaze darted around, and then she spied a hippy place over the road. "Can we go there?"

It was a hole-in-the-wall joint that had signs out the front saying "vegetarian" and "half-price Mondays." Not somewhere he'd ever consider going. But Mae's eyes were bright with hope and his heart swelled to see it, so he said, "Sure," before he'd even thought it through.

"This is adorable," she said once they were seated.

He wasn't sure he'd call any place that served food adorable, but what he did know was that the air was stuffy, the chairs were hard, and the tables were small. Mae's dimples were showing, though, and he decided that the hard chairs were worth the sight.

After they'd ordered, he reached into a satchel he'd brought with him and laid five pieces of printed paper on the Formica tabletop.

Mae ran a finger across the top page. "What's this?"

"I had Rosario print out my schedule for the week. It will help as we discuss our plans."

She leafed through the pages. "You sure it wasn't to intimidate me?"

One corner of his mouth pulled up, and he had to fight to keep the smile at bay. That had definitely been part of it, and she'd seen right through him. He wanted her to see how busy this job was, how complicated it was, so she could just agree to sell to him. But mainly, they needed to discuss how this shadowing would work, and this seemed to be the easiest way.

"I cleared this morning to help you settle in—"

"Except for the bunch of matching lawyers all in a row that you were going to exclude me from."

"—except for the meeting with the lawyers this morning." He spread the pages across the table. "This way you can see what your options are. You can choose which meetings you attend, and what hours will be most interesting to you."

"If you're doing all of this, then I will too."

That was the response he'd been expecting, however, his load was heavy and she wouldn't last the entire week if she tried to do everything. "If you burn out within a few days, you won't get to see a proper scope of our work. It'd be better to choose the things that most interest you, and then we'll work out what to do about the rest."

Her chin tipped up. "Are you saying I couldn't handle your schedule?"

"I'm not bragging about my hours. I've been trying to scale it back ever since Ashley died and haven't got it to the level I'm comfortable with yet. Though I do leave at six o'clock each night now, which allows Alfie some consistency in his routine. Whenever possible, I get the nanny to bring him in for a visit during the day but, often, that's difficult."

"Admirable," she said, her gaze not faltering. "But teachers are no strangers to a busy schedule."

Was he missing something? There was no way a teacher would put in the hours he did. "Don't you normally work nine till three? No need to be a hero and cram everything in just because you feel you have to—there's no judgment."

"Nine until three?" she said with a snort. "We dream of those hours. After the kids go home, teachers mark assessments, do lesson planning, answer emails from parents, attend in-service training, have meetings with the school administration or other key people, etcetera, etcetera, etcetera. Plus, that work also spills into the weekend and holidays, and now with easy access email and messaging platforms, families and senior management often expect us to be available twenty-four-seven."

Their food—something called a wellness bowl for her and a simple pasta for him—arrived and he moved the pages into a stack to make room while Mae chatted with the waitress. From her flushed cheecks, it looked as though he'd touched a nerve about her teaching schedule. It must be something she had to explain a lot, and he was sorry he'd made her do it again.

Once the waitress left, he reached out and laid a hand on her arm. "I didn't realize about your hours. I was seeing it from my own point of view and didn't think to ask what hours you normally worked, which made my comments patronizing."

Her warm gray eyes widened—from the apology…or the touch of his hand? He shouldn't have done it, should remove his hand, would never normally dream of touching someone in a professional setting. Technically, she didn't work for him, and he wasn't carrying out any business with a representative from another company. No, it was much worse. She was a Rutherford, and he was potentially shooting himself in the foot by making things messy. Because things were *bound* to get messy. And yet…neither of them had moved. Her skin was soft beneath his, warm, and the pulse at the base of her throat beat fast. What would it be like to kiss her? To feel all that vitality and life in his arms? Writhing beneath him?

The intensity of the image in his mind too

much to bear, he pulled his hand back, looking down at his pasta. That was not a path he could allow his mind to take. There was too much at stake.

He cleared his throat and picked up his cutlery. "Just so we're clear, my hours are eight till six. I used to work later, but I cut back when I became a single dad."

"Noted," she said and studiously picked up the printed pages containing his schedule, avoiding eye contact. "What's this note on the lunchtime slots?"

"I've blocked out lunch with you each day." His voice was tight, but there wasn't much he could do about it. "That way, we'll have a chance for you to ask questions or debrief after meetings."

"I appreciate that." She put the pages down and picked up her spoon, still not looking at him.

He shoved a forkful of pasta into his mouth and tried his best to ignore that his body was hungrier for Mae than for food.

FIVE

MAE ARRIVED FOR her second morning of shadowing Sebastian and stopped by Rosario's desk.

"Morning," she said and held out a cup.

Rosario reached for the cup. "Morning. What's this?"

"A French vanilla cappuccino made with oat milk." Mae had listened closely yesterday when Rosario had ordered a coffee and made a mental note. "Is it too early for it?"

"No," she said with feeling and then took a sip and sighed. "It's perfect timing."

Mae smiled. For this week to go smoothly, Rosario was the key person, even if Sebastian probably thought it was him. Besides, she liked the other woman.

"Before you go in," Rosario said, tilting her head to Sebastian's office, "you should know that there's…a situation unfolding."

Mae instinctively looked across the space, but

the closed door offered no clues. "Okay, thanks for the warning."

She opened the door and poked her head around. Sebastian was standing in the middle of the room with a baby in one arm.

"Alfie!" Mae rushed over, surprised at how happy she was to see him. "How are you?"

Alfie offered a quick smile and then turned his head into his father's shoulder. Apparently, just because they'd met a couple of times didn't mean they were friends.

"Morning, Mae," Sebastian said, sounding weary. She looked from the baby up to the father, noting the dark smudges under his eyes, and olive skin a little paler than usual.

"Do you normally bring him into work? I thought it was his nanny who brought him in."

"Never on my own, or I wouldn't get work done. Emily does bring him in sometimes." He blew out a long breath. "But she got sick overnight, and I took her up to the ER. Of course it meant waking Alfie too, so we're both pretty tired. Emily has a stomach bug. The doctor suggested she have a few days away from Alfie even after she feels better to ensure she's not contagious, so we don't know how long until she can come back."

Mae stroked Alfie's chubby little arm. "What will you do?"

"I have calls in to all the agencies, but there seems to be some sort of shortage of experienced nannies. Maybe they're all enjoying the spring weather somewhere, I don't know. For today, Ashley's parents are on their way down from upstate to help. They should be here soon." Sebastian walked to the chair behind his desk and sank into it, Alfie on his lap. "I've had to clear my morning again."

Her instinct was to offer to help, but she wasn't sure exactly how. Before she could think it through, raised voices from Rosario's office floated through the doorway. "I want to see him."

"I'm afraid that's not possible," Rosario's calm, firm voice countered.

"We had an appointment this morning and I'm here." The voice sounded like that of an older man. An annoyed older man. "I want to see him. Now."

Sebastian pinched the bridge of his nose, took a deep breath, then stood, Alfie still in his arms.

"Do you want me to…?" Mae said, putting her hands out, not really sure of the best course of action.

"No, it's fine," he said and opened the door, revealing a man of about seventy wearing a tweed coat. "Mr. Sheridan. I'm sorry about our meeting. As you can see—" he looked down at Alfie, who was starting to fuss, kicking his legs "—my hands are relatively full this morning, which is why my assistant changed our time."

The other man planted his feet. "Well, I'm here now."

"Okay, then come on in," Sebastian said, a determined smile plastered on his face.

Mae stepped back, out of the doorway, not really sure what she should do.

"Mr. Sheridan," Sebastian started, before Alfie covered his mouth with his chubby little hands. Sebastian removed them and adjusted the toddler. "Mr. Sheridan. Laurence, if I may?"

"You may not. I'm Mr. Sheridan to you, and I want the meeting I was promised."

For a suspended moment, Alfie seemed to stop breathing, his little face turning red, and then he let out a wail.

Mae stepped forward and stuck out her hand to their visitor. "Nice to meet you, Mr. Sheridan. I'm Mae."

He regarded her suspiciously. "I came for a meeting with him—" he jerked a thumb at Sebastian "—and I won't be foisted on someone else. I need to meet with the owner."

Sebastian turned sideways so he could speak over Alfie's head. "Then it's your lucky day. This is Mae Rutherford, and she owns 50 percent of the company."

Technically, she and Heath owned 25 percent each, but now wasn't the time for nuance. She grabbed a chair from in front of Sebastian's desk and took it over to her little wooden desk. She had no idea what she was doing. Her only aim was to smooth things out somehow. "Would you like to sit down?"

Mr. Sheridan looked from her to Sebastian and back again. "Thank you, I will."

As she took her seat on the opposite side, she met Sebastian's gaze over their visitor's head. He mouthed, "Just go with it."

She laced her fingers together on the desk in front of her and smiled as if she were meeting a student's parents at a parent-teacher conference. "How can I help you, Mr. Sheridan?"

He ran his hand over the wood. "This is a good desk. Solid."

She nodded. "Not too big, not too small."

"Exactly." He threw a look at the huge glass

monster of a desk on the other side of the room. "Too much desk for any one person, that one."

"Plus," Mae added, "I'd be looking at my own legs all day. I want to focus on the work instead."

He grinned. "You're not like the other suits."

"To be honest," she said, peeking over his head at Sebastian as he entertained Alfie with a bunch of pens, "I'm an elementary school teacher. My family owns half of this company, but I don't usually work in the office."

"Good to hear it. All these business people in their fancy suits and their hair slicked back like it's the forties. Gives me the heebie-jeebies."

Mae couldn't hold back the laugh. He'd summed up the lawyers at the meeting the day before. "They're great talkers," she said, "not so great at listening."

He slapped a hand on the desk. "That's it in a nutshell."

"I'm right here," Sebastian said, leaning a hip on his desk.

Mr. Sheridan turned to him. "Why *are* you still here?"

Sebastian's brows drew together comically. "It's my office."

Mae bit down a grin. "Actually, he's not so bad. Now, tell me why you're here, Mr. Sheridan."

"Larry. The name's Laurence, but you can call me Larry."

She caught sight of Sebastian mouthing, "Oh, come *on*," and grinned back at him.

"Okay, Larry. I'd love to try and help."

Almost forty minutes later, as she walked back in from seeing Larry out, she found Sebastian sitting on her desk, a drowsy Alfie still in his arms.

"That was impressive," he said.

"I didn't fix things." Larry had multiple offers for his small property, and he was ready to sell, but wanted a bunch of assurances. First and foremost, that his house wouldn't be pulled down and the land used to build a skyscraper. Turned out, that was exactly what Bellavista Holdings had planned. A stalemate.

"You got him to discuss his terms and start to consider he might need to compromise, which is more than anyone else here has been able to do."

"I feel for him, though." It was the house he'd bought with his wife when they'd first married. They'd raised their kids there and he knew almost everyone in the neighborhood, who would all be affected by the decision. But the prime location meant that even if he sold to a private person, they'd likely be tempted to sell to a developer soon after. He was just trying to do his best for his community.

"Hello?" A soft voice came from the door and a middle-aged couple walked in, clearly trying not to make too much noise. "Is he asleep?"

Sebastian smiled. "Close. His eyes are starting to droop."

"Oh, my heart," the woman said, crossing to the baby and smoothing the hair from his face.

Sebastian looked down at his son too, and his features softened, his gaze full of love. Mae's father had been completely absent from her life, so fathers were always a curiosity to her. When her mother had found she was pregnant for the second time, she'd taken two-year-old Heath and disappeared to protect them all, and Mae was both grateful and proud. It had left her fascinated by fathers with their babies—nothing quite tugged at her heart the way Sebastian unashamedly loving his son did.

"Can I hold him?" the woman asked.

"Sure." He carefully transferred Alfie to his grandmother's arms. "He might be too sleepy to be excited now, but once he wakes up and realizes you're here, he's going to be beside himself."

"My sweet baby," she whispered and kissed the soft, wispy hair on his head.

Sebastian waved a hand toward Mae. "This is Mae Rutherford, though I think she prefers Mae Dunstan. One of Joseph's missing children. Mae, this is Amanda and Barry, Ashley's parents and Alfie's grandparents."

"Oh," Amanda said, eyeing her eagerly, "so lovely to meet you. I have to admit, after reading about your reappearance I've been a little curious."

"A *little* curious?" Barry said, chuckling. "She's been following any crumbs of the story she can find."

Amanda blushed. "Well, we have a family interest. You're the people who share Sebastian's company. And our little Alfie will inherit it after him, so you'll have to excuse me for wanting to snoop a bit."

"It's fine," Mae said. "I'm sure I'd do the same in your position." In fact, she and her brother had been raised to be suspicious, so they would have done much more investigating than simply following the crumbs of a story.

Amanda turned back to Sebastian. "What's the latest about Emily?"

"She's doing okay. She's gone to stay with her parents, and the doctor advised that we should wait a few days after the last time she has symptoms before she starts caring for Alfie again."

"Glad to hear she's okay," Barry said. "You said you're trying to get an agency nanny?"

Sebastian nodded, wrapping a hand behind his neck. "I'm expecting a call back soon. They said they'd have someone here by the end of the day."

"You know," Amanda said, "we could take him. It's only a couple of weeks before our monthly days with him anyway, so we could bump that visit up. The nursery at our house is always ready, Sebastian, just in case you need us."

"She means," Barry said, "just in case she gets the chance to have an extra day or two with Alfie."

Amanda grinned and held the baby a little tighter for a moment. "I can't deny that."

"Well, if you're sure," Sebastian said. "It would certainly be less disruption for Alfie to go to a familiar environment with people he loves than adjust to a new nanny for only a few days."

"Oh, we're sure," Amanda said, her eyes lighting up.

"Right, then." Sebastian went behind his desk to grab his suit jacket. "We'll head back to my place now and pack his bags."

Mae watched everything unfold in front of her, feeling more like a casual observer than a part of the scene. She was here to shadow Sebastian, but this was a private family situation, so perhaps she could hang out in his office in case any other Larrys arrived. "Is there anything specific you want me to do here while you're gone?"

Sebastian frowned and glanced at his desk. "Not really. There's nothing you're up to speed with to work on. I still have some time cleared this morning, so why don't you come with us, and we'll have our working lunch early today?"

"I can do that," Mae said and grabbed her bag.

She, Sebastian, and Alfie caught a cab over to his apartment while his in-laws followed in their car. They didn't chat much, since Sebastian was focused on Alfie in his baby seat. He was talking to his son, telling him about the trip he was about to have with his grandparents and all the toys he'd pack to take with him, and when he told him how much he loved him, Mae had to swallow past the lump in her throat.

Packing bags went fairly smoothly, partly because Sebastian seemed to be in a routine of leaving each weekend, but he also just seemed to know where everything was. Of course, being a single parent meant he had to be on top of his kid's things. Still, since he had a full-time nanny, she'd expected he'd stumble a few times.

Amanda fed Alfie a banana while Sebastian got things ready, and by the time they waved Alfie and his grandparents off at the door, she could see the strain around Sebastian's eyes. They were left standing together in front of the closed door, neither of them speaking for a couple of moments.

It was different than the stress on his face when she'd arrived at the office this morning—that had been more about the frustration of trying to do too many things at once and not succeeding at all. This stress, though. This was deeper.

When children arrived on their first day of school, they were often excited to see all the new things. But the parents? They tended to fall into one of two groups. Those that blinked back their emotions and pretended everything was fine. And those that needed reassurance that they and their child would be okay. The expression on Sebastian's face seemed to put him squarely in the second group. Seeing his uncertainty pulled fiercely at her heartstrings.

"Does he go with them often?" she asked gently.

He loosened the tie at his neck. "They come down and spend a day with him every couple of weeks, and we planned that he'd do an overnight trip to their place every month, but I often manage to find an excuse to put that off. Luckily, they're understanding."

"Do you want to talk about it?"

He blinked hard and looked at her, confused. "Talk about it? I'm fine. Really."

"Okay, then," she said, not believing him for a minute.

"It's a bit early to go for lunch." He undid his white shirt's cuff buttons and rolled the sleeves up to his elbows. "Do you want a coffee here first? Or we could go back to the office."

After a hectic twelve hours, taking his nanny to the ER and having Alfie at work, then having his son leave for a few days, she could see that he needed a beat to catch his breath. That was something she could help with.

"A coffee would be great, thanks."

She followed him into the kitchen and leaned back against the counter as he operated a state-of-the-art coffee machine. He talked as he worked, explaining something about Bellavista Holdings, his talking getting faster as he went, until she stepped close and laid a hand on his forearm.

"Sebastian," she said.

He looked up sharply.

"It's okay to be sad."

"About the deal with Johnson Developments?" he said slowly, as if he was missing something.

"About your little boy leaving with his grandparents." She withdrew her hand and let her arms hang at her sides, wishing she could do more.

He shrugged his broad shoulders and went back to finishing up with the coffee. "I've been away from him before."

"Thanks." She accepted the mug he handed her. "Just because you've been away from him before doesn't mean that this time isn't hard."

He picked up the second brew, wrapping his long fingers around the mug, then he closed his eyes for several seconds before opening them again. "It's always hard."

"Did it get worse after your wife passed?"

"From the day he was born, I never really wanted to leave him. But while Ashley was alive, it was bearable...at least it was until she got sick." He turned to face her, resting his hip on the counter. "But since Ashley died, I feel this primal need to be there for him all the time."

The load on his shoulders was huge—he was trying not to let anything slip with the company or his son—and her heart ached for him. "I guess it's harder because Ashley's parents are hardly just around the corner. And your father wouldn't be any help."

He turned so his buttocks rested back on the counter, then he crossed his legs at the ankle. "I keep Alfie away from my father as much as I can. I can't think of a worse role model." One corner of his mouth hitched up. "Except, of course, your father. He was an absolute asshole."

"I've heard that," she said drily and grinned, mainly because Sebastian had broken the tension, but also because it was a relief that someone wasn't sugarcoating the truth. "Can't say

I'm sorry to never have met him. What about your mother? Did you say she'd moved away?"

A humorless smile flashed across his face for a moment as he placed his mug on the counter. "She walked out when I was about nine."

She blinked, trying to make sense of it. "Your mother left you with your father? A man who everyone says is a despicable human being?"

He placed his hands back on the counter, fingers splayed, in a move that should have been casual but somehow looked formal since he was still in a crisp white business shirt and dark pants. "She decided that I was just like him, and she wasn't putting up with two of us. Moved out, met a guy richer than my father, and moved to Texas. I've barely seen her since."

"You are *kidding* me," she said, her skin growing cold.

His beautiful mouth twisted. "Wish I was."

"Holy hell. At least I had one good parent." As if pulled by a magnetic force, she moved closer to Sebastian. The body heat emanating from him called her to move even closer, but she dared not. "Hang on, if you were raised just by Christopher, how did you turn out…" Her voice dried up as she realized she was rushing headlong into saying something that would give away her growing fascination with him.

He grinned, his eyes shining. "Mae Dunstan, were you about to compliment me?"

"Don't let it go to your head," she said dismissively. "From what I hear, the bar to be a better person than your father is a very low one."

The lines around his eyes crinkled. "It was still a compliment."

"It might have been," she said, looking at her nails and feigning disinterest. "We'll never know now."

He reached for the hand she was holding up and, unable to resist, she reached back. He slid his fingers between hers, the intimacy of the move sending a shiver racing across her skin, the heat of his palm against hers making her heart quicken.

"I choose to believe it was going to be a compliment," he murmured, his voice low, "and that you're finally starting to believe that I'm not full of nefarious plans."

She was drowning in his blue, blue eyes, trying not to get carried away and read too much into the situation, trying to keep things light.

"Would an honest, straight-up guy use words like nefarious?"

"This one does." He tugged her closer, until her feet bumped against his. "This one uses a whole heap of words that might surprise you."

"Yeah?" she said, but her voice sounded breathy to her own ears.

"We could start with *want*."

Her heart skipped a beat, and the whole world seemed suspended before it kicked back in and thudded against her ribs. "Want?"

"It's been going around and around in my mind since we first talked on that moonless night." The intensity in his gaze was scorching. "Before I even saw you."

She swallowed. "What did you want?"

"To touch you." He released her hand and wrapped an arm around her back, sending sparks through her blood. "To kiss you."

She took the last step to close the gap between them and looked up into his eyes, with less than an inch separating their bodies. "I wanted things too."

He swiped a thumb along her bottom lip. "Whatever it is, you can have it."

"That's a hell of a promise. You don't know what I'm going to ask."

"With you looking at me like that? I don't care." His voice was deep and smooth, and she started to sway as if hypnotized, and then she was being lifted and placed onto the counter, and he was standing in the V of her legs, his uneven breath on her mouth. "Tell me what you've been wanting."

"I want…" She had to fill her lungs to make a sound. "I want…"

"Tell me, Mae." His chest rose and fell, rose and fell, working overtime. "Tell me what you want, and I promise—"

"To touch you," she said on a whisper. "And I want you to touch me."

A groan was ripped from his throat and he leaned in and kissed her. It was hard and it was hungry and it was everything she'd dreamed it would be. She lifted her legs and locked them together behind his hips, holding him against her and spearing her fingers into his hair. His mouth was hot, decadent, and he held the sides of her face in his hands as if she were precious.

Then his hands roamed down, undoing the buttons on her jacket and slipping underneath it, sliding over the smooth cotton of her shirt, leaving a trail of fireworks despite the bar-rier to her skin. She felt his fingers spread out on her back as he leaned her backward. She'd never had a kiss go from zero to one hundred so fast, and she was trying to keep up, wanting more, wanting everything he had. His erection pressed against her, and an insistent pulse beat at her core as she started thinking about where they could move to, and how far away his bedroom was. Then she was struck by the thought that the bedroom would have been his and Ashley's...

She looked around the kitchen with new eyes, spotting a collage of photos on the refrigerator—Sebastian with a tiny Alfie, Sebastian and Ashley, the two of them with Alfie... She was in another woman's kitchen, another woman's apartment. It had been long enough for Sebastian to move on, but this still felt... wrong. And then she remembered everyone else who would be upset by this kiss, including her own family, and it was as if the whole world had crowded into her brain, and the moment, their connection, was lost.

She pulled back, dragging in air to fill her lungs, needing a moment to think things through. This wasn't a random hookup; anything they did together had consequences for a range of people. If this was going to happen, it couldn't happen on impulse, when he'd been feeling vulnerable and she'd tried to cheer him up. The whole thing was a hot mess on so many levels.

"What's wrong?" He dipped his head to meet her eyes. "Hey, did I do something wrong?"

"No, no. I just…" Her gaze drifted to the fridge again. "We shouldn't be doing this."

He eased back, then cocked his head to the side. "Why not? We're consenting adults."

She bit down on her lip, wondering how a person should bring up a dead wife with a man she'd just kissed. "This might sound weird to you, but this feels like Ashley's home, and…"

He laid a finger over her lips and sighed. "That doesn't sound weird. In fact, I haven't brought another woman here to the apartment for that reason. This kiss…" He looked up at the ceiling. "This was unexpected."

"Definitely unexpected. And possibly unwise."

He winced. "Now that the blood is starting to return to my brain, I think you might be right. Unwise."

"My brother, my aunt, your father, they'd all be horrified that we were blurring the lines," she said, pushing the point home. "Even Alfie's grandmother commented on the company being Alfie's future inheritance. This situation is bigger than the two of us."

"You're right. One hundred percent. And yet..." He cupped the side of her face and she leaned into the touch. "It's hard to make myself care about any of them right now."

She pressed her palm against his chest—the solid muscle, the heat emanating through his snowy white shirt—maybe instinctively, to hold him at bay, but found herself gripping his shirt in her fist and pulling him down again. He came willingly.

This time, when he captured her mouth, it was slow, gentle, honoring her, tempting her. And after only a few moments, he broke the kiss, leaning his forehead against hers, his warm breath fanning across her cheeks.

"I can't think of anything I want less than to end this kiss, but if we're going to stop, we probably should head back to the office. We need some sort of impediment, like being in an office with no privacy, to stop us from taking this further."

Everything inside her rose up to object. It felt wrong to be kissing him here, now, at all, but it felt just as wrong to not be kissing him.

This was a lose-lose situation and was really just about picking the lesser of two evils. Which meant they had to stop.

She slid down from the counter and began straightening her clothes. "And if we're serious about not taking this further, then we need to go now. Like, right now."

His expressive eyes filled with regret, and he nodded. "Let's go."

As they walked out the door of his apartment and headed down to the sidewalk to hail a cab, she'd never wanted to throw caution to the wind more in her life and turn right back around.

SIX

FOR THE REST of the day, Sebastian focused on his work and nothing else. Or he tried to. Mae was sitting at her desk. In the same room. Lighting up the space as if she were the midday sun. He could walk over there and kiss her if he wanted to.

And he wanted to.

I want you to touch me.

He'd almost combusted on the spot when she'd said that. And now none of the figures on the spreadsheet made sense.

Instead of the working lunch he'd planned, they'd ordered sandwiches from a place that delivered and eaten at their desks. To keep her occupied, he'd told her to ask Rosario for any company files she wanted. The two women had carried some boxes of old files in, and Mae was also going through files on the company server. He'd had a meeting in the boardroom, but Mae had been absorbed in something she'd found, so she'd waved him away and kept reading.

It was annoying that she could concentrate on work so well when he was still consumed by their kiss.

Rosario came through and picked up a couple of packages off his desk that needed sending. "I'm heading out—I'll see you both in the morning."

Surprised, he glanced at the clock. Six o'clock. "I lost track of time in the spreadsheet." Although he was lying about what had consumed his thoughts so much, he wondered if it was obvious to anyone else. "Thanks, Rosario. I'll see you in the morning."

After she left, he stretched his arms over his head in an effort to look casual. "I'm thinking of working late to make up for the time I lost this morning." Another lie. Alfie was with his grandparents. The house would be empty, nothing to rush home for. And worst of all, the kitchen would be full of memories of Mae sitting on the counter, kissing him as though she would die if she didn't. No one had ever kissed him with so much desperation.

Mae put the lid back on an open box and

stood. "Have fun. I have somewhere I need to be."

"Well, that sounds mysterious." And, again, here he was, drowning in memories of their kiss while she seemed to be going about her day and evening, even going out to socialize.

She flashed him a smile, her dimples peeking out. "I'm dropping over to see my mother's family."

He frowned. For some reason, he only ever thought of her as a product of the Rutherford side of her family. "Did you know them growing up?"

"No," she said, grabbing her satchel. "When my mother ran, she cut all ties. She never saw them again."

Well, now he felt like a louse. Of course she wasn't thinking of their kiss when she had this on her mind. He turned his computer screen away and leaned back in his chair. "Are you going for dinner?"

"Just a visit." She picked up her coat and draped it over her arm. "Joseph Rutherford really screwed them over on a number of levels. The O'Donohue family lost their daughter and sister, but he also systematically harassed them after she left, just in case they knew something. Or maybe it was petty revenge—who knows?"

"As previously mentioned, I can attest to the fact that he was an asshole."

She tipped her head in acknowledgment and leaned a hip on the corner of her desk. "So now Heath and I have inherited all this money, and we want to share it with them."

He could imagine how well that had gone down. "Let me guess, they don't want a cent of anything that Joseph owned?"

"That's a big part of it, but they think of it as our money and say we should keep it."

Large amounts of money affected people in different ways. Some were keen to share it, while others would throw their best friend under the bus to get their hands on it. Still others didn't like to touch it. For them, small amounts were fine, but once large sums were mentioned, they took a big step back. And given their front-row view of Joseph Rutherford's use of money, it probably wasn't surprising that her mother's family wanted nothing to do with it. Mae seemed confused by their reaction, though. "You see it differently?"

"It's more than we can use, and the O'Donohues have suffered terribly because of Joseph. At the very least, we should be able to make some reparations with his money." She lifted a hand, palm out.

It was a good justification. "You know, if he was still alive, they'd have the chance to sue him for stalking and harassment, so giving them a settlement seems very reasonable."

"Easier said than done," she said, rolling her eyes.

He rested his elbows on the chair's armrests and steepled his fingers under his chin as he thought the problem through. "Do you have ideas about how to get them to accept it?"

"Not really. I was going to try logic again, but Heath has tried a few times already and it hasn't worked so far. I said I'd take over trying." She tucked some long, dark hair behind her ear. "One of the underhanded things Joseph did was buy the company that my grandparents and three of my uncles worked for. He did it so he could get reports on them from their managers—looking for suspicious vacations, etcetera. But that now means that Heath and I own that company. I'd be very happy to hand it over—"

"You can't," he said, interrupting her. "That would insult their pride. They don't want a handout from their newly discovered grand-children. They'll want to give, not take."

"That's the same conclusion we came to, so we haven't even offered it." She looked so downcast that he felt compelled to fix this for her. Offer her something uncomplicated that she could accept.

"What if you took them on as consultants?" he said, sitting up straight. "Pay them for their expertise about the business."

She fiddled with the strap of her bag. "Would that be enough money?"

"Some consultants get paid an exorbitant fee. The price can be the amount you want to give them, and then they have earned it, not been handed it."

She turned to the window for a long moment before turning back to him again. "That could work. I don't suppose...?"

"As it happens," he said, grinning, "I have a free night if you want me."

Her eyes flared and everything around them stilled. He hadn't meant to remind them both of the kiss that morning, of everything they'd said they wanted, but now that it was there, it was like a living, pulsing thing between them.

"I didn't mean——"

She held up a hand. "I know you didn't. And, yes, thank you for your offer, I'd love to have someone with a good business brain there when I talk to them about being paid consultants."

He shut his laptop and stood. "Then I'm at your service."

They caught a taxi over to her grandparents' house in Brooklyn, and together, she and Sebastian laid out the plan to her mother's family. The O'Donohues were grateful for the offer, but saw through it immediately and graciously declined. Disappointed, but not surprised, she and Sebastian said goodbye and then shared a taxi back to Sarah's place. He'd said he'd take it on to his place after it dropped her off, but as it pulled over, he found himself paying the driver and getting out with her.

"Sebastian?" Mae said as he came to stand on the sidewalk beside her.

"It's a nice night." He rocked back on his heels. "Thought I'd walk some of the way home."

She looked up at the exterior of the building, then back to him. "I'd invite you up…"

"You can't." The very idea was ludicrous. "I'm not welcome in the enemy camp."

"I wouldn't say *enemy*," she said diplomatically.

"Really?" He allowed his incredulity to flow into his voice. "What would you say?"

She opened her mouth, but no words came out.

He chuckled. "It's okay, Mae. You don't have to spare my feelings. I've lived in the middle of this family feud my entire life. It's the same at my father's place."

Her expression was suddenly full of sympathy as she nodded. "Will you be okay at home tonight?"

He put on a mock stern face. "Are you seriously asking if I'll be okay in my own apartment overnight?"

"You know what I mean," she said, not diverted by his teasing.

He did. She wondered of he'd be okay without Alfie. "I'll be fine. Amanda has already sent through a bunch of videos of the things he's done this afternoon, so I'll console myself by watching those." He was being tongue-in-cheek, but there was an element of truth in there too.

"Thank you for coming with me tonight and trying." She pulled her bottom lip into her mouth and let her front teeth scrape over it as she released it.

He sank his hands into his pockets, willing himself not to respond. "It wasn't a problem. I liked your grandparents. They're stubborn, but that's not a bad thing."

"Well, good night." She leaned forward and kissed his cheek, and as she did, the world faded away. The traffic sounds disappeared; the other people on the sidewalk and the buildings all evaporated from his awareness. All he could see was Mae. All he could hear was her breathing so close to his ear. She seemed to have frozen, perhaps waiting for him to make a move. Perhaps she was as paralyzed by whatever was between them as he was.

"Mae," he said, his voice rasping. "I want…"

"I know," she said near his ear. "I want too."

She pulled back and met his gaze. "But we won't. We can't. We're fighting over a company."

"Are we fighting, though?" He had to ask the question that had been bouncing around in his brain. "It feels like we're on the same page most of the time."

She arched an eyebrow. "You still want Heath and me to sell you half the company, right?"

"It's the only thing that makes sense." Getting to know Mae had only supported that conclusion.

"Then yes—" she tipped up her chin "—
we're still fighting."

She had the most beautiful chin. Rounded,
with skin that was silky smooth, and he wanted
to cup it in his hand and draw her face toward
him so he could kiss her senseless. His breathing
was labored, as if they were striding along the
pavement, not standing still, and hers seemed to
be uneven too. Who were they kidding?

"Not sure how many business fights you've
been in," he said, knowing the answer. "I've
been in quite a few, and none of them have felt
like this."

"Felt like what?" she asked, her voice faint.

"The wanting."

She stared into his eyes for a second too long.
"And that's exactly why we're not going to
complicate it even more."

"You're right. Good point." He kept forgetting that, and he really needed to do something
now to get them back on track. "I'm totally out
of line. I was emotional today because of Alfie
leaving. I don't know what to do with myself
tonight because he's gone, and I've gotten carried away. I shouldn't use all of that to complicate things between us."

"That's all this has been?" she challenged, her beautiful gray eyes stormy.

"Yes." *No.* "Sure."

She gave a quick shake of her head. "You're kidding yourself."

"Well, what's your suggestion, then, Mae? What do we do about it?"

She simply looked at him for an eternity, her eyes unreadable. "How about this? Heath is staying at Freya's place and Sarah is out until late. I'm going up now, and on the way through, I'm going to tell the doorman that a guy named Sebastian Newport might be dropping by, and if he does, to send him up."

He drew in a sharp breath. "If he doesn't drop by?"

"Then I'll see him at the office tomorrow."

"And if he does?"

"Then two consenting adults would have to work out what they're going to do about the inconvenient thing that's between them." She turned and said, over her shoulder, "'Night, Sebastian."

He watched her walk to the door, stop to say a few words to the doorman, then disappear into the building. And he'd never been so torn in his life.

★ ★ ★

Once she'd made it inside Sarah's apartment, her heart pounding, Mae couldn't make herself leave the foyer. She'd just crossed a huge line with Sebastian. Dropping her bag on the floor, she drew in a shuddering breath. They were in an impossible situation, and inviting Sebastian Newport upstairs had been a very bad idea, and yet...a little kernel of hope flickered in her chest. Hope that he'd be as reckless as she'd been.

She groaned and pinched the bridge of her nose. "This is ridiculous," she whispered.

Getting her hopes up was just setting herself up for disappointment since she had zero idea what Sebastian would do. She told herself to head for the kitchen and make a coffee, or sit on the sofa, or something. Anything. Yet she remained with her feet planted on the tiled foyer floor...hovering. Wishing. Wanting.

So much wanting.

Footsteps sounded outside and then a sharp double-knock. Mae's heart stalled and then burst back to life, beating double time. He'd actually followed her. She reached for the door, then hesitated, her belly filling with butterflies. She should have used the few minutes

before he'd arrived to brush her hair or re-
fresh her lipstick. Maybe change into something
new. Pop a breath mint. But it was too late, so
she smoothed her hands over her trousers and
tucked her hair behind her ears, hoping she was
enough as she was. Then she took a deep breath
and opened the door.

Sebastian strode in, and she took a step back
because he didn't seem to be stopping. She
wasn't fast enough, though, because he crashed
into her, grasping her face with his hands as his
mouth landed on hers, hot and hungry. Suddenly light-headed, she wrapped an arm around
his waist to keep her balance and kissed him
back. Heat licked through her body, a deep
need, unlike anything she could remember feeling. Without breaking the kiss, he kicked the
door closed behind him and slid his hands to
her thighs, lifting her. While she wrapped her
legs around him, locking her ankles, he turned
and walked her backward until her shoulders
hit the door with a light thud. The exquisite
pressure of the hard planes of his torso pushing
up against her breasts made her moan, but their
kiss swallowed the sound.

When they finally wrenched themselves
apart—moments? Minutes? A lifetime?— later,

she rested the pad of her thumb against his bottom lip and whispered, "You came."

He stared at her for a beat, his blue gaze unreadable, their heavy breathing the only sound in the apartment.

"Here are my terms," he said, his focus on her unwavering. "We agree that this is not the start of something. It is a onetime only deal. We shouldn't have started this in my kitchen, but since we did, we finish it now." He adjusted her weight by placing his forearms under her buttocks. "There will be no repeats—we just get it out of our systems and move on. And we don't talk about it after I leave this apartment tonight. Those terms acceptable to you?"

She would have agreed to fly to the moon in that moment if it had been a condition for him to start kissing her again. "Deal."

He lowered his head, his mouth finding hers for another brief kiss that scorched her system. "Where's your room?" he asked, his voice unsteady.

She unlocked her ankles and slid down his body, relishing the feel of him so close. "This way." She took his hand as she stepped away, but he didn't follow. "Sebastian?"

"Are you sure, Mae?" His gaze was intense,

but wary. "Less than ten minutes ago, down on the sidewalk, we agreed this shouldn't happen." He lifted their joined hands and gently kissed her knuckles. "Us getting carried away and you regretting it in the morning is not my idea of a good time, so I need to know that you're sure."

The air around them was heavy, as if carrying the weight of this moment. Of her choice. But there was no choice to be made. There was only the need, and the want that thrummed between them. She knew why he was checking—she'd been the one to pull away in the kitchen. That kiss had been unexpected and overwhelming, and that combination meant that she'd needed to step back to give herself a chance to think things through. To process. She was done processing now.

"That conversation was about why we shouldn't do this. What we didn't cover was why we should."

He cocked a brow. "Yeah? Got many reasons on that list?"

"Just the one," she said through a dry throat. "Right now, I feel like I'll die if I don't have you even once."

A slow smile spread across his face. "Lead the way."

Making it through the apartment took much longer than it should have. Sebastian caught her on the staircase and turned her in his arms, the extra height of the stair meaning she didn't have to stretch up to kiss him. And once they reached the hall, the absence of his touch was too much to bear, so she turned and reached for him, and he pulled her tight and kissed her hard.

Somehow they made it to her room, and as soon as they were through the door, she was in his arms again, his breath hot near her ear. "Now, where were we?"

"Where were we?" she asked, trying to get her brain to work, which was difficult when she could smell the intoxicating, warm musk of his skin. "You were asking if I was sure?"

"Earlier." He sucked her earlobe into his mouth and gently bit down.

Her blood fizzed through her body like champagne. "Deciding if you were coming upstairs?"

"Earlier."

Everything outside this room was a distant memory, but she forced her mind to work. "When we were in your kitchen?"

"That's the one," he murmured against her skin. "Tell me what you want, Mae."

The possibilities flooded her mind, and she swayed, her grip on his shoulders the only thing keeping her upright.

"Everything," she whispered. "I want to touch you, and be touched by you. To kiss and be kissed by you. To drown with you. I want everything you have to offer."

"Done." He kissed her again, pressing his thigh between her legs, providing delicious pressure where she craved it the most.

"And what about you?" Her hands roamed over his back, his sides, wherever she could reach, learning the shape of him, committing it to memory. "What do you want?"

His eyes flared. "I want to hear you say my name."

"Sebastian?" she said, knowing she was missing something, since she'd used his name countless times over the past few days.

"Not like that." He leaned in, murmuring at her ear, sending sparks zinging across her skin. "I want to hear you moaning it when you're lost to sensation. Screaming it when you find your release. I want my name to be your whole world for tonight."

As she snaked her hand down his chest, across the flat of his abdomen, and farther to the bulge of his erection, she whispered, "I don't think that's going to be a problem." His breath hissed out from between closed teeth. She traced the outline of his shape, teasing him, building, wanting him to be as desperate as she was. Then she palmed him through his trousers, cupping him, and his hips bucked, thrusting into her hand.

She found his belt and was fiddling with the buckle when his hands came down to stop hers. He swore savagely under his breath.

"I don't have a condom," he rasped. "Didn't need them when I was married and haven't been seeing anyone since. I'm assuming, since you haven't been in the country long...?"

Her stomach sank and she winced. "I didn't bring them from Australia and haven't had a reason to buy any since I arrived." Which right now seemed like a massive oversight. "I don't want to stop to get some, though."

"I'm not even stopping for earthquakes or hurricanes," he said and kissed her.

The intensity of the kiss kicked up a notch, setting her aflame. The pads of his thumbs stroked over the front of her bra, but her hands were greedier, trying to touch all of him through his clothes at once.

Breaking the kiss, he turned her and pushed against the closed door, his arms coming around from behind to find the button and zipper at the top of her pants. He released the closure and slowly pushed them down, taking her underpants with them, smoothing his hands over her bare buttocks as he went. A rush of cold air hit her flesh and her head swam.

"I knew your ass would be delectable." He kissed one cheek, his tongue flicking out, and then he softly bit her.

All the air left her lungs in one long whoosh and her legs swayed. "Maybe give a girl a little warning next time?" she said once her lungs were working again.

He stood, his front sliding up her back, and then his breath was at her ear. "Now where would the fun be in that?"

She coughed out a laugh.

He undid the buttons of her shirt and tugged the sides apart. He wrapped one arm around her stomach, and the other up and over her shoulder, sliding his hand down into the cup of her bra. With his body pressing into her from behind, the hand holding her against him started to inch downward, overwhelming her with sensation. And then his hand reached the juncture of her thighs and he cupped her, pressing lightly.

"Oh, God," she said, her vision swimming.

"What was that?" he murmured beside her ear. "Was that my name you were trying to say?"

She started to reply but broke off as he gently sucked at the sensitive skin on the side of her neck, and, this time, had no trouble remembering to say his name. Every nerve ending was sensitized, every inch of her skin yearning for his touch. The hand he'd placed between her legs began to move in a slow, rhythmic pattern, and the hand still inside the cup of her bra explored, gripped, caressed. Her head dropped back onto his shoulder and she melted into him. Her entire universe was Sebastian—his hands, his mouth, his hard body behind her.

"Sebastian," she whispered, unable to summon her full voice, but needing to say his name, to add the extra layer of connection between them.

"An improvement," he murmured, "but I think we can do better."

The toe of his shoe nudged her feet farther apart as he slid a long, strong finger down low, then another, moving into the slickness he'd created, driving her out of her mind. Her knees buckled, and the hand at her breast moved down until his arm wrapped tightly around her waist, taking her weight onto his frame. Near her ear, his breathing was ragged as he talked dirty and whispered sweet nothings in equal measure. She tried to focus on everything she was feeling, to commit it all to memory. Since their deal was for this one night only, she wanted to remember every second. But it was no use—she was too lost to sensation, overwhelmed by the rising, swirling currents inside. And as her world came apart, his name was wrenched from her throat, the only word that made sense, the only thing that seemed real.

For long moments, she simply stood, the sound of her harsh breathing filling the room as she leaned back against him. Once she could breathe freely again, she opened her eyes and turned in his arms. "That was…"

"Yeah," he said with a satisfied smile. "It was."

"And now it's my turn." She pushed against his shoulders, and he dropped his arms.

He cocked a brow. "You can barely stand on your own."

"I'm recovering fast," she said, grinning.

She unbuttoned his shirt and pushed the fabric back over his shoulders and down to his wrists. She paused as she undid the cuffs, then he slid his arms free. The shirt hung from his waist, its tails still tucked into his trousers and secured by his belt, but she didn't care; she had free rein to explore every inch of the warm olive skin of his chest. She ran an exploratory hand over the crisp hair covering his pecs, down over the solid muscles of his abdomen, loving the way his breathing matched her movements.

Leaning in, she allowed herself the luxury of pressing a kiss to his collarbone, then the base of his throat. His pulse throbbed there, strong and fast. She slid her hands down his sides, bringing them to rest on his hips, and they anchored her as she explored his chest with her lips, her tongue, her teeth. She dropped lower, onto her knees, and felt a shudder run through his body.

Clasping the zipper, she undid his trousers and let them pool at his ankles, then hooked her thumbs in the sides of his briefs and lowered them to the floor. As she leaned back, he stepped out of the discarded clothes, shoving them to the side. Looking up, she met his eyes and then took a moment to let her gaze roam down, over the expanse of skin on display, and her breath caught high in her throat.

Then she brought her attention to his erection, encircling it with one hand as the other rested on the solid muscles of his thigh. The skin was soft and burning hot, and as she moved her fingers lightly, Sebastian groaned and speared his fingers through her hair.

She looked up and smiled. "Let's see if I can make you say *my* name."

Then she leaned forward and took him in her mouth and he gasped. She experimented a little, looking for sensations and rhythms that he liked, peeking up at his face to gauge her success. His eyes were closed, and his chest was rising and falling quickly with every breath.

"Mae," he said, his voice tortured, and she grinned.

She leaned back, releasing him, and before he could question her or complain, she gently pushed him back onto the bed. She wanted him stable for what she had planned.

His eyes flashed to hers, but she crawled onto the bed with him, over him, and his mouth curved into a lazy smile. "Come here," he said, then he pulled her close and groaned.

The scorching heat of him against her bare

skin sent a shiver down her spine, but she kept her eye on the prize. "Not a chance," she said, smiling back. "I'm going to finish what I started."

She kissed a trail over his chest, down his stomach, her nails scraping across his abdomen as she went. And when she reached his erection again, hot and solid in her hand, in her mouth, she returned to her experimentation, more confident now that she knew how he liked to be touched.

"Goddamn it, Mae, you're going to kill me." She glanced up to find him propped up on his elbows, watching her, his blue eyes dark with desire, his jaw tensing and releasing.

She stopped what she was doing long enough to echo his words from earlier. "A good use of my name, but I think we can do better."

As she took him into her mouth again, her fingers and palms working as well, he flopped back onto the bed, groaning. It was gratifying to know that he was as powerless and as lost to need as she was.

As his need built, she watched his beautiful body fill with tension, his muscles cording, and his arms moving restlessly, from cradling her head, to grasping handfuls of the bed cov-

ers, and back to tangling his fingers in her hair.
As he found his release, he cried out her name,
and she'd never felt so triumphant in her life.

SEVEN

THE NEXT MORNING, Mae walked downstairs, hoping that no one would guess from the smile she was attempting to hide that Sebastian had spent the night. She'd reluctantly sneaked him out the front door just after four o'clock, when everything was quiet. With a gentle kiss in front of the elevator, he'd whispered, "See you at work," and was gone. Sleep had been impossible after that—she'd lain awake replaying every second of their time together.

She ran into Heath at the front door. He mainly spent his nights at Freya's place, but in the mornings, when she left for her job as a forensic accountant at the FBI headquarters, he headed over to Sarah's. He and Sarah were still going through various business files and legal details about the inheritance during the day, and she'd be doing that this week with them too, if the opportunity to shadow Sebastian hadn't come up. She loved her brother and was coming to love her aunt, but this time with Sebastian? It was precious—and not only because she stood to learn the ropes of the company she'd partially inherited.

Heath held up a paper bag. "I come bearing bagels."

She snatched the bag and opened it to draw in the scent. "See, this is why you're my favorite brother."

"From a pool of one," he pointed out. "Though, to be fair, that's the reason you're my favorite sister."

She grinned and headed for the kitchen, where she found Sarah making coffee and chatting to Lauren.

"Morning," her aunt said.

Mae handed her the bag. "Heath brought bagels."

"And *that's* why he's my favorite nephew." Sarah took the bag from Mae and kissed Heath's cheek.

Heath pumped a fist. "Man, I'm really creaming the competition in the categories where I'm the only candidate."

Lauren chuckled as she took a mug of coffee

Sarah handed her. "Morning, Heath. Morning, Mae."

Heath pointed at Lauren. "I wasn't sure if you'd be here for breakfast or not, so I got enough bagels just in case. I guess that makes me—" he raised his eyebrows hopefully "—your favorite future son-in-law?"

"Maybe," Lauren deadpanned. "So far, you're ahead of both of Freya's ex-husbands, but let's see how it goes, hey?"

Heath clutched his chest. "I'm wounded."

Mae grinned and began pulling bagel toppings from the fridge. Over the years, people had sometimes commented on how she'd missed out on having an extended family, growing up with just a mother and a brother, but the three of them had always been close. Now that she had Sarah, as well as all the O'Donohues from her mother's side, and even Lauren living downstairs—all of a sudden she had a bounty of riches in terms of family. Her heart was full from having them all in her life, and she just wished her mother was here to see it, to be part of it.

Her thoughts drifted to Sebastian, alone in his apartment. He'd been abandoned by his mother, his wife had died, and his father was horrible. Now, with his son gone for a few days, he had no family at all. It made no sense how much luck and arbitrary circumstances affected whether a person had family around them or not.

I'm not welcome in the enemy camp.

They walked through the kitchen to the dining table, carrying food, coffee mugs, and plates.

As she took her seat, Mae looked at the other three. "Can I bring a plus one to the dinner on Friday?"

Sarah's eyes lit up. "Of course you can."

Her brother frowned, and she could see his wheels turning. "Who?"

She grabbed a bagel and put it on her plate, attempting to look casual. "Sebastian."

Sarah's butter knife clattered onto her plate. "Sebastian *Newport*?"

Lauren's concerned gaze cut to Sarah then back to Mae, but she remained silent.

"Yes," she said simply and cut her bagel.

Sarah and Heath exchanged a glance, before Sarah said, "You said you were there to investigate, not...make friends."

Her brother was very still. "I don't trust him."

That didn't surprise her. Their entire childhood had revolved around them hiding from their father and being suspicious about new people in case they were private investigators. They'd changed identities more than once and moved around a lot. If Heath *hadn't* been suspicious it would have been weird.

"I'm not sure I trust him either, but I do know that there's a lot of bad blood between the families, and the cause was our father and his. Not him, and not us. If we're going to find a way forward, we at least need to find a way to talk to each other that's not combative."

Heath regarded her in silence for a long moment. "You know what you're doing?"

Honestly, she had no idea what she was doing, or what she was feeling, but she said, "Absolutely."

He nodded and went back to his breakfast.

Lauren cut into a banana and arranged the slices on her bagel. "It doesn't have much to do with me, but in case anyone's interested, I won't mind if there's an extra person at my daughter's engagement dinner."

Mae threw her a grateful smile, and Lauren gave a small nod before biting into her breakfast.

"I'll extend the booking," Sarah said with a valiant attempt at a smile.

"Thank you," Mae said and stood, snagging the bagel from her plate. She kissed both her brother and aunt on the cheek, mouthed "Thank you" to Lauren, took her plate back to the kitchen and went to her room to get dressed for work. The room where the sheets were still rumpled from her encounter with Sebastian. She bet they still smelled like him too.

Less than an hour later, she walked through Rosario's office, placing a French vanilla cappuccino, with oat milk, and a paper bag containing a pastry on her desk.

"Mae, I'm so glad you came to work here," Rosario said with a smile that bordered on adoration. "Best boss ever."

"Hey." Sebastian appeared in the doorway. "You know she doesn't actually work here. I'm still your boss."

Rosario lifted her hands, palms out. "You don't bring me coffee. My loyalty is fickle."

Mae went to her shared office and headed for her little wooden desk. "Morning, Sebastian."

"It's all making sense now," he said, one side of his mouth hitched up. "You agreed to shadow me so you could woo my staff into switching loyalties. You were the one with the nefarious plan."

"I can write down the way she likes her coffee for you if you think it would help," she said sweetly, and heard his chuckle from behind her.

As she sat down at her desk, she noticed a square box tied with a red ribbon. She glanced at Sebastian, who gave her a self-satisfied smile, and opened it to find an assortment colored pens, sticky notes, striped paper clips, highlighters, and a bright-orange notebook.

She gasped. "You got me stationery?"

"I had some spare time this morning without Alfie at home, so I left early. When I passed a stationery store, I remembered you said how much you like it." He casually shrugged one shoulder. "I figured you needed some for your desk."

"Thank you," she said, lifting each item out of the box and admiring its beauty.

He rubbed a hand across his jaw. "No need to be too grateful—it went on the office expenses."

It was more than that, though. He'd thought about her and had stopped to pick out some things he thought she'd like. Her heart swelled in her chest. She lined each of the items up along the side of her desk, then folded her hands, looking at them. Then she looked back up at him and smiled. "What's on the agenda today?"

"Back-to-back meetings I'm afraid." He swiveled in his chair to face his computer screen. "First one starting in ten minutes in our boardroom, then we're darting across town for the next. No time for one of our lunches either, since we're catching up from yesterday. We'll just grab something on the go."

No time to go out for lunch? That was when she was going to ask him about the engagement dinner. Maybe she should just get it over with now instead. "Sebastian?"

"Mm-hmm?" he said as he stood and started collecting things he'd need for the meeting.

"Are you busy Friday night?"

His brows drew together. "Not really. Amanda and Barry are keeping Alfie over the weekend."

"Then you should come to dinner with us," she said brightly.

"Who is 'us' exactly?" He looked over, his deep blue eyes narrowed.

She counted off on her fingers. "Heath, Freya, Lauren, who is Freya's mom and Sarah's best friend, Sarah, and me."

"You want me to have dinner with the heart of the Rutherford family?" He put his things down again and crossed his arms. The action brought her attention to his fresh white shirt, and the muscular chest beneath it that had been pressed against her breasts the night before. Suddenly, there wasn't enough oxygen in the room.

"Yes," she managed to whisper.

"Why?" he said, his voice full of incredulity.

She shook herself and forced her attention back to the conversation at hand. "Because we're toasting Heath and Freya's engagement."

"Sure," he said pointedly, "but why invite *me* to it?"

"Because I think we need to move past this idea of who is from what family and preconceptions about things and just meet each other as people." Was she the only one who saw it like that? How people were just people and should be judged on their own merits?

He was still clearly less than convinced. "Now who has a secret agenda?"

"Lord above," she muttered to herself. "What *possible* secret agenda could I have to invite you to dinner?"

"I can't imagine, Mae." His voice was taut, his jaw set. "You tell me."

She'd already offered him the justification that Heath and Sarah had accepted, yet he wanted more. What else could she tell him when he wouldn't see the need to build bridges between their families? Gazes locked, they waited, as if in a standoff.

A little voice inside her mind nudged her to acknowledge the truth. Yes, there was a need to bring the families together, but there was something deeper that she was scared to admit. Something terrifying. And now that she'd realized what it was, she could no longer be a coward. She needed to say it out loud.

She blinked and then softly said, "I'd like you to be there."

He held her gaze a moment longer and then nodded. "Then I'll come."

Sebastian arrived at the hotel at five minutes to seven to find Mae already waiting for him on the sidewalk, beside the door. She was wearing a lilac wraparound dress that hugged her curves so close he almost stumbled on the pavement. The vibrant color complemented her dark brown hair, and her gray eyes took on the lavender tones in the dress, and he had the thought that she should be on the big screen. Had he once thought she wasn't traditionally beautiful? He'd never seen anyone look more exquisite.

He reached her and leaned down to kiss her cheek, drinking her in. "Hello, Mae."

She grabbed his forearms and went up on her tiptoes to kiss his cheek in return. "I'm so glad you made it."

When they separated, she was looking up at him, smiling widely, her dimples twinkling in her cheeks. Her joy was infectious, so he smiled back. "Thanks for inviting me."

"Come on, let's go in." She led the way through the ornate marble lobby with expansive ceilings. Everyone knew this hotel, and Seb had often thought about staying a weekend here just for the experience, but had never seemed to find the time.

Mae took him off to one side, then led him into the hotel restaurant, finally stopping at a private dining room. The room was small but lavishly decorated, from its crimson fabric wallpaper to its elaborate chandelier. The tabletop was marble, and the seats of the chairs were upholstered in the same crimson fabric as the walls. It would have been a comfortable room to spend a few hours, except for the four sets of eyes that had watched his approach and were glued to him now.

"This is Sebastian," Mae said. "I think you know everyone except Lauren?"

He nodded. "Sarah and I have crossed paths

a number of times over the years, and I met Heath and Freya only a few months ago."

Some stilted small talk followed, in which he tried to make nice with people he was in the middle of a battle of wills with. Entrées came and were cleared away, and Seb continued to chat, mainly with Sarah and Lauren, both of whom were clearly assessing him.

Once the waiter had refilled all their glasses with champagne, Sarah raised hers and said, "To Freya and Heath."

Seb joined in the chorus of the others repeating, "To Freya and Heath," and then half listened to the discussion about wedding plans. Most of his attention was on Mae, at his side. Every time she moved, she brushed his shoulder or his arm, and it was throwing him off-balance.

The waiter brought their main course, and Seb glanced across the table to find Heath staring at him. In a business context, he'd take on Heath Dunstan, no question. But, despite their joint business interests, this was not a business setting, and Seb didn't know what the rules were. Mae turned to speak to Lauren, at her other side, and casually brushed against Seb's arm again, and he watched Heath pointedly follow the casual contact.

"Mae," Heath said, "can I have a quick word?"

"Not just now," Mae said, using a sweet voice that Seb was coming to recognize as the one she used when she knew exactly what she was doing to mess up someone else's plans.

"Heath," Sarah said, snagging Heath's attention away. "I was just talking to Freya about a proper engagement party."

"I thought that's what this was," he said.

"No, this is a small family gathering. I've been thinking about something bigger, with all your friends. I'll take care of everything, of course, plan all the details."

Heath and Freya exchanged horrified looks.

"Here's the thing, Sarah," Heath said gently. "Freya and I both hate parties. We've attended your others because they're yours, and we love you, but it's no kindness to us to throw us a party."

Lauren laughed behind her hand, and made eye contact with Sarah, toning down her amusement to offer unspoken support once she saw how crestfallen Sarah was. Seb watched the two older women a bit longer. Hadn't Mae said they were best friends? There was something too attentive between them for mere friendship. They both always seemed attuned to the other no matter who was talking or where they were. If those two weren't secretly a couple already, then they should be. He checked out the others around the table and wondered if they all knew.

Across from him, Heath put down his cutlery. "Are we going to talk about the elephant in the room?"

Seb stilled. Had Heath just worked it out? Or had Seb given it away by watching the women too closely?

Freya made a valiant effort to redirect the conversation to the history of the room they were sitting in, but Heath persisted, saying, "Everyone here is okay that there's something going on between these two?"

Seb was horrified to realize that Heath was waving a hand at Mae and him. He hadn't expected to be welcomed with open arms, not when their families had been fighting for years, but it still felt like a punch to the gut that he was deemed so wildly unsuitable for Mae.

"There's nothing between us," Mae said, but she undermined the statement by putting a reassuring hand on his thigh. Heath didn't miss the move.

Sarah leaned forward. "Heath, this is hardly the place..."

"I'm okay with it," Lauren said and took a slug of wine.

"What?" Heath said. "After everything you put me through when I wanted to be with Freya?"

"Freya's my daughter." Lauren gave the table an enigmatic smile. "Besides, I've mellowed."

"You have not," Heath said.

Lauren raised her glass to Seb down the table. "Single parents have to stick together."

Seb tried to smother a smile, but was unsuccessful, so he simply raised his champagne glass back to her. He knew that would probably infuriate Mae's brother more, but there weren't a lot of good options given the circumstances.

Hoping to defuse the situation, Seb pushed his chair back. "If you'll all excuse me for a minute, I need to find the restroom."

Before he was even out of earshot, he heard Mae telling Heath to let it go. He blew out a long breath. He'd known coming tonight would be a disaster, but when Mae had said she wanted him here, he'd found that he couldn't say no. He seemed to have an ongoing issue with his ability to deny Mae Dunstan anything she asked for.

When he was done and walking back through the hotel lobby, he saw Heath waiting for him up ahead and groaned.

Heath stepped into his path and didn't bother with a greeting. "I don't know what sort of game you're playing with my sister."

Seb sank his hands into his pockets and prayed for strength. "I'm not playing a game."

Heath took an infinitesimal step forward. "You should know that when my mother found out she was pregnant with Mae, she took me and ran. Changed our names, falsified Mae's birth certificate, moved countries with us several times, all to keep the two of us safe."

"I know that," Seb said, confused. Everyone in the state knew that. His cell in his pocket vibrated but he ignored it—the man in front of him needed all his attention.

"Then," Heath said, menace in his eyes, "you'll understand that after all my mother's efforts to protect her, I'll be *damned* if I'm going to let you walk into my sister's life and take advantage of her. It would be dishonoring my mother's sacrifice if I allowed it."

Part of him was glad that Mae had someone

in her life willing to go to bat for her—except for the short period of his marriage, Seb had never had that, and Mae deserved all the support. The other part wanted to de-escalate the situation, get through the dinner, and go home. His cell vibrated again, and again he ignored it. "I know what she's been through—"

"You don't know anything about what we've been through," Heath said, then turned on his heel and strode away.

Seb watched him leave, then rolled his shoulders back, trying to release some tension. His cell vibrated again. He drew it out and found a message from Mae.

Where are you?

Torn, his thumbs hovered over the cell.

Maybe it's best for everyone if I leave.

The reply was instant.

Is Heath with you?

He almost grinned at how fast her mind went to her brother. She must have suspected what he'd been up to, which also meant there was no point avoiding or sugarcoating the truth.

Not anymore.

I will kill him.

Seb rubbed a hand behind his neck, even less keen to return to the table now that he knew that fratricide was being contemplated. While he was still working out a plan, he saw Mae striding toward him, dragging Heath by the hand.

When she reached him, she dropped her brother's hand and looked from Heath to Seb, and back again. "What the hell, Heath?"

"I could say the same to you." He pointed at Seb while keeping his eyes on Mae. "What exactly is going on between you two?"

"I'll tell you what." Security near the front door looked over, so she dropped her voice to a harsh whisper. "None of your business is what's happening."

Heath angled his shoulders to exclude Sebastian, and, if anything, Seb was grateful. Mae wasn't in danger, and there were about a thousand places Seb would rather be right now. But she wanted him there, so he waited.

"Since when do we keep secrets?" Heath hissed.

Mae's eyes widened and even Seb could see that that had been a trigger of some kind.

"Since you started it." Her voice was laced with barely contained anger. "Finding out about our father and Sarah. The inheritance. You did it on your own, without telling me, until it was pretty much all settled."

Heath rocked back, shock all over his face. "Hang on, that's not fair. You know why that was."

"I know your own justification for it, sure," she said, pointing a finger at his chest. "Now I'm doing my version of how to approach all of this on my own. So you can back off."

"But—"

"I. Said. Back. Off." Her voice was low and lethal and both men took a small step back.

Heath glared at his sister for a long moment, then headed back to their private dining room.

Once he was out of sight, Mae's face filled with pain and her shoulders slumped. Sebastian reached for her and brought her into the circle of his arms, holding her tight. She felt good there. Right. As if nothing in the world could be bad as long as she was there.

"You don't fight with him often, do you?"

"No," she said against his shoulder as her arms wrapped around his back. "But that one had been coming for a long time. I hadn't forgiven him for keeping secrets. Still, I shouldn't have done it here, or in front of you." She tipped her head back. "I'm sorry. That must have been uncomfortable to see."

"Not as uncomfortable as it would have been for you to be in the middle of it."

"And what's worse is I'll have to apologize to him later. He was out of line, but I shouldn't have lost my cool. Not in public, anyway."

"Do you want me to get you out of here?"

She sighed and pulled back. "Thank you for offering, but no. We need to go back, finish the dinner, and then I can go. It's not just Heath's night, it's Freya's too, and I really like her."

"Then, let's go." They disentangled themselves and walked back to their table with a respectful distance between them, but the imprint of her body still hummed against his.

Sarah and Lauren watched their approach, one with an expression of concern and the other looking intrigued. They took their seats as Freya was whispering to Heath, her brows drawn together, but her fiancé merely gave a curt shake of his head and mouthed, "Later."

The whole scene was excruciating, even compared to dinners with his father. The difference was that he hadn't cared about his father from quite a young age, so he could easily dismiss or ignore whatever he was saying. He'd grown very accustomed to tuning his father out. But, he realized, he cared a lot about Mae. He didn't want to be the cause of a rift with her family, especially with her brother after all they'd been through together.

Worst of all, what if Heath had been right? Seb hadn't set out to take advantage of Mae, but maybe, subconsciously, that was part of what he'd been doing? He was Christopher Newport's son, after all. Even his own mother thought he was like Christopher, so perhaps he'd been kidding himself about his own motives all this time?

While stilted conversation went back and forth around the table, Seb took his cell from his pocket, set it on his thigh, and typed a message to Mae.

I don't belong here. I should leave.

He heard her phone vibrate and saw her look down seconds before his cell vibrated on his thigh.

You can't.

He turned to her and raised his eyebrows, snagging his water glass at the same time for cover. His phone vibrated again.

You said, whatever I want, I could have it.

A bolt of heat shot through his system.

Mae...

He didn't know if that had been a warning or a plea, but, either way, he couldn't look at her.

You promised. And I've decided. I want you. Tonight.

He almost choked, and took another sip of water. He checked the table, but no one seemed to be paying them attention. But then he had a horrible moment of doubt. Surely, she wouldn't use him to get back at her family? This had to be about more. But he had to check.

Is this because you're mad at your family?

She leaned over and whispered in his ear, "I want what I asked for before, but more. So much more. I've wanted it since we were in your kitchen." He felt her hand on his side. Clearly, she wasn't bothering to hide things from the others now, and he had no idea how he felt about that. His cell vibrated again.

Check your jacket pocket.

He slid a hand into his pocket and found the hard, smooth surface of a hotel room key card. He put more effort into keeping a poker face at that moment than he ever had in his business negotiations. When had she even booked a room? His hand was unsteady as he typed on his cell.

Are you seriously doing this?

From the corner of his eye, he saw her smile.

No one ever accused me of being sensible.

With that, Mae stood and gathered her purse from under her chair. "I'm feeling tired, so I'm going to make it an early night. Congratulations again, Freya and Heath. I can't tell you how much I'm looking forward to having a sister. Sebastian, would you see me home?"

"Yeah, sure. Thanks for having me tonight," he said to the others. "It was an honor to be invited." He pushed his chair out and stood beside her, feeling as if the rug had been ripped out from underneath him. "After you," he said, mainly because he didn't know where they were going.

They walked out, side by side, and once they reached the lobby, she took his hand and changed direction, heading for the bank of elevators. And just like that, Sebastian was dizzy with want.

EIGHT

As they neared the door to the room she'd booked, Mae slowed down and tried to catch her breath. Since she knew the room number, she'd been the one leading the way, but it was somehow important that Sebastian be the one to open the door. There was a second card in her purse, but him doing the honors would make this a choice they were making together.

His hand was still wrapped tightly around hers, and when they stopped, he produced the key card from his pocket. He held it aloft for a beat, and when she nodded, he inserted the card, pushed open the door, and held it for her to enter.

A few steps inside, the sound of a soft click from behind told her that the door had been closed, and she turned, hoping he'd dispense with preliminaries like last time. Instead, he stood there, magnificent, his chest rising and falling, with an intensity in his features she didn't understand.

"Mae, I need to check something. Is this really what you want?" Small frown lines appeared across his brow and he lifted a hand to absently rub at them, before dropping it back to his side again. "Am I really what you want?"

Caught off guard, she almost laughed at how ludicrous the question was, but stopped herself in time. "It was your pocket that I slid the card into." She'd thought that was a pretty clear signal. "Besides, who else would I want here?"

"It's..." He blew out a breath. "We had our deal in place—that last time was a one-time-only deal. Then you argue with your brother about me and now here we are."

"Sebastian, no—"

"I need to know that you want this—" his eyes narrowed, assessing her "—and it's not you proving something to yourself or whatever."

That explanation made sense, but was there more to it? She bit down on her lip, thinking it through. Had *he* been swept away with her putting the card in his pocket and wanting to get out of the dinner...and was he now having second thoughts?

"Sebastian, do you want to be here? You laid

out your terms that night at my aunt's apartment, and I'm the one who's crossed the line by inviting you here. If you'd rather leave, it's fine. Honestly." She tried to emanate I'll-be-fine vibes, when that was the opposite of how she felt inside, but he deserved have the choice to walk away if he wanted to.

He drew in a shuddering breath. "Mae, I really want to be here. In fact, I'm so far beyond want right now that I can hardly see straight. Which is why I need to know that you do too."

A weight slid from her shoulders and her body felt as if it were filled with champagne bubbles. *He wanted her.* Wanted this.

"I paid for this room before Heath was being a jerk," she said, taking a small step closer.

He cocked his head to the side. "When, exactly?"

"Before you arrived. I got here early and took the room." She'd come with Sarah and Lauren but had told them to go ahead to the private dining room, taking the chance to sneak over to reception.

His eyebrows shot up. "You had this planned?"

"Not planned, exactly." Planned sounded too definite. But hoped? Absolutely. "Let's say I was keeping my options open."

He reached into his back pocket, pulled out his wallet and produced a condom. "Maybe I was keeping my options open as well."

Arching an eyebrow, Mae lifted her purse in front of her chest and pulled out an entire box of condoms.

Sebastian laughed. "When you're in, you go all in."

"I'm what you might call an all-or-nothing kinda gal," she said, fluttering her lashes.

"I've noticed." One corner of his mouth hitched up.

She hesitated. "Noticed it in a bad way?"

He closed the distance between them and slid his arms around her waist. "I like it."

"Well, then you're going to love this," she said and began unbuttoning his shirt.

He leaned in, pausing when his mouth was so close that his breath fanned over hers, and said, "You're right. I do."

And then he kissed her and she was once again drowning in her need for him. His tongue pushed against her lips—seductive, carnal—and she forgot about the buttons on his shirt, winding her hands up behind his neck, holding his head in place.

She'd kissed and been kissed before, but it

had been nothing compared to kissing Sebastian. The need he didn't attempt to disguise, the desperation she couldn't have hidden if she'd wanted to. He slid his hands down to her hips, pressing her closer as she speared his hair with her fingers, giving her all and taking as much from him.

Eventually, she dragged her head back, sucking in lungfuls of air, almost dizzy with wanting.

"I have to tell you," Sebastian said around his own panting breaths, "I'm feeling torn about this dress."

She glanced down. "You don't like it?"

When she'd bought it, the dress had made her feel good about herself, flattering her nicely. And when she'd put it on earlier in the evening, she'd thought of him and smiled at herself in the mirror, hoping he'd be taking it off later.

"I'm torn," he said, toying with the neckline, "because I like it so much that I'm a little sad it has to go. But it does. Have to go. Now."

Her knees buckled, and she swayed in the safety of his arms. "There are two ties. The one you can see on my left side, and, on my right, there's a secret hook as well as the tie."

"Now, that is useful information." He kissed

her again, a quick, scorching press of his lips to hers and then dipped his head to focus on the task. He pulled at the first tie, and one side of her dress dropped, leaving a length of material wrapped against her torso. The light pressure of his fingers at her side as he searched for the hook was torture—the touch, muffled by the fabric, was nowhere near enough. And then he found the hook, unclasped it, and the rest of the dress unraveled from around her.

As he slid the two panels of soft material apart, the pads of his fingers brushed lightly against her ribs, leaving a trail of sparks on her bare skin, and she gasped. Too soon, his fingers were gone, and then his hands were on her shoulders, slowly easing the dress down her arms. In moments, her dress was gone, leaving cool air swirling against her flesh.

Surprised, and impressed, that he'd worked it out so easily, she gave him a lazy smile. "That was fast."

"I can be fast when it's important. And this was very important." He leaned past her and carefully draped her dress on the hotel room's plush velvet chair.

As his gaze roamed her body, he set his warm, strong hands on her shoulders, first tracing circles and patterns, then moving down her arms, across her back, and a soft moan escaped her lips.

She glanced up at him, mesmerized by the wonder and appreciation she found in his features. "What do you want, Sebastian?"

"I want to see you this time," he said without hesitation.

Meeting his eyes, she reached behind her back and found the clasp on her bra. It took her a few seconds to release the catch—despite only having one glass of champagne at dinner, she was feeling more than a little inebriated. It had nothing to do with the champagne. She was drunk on him. It was all him. It was Sebastian's effect on her, making her fingers tremble, making her light-headed.

She pulled her arms from the lace straps, and let the bra fall from her fingertips to the floor. Then she hooked her thumbs in the sides of the matching underwear and slid them down to her ankles before kicking them away, along with her shoes. Sebastian's eyes flared as he drank her in, and she stood tall, feeling beautiful under his gaze.

"Mae," he said, his voice a hoarse whisper.

"You're..." He stopped, cleared his throat, and tried again. "Everything about you is exquisite."

He reached for her and she melted into him, tugging at his belt buckle even as he kissed her, wanting to remove the last fabric barrier between them. On one especially rough tug on his belt, he laughed and laid his hands over hers, stopping her until she looked up at him.

"What about you?" Releasing her hands, he cupped her face and brushed a featherlight kiss on her lips. "What do you want?"

"I want..." She had no idea if this was another onetime deal or if it was the start of something, but just in case, she wanted to experience everything with him at least once. "I want you inside me this time."

"Well," he said, swallowing hard, "it would be a shame to waste all those condoms."

This time, when he kissed her, his hands had free rein over her body, and he took full advantage, from teasing her breasts to skimming across her stomach until he reached the delta of her thighs, an area he gave special attention to until she was writhing against him.

When his hands moved on again, she wrenched away and sternly said, "Trousers, Sebastian."

Grinning, he dispensed with his pants, and

she allowed her gaze to roam over him, from the rigid erection he'd just freed, to his strong, muscular legs, up to his chest with its expanse of olive skin, dusted with dark hair.

"My turn," she said and scraped her nails across his pecs.

As a shiver ran through his body, he dropped his hands. "No argument here."

She circled behind him and pressed a kiss to the spot between his shoulder blades. Last time, everything had happened so fast that there hadn't been time to stop and smell the roses. Or, more precisely, to smell him. She pressed the side of her face against his back, luxuriating in the feel of his skin, the heady scent of him. He remained still, giving her the space to explore as she chose, so she traced her nails down into the arch of his lower back then over the rise of his ass cheeks, caressing them for the pure pleasure of it.

Circling around again, she found his eyes closed, the tension in his expression betraying what it cost him to stay still while she played. She stood up on tiptoe and touched her lips to the sculpted perfection of his mouth, and his arms were suddenly around her, lifting her off the ground as he kissed her hungrily, then gently lowered her to stand again, all without breaking the kiss.

"My turn?" he asked when they came up for air.

"Nearly," she said, snaking her hand down to grasp his erection. He already felt familiar, velvety and hot, and she stroked him the way he liked it. Knowing how Sebastian liked to be touched, having the freedom to simply reach out and do it was exhilarating.

He brushed his mouth over the shell of her ear and, his voice gravel-rough, said, "Now it's my turn."

"For now," she conceded, releasing him.

He drew her earlobe into the heat of his mouth and scraped his teeth across its flesh, igniting fireworks in her blood. Then he kissed his way down the side of her face, her neck, nipping at her collarbone before circling the peak of her breast with his tongue. Her heart raced in an erratic beat, but before she could find her equilibrium, he'd moved on, sweeping kisses across her stomach and then kneeling before her. As he threw her a smoldering glance, she steadied herself with her hands on his shoulders and held her breath. He parted her with his fingers, then rubbed her with his thumb, using downward strokes. She made a loud, involuntary noise but couldn't make herself care. All that mattered was Sebastian and what he was doing. Then, slowly, oh so slowly, he leaned forward and his tongue swept the path his thumb had taken.

"Sebastian," she said on a strangled breath.

Without missing a beat, he gripped her hips to steady her, his mouth making blissful magic, and the world around her dissolved into a burst of light and sensation.

She was vaguely aware of him lifting and moving her, and when she blinked her eyes open, she was straddling his lap on the side of the bed. She smiled, feeling pretty good about the world.

"Hey," he said softly.

"Hey, you." She reached her arms above her head to stretch, her muscles still buzzing.

"Whoa," he said. "You might want to give a guy some warning if you're going to do that. My entire system could have overloaded."

She pushed gently at his shoulder. "I think you can take it."

"Think of my poor heart," he said, hand on his chest, all faux dramatics, even though his jaw was tense and his muscles were bunched. It was costing him to be light and charming when his body was screaming for release.

Grinning, she maneuvered and wriggled until she was tighter against him, and all traces of humor evaporated from his features.

"This," he hissed through his teeth. "This is what I want."

"Just this?" she said innocently, squirming just a little.

His breath caught. "Maybe you're right and I can handle more."

"Care to prove it?" she said, raising an eyebrow in challenge.

Eyes dancing, he lay back on the bed, and she lifted herself on her hands and knees above him, leaning down for his kiss, the heat rising inside her again as his hands stroked and teased her flesh. Just as the urgency began to creep back into her blood, he changed their positions and then stood, taking all his warmth and beauty with him. He held up one finger before disappearing for intolerable seconds, and then he was back, sheathed, and she pulled him down to her on the bed, needing the feel of his skin on hers again. As he kissed her, he rolled her beneath him, his delicious weight pressing her into the mattress. Everything inside her began to feel frantic, needing him more than anything, wanting it all, whatever *it all* was.

Honestly, it all came down to him. Sebastian. Lately, it seemed that it always did.

She reached a hand and laid it on the side of his precious face, wanting to appreciate the moment, commit this view of him to memory. He stilled for endless seconds, seemingly lost in the moment with her, the only sound in the room their heavy breathing. And then he whispered her name and reached down to guide himself inside her, and she wrapped her legs around his waist, shifting to adjust, reveling in the intimacy of the contact.

He began to move, and she caught his rhythm and moved with him, the coiled tightness inside coming faster than she'd expected, growing stronger, until the world exploded and she clung to Sebastian as if he was the only thing anchoring her to reality.

As he chased his own peak, Sebastian continued his rhythm, and in his moment of release, he called out her name.

When she drifted off to sleep a little later, it was that moment that she replayed in her mind, and she smiled.

★ ★ ★

Mae woke slowly, stretching catlike before opening her eyes. Spontaneous stays in expensive hotels were one aspect of being rich she could definitely get used to. She rolled over to find Sebastian already awake and sitting up on the bed.

She smiled sleepily. "You're awake early."

"I have a toddler," Sebastian said with an eyebrow quirked. "This is not early."

As her brain began to engage, she frowned. He was wearing the same shirt and pants from dinner the night before, though they were more rumpled now. "You're covered in all those clothes." She slid a hand across his covered stomach. "Can't say I approve of that."

He lifted two cups. "I had to put the clothes on to get the coffee."

"Then I do approve." She sat up, stretched again, and took the coffee he handed her. He'd brought her a Grande Americano, just as she liked it? "This is an excellent way to start a day. Much better than sneaking you out of Sarah's apartment at 4:00 a.m."

"Also better than sneaking out of a family dinner that turned messy."

She sighed. "I'm so sorry about that. It must have been awful for you."

"It wasn't all bad." He shrugged. "Freya seems great. And I liked Lauren."

"She was definitely on our side, which surprised me."

Sebastian sipped his coffee, his gaze thoughtful. "Is there something between Sarah and Lauren?"

"I think there's a lot between Sarah and Lauren. They're boss and employee, but most importantly they're pretty much best friends." They always seemed in sync with each other, the way long-term friends often were.

He cocked his head to the side. "Nothing more than that?"

"I don't think so." She pulled her legs up under the covers so she could wrap her free arm around them. "Why?"

"I just thought I saw a…connection."

Mae considered it, thinking back over the interactions she'd seen between the two women. "I doubt it. They've been friends since before Freya was born, so if there was something there, surely they would have acted on it by now?"

"Maybe," he said.

"Though that does make me think I should

try some matchmaking for Sarah. I love to see people find their person."

"I'm glad you think that, because I have something to ask."

"Me too," she said and took a sip of coffee, savoring the deep, rich taste. "I was thinking about coming into the office again and doing another week." The week had gone so quickly, and there were a couple of things she hadn't been able to resolve during that time. Larry Sheridan's situation was one—she wanted to ensure that he was okay with whatever Bellavista decided to do—and a couple of changes she'd been supporting Rosario in making with the admin staff.

"I have a better plan." He reached over and took her hand and his gaze became more intense. "We should get married."

Mae blinked. She hadn't been awake long, and her brain wasn't firing on all cylinders yet, but it sounded like he'd just…proposed? That made zero sense.

"This is from left field," she said carefully. "When did you decide this?"

A frown line appeared between his brows. "Last night your brother accused me of taking advantage of you."

Mae shot up from under the covers. "Heath said *what*?"

"It's okay," he said, holding up a hand. "Under the circumstances, it wasn't completely out of line."

"Yes, it was." Because of the way she and Heath had grown up, with the two of them and their mother keeping their identities secret, and only being able to rely on each other, they'd all tended to be overinvolved in each other's lives. And since their mother's death, when it had become just the two of them, she and Heath had looked out for each other more than most siblings, which could lead to overstepping. It was time to end that. She'd be having a word with her brother in the very near future. Again. "I'm sorry he said that to you. I know it's not true, and that's all that matters."

He swallowed hard and looked down at their joined hands. "Even though it wasn't my intention, it did start me wondering if I've been subconsciously taking advantage of you. I mean, I do have my father's genes, and that's what he'd do. But if we get married, it puts us on even footing, which fixes everything."

"Fixes everything?" She tried to put all that together in her head, but it didn't add up. She took a slug of coffee, set the cup on the side table, and said, "Okay, explain that to me."

He twisted so he was completely facing her. "If we're married, then there's no question of motives anymore. We'd be on the same team. It won't be the Rutherford-Dunstan family versus the Newport family, it would just be Mae and Seb, the dynamic duo." His eyes filled with enthusiasm, and he tugged on her hand, inviting her to join his excitement. "When you split your inheritance with Heath, you could ask for Joseph's shares of Bellavista, and once my father retires, the two of us would own the entire company. I'll help you learn everything you need to know, and we can run it together. And Alfie and our future kids will inherit the combined company."

Mae stared at him with growing horror. "Is this a proposal for a marriage or a proposal for a business merger?"

He shrugged that away, seemingly unconcerned. "Why can't we have the best of both worlds?"

The coffee in her stomach turned sour. Was there a chance that she'd been right in her suspicions at the start? That he was playing a long con, and this was another step in his plan? "Sebastian," she said slowly, "I don't think this is a good idea."

He stilled, the passion in his eyes ebbing. "You seemed to like being with me, though."

"Sure, but that's not really enough to be considering a lifelong commitment." And it felt weird to even have to spell that out.

"It's all relative. Ashley and I grew to love each other more once we were married, but if I compare my feelings at the time of making a commitment..." He shrugged one shoulder. "I already feel closer to you than when she and I got engaged."

There was silence in the room for several beats as she wondered if this was what rich people were really like—very little about how rich people operated made sense to her—or if this was just a Sebastian thing. Either way, this conversation was getting surreal. He really was speaking as though he believed intimate relationships were transactional. She needed a moment to think, and this wasn't a conversation she wanted to have while she was naked and he was dressed. Stepping from the bed, she slipped on her underwear and the lilac dress, then, taking his hand, drew him to the armchairs off to the side.

"I haven't had a committed relationship before," she said once they were seated. "It didn't seem right when I couldn't share the truth about who I was and knowing we might have to move with little notice again, so I kept things light when I was involved with someone. So, I'm definitely no expert, but, Sebastian, I don't think this is how proposals are supposed to work."

His gaze on her was unwavering. "Well, I've only ever done the one proposal before now, so I'm no expert either, but I think they should work however we want them to work. It's just between us."

So many thoughts were crowding her brain that it was difficult to separate them. She tucked her hair behind her ears. "You've raised a few different things here, and they seem to be all tangled together." The only thing to do really was to address them one by one, and the easiest one to start with was the company. "Sebastian, I don't want to work at Bellavista. Being a businessperson is who you are, but it's not who I am."

He tipped his chin. "You just asked to come back for another week," he said, surprised. "I've seen you in the office, and you clearly love it. Plus, Rosario tells me that all the people you met so far only had great things to say about you. You're a natural."

Rosario was lovely to have passed nice feedback about her to Sebastian, but working in an office for the rest of her career, chasing profits instead of doing good, going to meetings with those smug, hungry lawyers and people like them, sounded awful. "A main reason is I wanted to follow up on Larry—I'm the sort of person who finishes what I start. And—" she glanced down, butterflies filling her stomach "—to be completely honest, I wasn't ready to say goodbye to you."

It shouldn't have been awkward to say, not after he'd just proposed, but his idea of marriage was about business, and she was admitting something deeper. But then he was there, kneeling in front of her, and he tipped up her chin with one finger. She looked into his deep blue eyes, and found herself trapped by the emotion there.

"Mae," he said, his voice gentle, "I told you that you could ask for anything you wanted. You didn't have to invent a story about coming into the office. Why not just ask to keep seeing me?"

"I thought that was just about…" She didn't

want to say aloud that she thought he'd only been talking about sex, in case she'd misjudged him.

"It's about everything," he said simply.

Unable to help herself, she leaned forward, and he met her halfway. The kiss was sweet and soft and full of tenderness and promises.

When they pulled apart, she laid her hand on the side of his face. "Here's a counteroffer. What you and I have had so far has been hurried and clandestine. What I'd really like is for us to start dating. I appreciate that part of your reasoning for the marriage proposal was to protect me, but it's been just over a week since we met, Sebastian. Regular people don't get married that quickly."

He huffed out a laugh. "You might be right. Okay, dating it is." He leaned in and kissed her again and then murmured against her lips, "What time is checkout?"

"I arranged a late checkout when I booked the room last night."

His eyes widened comically. "Miss Dunstan, were you planning on seducing me this morning?"

"You bet I am," she said and let him lead her back to the bed.

★ ★ ★

Three weeks into their new dating arrangement, Mae decided to surprise Sebastian for lunch. They'd managed to spend some time together most days, getting to know each other more like a normal couple, and she'd spent some time with Alfie, too. She and Sebastian had managed to have lunch a couple of times a week, and dinner at his place after Alfie went to bed, and he'd left a few gaps in his daily schedule to meet up with her. She hadn't stayed the night with him, though. After his proposal, she was wary of sending mixed signals, so she was trying to keep them firmly in the "just dating" territory. But the warm call of his body every day was making it harder to say no, and to leave his apartment and head home.

She'd spent the rest of her time with either Heath or Sarah, dealing with the rest of their inheritance. On Thursday, she'd passed the morning at the office of their charitable trust, which was easily her favorite of the offices, and had some free time before an afternoon meeting with Sarah.

There were options to fill her time, but she was always itching to see Sebastian nowadays...

In the past, if things were going this well, she

would have split and run because she was raised to believe that if it looks too good to be true, it probably is. She was trying to be optimistic, though. To believe in Sebastian. Believe in the two of them together.

So she drew in a breath and decided to drop in and see him in her free window of time.

When she reached Rosario's desk, the other woman was on the phone. Mae put the cappuccino she'd brought in front of her, and when Rosario held up a finger, Mae nodded and stood back to wait. She put the call on hold. "It's great to see you, Mae."

"You too, Rosario. Is Sebastian in?"

She shook her head. "He's having lunch with Ashley's parents. Since it's her birthday, the first one since she died, I think they were going to do something to commemorate it."

"Oh, of course," Mae said, trying not to betray her feelings. Maybe it was nothing, but was it weird that Sebastian hadn't mentioned this at all? She'd seen him last night and he'd sent a text at 7 a.m. to say good morning, but there had been no mention of something this big. She considered the other side of the story, for balance. Perhaps he was thinking it would be awkward for her? Still, she was going to have to mention to him that secrets were a deal breaker for her.

Rosario pointed to her headset. "Give me a minute to finish this call before you go, though. I was hoping to talk to you today."

"Sure," Mae said and glanced out the window.

An older man with gold-rimmed glasses and an angry face stormed in, pushed past her, and opened the door to Sebastian's office.

He stomped back and scowled at Rosario. "Where is he?"

"I'm sorry. I need to put you on hold again for a moment," Rosario said into the headset's microphone. To the man, she said, "Mr. Newport, he's not available right now."

Mae was suddenly on full alert. This was Sebastian's father, Christopher Newport. Sebastian looked nothing like this pasty-faced man with sandy hair—he must have taken after his mother in looks.

"I can see that," Christopher said. "I asked *where* he was."

Rosario didn't flinch or falter. "I'm afraid he didn't tell me. I'm only his assistant."

"This is unacceptable—" He froze as he caught sight of Mae waiting to the side, all color draining from his face. His mouth opened and then closed again.

In the background, Mae heard Rosario going back to her call and ending it. "Mr. Newport, I can take a message and pass it to Sebastian when he gets back."

Christopher didn't take his focus from Mae. "I assume you're Joseph's other missing brat. At least you look more like the Rutherfords than your brother."

Mae weighed her options. Even if she hadn't already known what sort of man Christopher was, it was clear now that nothing good was going to come out of his mouth and she should step outside until he was gone. But this man had been her father's business partner and rival, and she expected to see something of her father in him—more than she'd seen anything of her father in his sister, Sarah, so morbid curiosity kept her there.

Besides, this was Sebastian's father and observing him for a few moments might give her more of an insight into the man who occupied her every waking thought.

And so she stuck out her hand. "Good to meet you, Mr. Newport. I'm Mae Dunstan."

He stared at her hand without reaching for

it, then looked back up at her. "I'd heard rumors that Sebastian was taking a leaf out of my book, but I didn't believe it."

"I'm sorry," she said. "I'm not sure what you're referring to."

He smirked. "You look like your aunt."

She'd heard that often enough, but it still didn't make sense. "So I believe. Not sure how that relates to Sebastian."

He tipped his head to the side in what he probably thought was a suave gesture. "Sarah and I used to be together."

"You and Sarah?" she said, incredulous.

"What? You think I wasn't good enough for her? She was obsessed with me back in the day."

Magnificent Sarah, obsessed with this buffoon? "I find that hard to believe."

He lifted his chin in the air. "I almost had her father convinced to leave his share of Bellavista to her. Then once I married her the whole company would have been mine."

A creeping chill spread across her skin. Something about his words seemed very off. "What about Joseph?"

"Your father was a jerk." He'd spat the words with contempt. "And stupid too. Sarah was the brains of the family, and their father knew it.

And if I'd pulled my plan off, you and your brother would never have seen a cent either."

"That's an interesting story, but you obviously didn't pull it off. Heath and I inherited everything, so something went wrong."

His eyes shifted to the doorway. "I changed my mind," he said with less bluster.

"She dumped you, didn't she?" His shoulders bunched up and Mae smiled. "Took her a while, but she ended up seeing through you."

"She didn't see anything. I decided to tell her the reality of our situation and she freaked out. She might have been smart but she was naive about the world."

"Hang on, you had a grand plan to get control of the company by seducing and marrying Sarah, then getting her father to change his will to leave his share to her. And then, what? You ruined it all—why? Did you fall for her and tell her everything? And she realized what a contemptible human being you are and walked out. Is that it?" She could see from the look in his eyes that she'd put it all together.

"Don't look so self-righteous. Sounds like you and Sebastian are doing the exact same thing to *your* brother."

"Wait, what? I would never try and cut Heath out of his share."

"Right. Then it's just Sebastian working alone. Hopefully he'll propose soon and all this can be yours." He swept an arm around the office.

The cold, sinking feeling she'd had through the entire conversation finally became a sharp bar of ice in her gut. She glanced at Rosario and back again.

Christopher guffawed. "Oh, that is rich. He's already proposed, hasn't he? Gotta hand it to the kid. I often wondered if he had too much of his mother in him to do anything good with the company, but looks like he's got it all shored up. Welcome to the family, sweetheart."

He walked out the door, laughing. Mae didn't move. She felt like a grenade had just gone off and she wasn't sure if she'd survived or not.

Rosario rushed around the desk and put an arm around Mae's shoulders to guide her to a chair. "I'm so sorry. I hate him—we all do. Most of us only stay for Sebastian. Just ignore everything he said. He shoots his mouth off all the time, and I don't think he knows what he's saying half the time."

Mae found a smile to reassure Rosario that

she was okay. She needed to talk to Sebastian, but she couldn't call or text him if he was at some sort of memorial for Ashley.

"I might just leave Sebastian a note on his desk, if that's okay."

"Of course it is. And I'll tell him that you were here if he calls to check in."

"Thank you."

But what could she say in a note?

If the proverbial apple had fallen right at the base of the tree, then there was nothing left to say. And if it hadn't? She squeezed her eyes shut and tried to ignore every instinct she had, because they were all screaming to run.

Don't look back, don't falter, just run.

She opened her eyes, picked up a pen, and started writing.

NINE

SEBASTIAN OPENED HIS car door, sank into the driver's seat, and leaned his head back on the headrest with his eyes closed. The lunch with Ashley's parents, extended family, and assorted friends for her birthday had emotionally wiped him out. Such a senseless waste of life to cancer—their daughter, their cousin or niece, their friend, Alfie's mother, his wife.

He missed Ashley's companionship, her sensible advice, and most of all, he missed parenting with her. Every time Alfie hit a milestone, it was bittersweet because Ashley couldn't see it. They might not have started as a love match, but they'd come to love each other, especially through Alfie.

Alfie had been the center of attention today, and Ashley's friends and cousins had taken turns holding him, needing that connection to her. They'd prearranged that Amanda and Barry would keep him overnight and bring him back in the morning, since they needed to hold their daughter's son more than anyone today.

His cell rang and Rosario's name flashed up. There had been a message from her earlier to call and he'd planned on using the drive back to do it anyway. He started the car and answered the call. "Hey, Rosario. I'm just heading off now."

"I know this is a terrible time to bother you, but something's happened you'll probably want to know about."

He stifled a groan. "If that's the architect about the plans I said I'd have back this morning, tell her—"

"It's Mae."

He broke off immediately, heart in his mouth. "What about Mae?"

"She came in to surprise you for lunch and ran into your father. He was as unpleasant as you'd expect, but he's suggested to her that you're seducing her to get her shares in the company."

He almost ran off the road. "You *have* to be kidding me."

"It was like a slow-motion train wreck. I

watched it happening, could see it getting worse, but there was nothing I could do. I'm sorry."

"None of this is your fault, Rosario. Not a thing." The fault was all his father's. "Why would he even say that? If he really thinks I'm playing a game, why would he alert her?"

"Honestly, I think he just got carried away with his story about dating Sarah when he was young and being a blowhard, and totally lost sight of who his audience was. But, yeah, if you *were* capable of something like that and were using Mae, then he'd have shot the Newport plan in the foot."

Seb gripped the steering wheel tighter. "How did Mae take it?"

"She seemed rattled. I tried to talk to her after, but I think she just wanted to get out of the office." She drew in a breath. "There's something else."

"Hit me," he said and braced himself.

"Mae asked where you were and I assumed she knew about the lunch for Ashley and had just forgotten, so I told her. I'm sorry if I've put my foot in it."

He winced as he made a left-hand turn. Poor Mae, double blindsided without him there to explain. "Again, that's not on you. That one's on me. Do you know where she went?"

"She didn't say, but she did leave you a note on your desk."

"I'm on my way. And thanks for the heads-up."

He disconnected and tried Mae's number. She didn't pick up, so he left a message, apologizing for not being around today and asking her to call him. He should have been up front about today, and at the very least told her in the text he'd sent her this morning where he was going, but he'd needed some time to get his head around the day first. Once he'd arrived there, he'd realized why.

They'd all visited the grave site first, in a picturesque cemetery partway between Manhattan and her parents' place, and then had lunch together at a local café to reminisce. Laying the flowers at her graveside, his feelings had suddenly made sense. He was there to say goodbye to Ashley before moving into the future with Mae. Having a future with Mae without doing this first would have felt like a betrayal of his first marriage. He'd needed to tell Ashley.

The others had let him have some time alone to stand beside the marble headstone, which he'd appreciated. He'd given her an update on Alfie, told her how proud she'd be of her son, promised her he was still prioritizing finding work-life balance. And then he'd asked for her blessing to move on with Mae.

In that moment, as he'd told Ashley about her, he had been hit with a bone-deep certainty that he loved Mae. He'd told Ashley that he loved her too, but that his love for Mae was different. Ashley would have understood—they'd never lied to each other about their feelings, and she'd known that he loved her as his best friend, his ally, and the mother of his son.

Mae, though? She was everything. His here and now, his future, his everything. He could barely breathe when he thought of her.

He tried her cell again a few times on the drive back, but she still wasn't answering. Once he finally reached the Bellavista headquarters, he had to force himself not to run to his office to find her note. He smiled and exchanged greetings with various people in the hallways and told someone from accounts that it was okay to send through some files.

When he stepped through to Rosario's office, she said, "I've cleared your afternoon."

"You are an angel," he said, without stopping.

In the middle of his glass-top desk was a folded slip of paper with his name written in her neat handwriting. Barely restraining himself from lunging at it, he picked it up in controlled movements and opened it.

> *Sebastian,*
> *Rosario told me where you are, and I'm sorry you have to go through this, because Ashley's birthday will be a rough day for you.*
> *I haven't called or texted because I didn't want to interrupt, but the thing is, I'm mad at you, but I don't want you to see me mad on a day like today. So, I hope you're okay, and tomorrow we need to talk.*
> *Mae*

His stomach turned over and made a new knot. This mess needed fixing, now. First, he had to find her.

He was still holding the piece of paper in his hand when his father blustered past Rosario and into his office.

"There you are," he said in his too-loud voice. A voice that had grated on Seb his whole life. "I've been looking for you. What's the point of having a personal assistant if they don't know where you are?"

Seb folded the note and put it in his shirt pocket. "Dad, it's not the time."

His father stabbed a finger in the air in the general direction of a wall clock. "These are business hours and I need an update on the Sheridan property, which is a business matter, so this *is* the time."

Seb glanced up at him, the man who'd sucked any joy from most things in his life and who might now have ruined his future. "What did you say to her?"

"Who? Rutherford's daughter?" He flicked a hand as if this was beneath his notice. "Nothing much. I'll give her one thing, though. She at least looks like the Rutherfords. Still not convinced her brother's part of their gene pool. Not that their features sit well on her. Not really a looker, is she?" His father laughed.

Seb drew in a breath through his nose. Blowing his top at his father wouldn't help anything—besides maybe his mood—and would only waste time. The day his father handed over the reins of the company and stepped away couldn't come soon enough. On that day, Seb was going to tell him exactly what he thought of him and then walk away from him forever.

Today, however, yelling at his father would only delay finding Mae.

So all he said was, "You're an ass," and then pushed past him and out the door. Finding Mae was all he cared about. Any interaction with his father would have left her feeling awful, which meant he didn't want to wait until tomorrow, as her note had suggested. He needed to check if she was okay today. Now. If she really didn't want to talk, then he could wait, but only when he knew she was fine.

As he stepped out of the building onto the sidewalk, he tried her number again, and she still didn't answer. So he did the unthinkable. He called Heath.

"Newport," Heath said on answering, his tone dry. "What a *delightful* surprise."

He didn't bother with niceties. "Have you seen Mae today?"

There was silence on the line, and he was just starting to wonder if Heath had walked off without disconnecting to annoy him, when Mae's voice came on. "Sebastian?"

"Thank goodness," he said, his shoulders slumping in relief. "I've been trying to call."

"My cell is turned off. I didn't want to talk

to anyone, and I thought you'd be busy for the rest of the day."

It was so good to hear her voice again. "Where are you?"

She hesitated before admitting, "At Freya's place in Queens."

"Can I come over there and see you?"

"You'd better not." Her voice had dropped to practically a whisper. "Everyone here is pretty anti-Newport at the moment."

And that was fair. His father made enemies more easily than he made friends. But he still wanted to see her. Emily, the nanny, was having some friends over to his apartment while Alfie was away, so his options were limited. "I'm going back to the office," he eventually said. "When you're done at Freya's, come and see me, no matter how late."

"I don't know, Sebastian." Her voice wavered. "I wanted a bit of time to think it all through."

"Alfie's with Amanda and Barry, so I'll wait the rest of the evening. Hell, I'll wait all night, just in case you decide to come."

"I'll see," she said and disconnected.

Seb dragged himself back up to his office and closed the door behind him. Mae's desk was still sitting at the window. He couldn't imagine his office without it now. What he wouldn't give to see her there, smiling across at him.

When the rest of the staff left for the night, Seb ordered in dinner and worked through his backlog of paperwork, trying not to check the clock every five minutes.

Just before midnight, Mae arrived.

"Hello," she said softly from the door. "I wasn't sure you'd be here this late."

"Hello," he said, drinking her in. "I told you I'd wait until morning, if necessary." She was so beautiful that his chest ached to look at her. "You want to come in?"

She wandered over to her desk and sat on its edge. "Your father said some things to me today," she said without preamble.

"I heard." He stayed in his chair, not wanting to spook her away now that she was so close. "I'm sorry about that. It was unforgivable. He's a despicable human being."

"No argument from me. He said he dated Sarah when they were younger, and he tried to manipulate the situation to get his hands on the Rutherfords' half. Something that Heath has confirmed. Did you know about that?" she asked, her chin tipping up.

"I've heard the story a few hundred times, yes."

"He also seemed to think you might be using the same playbook with me." Her gaze on him was laser sharp as she watched for his reaction, testing his father's theory against what she could see.

"Mae, after everything we've been through so far, you can't still suspect me of running a long con?"

She shrugged one shoulder. "My mother taught us to be suspicious precisely because of our father, and people like your father."

"I'm not him." He speared his fingers through his hair. He didn't just want to smooth this out so they could move on. He'd never really had anyone in his corner before, someone completely on his side, believing in him. To an extent, Ashley had been, but he kept her shielded from a lot of his family stuff, so she hadn't needed to take a stand by his side. With Mae, it was as if his chest had been ripped open from the start, with his beating heart on offer to her, vulnerable to her. More than anything, he wanted her to see him for who he really was. To look into his heart and know. To believe him. Believe in him.

He stood and crossed the distance to her desk.

Not wanting to touch her yet, to risk swaying her through their chemistry, he shoved his hands in his pockets and left a couple of feet between them.

"I realized today that I love you, Mae. The only other person in my life I've ever really loved this much is Alfie, and I thought that was different because it's how you feel about your child. But, Mae, I love you with the same intensity. I'd die for you. I know you think we've been going too fast, and I'm not expecting you feel the same, because it's too soon for you." He paused, sucked in a breath and opened his heart to her. "All I want is for you to see me. Neither of my parents ever saw me, and I'd kept parts of myself hidden from Ashley, so she never had the chance to see me even if she'd wanted to. You've been different from the start, though. I've kept nothing hidden. I need you to see the real me and that I'm nothing like my father."

Mae rose and took his hand, threading her fingers through his. "I do see you." She placed a palm firmly on his chest. "And I see your heart. I just sometimes get tangled in my own head. The programming my mother instilled to keep me safe hurts even as it helps. And being in this world—my father's world—was bound to trigger it more than normal."

He closed the distance separating them. "Not sure if you noticed that I slipped into that speech that I love you."

A corner of her mouth hitched up. "I did happen to notice that."

"You don't need to say it back," he clarified, in case she thought he was pressuring her. "I just needed you to know."

She drew in a trembling breath. "You were right that this is going too fast for me—I'm not in the same place as you. I'm not sure I *can* be in that place. If I can ever be as open and vulnerable as you just were."

"I'm willing to take the chance." Mae was worth the chance.

He rested his forehead against hers and slid a hand behind her neck, a shiver running up his spine at just being able to touch her again. She lifted herself up on her tiptoes and leaned into him, kissing him, drawing out the desire that was always near the surface when he was around her. Breathing her name, he kissed her back.

When they came up for oxygen, he said, "Come to the Hamptons with me. Alfie and I will be heading up tomorrow."

She grinned, her dimples flashing. "You mean today?"

He glanced at his wristwatch. "I guess I do. Amanda and Barry are bringing Alfie back during the day, and then we'll head up after I finish work. Come with us." In the weeks they'd been dating, they'd spent most of the first weekend in the hotel bed after her family's disastrous dinner, and the next weekend, she'd said she had something on. But they could spend this weekend together, with no Rutherfords, no nanny, no work. Just them. "Spend the weekend with us. Alfie can sometimes be a handful when he's awake, but he has an early bedtime."

She chewed her bottom lip and then nodded. "Okay. I'd like that."

He kissed her again and the world seemed a whole lot brighter.

They made it up to Sebastian's house in the Hamptons just at sunset the next day, and Mae was hit with a strong sense of déjà vu. The first time she'd been in this driveway, she'd just walked over from Sarah's house next door to confront Sebastian and get some answers, and the second time had been when she'd accepted a ride back to Manhattan with a man she barely knew. This third time, she was arriving as an invited guest to stay the weekend with the man she wanted to spend every waking and nonwaking moment with.

Alfie had fallen asleep in the car, so Sebastian transferred him straight into his crib in the nursery while Mae carried in her bag and some of the food bags she'd brought.

Within an hour, they were out back, sitting by the pool in wooden deck chairs, a glass of white wine each, and the baby monitor on the small table between them. The pool lights cast a glow around her, the balminess of the summer night nothing compared to the warmth flooding through her.

"So this is what this side of the hedge looks like," she said.

Sebastian indicated a spot farther down the paved pathway with his glass. "That's where I was standing. And I think it's almost as dark now as it was that night."

"It was a moonless night," she said, looking up at the small sliver of moon in the sky, It seemed like forever ago. "I couldn't see a thing on my side of the hedge, let alone you over here."

He nodded sagely. "Good for all the hiding you were trying to accomplish."

"And I was very successful at it, except from the chatty neighbor with the voice like melted chocolate."

He glanced over, eyes comically wide. "Mae Dunstan, was that another compliment? I need to bring you to the Hamptons more often—it agrees with you."

She chuckled, happier than she could remember being in a long time. "It's certainly more relaxed here," she said as she stretched her legs out and flexed a foot. "That aspect of it reminds me of home."

"Are you thinking of going back to Noosa?" he asked, tapping his nails against the side of his glass.

"Not sure I can. Sarah's lawyers are working on it, but I was in Australia under a false identity, so I'd have to apply for a visa again." She'd originally just taken leave from her teaching job, but with the citizenship and visa situation, she'd had to resign so they could fill her position. "Heath seems to be putting down roots here—he's even selling his beach bar in Noosa—so New York seems as good a place as any to set up a life."

"From my own selfish perspective, I'm glad to hear it." He reached for her hand and linked their fingers. "What about what you'll do here—have you thought more about that? Perhaps run a certain company with a man who has a voice like melted chocolate?"

"If you're going to let the compliments go to your head, I'll be more careful handing them out." She grinned, knowing full well that never complimenting Sebastian again would be impossible. "I still don't see myself working at Bellavista Holdings. But I've been thinking more about what you said that first night—working out what I want to do with this financial privilege I inherited."

"And what is that?" he asked, rubbing his thumb along the back of her hand.

"I still want to do good in the world." She was embarrassed to voice those words aloud—it sounded like an impossibly naive thing to say—but she knew Sebastian would take her seriously.

"I have no doubts at all that you'll do it," he said, his tone so strong and sure that it brought tears to her eyes.

She blinked a few times to clear her eyes, then decided to divert the focus to him. "What about you? Do you ever think about the world you're leaving for Alfie and want to do something good? What do *you* want? You know, if you'd been born to another family that didn't own half a property development company, what would you want to do?"

He took a sip of wine as he thought. "To be honest, I think it would still be the same. I like the world of property development. I like seeing evidence of what I've achieved, and helping to change the landscape of the city. I can't even imagine myself not doing it."

He did seem well suited to the work, and his staff respected and liked him. She took another sip of her wine. "Before I can do good in the world, though, I still want to do something for my mother's family, especially my grandparents. It just seems wrong that they suffered so much from my father harassing them and losing their daughter. His money should *do* something for them."

He shrugged. "When I met them, they were pretty adamant about letting you and Heath keep the money."

"Which is why I need a plan." She and Heath were in one-hundred-percent agreement that the O'Donohue family deserved a share of the money; the only question was finding a way to give it to them that they'd willingly accept.

"As a father," Sebastian said, glancing at the baby monitor, "I think about Alfie's future more than my own now, and money is framed that way in my mind, like I'm thinking a few steps ahead. So maybe you could talk to your grandparents about setting up college funds or trust funds for the grandchildren. That moves money into their family, while bypassing their concerns about the adults profiting."

The beauty of the idea unfurled in her imagination. "You know, I think that would work. You are a genius, Sebastian."

"Another compliment," he said, raising his glass to her. "We are definitely coming back here every weekend."

"I could get on board with that," she said, leaning back to look at the twinkling stars. It was such an amazing place that she could imagine spending a lot of time here. "I've been thinking more about the company Heath and I own that my grandparents and uncles work for."

"I remember it. We tried to offer them paid consultancies and they outright rejected the offer."

Her grandparents had been far more curious about Sebastian and his connection to her than they had been about the offer. "What if we broke up the company? I was reading some stories where employees banded together to buy the company they worked for. What if we combined that idea with that thing some businesses do where they hand out stocks as bonuses?"

"You want to give the employees stock bonuses that will total the entire capital of the company?" he said, his voice full of amused wonder.

"Pretty much. Maybe offer 5 percent of stock to each of twenty long-term employees, which would of course include my grandparents and uncles, and those twenty become like a co-op, and run it together. If it's treated like a bonus and goes to other staff as well, then it's all aboveboard and my grandparents would still have the option of giving their shares away to other employees if they didn't want them." She hadn't been able to stop thinking about it since she'd found the stories online. "What do you think—is it doable?"

Sebastian set his arms wide on the arms of his chair. "I think, Mae, that your mind is an amazing thing, and that your idea has some interesting possibilities that we will discuss. Tomorrow.

But right now, I think you should come over here and join me on this chair." He was smiling; she could hear it in his voice.

"Why would I do that when I have a perfectly good one over here?" she said in a breathy voice, all faux cluelessness.

"This one has me," he said simply, but with certainty.

Laughing, she stood, finished the wine and then deposited the glass on the small table. "You might need to scooch over a bit so I have some room."

"I'm afraid that's not possible," he said, snagging her hand and drawing her down on top of him. "Sharing this chair is a contact sport. Full-body contact, to be precise."

She stretched out against him. "I think I can live with that," she said and kissed him.

TEN

JUST OVER TWO weeks later, Mae let herself into Sarah's apartment, feeling pretty pleased with herself. With Heath's blessing, she and one of the lawyers had set up generous funds for each of her cousins that could be used for education or other purposes their grandparents approved. Her mother's parents had finally been happy with a money-related plan when she'd explained that it was for their grandchildren. She still had plans to distribute the company's stock with them as well, but she was taking it one step at a time. Once her family's needs had been squared away, she'd turned her attention to finding a solution for Larry Sheridan, and this morning, the pieces had finally fallen into place.

She found Heath and Sarah at the table in the formal dining room, documents spread across its entire surface.

"I'd really like Freya's take on this one," Sarah said.

Heath glanced up. "She said she'll meet me here after work, so we can get her to look at it then. I never thought having a forensic accountant in the family would come in so handy."

Mae dropped her bag on a small table nearby, and Sarah looked up, saw her, and smiled.

"You were out early this morning," her aunt said. "Gone before I even made it to breakfast."

"There were a couple of last-minute things I wanted to check out or clear with people before I present my plan to you both."

Heath sat back. "That sounds intriguing. And vaguely alarming."

Mae slid into a chair across from them and squared her shoulders. "Our charitable trust was set up as a tax write-off, and historically, it just donates minimal amounts to established organizations. I'd like to change that so that we take on projects of our own as well."

"Like what?" Sarah asked, tapping a pen against the papers under her hands.

Mae bit down a grin and tried to appear like a serious businesswoman for her pitch. "There's an old house in Brooklyn that's on the market. The owner is Larry Sheridan, and he originally bought the house when he married and lived there with his wife and raised a family. Now he's widowed and retired and needs to downsize, but wants his house to somehow do good for his neighborhood. I spent some time talking to him and a few of his neighbors, and I think this would be a perfect opportunity for us to do something good."

Her brother leaned forward, resting his arms on the table. "What are you thinking we do with it?"

"The yard would make a great playground for the local kids." She'd spoken to a bunch of the kids from Larry's neighborhood and realized how much she'd missed working with children. They'd been enthusiastic and creative with their ideas of what their neighborhood needed. "And if we do some alterations to the house, we could make it a community center."

"I like that," Heath said, running a hand over his chin as he thought.

"Thank you." She beamed at him. "Sebastian inspired me."

Heath and Sarah exchanged a glance.

"What?" Mae said.

"You already know what we're going to say," Heath said, gentling his voice as if she were a child getting bad news. "We don't trust him. He's been trying to influence your decisions since that first night, when you met through the hedge."

Mae frowned. How had the conversation gone from her exciting plan to an attack on Sebastian? "He didn't tell me to take on this project specifically. He doesn't even know about it yet—I wanted to run it by you two first. He just helped me think about what I wanted to do with my life, and that's when I realized I wanted to do something with the charitable trust."

"So after all this time of having you shadow him, and then dating," Heath said, "he's managed to convince you that you don't want anything to do with a business that he's trying to get control of?"

She crossed her arms and steadied her voice. "That wasn't his aim at all." If they knew Sebastian the way she did, they wouldn't be questioning his motives. "In fact, he proposed to me weeks ago and suggested I could work in the company with him if I wanted."

Sarah was suddenly alert. "Proposed? What, exactly, did he say?"

Mae winced as she realized how that would sound to Sarah and what memories it would trigger. "I know where you're going with this, because I met Christopher and he told me what happened between you two."

"Oh, did he, now?" her aunt said, her voice full of disdain, though Mae knew it wasn't for her.

"And at face value, Sebastian's suggestion was similar, but the motivation was completely different. He loves me." Her chest warmed as she said those words aloud for the first time.

"Christopher said he loved me too," Sarah said, her lips tightening.

Heath watched the exchange, then jumped in. "So, let me get this straight. A man from a family that we have an intergenerational feud with…" He held up one finger. "…gets a private investigator to compile a thick dossier on you…" Another finger. "…then *accidentally* meets you on a night when everyone knows where you would be…" A third finger. "…then convinces you to share his office for a week and gets you on-site…" A fourth finger. "Then he starts dating you and proclaiming his love…" He held up a thumb. "And then—" he held up a finger from the other hand "—uses the *exact same strategy* his father used on Sarah forty years earlier to scam our family and gain control of the company that started this whole feud."

Mae shifted her weight. "When you put it like that, it doesn't sound great, but that's not how things really happened. Some of those things were my decision."

Gently, Sarah said, "Tell me you at least saw the dossier he has on you? So you know what information he's been working with?"

Mae thought back and couldn't remember it ever being mentioned once she'd started at the office. "I never asked to see it."

Heath and Sarah exchanged another glance.

"I don't know what you're implying," Mae said. "Sebastian and I have no secrets. I told him that secrets were a deal breaker for me."

Sarah nodded. "Then would it hurt to take a look at the dossier?"

Mae pulled out her cell. "I'll call him now and ask to see it."

Heath frowned and looked down at his hands.

"What now?" Mae asked, exasperated.

Sighing, Heath met her eyes. "If there's anything there and you give him notice, he'll doctor the file."

"Assuming he hasn't already," Sarah added.

"Okay," Mae said, standing. She'd had enough of this questioning of Sebastian's motives. "Let's go."

"Now?" Heath said, glancing around at all the pages they'd laid out.

"Right now." Mae used the voice she saved for times her class needed to be pulled back into order.

Instead of standing, Sarah rested her elbows on the table and cupped her chin with her two hands. "Why are you fighting so hard about this, Mae?"

"Because I think I might have a future with Sebastian," she admitted, "and that's not going to work if you two keep trying to sow seeds of doubt for the rest of my life."

"You're serious about him?" Heath asked, gaze unwavering.

Her gaze didn't waver either. "I am."

Heath's eyes narrowed a fraction. "And you have enough faith in him that you're willing to take us there, giving him no warning."

"I believe in him," she said simply. "He's a good man."

Heath pushed his chair back and stood. "Okay then."

Sebastian rose from his chair and circled around his desk to see the photos his site surveyor, Lisandro, had opened on a tablet.

"This one," Lisandro said, "lines up with the drawings."

Sebastian nodded. "Send it to me."

From the distance, he heard Mae's voice floating down the hallway and he found himself smiling. She'd left before he'd woken this morning. He'd missed her being the first thing he saw more than he could have guessed.

"Lisandro, do you mind if we postpone this?" he said, straightening. "I need to check on something."

Lisandro picked up the tablet, saw Mae come into Rosario's office, and smothered a grin. "No problem."

Seb had been catching various members of his staff giving similar reactions when Mae walked into the room, and he could hardly blame them. He was well aware that his expression changed when she was around. His whole being transformed whenever he saw her. Hell, whenever he even thought about her, his pulse picked up speed, and his heart swelled in his chest, as if she'd cast a spell over him.

After Lisandro left, Seb crossed to the door to greet Mae, only then realizing that she had her brother and aunt with her. The happy glow he'd felt ebbed away, replaced by caution. These two people were no fans of his.

"Good to see you all," he said and stepped to the side of his doorway. "If you're here to see me, you'd better come in."

The three of them filed into his office. Mae came over and kissed his cheek, her dimples flashing. The other two seemed less pleased.

"Why does this feel like an ambush?" he asked, only half joking.

"Nothing nefarious," she said, and her use of the word from previous conversations about secrets and cons put him on alert. She slid her hand into his. "We just dropped by because I'd like to see the file that your private investigators compiled about me."

Mae was still smiling at him, but it was strained now, and the other two were wearing poker faces.

"Right now?" he asked.

She nodded. "If it's no trouble."

They were here about an outdated briefing file put together long before he'd met her by a team of private investigators who were no longer working the case? What did they think they were going to find? Hacked documents of national importance?

He cocked his head, trying to understand. "Why didn't you just ask when you were here? Doing it this way feels like a test of some kind."

"Does it?" Heath asked, eyes narrowed. "Is it a test you can pass?"

Seb looked from person to person, trying to read the situation. There was an undercurrent here that he was missing. He caught Mae's eye. "Can I talk to you for a minute?"

Heath crossed his arms over his chest. "What is it with you always wanting to talk to people in private?"

"Heath, don't," Mae said to her brother, then turned back to Seb. "Of course."

Unwilling to leave her suspicious family members alone in his office, he drew her down to the other end of the room. "What the hell is going on here, Mae?"

"Sorry," she said, her shoulders slumping. "This is bigger than I'd intended—I sort of lost control of the situation along the way."

"What situation is that?"

She tipped her chin so she was looking directly in his eyes. "I was defending you, saying you had nothing to hide, and we somehow ended up here."

"Right," he said, wrapping a hand around

the back of his neck. "But why did I need defending, exactly?"

She closed her eyes and winced, as if realizing she'd just given away more than she'd intended. Then she opened them again and her beautiful gray eyes were clear and certain. "If we want a future together, then we need everything out in the open once and for all. No room for doubts. So I wanted to prove to them that you're an open book to me."

Seb sighed, all the fight leaving his body. "Okay, sure." He turned his head to the door. "Rosario? Can you get the private investigator's file on Mae, please?"

"Can do," his assistant called back, then her tone changed as she said, "Mr. Newport, I'm afraid this isn't a good time."

From Rosario's office, his father's voice boomed, "I'll go in there whether or not it's convenient to you or my son." Then Christopher appeared in the doorway, scowling. "What the hell happened to the Sheridan property?"

Seb cast his mind around, working out what his father could mean. "Nothing, as far as I know. I was just meeting with Lisandro, the site surveyor, who was out there a couple of days ago—"

"Well," his father interjected, "something's happened. I just got off the phone with Laurence Sheridan and he says he's not signing the contract. Has another buyer."

Seb's gut twisted. "I don't know anything about this."

"You should know everything about that property," his father spat. "We'll lose a mountain of money if this doesn't come off. We've already invested too much."

Seb racked his brain. He'd spoken to Laurence Sheridan himself last week. The man had been disappointed that Mae wasn't there, but they'd ended up having a productive conversation, and Seb had asked the lawyers to draw up the contract.

Mae stepped out from behind him, into the center of the room, chin tipped up. "It was me."

Seb frowned. "What was you?"

"I'm going to buy the property for our charitable trust. We're going to build a playground for the kids, and a community center, and make it into something that contributes to the neighborhood."

Seb's blood chilled as he absorbed what she was admitting. "You met him here in my office and then used information you learned while speaking to him on behalf of Bellavista Holdings to follow up outside the company and then bought the property?"

Her mouth opened but no words came out. She simply stared at him, a deer in headlights. He wasn't sure she knew what lines she'd crossed, but she was clearly picking up from his tone that there was a significant problem.

His father swore loudly. "You stupid girl. Besides the fact that you just lost your own company's money, you can't take information you got while here and undercut it with your own offer. You idiotic—"

Seb stepped forward to stand between Mae and his father just as Sarah drew in an audible breath from her position near the door.

"Stop right there," she said, her voice threaded with steel.

His father froze, then very slowly turned and caught sight of Sarah for the first time. "Sarah," he said, his voice hoarse.

"Don't you dare attack Mae over what's the right thing to do. You have fewer morals and ethics than a slab of concrete." Her expression was one of complete disdain and disgust.

"Sarah," his father repeated, looking in danger of swaying on his feet. "I—"

She prowled closer, pointing a finger at his chest. "You have never done a principled thing in your entire life, Christopher Newport, and you have the gall to stand there and yell at a woman who is trying her best to do something good."

His father took a step back and Sebastian blinked. He'd never seen his father back down from anyone. He was starting to wonder if he'd dozed off at his desk and this entire meeting was an elaborate, bizarre dream.

Sarah turned to Mae, her gaze softening. "He's right, though. When you told us about the plan, you left this very important part out."

"Wait, what?" Stunned, Seb looked down at Mae. "You've been working on a plan and told them, but you didn't talk to me about it? Even though it's a property you know I'm in the process of buying?" The betrayal bit so deep he almost stumbled. He straightened his spine, tensing himself. This couldn't be true.

How had he been so blind?

Mae's loyalty was to her brother and aunt, and likely always would be. To be fair to her, he was the one who'd said he loved her, the one who'd proposed marriage. She'd never professed her love for him and had fought to keep their relationship status casual.

She'd been accusing him or questioning him about whether he was conning her since the first morning she'd arrived on his doorstep. Had that been to cover her own agenda?

The lady doth protest too much.

The words rang in his mind like a slap in the face. Had she been stringing him along, holding him at arm's length this entire time? Playing with him? Maybe not to get her hands on Laurence Sheridan's property, but he could suddenly clearly see that there was a huge imbalance in their relationship. He'd opened himself to her, prioritized her over everyone, let Alfie get to know her, even told Ashley about her. In return, she still wasn't on his team. She'd been able to just cut him out of something this huge and see no problem in her priorities.

He'd thought that, for the first time in his life, someone had seen the real him; he'd have someone he could support who would love and support him back. Maybe that had been an unrealistic fantasy, but the little boy whose mother had left him with a monster of a father had clearly been too desperate for things to work out with Mae. So desperate that he'd read the situation—and her—all wrong.

"You inspired the whole plan," Mae said, her eyes wary now. "When we were talking about what I want to do and I said I wanted to make the world a better place and you said I should go for it." She threw out a hand. "Well, that's what this is."

His ears buzzed. Even aside from the personal element, there were layers to the corporate angle of this situation that he needed to address, and he had no idea where to even start.

"You idiot!" his father bellowed at Mae. "You have no idea what you've—"

Seb turned to his father and snarled, "You heard Sarah. You have no ground to stand on in attacking Mae. She's one hundred times the person you are, you pitiful excuse for a human being."

His father straightened to his full height, seeming to swell to the size of a much larger man. Seb had seen the same move countless times in his life, and it suddenly struck him that he was done. Done with his father, done with this company, done with everything.

Done.

There was no way he was going to stand side by side with his father against Mae. In fact, he didn't want to be on the same side as his father at all. His father had never been on his team. The only team Seb had was with Alfie.

He held up a hand. "Before you say anything, listen, because you may as well save your breath. I'm out. I'll hand over the projects I'm in the middle of to the team, and then I'm walking out that door. And once I've gone, I don't ever want to see you again."

His father's face was scarlet, his breath audible. "You can't walk out!" he yelled. "This company is our family legacy."

"I don't want it," Seb said and slid his hands into his pockets.

"If you leave," his father said, his face turning ugly, "I'll disinherit you. Cut you and that crying baby of yours out of my will entirely."

"Great." The relief he suddenly felt was dizzying. "Then at least we're clear about that."

His father stepped toward him with a raised arm, his eyes bulging, face so red it was starting to look purple. "You ungrateful—"

Sarah jumped between them. "Christopher!"

His gaze slid down to Sarah's, and he drew in

an unsteady breath. "Sarah," he said, his voice cracking on her name, "you—"

"There is *nothing* you could say that I want to hear. It's time you left." She swung her arm and pointed at the door.

His father shot a baffled look around the room. "But this is my—"

"Out," she said, and with only another moment's hesitation, he left.

After he went through the door, no one moved or said anything for a long moment. Seb was reeling. He'd just crashed and burned his career, and given up the company he'd planned on leaving Alfie one day. His father appeared to still be in love with Sarah, and Mae's family hated Seb more than ever.

Worst of all, Mae had undermined him, and he'd realized their entire relationship had been one-sided. He glanced down, half expecting flames to burst through the floors.

Sarah blew out a breath. "I think we should get going." She headed for the door, then paused, with a hand on the doorjamb. "Good luck, Sebastian."

"Yeah, I have places to be," Heath said and followed his aunt.

"Sebastian," Mae said softly from his side. "I'm sorry."

He couldn't look at her. He knew that if he saw her, he'd fall at her feet and accept any crumbs of attention that she was willing to throw his way, and he couldn't live like that.

"I know," he said through a tight jaw, forcing a smile. "Look, I have a lot to do here. I need to tie things up and hand projects over, say good-bye to the staff, and a million other things."

"Do you want me to go?"

His heart screamed *no*, but following his heart for the first time in his life had led to this mess. He'd always tried to keep his heart protected—only Alfie had really breached its defenses. Then along came a brunette with an Australian accent and an infectiously positive attitude to life and, without hesitation, he'd handed her his still-beating heart and thrown a grenade into his life.

What would that life even look like now? And, more importantly, *who was he* without his grandfather's company? He'd lived and breathed Bellavista Holdings since he was old enough to say the words. And he had no idea where to even start finding those answers.

The only thing he knew for sure was his devotion to Alfie.

"That would probably be best," he said, still not looking up as she slipped out the door.

ELEVEN

THAT NIGHT, MAE sat at the marble-topped table Sebastian had reserved at a chic SoHo rooftop restaurant and straightened her napkin and cutlery again. He'd booked this place a couple of weeks ago, when things had been bright and sparkly between them. Now the timing seemed excruciating. In fact, she wasn't even certain that he was coming. She'd sent him several texts to confirm and he hadn't replied. She took a mouthful of the wine she'd ordered when she'd arrived.

She glanced past the lush greenery that spilled from pots and climbed posts, looking for a familiar tall frame. The sounds of glasses clinking and laughter from other tables blended with the soft bubbling from the water fountains, and all of it made the wriggling bundle of nerves in her stomach ratchet up several notches. Where was he?

Something had changed between them in his office today. She knew the moment it had happened—his features had morphed from confusion to granite, hard and cold. It had been more than cutting himself off from his father, something that they would have discussed and she could have comforted him about only yesterday. No, this was something concerning Sebastian and her, and she couldn't remember being this agonizingly worried about anything before, which, given her childhood, was saying something.

Movement in her peripheral vision snagged her attention, and then Sebastian was there, devastating in a charcoal jacket over a deep green shirt that set off his tan skin, his dark wavy hair sitting formally in place. His expression was troubled, and as their gazes met, he smiled with exquisite politeness.

"Sorry, I'm late," he said as he took his seat.

Nothing about his approach or lack of greeting eased her nerves. "Did you get Alfie to bed okay?"

Seb nodded. "He had a big day at a baby gym with Emily, so he crashed pretty quickly."

"Oh, good." So it wasn't Alfie that had held

him up. "Do you want to order dinner or start with a cocktail?"

"We may as well jump straight to dinner," he said and picked up the menu.

It didn't appear that they were going to linger over their night. She'd already scanned the menu several times, so she used the time to surreptitiously observe him. Ocean-blue eyes flickering back and forth as he read the options, that beautiful mouth, which she'd felt all over her body, now tense and unyielding.

The waiter came and they placed their orders, and he filled Sebastian's glass from the bottle Mae had ordered. She sipped her wine, wondering how to break the tension.

"Mae," he said, looking at her properly for the first time. "I apologize for my father. Yelling at you like that was inexcusable."

"I appreciate you saying that, but it's not your responsibility to apologize for him." She ran her finger through the condensation on the side of her wineglass. "I liked your defense of me." It had been worth having someone yell at her to hear his words.

She's one hundred times the person you are.

"It was true," he said and shifted his weight in his seat.

"Have you heard from your father since…"
The dumpster fire that I triggered in your office…

He gave a curt shake of his head. "And I don't expect to. He's probably still in shock that I rejected the most important thing in his life." His broad shoulders lifted in a shrug. "Plus, he has nothing to hold over my head anymore, and he doesn't like any conversation where he's not automatically on top."

"Do you really think he'll cut you out of his will?" She'd been shocked at how quickly and easily that had happened.

"I'm certain of it. I'm literally no use to him anymore."

He didn't seem particularly worried. Six months ago, she'd been a teacher with no savings to speak of, and Sebastian had been the classic rich guy who'd inherit even more wealth, and now she was the one who'd inherited money beyond her dreams, and Sebastian was about to lose most of his. Sometimes the world was unpredictable.

There had been something else unexpected in that conversation. "You know, Christopher reacted weirdly to Sarah."

"That caught me by surprise," he said, leaning back in his chair. "The only thing I can think of is that he's still in love with her after all these years."

The first time she'd met Christopher, he'd talked of Sarah. "He told me that when they were younger, he was conning her, and then he decided to tell her everything, and that's when she dumped him. So maybe it started as a con but he fell for his mark."

He took a sip of his wine and put the glass back on the table before replying, "Makes sense."

"Do you know what you'll do now?" she asked, wishing she could cross this divide of polite conversation.

"No idea, to be honest. I'll take some time and think it through." He looked at her and there was finally a glimmer of the real him showing, sharing something real, so she took a deep breath and forged ahead.

"Sebastian, what changed between us today? I know it was wrong to show up like that, and I wish I could take it back, that we could start today again. You were right that it turned into a test, but you have to believe that's not what I meant it to be."

He turned to look out over the expansive views and twinkling lights, but she had a feeling he wasn't seeing any of it. A slight breeze rumpled his hair, and she yearned to reach over and smooth it.

"You told me once," he finally said, turning back to her, "that you'd never had a committed relationship before, and I thought at the time that it would be me. I'd be the one you'd fall in love with and commit to." A deep groove appeared between his brows. "But I don't think it will be. Maybe it's the way you grew up, always keeping people on the outside of your core family. Not trusting anyone completely except Heath, and maybe now Sarah, and having to keep your guard up around everyone else. I wish it weren't this way, but I think I'll always be part of 'everyone else.'"

"How can you possibly think that?" she said, dumbfounded by the direction of his thoughts. *This* is what was troubling him? "I've let you in so much."

He pinned her with an intense stare. "Do you love me, Mae?"

She hesitated. How did you even know if you were in love? She had feelings for him, absolutely, but he was right that she'd never formed a deep attachment to anyone outside her family—they moved around far too often when she was growing up for that. So if she'd never loved before, how could she even recognize it now?

Sebastian nodded. "There's my answer. I've said from early on that I'd give you anything. *Everything.* But it hasn't been a two-way street, has it? You've wanted to keep things light between us, and I don't mind going slow if that's what you need, but, Mae, I don't get a sense that you truly believe we're going somewhere. You've been testing me in a range of ways since we met. Always asking if I'm conning you, or trying to trip me up, or bringing your brother to my office to demand to see an old document. I can't build a life with someone who's always expecting the worst of me. I've had two parents who saw me that way. It would destroy me to spend my life with someone else who did."

Her stomach turned. "I don't think the worst of you. I think you're amazing."

"Can you really deny it?" he challenged. "Deny that every time something happened between us, that your first thought was you couldn't trust me for some reason? That I was trying to con you or manipulate you in some way?"

She ran back through the time they'd been together, and her doubts, and her fears about trusting him, and she had to admit that it was true—every time something had happened, she'd questioned his motivations, either in her head or by asking him directly. And, looking at it from his perspective, that had been grossly unfair. He was a good man, and he'd shown her over and over that he could be trusted.

"I'll do better." She leaned forward and reached for his hand across the table. He took it and squeezed her fingers, holding tight. "I can change."

"I have Alfie, Mae," he said and released her hand. "Taking on a serious relationship based on a promise that the other person can change is a risk I can't take. He's already lost his mother. I don't want to be casual with you for a couple of years, have Alfie come to love you and then find that I don't pass some test you've given me, and you leave. Alfie would be devastated all over again."

Panic was rising from her toes all the way up through her body, and she swallowed hard, trying to contain it. Was he really saying that it was over? That *they* were over?

"Where does that leave us?" she asked and bit down on her lip to stop it from trembling. "Do you still love me?"

He sighed, and it was a bone-deep, sad and weary sound. "I can't turn it off like a faucet, so yes, I still love you. But this relationship isn't going to work for me. We need to end things here, tonight."

Her chest started to crumble in on itself, folding into blackness, disappearing, threatening to suck down and destroy her.

Sebastian's cell sounded from his jacket pocket. He never ignored a call when Alfie wasn't with him, so she wasn't surprised when he drew it out and looked at the screen.

"It's my father's number," he said, frowning, but he didn't move to take the call.

"Are you going to answer it?"

"Can't see the point," he said, and his finger moved to dismiss the call.

"Answer," she said quickly. "Don't get caught in regret later. If he acts like a jerk, then disconnect, but at least answer." Sebastian had already lost so much today. If there was a chance that his father had realized what he'd done and wanted to make amends, then she didn't want Sebastian to miss the opportunity to lose one less thing.

He frowned at her, looked down at his screen, and then answered.

Mae tried to give him some privacy by looking at the panoramic view, but his voice, unusually staccato, broke through. He was already standing as he disconnected.

"What's wrong?" she asked.

"The hospital found my number on my father's phone when they were looking for a next of kin. He's had a heart attack. He's not conscious but they're working on him."

"Oh, God."

"Look, I have to go." He moved around to her chair and bent to press a kiss to her cheek. "If you need me, you know where to reach me."

"It's not like we won't ever see each other—you have a house next door to my aunt's," she said lightly, unable to bear the tension surrounding them.

He gave her a tight smile. "Be happy, Mae."

And then he left, taking a part of her with him.

Mae made it home and checked a few rooms before she found Sarah in her favorite blue wingback.

"Hey, sweetheart," her aunt said. "How was your dinner?"

Ducking the question for now, Mae crouched

beside the chair. "I know you don't like Christopher much, but given your complicated history, you should know that he's had a heart attack and has been taken to hospital. Sebastian is on his way there now."

Sarah's eyebrows shot up, then she let out a breath. "I'm sad to hear it, but it's been a long time since I loved, or even liked, Christopher Newport."

"I think he loved you too," she said, thinking back over the conversation with Sebastian. "Maybe even still does."

Sarah smiled sadly. "Love is wanting more for the other person than you do for yourself."

That sounded borderline unhealthy. She might not know what love was, but it couldn't all be about giving and not looking after yourself. Sebastian had just ended things with her for his own sake, and she didn't doubt at all that he loved her.

"Surely, that's not true," she said, thinking it through. "Well, maybe it is, but it's only part of the truth. Love is more complicated than that. Heath and Freya prioritize each other, but they also prioritize themselves. That's why they work so well together."

Sarah tipped her head in acknowledgment. "Heath and Freya are two of the lucky ones."

Mae moved across to a small sofa and sank into the cushions there. "Can I ask you something? It feels a bit out of line, maybe too personal."

"You can absolutely ask." She picked up a mug from a side table, took a sip, and replaced it. "I reserve the right to not answer, but I can't imagine anything I won't tell you."

"Have you been in love with Lauren for all these years?"

Sarah stilled, her eyes going big and round like those of an owl. "That's a strange question."

"You're not together, are you?" Mae asked, suddenly worried she'd put her foot in it and was talking about a relationship that they were trying to keep secret.

"*Lauren and me?* Of course not." Her eyes slid to the door and back. "Why would you think that?"

"But you're in love with her," Mae said, even more sure. Sebastian had been the only one to see it. The kid who'd had no love in his life had grown into a man who could spot love when no one else could.

And offer it to someone as undeserving as her.

Sarah fixed her with a stern glare. "It would be very inappropriate for me, as her employer, to have feelings for her."

"Freya told me about her father, that Lauren was the family's housekeeper, and when they found out she was pregnant, Freya's biological father and his wife kicked Lauren out."

"Asshole." Sarah scowled. "Heath fixed that situation a few months ago, though."

"I heard that too, but also that you fixed things for Lauren at the time. Took her in when she was pregnant, gave her a job as your chauffeur, and yelled at her former boss until he agreed to pay child support for Freya."

Sarah smiled. "Ah, that was a satisfying day."

"And," Mae said, bringing her point home, "that's why you've never told her that you love her, isn't it?"

Sarah opened her mouth, clearly about to deny it, and then appeared to give in. She lifted her mug and took another mouthful, this time keeping the mug in her hands. "She's already had to put up with the advances of one boss— she certainly doesn't need that in her life again."

That was a reasonable position to take, except that—depending on how long it had taken them to fall in love—it might have been twenty years, maybe even twenty-five or more. That amount of pining should be illegal. Logic was the key, though. If Sarah could be swayed by pure emotion, she would have said something already.

Love is wanting more for the other person than you do for yourself.

Mae's heart broke a little more, thinking of Sarah being in love with Lauren for most of the time that Mae had been alive, seeing her every day, and loving her so much that she'd rather Lauren was comfortable and safe in her job.

"You have a very different power dynamic between you," Mae said, tucking her feet underneath her legs. "You're good friends. And she'd know that if she didn't return your feelings, her job wouldn't be at risk."

Sarah looked shocked. "Of course it wouldn't be at risk."

"Then tell her." While her own heart was raw and bleeding, she needed to see at least one other couple finding happiness. "What have you got to lose?"

"Have you told Sebastian that you love him?" Sarah said pointedly.

She recognized an attempt at diversion when she saw one. She and Heath were the masters at diversion—they'd practiced it most of their lives whenever someone asked an awkward question about their history. "That's different."

"Oh, is it?" Her aunt narrowed her eyes. "Please do tell."

Mae looked at her aunt, her face so similar to the one she saw in the mirror each day, and gave up. It would be good to tell someone. "We've already tried a relationship, but it exploded."

"Oh, Mae. I'm sorry." Sarah pushed to her feet and joined Mae on the small sofa, placing an arm around her shoulders. "But he knows you love him, right?"

"How do you know I do?" she asked, curious. Why would Sarah think that if Mae hadn't been sure?

Sarah grinned. "That defense you mounted for him today. That came from a place of love."

Mae digested that. It might not be a perfect definition of love, but, she really did need to be honest with herself—whatever definition she used, she absolutely, one hundred percent, completely loved Sebastian. Hell of a time to realize it, obviously.

She rested her head on Sarah's shoulder. "I

do love him, and, no, I haven't told him. In fact, I didn't even reply when he point-blank asked me at dinner tonight." She winced at the memory. "He's been much smarter and braver about it than I have."

"I was wrong about him." Sarah stroked a hand over Mae's hair. "Maybe I was too caught up in my distrust of his father, but I saw the way he looked at you today, the way he defended you to his father. The same way you defended him to us. That man loves you, and he has a good heart."

A tear slipped out the corner of Mae's eye, and then another. She swiped them away, but they were coming too thick and fast, so she spoke through them. "It's too late. He ended things with me tonight."

Sarah sat with her until the tears stopped and then twisted to face her. "You said he's at the hospital with Christopher?"

"Yes, he was heading over when I came up here," she said, scrubbing at her face with the inside of her wrist.

"Regardless of what happened at dinner to-night, they have no other family, so Sebastian has no one."

Mae had been thinking about that after she

left the restaurant, but had decided she was the last person he'd want to see. Now that she'd released some of her emotions, though, she could see more clearly. She needed to check on him. If he didn't want her there, she'd leave. But she couldn't leave him alone at the hospital.

She drew in a shuddering breath and stood. "On my way. And you have someone to talk to as well."

Sarah opened her mouth, as if to deflect again, then closed it and nodded.

Mae smiled.

She caught a taxi, and, when she arrived at the hospital, searched through the emergency department until she spotted him. Her heart tripped over itself at the sight of him. How had she ever doubted that she loved him? He had his head in his hands, so he didn't see her approach.

She plopped down onto the seat beside him. "Today has been wild."

Startled, he looked up. "Okay, you have to stop ambushing me or there will be two Newport men in there with heart attacks."

"Any news?" She bumped his shoulder with hers, offering support but trying to keep the boundaries he'd set.

"No." He flipped his hand over to reveal

his cell. "They said they'd call when they have news or he's stable enough for a visitor, but where else can I go?"

"Let's go outside and get some air." She stood and held out a hand, and, after a quick glance at the doors to the treatment rooms, he took it.

They walked outside into a warm summer night.

"Not that I don't appreciate you coming," he said after a couple of minutes, "but why are you here? We left things between us in a fairly final place."

"Same reason you're here for your father." She stopped so she could see his beautiful face. "We're the same about that—we show up when people need us, regardless."

He held her gaze for a heavy moment and then pulled her into a hug. "Thank you."

They strolled in silence for a few more minutes until Sebastian let out a long sigh. "He probably doesn't even want me here. It's less than a day since he said he was disinheriting me, but he's my only family. I'm not even sure where my mother is living now, so, besides Alfie, he's the only family I have left."

"Families are complicated," she said, and given their entangled circumstances, she knew it was an understatement. "He's a horrible human being, but he's still your father, the man who raised you, so you're bound to be conflicted."

"Thank you for understanding." He cupped the side of her face with his large palm. "You always do."

She sucked her bottom lip into her mouth, keeping herself steady at the warm contact of his hand on her face, and waited until he dropped the hand and shoved it into his trouser pocket before she let herself take another full breath. They set off walking again, and she said, "Hey, here's some news for you."

He coughed out a laugh. "Not sure I can handle any more news."

"You'll like this one. You were right about Sarah and Lauren. Well, from Sarah's side anyway. I nudged her a bit—"

"I can imagine," he said, smiling.

"—and she's going to tell Lauren how she feels." It was the one bright spot in this wretched day.

"You've done a good thing, Mae. After seeing them together, there's no way it's one-sided. I'm glad for them."

"Me too." And since Sarah was going to tell Lauren how she felt, Mae needed to do the same. "This is really crappy timing, but there's something I need to say too."

He shrugged, as if resigned. "Go on then."

"You asked me at the restaurant if I loved you and I didn't reply straight away. That's because I'm not always great at recognizing how I feel about things." She stopped walking again and he stopped too, watching her intently. "But I do. I love you, Sebastian. So much."

He reached for her and pulled her face to his, their lips crashing in a kiss that was hungry and desperate, and she melted against him. Her brain was trying not to read anything into the kiss because the day had been turbulent, and it was just a kiss, after all, but her heart was full of hope. They broke away and he rested his forehead against hers as they caught their breath.

"Is there any chance for us?" she whispered.

He squeezed his eyes shut tightly and stepped back. "All my life I've had my guard up, even with Ashley. Always waiting for someone to leave or kick me while I'm down. I have no idea why I let you in so easily, but now that my guard is up again, I don't think I can bring it back down. I am sure I don't want to. I love you, Mae, but I can't spend my life constantly proving myself to you."

That was fair. It might break her heart but she couldn't blame him for needing to protect himself and his precious son.

His cell chirruped in his pocket and, lightning fast, he had it out and at his ear. She watched the conversation, watched the color drain from his face, and then he disconnected and carefully put the cell back in his pocket.

"Sebastian?" she said gently.

"It was too late." He looked at her, his eyes wide and unseeing. "They couldn't save him."

She pulled him close and wrapped her arms around him. "I'm so sorry."

"This doesn't seem real." He rubbed his hands over his face, as if trying to wake himself up. "And it's all so messy, I don't know what I'm supposed to feel."

She took his hands and held them between hers. "There's no 'supposed to' in these situations. How do you feel?"

"Numb."

"That's probably normal." Unlike Sebastian and his father, Mae had been very close to her mother, and when she died after being hit by a car, Mae had felt numb for days.

He looked back at the hospital over his shoulder. "They said I could go inside and say goodbye and collect his personal things."

"You want me to come with you?"

He released her hands and stepped back, his face blank. He stuffed his hands into his pockets. "I think I should do this alone."

She'd expected that, and she tried not to care that it stung, because he really did need some time alone to say goodbye to his father. "Call if you need anything."

He nodded, turned, and left.

She watched him walk away from this little moment outside time, and wondered if she'd ever feel this close to Sebastian Newport again.

TWELVE

MAE STEPPED OUT of the elevator at Bellavista Holdings just over a week later, surrounded by her aunt, her brother and future sister-in-law, and one of their lawyers. An invitation had arrived a couple of hours ago to attend a meeting in the boardroom. The message was from Rosario, and she'd apologized for the short notice and said they could bring along anyone they wanted, but mentioned nothing about the reason for the meeting. After a quick conversation, they'd decided that whatever the meeting was about, having Freya's forensic accounting brain and one lawyer would be useful, so Heath had rung Freya at work and asked if she could get away for a couple of hours, and Sarah had organized one of her lawyers to attend.

That left Mae to stew in her own thoughts. She hadn't seen Sebastian since the night at the hospital—the night his father had died. She'd composed hundreds of texts in her head since then, even started typing several of them, but had deleted them all. He'd made the decision to stay apart and she had to respect that, no matter how wrong it felt or how much she physically yearned to be near him.

Rosario was there waiting, and they had a quick, catch-up conversation as she showed them into the boardroom. She'd missed Rosario. Sebastian's assistant had become a good friend, and she was sorry to lose that.

Once in the boardroom, Rosario took Mae to a place beside the head of the table that had a coffee waiting. "Grande Americano. That's right, isn't it?"

Mae laughed and hugged her, saying, "Perfectly right, thank you," and took her seat. Heath, Freya, Sarah, and their lawyer all sat in a row beside her.

Within minutes, Sebastian entered, and her heart swooped and then clenched tight in her chest. He looked as commanding and in control as that first day in his office, and her body ached for all she'd lost. He was followed by a group of six women and men in suits, most she recognized from when she was shadowing Sebastian, but she couldn't remember any names.

Like the suits at the first meeting she'd attended in this room, they were all matching in their attire and their severe, slicked-back hair, and all looked smart, dispassionate, and focused.

Sebastian took the seat beside her, at the head of the oval table, and for a suspended moment, she was paralyzed with longing. His profile was heartbreakingly beautiful—how had she forgotten how beautiful it was? His woodsy cologne drifted over to surround her, teasing her senses, and his mouth moved to form words to the person on his other side, but she didn't hear any of them. All she could do was drink him in. And try to stop her hand from reaching out to touch the fire that burned so brightly from within him that it warmed her from where she was sitting.

Then he swung around and caught her gaze, and for a moment so tiny, so brief that she almost missed it, his eyes filled with pained longing that matched her own, then disappeared as his features smoothed out.

"Mae," he said, his voice as steady as a rock. Then looked beside her. "Heath. Thank you for coming. I know it was short notice." His gaze traveled to the others in her group, and he greeted them one by one, and she was glad, because she wouldn't have been able to get her voice to work—not without it giving away every foolish and messy thought inside her.

Sebastian shook out his wrists, bringing her attention to his strong, tan hands against the snowy white of his shirt cuffs, and leaned his forearms on the table as he took control of the meeting.

"I'm sure you're all aware that my father threatened to disinherit me," he said, and the room fell into deathly silence. "There's a chance he would have followed through, but he died before he could, so we'll never know." He paused, swallowed, then continued. "All we can do is move forward, and that means I've inherited his half share in Bellavista Holdings. The other 50 percent, of course, is jointly owned by Mae and Heath."

There was nodding around the table, and Sebastian made brief eye contact with everyone on her side. "Because of the way things were left with my father, I considered selling my share. Drawing a line under it. The company, and the rift between the descendants of the original owners, has caused too much pain over the generations." He looked over at Sarah and they exchanged a nod of acknowledgment.

"Instead," he said, straightening, "I'm bringing you a proposal today to turn this company and its capital into a force for good.

"Someone asked me a question recently, a question that was so sensible, so obvious, that it's replayed in my mind ever since. It was this—do you ever think about the world you're leaving for Alfie and want to do something good?"

Mae bit back a gasp, peeking around to see if anyone had realized it was her question, but they were all transfixed by Sebastian. Her pulse thudded in her ears as she turned back to him, desperate to know where he was taking this.

"The answer I found is that I want Alfie to grow up in a better world. Also, after just losing my father, I've done a lot of soul-searching about the sort of father I want to be. I want Alfie to grow up with a dad who sees the world the way good people see it." He glanced down at her, his mouth quirking at the corners. "The way Mae Dunstan sees it."

He held her gaze and she couldn't look away. The air was completely sucked from the room, and she couldn't draw breath, and the terrible truth was that she didn't care. As long as Sebastian was looking at her, as long as she was looking at him, within touching distance, nothing else mattered.

Heath cleared his throat. "So what's your proposal?"

Mae tore her gaze away and looked down at her hands crossed on the notepad.

"I want to change the company's vision statement to center on projects that improve quality of life in tangible ways. The perfect example of this new model would be purchasing Laurence Sheridan's property, which sits in a neighborhood that needs more communal spaces, and building a multilevel playground for the local children."

He drew something from his pocket, and the screen behind him flared to life, showing drawings of an amazing playground, with slides and swings, but also, a four-story wooden fort, with rope netting instead of walls, and interior stairs, climbing poles, and slides. Beside the fort was a metal climbing pyramid that was at least half as high, with a spiderweb of rope in all directions to make paths for a child's ascent. "These are initial ideas, and the plan is for the designers and architects to work with local children on the final design before commencing work."

"Good God," Freya whispered from the other side of Heath.

"In Mae's original idea, the plot would also have a community center. Our planner—" he nodded to a woman at the far end of the table "—suggested using the entire plot for the playground to maximize the opportunity, and buy a separate space for the Evelyne O'Donohue Community Center." Another slide flashed up behind him with a drawing of a welcoming building that had her mother's name emblazoned across the front, and she heard Heath's breath catch.

She looked from the screen to Sebastian and back again. He was still talking, and she tried to take it all in, her eyes swimming with the tears she was trying to blink back.

"Of course," he said, flicking the slide to one with graphs and numbers, "this is one idea, an example of the type of project the company would take on. To carry this out, we might take a commission from a charitable trust, or we might take it on as a pro bono case."

One of the suits took over and started explaining financial specifics, and Freya asked a couple of money-related questions, but Mae wasn't listening to any of it. Sebastian had turned everything around because of something she'd said? Her entire body trembled with the enormity of it.

She scribbled a note on the paper in front of her and slid it to him.

Did you call me sensible?

He subtly took the paper without looking away from the discussion in front of him. After a few seconds, he glanced down, saw her note, and scrawled something with his strong left hand beside it, and passed it back to her.

Very sensible. You're starting to blend in with all those suits on the other side of the table.

She smothered a grin and wrote her reply in big letters across the bottom of the page.

You take that back.

He looked at her then, and she was in danger of drowning in his blue, blue eyes. The meeting, the rapid-fire questions that were being asked and answered around the room faded away, and all there was in her entire world was Sebastian.

Someone called his name and he jerked, as if pulled from a trance. He turned to the suits and elaborated on a point that needed clarification, then he wrote on the notepad and slid it over to her.

It's good to see you, Mae.

He faced the table again and cleared his throat, and the other conversations died down. "That's the crux of it. Obviously, there's more that needs to be discussed and worked out, but I wanted to share the overall vision with you now. I realize it's very different to the company's past, but I'm committed to this new direction. I'll understand if you don't want to be part of it—profits will obviously go down. If you're not on board, I'd be happy to talk about buying you out, or we could split the company in two and I'll take my smaller company in this direction."

Mae looked at Heath beside her, then at the others on her team. Freya gave a subtle nod, meaning that the numbers at this early stage had passed her assessment. Sarah's eyes were wide and sparkling, and the corner of her mouth was hitched up, so she clearly approved. The lawyer gave a noncommittal head tilt, which she took to mean that there were no red flags. Finally, her gaze landed on her brother. They were literally half a world away from where they'd been less than a year ago, in an Australian beachside town, living as a bar owner and a teacher. They'd gone from just the two of them against the world, to Heath planning a life with Freya, having their aunt Sarah in their corner, and joining the large O'Donohue family. The enormity of the changes in such a short time made her head spin. But in this moment, it was just the two of them again, brother and sister, deciding their path forward. Did they focus on building more money that they didn't need, or did they join Sebastian in making the world a better place? There was no doubt in Mae's mind what the right path was, but Heath owned the shares with her and had a say about it.

Her brother's dark gaze softened, and he leaned over to whisper in her ear, "Your call."

Mae straightened her shoulders and turned back to the man she loved, bursting with pride for him. "The Rutherford-Dunstan side of the company would be thrilled to work with you in transforming Bellavista Holdings into your vision of what it could be."

A slow smile crept over Sebastian's face and her heart lurched in her chest.

"Thank you," he said, and she knew that was for her alone, for believing in him, the way he'd just shown he believed in her. Then he looked down the line at the others on her side of the table. "Just to be clear, the profits are going to slump to a trickle. We can still take on projects that will make us money if they also fit our new company vision, but I can't guarantee that stream of income."

Heath shrugged. "We have enough to live on already. This is what we want to do."

Sarah leaned forward. "My involvement as the executor of my brother's estate is all but over, but if you're looking for another investor in this new Bellavista Holdings, then I'm very open to that discussion."

The meeting wound up and, as her group was leaving, she tried to catch Sebastian's eye, but he was busy with the suits tightly crowded around him. Sarah linked her elbow through Mae's, and with a last look over her shoulder, Mae left the building, her head spinning.

Lauren was waiting on the curb with Sarah's black town car and the others started to pile in. "I think I'll walk," Mae said.

"You sure?" Heath asked beside her.

She nodded. "I need a moment to clear my head."

"Okay." He grabbed the door to lower himself in, then turned back and gave her a lopsided smile. "I like him," he said, then he was gone.

She filled her lungs with the New York air,

the sounds and the pollution, the buzzing energy, and the sparkle, and started to walk.

Her cell vibrated in her pocket. She took it out and saw Sebastian's name.

Where are you?

She glanced around.

About two buildings north of yours. I'm walking.

The reply was immediate.

Wait there.

With trembling fingers, she slipped the cell back into her pocket.

In an impossibly short time, she heard her name being called, and she turned to find him approaching, slowing from a jog to a walk, breathing heavily. He'd left his suit jacket somewhere behind, and his face was flushed from exertion.

"Did you run all that way?" she asked, confused.

"I might have." He rested his hands on his hips as he caught his breath. "Including the stairs, when the elevator was taking too long."

She smothered a smile. "You told me to wait, so there was no need to rush. I was right here. Waiting."

"There was a need," he said. He speared his fingers through his hair, leaving the dark waves rumpled. "I'd hoped to talk to you at the end of the meeting, but I turned around and you were gone."

Maybe she should have waited, but just because he'd changed his mind about the company didn't mean he thought any differently about her.

"It was a good meeting, Sebastian. A good proposal."

One side of his mouth hitched up. "You liked it?"

"I've never been prouder of anyone in my life than I was of you in that meeting today." Her chest swelled just remembering what he'd done, what he'd achieved in so little time, and what he wanted to do.

"Mae, I..." His voice trailed off and he turned to look at the traffic for what felt like an excruciatingly long time before looking back at her again. "I can't believe how badly I screwed up things between us. You should have been allowed to question me, to double-check things until you felt you could trust me, and I—"

She laid a hand on his arm, interrupting him. "No, Sebastian. You were right to call me out on that. My childhood was a training ground in the art of being suspicious, and then I landed in the middle of an ongoing feud between two families. That was a bad combination—a perfect storm."

"And I knew those things." He grabbed her hand from his arm, lacing their fingers together, and then let their joined hands hang across the space between them. "I should have been more patient, or...something."

"It wouldn't have helped. I was trapped in that spiral and couldn't even see through it enough to realize that it *was* a trap. And you caught the brunt of it all. I'm surprised you put up with it for as long as you did. You've been a saint."

He huffed out a laugh. "Hardly."

"Regardless, I'm glad you called me on it, or we'd still be stuck inside that spiral." Being with him now felt different. Even though they were just standing on the pavement, talking, her shoulders felt lighter with the freedom to trust him as her instincts had told her to all along.

Her guard wasn't up, not even a little bit, because she knew that no matter what happened from here, she'd never need it around Sebastian.

"So, you don't doubt my motives for today?" He cocked his head, watching her closely. "Think I might have an ulterior plan?"

"Honestly, it didn't even cross my mind. Not once. I can see your heart, Sebastian." She placed her free hand on the left side of his chest, feeling the steady thump-thump beneath her palm. "You were showing me right from the start. You showed me who you were, and I'm sorry I didn't see clearly then. But I see it now. The real Sebastian is shining from your eyes. It's in the way you care for Alfie. The way you went straight to the hospital despite the appalling way your father treated you your whole life. It's in the way you were open enough to new ideas that you changed the whole damn company. It's in the way you've treated me every second we've been together. Your heart is huge, Sebastian. And I trust it."

"Thank you," he said, his voice hoarse, and he captured the hand that sat on his chest so their four joined hands formed a cross between them.

The way he was looking at her now, the way

he was holding both her hands tightly, it was dangerous. It was letting a glimmer of hope spark back to life. "You," she began, but her voice shook, so she stopped and tried again. "You told me I could ask for anything...?"

His gaze didn't waver. "That still stands. You ask, and I promise I'll give it to you."

"I want a life with you. With you and Alfie. Everything else is negotiable, as long as we're together."

She felt a shudder run through his body and watched him close his eyes tight for a long moment. "Done." He leaned forward and brushed the gentlest of kisses on her lips. "The easiest promise to fulfill, because it's what I want too. Though I have to warn you that my negotiation skills are highly tuned, so get ready for some intense rounds of talks at the kitchen table. Where we live, who cooks dinner, what we watch on TV, where we vacation—"

"I'm not worried." She raised one brow. "I have bargaining chips."

"That you do," he said and released one hand to snake around her back and draw her closer for another kiss. This one was deeper, needier, and she felt the dampness on her cheeks from her own tears at the sheer joy of kissing him again.

Even once the kiss ended, they stayed tangled together, and she rested her head on his chest, her arms tight around his waist, luxuriating in the feel of him.

"You know," she said as a thought occurred to her, "I never did get to see that dossier about myself."

"It's outdated," he said, shrugging. "I'll write you a new one."

She arched her neck back so she could see his face. "What would it say?"

He didn't hesitate. "Mae Dunstan is a woman who is not at all sensible yet is quite often the most sensible person in the room." He cupped the side of her face with his palm. "She has dimples in her cheeks and starlight in her eyes, and my love for her is bigger than I thought love could possibly be." He dropped a kiss on her nose. "I'd accompany the written report with a photo of you in that lilac wraparound dress you wore to your brother's engagement dinner. Tell me you still have that dress."

"Of course I do. It's my favorite dress." It reminded her of Sebastian. She made a mental note to wear the dress again soon. "That's a good dossier report, but it needs a matching piece. One on you."

A group of people bumped them as they pushed past, but Sebastian barely seemed to notice. "What would it say?"

She thought for a moment. "Sebastian Newport is a serious businessman who sometimes surprises everyone by making unbusinesslike decisions. He has eyes the color of the ocean and a mouth that's pure, sculpted perfection, and my love for him is deep and trusting and endless. I'd accompany it with a photo of you with your blue shirt unbuttoned and your tie askew."

He frowned, as if confused. "You forgot a voice like melted chocolate."

A laugh gurgled up and burst from her throat. "You remember that?"

"I remember every compliment you ever gave me, Mae. To be fair, there weren't that many, so it's not hard. Mostly, you described me with words like nefarious," he said, his expression angelic.

"Hey, that one was yours. But point taken. If it helps, there was pretty much a constant stream of complimentary thoughts in my head. I'll have to remember to start saying them aloud."

He chuckled, shaking his head. "I love you, Mae."

"I love you more," she said and kissed him, ignoring all the bustling people on the sidewalk and the traffic noise and everything else except Sebastian.

EPILOGUE

MAE CARRIED TWO pies out the back door of Sarah's Hamptons house, Alfie darting around her feet. Alfie's third birthday party was underway—her mother's family and Alfie's grandparents had all made the trip, so the backyard next door was packed. To make up for asking people to come this far out from Manhattan, they'd offered everyone beds for the night. Fortunately, between them, they had enough space. Around the time they'd married, Heath and Freya had offered the neighbors on either side of them exorbitant sums of money to sell so they could have a strip of three houses in the family. Both owners had refused, but the people with the place across the street had heard the story and stopped by. The house's owners had made a good profit, and Heath and Freya had landed a home over the road from the rest of the family. Sarah and Lauren spent a lot of time in the

Hamptons now, and since Freya had given birth to their baby girl, Stella, she, Heath, and the baby had been out here a lot too. So Mae and Sebastian tried to get out as often as they could.

Her cell dinged, and with a bit of juggling, she saw the message from Sebastian.

Where are you? Amanda and Barry want to see Alfie.

She smiled and wrote her reply with one thumb.

On my way back. At hedge gate.

Sarah and Lauren caught up to her, their hands linked and their faces radiating the joy of new love. Well, love that was new in the sense that it had been over two decades in the making.

"Need any help?" Sarah asked.

Mae threw her a grateful smile. "Amanda and Barry are looking for Alfie."

"On it," Lauren said and held out a hand to the little boy. "Come on, Alfie, let's find your grandparents."

"*Yesss!*" Alfie said and grabbed both the hands offered.

Mae watched them walk through the little gate, her heart so full it barely fit in her chest. Alfie's happiness, Sarah and Lauren finally finding each other, that little gate…

After she'd moved in with Sebastian, she'd found a pair of pruning shears and cut a hole in the shrubbery, around the exact spot where she and Sebastian had had their first ever conversation. The gap had been just big enough to squeeze through—it was harder work to cut through a thick hedge than she'd expected—but she'd been happy with her work. Soon after, Sebastian had widened the opening and installed a cute little wrought-iron gate. Mae loved that gate. It wasn't just about the ease of access, it was symbolic of this large family— *her* large family. A shortcut to her aunt next door, with her brother and his wife just across the street. She had more people she loved, and who loved her, than she'd ever dreamed possible. Sebastian, too, had gone from a unit of just him, his son, and his father, to losing that one parent and now being surrounded by this chaotic, loving extended family.

Heath and Freya appeared with a sleeping Stella resting on Freya's chest, snuggled tightly in a wrap, and Mae's heart melted a little more.

"Hey," Heath said, "Sebastian was looking for you."

"I spoke to him," she said, her gaze still on her sweet little niece. "He wanted Alfie for Amanda and Barry. Sarah and Lauren have taken him through."

Heath edged closer. "Can I help with those pies?"

"I'm fine—" she began, but Heath took them anyway.

"What are they?" He took a deep sniff. "One cherry and one…?"

"Apple." Alfie's favorite. "A special request from the birthday boy."

"Excellent," he said as he turned and headed back to the party.

Knowing the birthday boy's uncle would get the first slice, Mae shared a look with Freya.

Freya raised an upturned palm. "Sometimes I think it's his newfound obsession with pie, not me, that keeps him in the country."

Mae laughed, partly because it was so ludicrous—anyone who saw the way Heath and Freya looked at each other knew the truth. Even so, she slid Freya a sly grin. "Let's hope he never has to choose."

"Let's hope," Freya said, smiling, and followed her husband back to the festivities.

Alone for the first time that day, Mae took a moment to look over the party, feeling like the luckiest person in the world.

Her cell pinged.

Happy?

A buzz zipped through her bloodstream at the sight of Sebastian's name on her screen.

Very.

Close your eyes.

She did as he asked but couldn't keep the smile from spreading across her face.

Within moments, she felt his arms slide around her waist and she leaned back into his solid strength. She'd never had a home with long-term security and stability. In the circle of Sebastian's arms, though, she'd found her home.

"How happy?" he murmured at her ear.

Her eyes drifted closed. "Deliriously."

"Me too," he said and kissed her temple. "Which got me thinking. We said we'd wait to talk about having another child until Alfie was used to you and the new arrangement."

She nodded. It had been one of their negotiations about what they wanted from their future. "When everyone else is used to it too, especially Amanda and Barry."

"And they are inside right now telling everyone that you're their daughter-in-law. Though there's some debate, especially among your cousins, about whether you're actually a daughter-in-law-in-law."

Mae laced her fingers through his. Ashley's parents had been grieving a daughter, and Mae had been missing her mother. They'd quickly bonded. Mae had gone from growing up with only a mother and a brother, and then just having a brother, to now also having honorary parents-in-law, her aunt Sarah and Lauren, a sister-in-law in Freya, her mother's large family, and best of all, Sebastian and Alfie—the loves of her life.

"So," Sebastian said, "I'm ready."

The world stilled. She turned in his arms. "You are?"

"Whenever you want to start trying for a little sibling for Alfie, I'm ready."

She stood on her tiptoes and kissed him. A

breeze danced around them and the leaves of the shrubbery rustled, and Mae felt completely at peace. She had family and a life here—she had roots—and would never need to run again. And more than that, she had a future.

"I'm ready too," she said. "But for now, let's go back to our guests. We're missing out on all the fun."

"And the apple pie," Sebastian said. "Let's find out if your brother left some for anyone else."

They stepped out of the gap in the hedge, into their own backyard and their future. Together.

★ ★ ★ ★ ★

Falling For The Enemy
Katherine Garbera

MILLS & BOON

Dear Reader,

It's bittersweet to be writing this particular letter to you. This is the last Harlequin Desire novel that I will be writing and the last book in the Gilbert Curse series. Some of the very first books I read as a thirteen-year-old were Harlequin Desire novels by Elizabeth Lowell, Joan Hohl, Stephanie James, Joan Johnston and Peggy Moreland. I loved this line from the moment I picked up my first one in the used bookstore.

I was addicted to the strong heroes and the feisty heroines who were more than their match. Their love stories were so deeply emotional and shaped in me the kind of relationship I wanted as an adult. I was never willing to settle for a man who couldn't be everything that those heroes had been. Loving, supportive, sexy and willing to bend and meet the heroines halfway.

I am so happy that I've been able to write seventy titles for Harlequin Desire and I loved every one of them. Thank you so much for reading my books and enabling me to keep telling stories that embodied so much of what I learned to love about romance as a teenager.

I'm pretty excited that Rory Gilbert's story is my last one. She was such a fun heroine to write. My first attempt at a *Sleeping Beauty*–inspired story. I love how fierce and brave she is and wish I could face the world with that kind of courage every day—I do sometimes, but not always.

Kit was great too. A man conflicted by his past and what he's always been told and truly believes and this woman who has knocked him off-kilter.

Thank you for reading the Gilbert Curse series and all of my series since my first book, *The Bachelor Next Door*. I have truly loved sharing this ride with you.

Happy reading,

Katherine

DEDICATION

To my Harlequin Desire friends who have made
the journey so much fun, especially Karen Booth,
Joanne Rock, Joss Wood and Reese Ryan.
Our monthly chats are the best and I'm lucky
to call you all my friends.

To all of the authors who wrote
for Harlequin Desire—for the great reads,
inspiring characters and stories that lingered
long after I closed the books.

ONE

THE GILBERT SISTER was the key.

Somehow when Kit Palmer referred to his teenage crush, the woman whose life had been ruined by his older brother and a family grudge, it was easier to pretend she was a stranger. Like there was distance between them despite their tragic connections.

If he was brutally honest with himself, he knew that there was no putting distance between Aurora Gilbert and himself. When she, her brother and her cousin moved to Gilbert Manor and he saw her for the first time, he'd fallen.

Hard.

It hadn't mattered to his eight-year-old self that he and his family lived in the old factory houses on the outskirts of Gilbert Corners or that his father was the shift manager at the old factory. As a child he hadn't seen that they were

in any way different, and at that summer party
where all the kids from Gilbert Manufacturing families played together, he'd found himself
alone with Rory for the first time.

She'd been brave and fearless, and when the
older kids, including his brother, had walked
across the river that surrounded Gilbert Manor
and flowed through the town, Kit had hesitated. He didn't know how to swim and didn't
want to be left behind but... Rory had held out
her hand to him. Taken his palm in hers and
said, "We can do this together."

And they had. And in that moment, his life
had changed.

Which was why he was referring to her as
Dash's sister and not his childhood heroine. She
was the key to reckoning with his past. As long
as she was a Gilbert, nothing else could matter.

Kit's family hadn't stayed in the factory houses
for long. His father and his brother were ambi-
tious and started moving up in Gilbert Manufacturing, until old Lance Gilbert promised
Kit's brother, Declan Orr, the position of CEO
of Gilbert Manufacturing. Finally, they had arrived and would be a force to be reckoned with
in Gilbert Corners.

But the car crash had changed all of that. The

factory had closed down, and in his grief his father had bought up shares in Gilbert Manufacturing, mortgaging their house and selling assets to take over the company and the position that had been promised to Declan. Something that Dash Gilbert had gotten wind of and had used to lure his father deeper into debt until all that was left of their assets was the deed to that crappy, run-down factory-provided duplex.

Now as he sat in front of the house that held too many mixed memories, watching as his new neighbor Rory Gilbert moved in, he couldn't help but think that he might finally have everything he needed to destroy Dash Gilbert, cure the bad karma that the Gilberts had passed on to his family and at long last get over the woman who was at the heart of his plan.

There was a rap on his car window and he turned, surprised to see Rory Gilbert standing there. Her hair had darkened over the years from that white blond she'd had as a child to a dark honey-blond. She had a heart-shaped face and pretty blue eyes. Her mouth was full, her nose delicate and she quirked her head to the side as she waited for him to open the window. He turned off the car and got out.

"Can I help you?"

"Yes, that's what I hired you for," she said.

Hired him. "I think you've got the wrong guy. I'm not a mover."

"Oh, I know that," she murmured. Her voice was as he remembered, light and lilting, sweetly melodic. "But you are here for the thing that I hired you for, right?"

He had absolutely no idea what she was talking about, but before he could tell her so, her brother, Dash, walked out of the house with a sour look on his face.

Rory looped her arm through his. "Just pretend we're old friends and don't mention what you are really doing here. I hate lies but I can't take another minute of having my older brother and cousin telling me I am too fragile to do anything."

Her touch on his arm was electric and sent through him a pulse of awareness that he tamped down. He had no idea what Rory was up to, but if it meant irritating Dash then Kit was all in.

"Sure. My name is Kit, by the way."

"Kit. Great. Just follow my lead," she said.

He intended to do just that. He had been trying for years to come up with a plan to find something to use as leverage against Dash Gilbert, and he had known in his gut that the sister was the perfect ammunition, but nothing had come of it. Rory had been in a coma, and after his engagement had been broken almost eight years earlier, Dash had become a recluse.

"Dash, you heading off?"

"Not yet. Who's this?"

"This is one of my old friends, Kit," she told him. "Kit, this overbearing dude is my brother, Dash."

Kit hadn't met Dash Gilbert before. He'd been eighteen on the night of the ball that had culminated in the car crash that had taken his brother's life. He held his hand out to the man that Kit had wanted to destroy for the last ten years. However, when their eyes met, instead of the pure evil he'd expected to find, he saw an easy smile and a semi-exasperated look.

"I'm not overbearing," Dash said. "Well, not too much. This one thinks that six months from waking up from a coma she can climb Everest."

"Not Everest yet," Rory replied.

"Then what?"

"Well, I'd settle for being on my own and trying all the things I missed in the last ten years."

Dash stiffened. "I agreed to you living here but the other stuff—"

"Too late," Rory said. "That's why Kit's here."

"Why *am* I here?"

"To help me experience all the things I missed in the last ten years," Rory explained.

"The hell he is," Dash said.

Rory wasn't going to argue with her brother in front of Kit. He wasn't at all what she was expecting but she'd hired him from a website that had offered discreet help for anyone experiencing extreme anxiety or problems leaving their home. Everything from the everyday stress of ordering a coffee to sex. Rory wasn't sure what she'd need, so had checked all the boxes. Frankly, after ten years in a coma, there was so much she didn't know. Like, did Lizzie and Gordo stay together? But also stuff like social media. The solutions, according to what she'd read, were designed to push her out of her comfort zone.

And she needed that.

As much as she'd been saying she wanted Dash and her cousin Conrad—who was like another older brother—to stop treating her like she was made of spun glass, a part of her had no idea how to do it.

Ten years in a coma had been hard to recover from. Physically, she was still stretching her limits and trying to regain her strength. If she overdid it and was on her feet for too long she had to use a cane. But those physical limitations were somehow easier than the mental ones. Rory had found it too easy to stay holed away in her suite of rooms at Gilbert Manor, with the staff eager to cater to her every need. She had started to really live in what she couldn't help but think of as her cushy tower. And, in many ways, she knew that she'd let herself fall into a second coma of sorts.

But *no more*. She'd used some of her inheritance to buy this half of the duplex and was determined to fix it up and make it into something that was hers. And as part of her grand plan, she'd hired Kit. But he was a bit more handsome than she'd been expecting. Okay, more than a bit. He had dark black hair that he wore short and spiky on top, and he had a light dusting of stubble that made him look stern until he smiled. A sigh escaped her as she continued to drink him in. He had a full, firm-looking mouth, which indicated that kissing him wasn't going to be a problem.

In fact, she couldn't help wondering what his mouth would feel like on hers, which stirred feelings that a twenty-eight-year-old woman should be able to handle. But while that might be her actual age, mentally she still felt like she was eighteen. Rory hadn't been sexually active before the accident, so she had a lot to catch up on.

So she'd hired Kit.

He was going to teach her everything she needed to know about modern dating and help her get over her fears of being touched. He was going to just help her do those things she was afraid of doing. Like going into Lulu's crowded coffee shop and ordering a coffee. Or going into the city to eat at Conrad's exclusive kitchen.

She'd tried to do it on her own, and knowing she'd see her cousin had gotten her out the door. But then she'd frozen. Part of it was the walking stick she still had to use. It was hard not to feel like everyone was staring at her. Which in Gilbert Corners was a very real fear since she was a Gilbert and everyone was aware she'd been in a coma for ten years.

She knew that fear had dominated her for too long, so when Dash made it clear he did not approve of her plans with Kit, Rory felt her hackles go up.

Pulling her arm from Kit's, she squared her

shoulders and faced off with her brother. "Dash, I know, in your eyes, I'm still that little sister who was sleeping for too long. So I get that you want to protect me, but you are slowly smothering me. I need someone who will help me embrace all of the things that I'm a little bit scared to try but that I know I have to do."

"And you think this guy is the one?" Dash asked stiffly.

"I do," Rory assured him. "He's not a stranger. As I said, we're friends."

She glanced back at Kit. His mouth was a firm line and when their eyes met for a moment, she wasn't sure what she read in his gaze. But then he gave her a nod and a wink.

He turned to her brother. "I give you my word that I will not let any harm come to her," he promised.

"That's not necessary," Rory said. If she'd learned anything from Elle and Indy, her soon-to-be sister/cousin-in-law, it was that women didn't need a man to back them up. Rory was doing this for *herself*. That said, it was nice to have Kit along for those panicked moments she knew would come. Case in point…she'd already had an anxiety attack as she'd entered the house that she planned to make over.

As a coping mechanism, she'd stood there, doing box breathing and then singing that one song that always cheered her up. "Island in the Sun" by Weezer. She'd just sung it over and over until she'd heard the moving truck outside. Then she shoved her anxiety into a box, like her therapist had said to, flashed a smile and met the movers.

She hoped that doing stuff with Kit, living in this house on her own, finding her voice and strength again would slowly start to feel normal. That maybe she'd be able to face her fears and not worry about crying or shaking or having to sing "Island in the Sun" over and over again.

"Fine. But I'll be keeping tabs on both of you," Dash warned. "And, Kit, I'll need your full name."

"No, you won't!" Rory protested. "He has nothing to do with you."

Dash gave Kit a tight smile as he took Rory's arm in a firm but gentle grip. "Will you excuse us for a moment?"

He didn't wait for Kit to answer but just led Rory out of Kit's earshot. "You're a Gilbert and a very wealthy woman," he whispered. "It's irresponsible for you to spend time with someone we don't know. Just let me have him checked out."

"No. Dash, I mean it. You know I wanted to move across the country so I'd be forced to stand on my own. However, I stayed here in Gilbert Corners because I love you and I want us to be the family I remember. But you have to let me do this my way."

It would be easy to give in to Dash's demands and stay locked up inside Gilbert Manor for the rest of her life. She'd have a nice, safe life, one where everyone took care of her, but Rory was beginning to realize she wanted more.

When she'd first awoken from her coma, she'd felt eighteen, scared and unsure. But over the last few months, she'd started to realize she wanted to be a twenty-eight-year-old woman. Not that frightened, protected girl.

"I hate this," Dash bit out.

She hugged her older brother, knowing that as much as he might not want to let her do this on her own, he was going to.

"Thank you."

He just sort of grunted and hugged her back, and when he walked away, past Kit, he said something to the other man that Rory couldn't hear. Then he got into his car and drove away.

And she was left with this stranger whom she was counting on to help her find herself.

★ ★ ★

Kit smiled at Rory as her brother walked past him, pausing to warn Kit that if he hurt Rory he'd come after him, and then left.

Now what? He had no idea what exactly the person that Rory had hired was meant to do, and as much as he had wanted to use her to ruin Dash, it felt wrong now. Rory's smile sort of melted away as soon as her brother was gone and he heard her muttering what sounded like a Weezer song under her breath. And in that moment, he realized that using Rory wasn't going to be something he could do.

For one thing, despite the bad history between their families, he still liked her. For a second, he wanted to help her rebuild her strength and transform back into that brave, fearless girl she'd once been…

Kit blew out a frustrated breath. It seemed like every time he was ready to wreak vengeance down on the Gilberts for what they'd done, there was some sort of universal intervention showing him that they had already wrecked themselves.

"Hey, it's okay," he said, walking over to her. She had one arm wrapped around her own waist, and the song sounded almost manic at the speed she was singing it at.

He put his arm around her, slowly recognizing that she was having an anxiety attack, having seen his own mother in a similar state more than once. Rory didn't seem to feel his touch and he pulled her close into the curve of his body. She closed her eyes and he drew her even tighter against him, ignoring his own reaction to her nearness. He started talking in a low, calm tone.

"We are on a tropical island, the sand under our feet is powdery soft and so white it almost seems like no one else has ever habited this place before. The sun on our skin is warm and soothing, not too hot. Your hand is in mine and when you look up, you see the blue waves washing gently on the shore. The breeze wraps around us, and as you exhale in one long breath, the stress gradually seeps away."

He stopped talking as her breathing started to slow and she stopped singing. He wasn't sure if she still needed him to talk her through this or not.

But she lifted her head and opened her eyes. Her blue eyes were bright and clear, but in his mind he knew they still had clouds in them. He had thought she was the key to Dash's undoing but she might be the key for him, the key to closure on the past and the anger and revenge he'd always wanted but had never been able to commit to.

He knew revenge was what his family needed and he'd always been the soft brother. The one who'd been more like their mom. Losing his brother and then watching his father's slow descent into alcoholism had changed Kit. Or had forced him to stop being the son that had never measured up in his father's eyes.

He just wasn't the type of man his father and brother had been. He had legally changed his name after Dash had ruined them and he'd chosen Palmer. He couldn't use someone else to get what he wanted; he knew that now.

"You okay?" he asked quietly.

"No, but I'm *better*. Thank you," she whispered. "I don't know if this is what you signed up for, but I have a feeling there are going to be a lot more moments like it."

"That's fine," he assured her. "But I have to tell you, I'm not the person you hired."

Her eyes widened. "You're not?"

"No. But I think we can help each other, which is why I showed up here today," he said.

Throwing out revenge meant nothing if he continued to lie to her. He couldn't let her think she'd hired him. That was deceit at its worst.

"Well...the person I hired was a stranger, which I thought would make it easier than someone who knows me and my entire family history."

"I can see why you'd want that." His conscience pricked at him, but he decided not to reveal that they'd known each other in the past, or that his brother had been involved in the car crash that had put her into a coma. If he did, he knew she'd shut him out. Rightly so? He had no idea.

"The movers are almost done here and I am supposed to be trying to leave the house more," she said, then hesitated, suddenly looking very nervous.

"Why don't we go to Java and get a coffee and talk?" she asked, the words running together in a rush. "But... Hang on a second. If you aren't the guy I hired, why *are* you here?"

"I am moving into the cottage next to yours," he said. Which was the partial truth. He had planned to move back into his childhood home. The home that had symbolized the last time he'd been happy. He might have had ulterior motives for returning to it, but now that he'd crossed paths with Rory Gilbert again, he knew that his plans were changing and he hoped that he'd be able to figure out what was next.

"You are? Well, then, we're neighbors. That's good," she said, scrunching her forehead in thought. "So...coffee?"

"Yes, we can have coffee if you like. What did you mean by you're *supposed* to go out?"

"I... I was in a coma for ten years—so tragic, right?" She tried to laugh it off, but her discomfort was obvious. "Anyway, I've been out of it for six months but have found myself unable to actually start living again. I mean at first I needed to recover my strength physically, but as you just saw... I'm not at my best," she said.

"I saw nothing of the sort. You handled yourself beautifully, standing up to your brother and championing your cause. Then when it was over you just needed some recovery time."

She let out a long, slow breath and nodded over at him, the smallest smile playing around her full mouth.

"I think I'm going to like having you as a neighbor, Kit," she said.

"I think I will like being neighbors, too."

They agreed to meet at two that afternoon

for coffee, and as he watched her walk back to the movers, an uneasy feeling settled in his chest. He knew that he was going to have to tell her who he was, but at this point in time, he knew it wouldn't help her. Of course, it wouldn't help him either.

TWO

INDY BELMONT WAS Rory's soon to be cousin-in-law. But she was also instrumental in revitalizing Gilbert Corners. She'd moved to this town about two years ago and brought her popular show |*Hometown, Home Again*|, which aired on the Home Living TV network, here to film. She'd started with Indy's Treasures, her bookshop on Main Street, and had slowly been working to get other projects off the ground.

When Rory had decided she had to leave Gilbert Manor, Indy and Elle had been her biggest supporters. And it had been Indy who had suggested possibly buying one of the Victorian-era duplexes and redoing it to help Rory adjust to being back in the world.

So, because she had a lot of love and respect for Indy, as soon as the movers left and she was alone in her new home, she was tempted to call her. She needed advice about Kit.

Kit.

He had the dreamiest brown eyes and she couldn't stop fantasizing about how his thick dark hair would feel beneath her fingers. She remembered when he'd wrapped his arms around her and helped calm her down with the soothing, deep timbre of his voice. His body had felt solid against hers...and she hadn't panicked.

She'd been so afraid she would when a man held her because the last memory she had of the night of the car crash was being forcibly kissed and held against the wall by Declan Orr, the man who had died in the car crash that had left her in a coma.

But in Kit's arms she hadn't felt scared. Maybe it had been his voice or the woodsy scent of his aftershave. Or perhaps it was the solid beating of his heart, which she had heard under her cheek. Whatever the reason...she couldn't stop thinking about him.

She was a bit bummed that he wasn't from the agency she'd hired, because the person they were sending was supposed to help her figure out how to kiss and have sex. All of her knowledge of that stuff had been a few brief make-out sessions in high school and then that one sexual attack that had scared her.

What was she going to do? Maybe this entire plan to meet Kit for coffee and talk to him again was a mistake.

But Elle, who was also her doctor, had said that mistakes were bound to happen. And that Rory would learn from them and become stronger by making them. Also, what was the worst that could happen?

That was what Conrad said to her every time they talked. Her cousin had been in the same car accident as Rory, and recovered, though it had left him badly scarred. He had confessed that it had taken him years to feel anything close to normal and he liked to do things that scared him. His advice to her was to go for anything that wouldn't land her back in the hospital.

So, what was the worst that could happen if she met Kit?

He might not show up. Fair enough and that would be fine. But, on the flip side, he might come through for her and prove to be that kind of man who could be an ally. Also fine.

And if he *did* show up, they might hit it off and then she'd want to kiss him and... Her mind whirled with the possibilities. She'd be in his arms again and this time their lips would meet. And that would be more than fine. She figured she had to have a first *real* kiss… Why not Kit?

Though he might not want to be her first-time guy.

It would not be the end of the world if that happened, but she wondered if she'd have the courage to ask someone else. But she was also supposed to be doing things that scared her, so in this case she was going to do it.

Rory got dressed, taking her time. She had a long, jagged scar on her leg. Things were different now, and she was trying to come to terms with the body she'd woken up in. So of course the scars were to be expected. But they just made her feel less like herself. The Rory she remembered had long, slim legs. These were flabby with cellulite on her thighs that Indy had reassured her everyone had.

Rory stood in front of the mirror in the wrap dress with the skirt that ended at the top of her knees. She saw the imperfections but shook her head, pushing those thoughts firmly out of her mind. She couldn't hate the flaws, because they made her who she was, and if Kit did…then he wasn't the man she was hoping he'd be.

She grabbed her purse, put on her sunglasses

and blew herself a kiss in the mirror before opening the front door and stepping outside.

This was it. Her new life started today and she was going to seize every opportunity that came to her.

No more hiding in her bed and being afraid of the outside world.

Kit slid his car into a spot in the public parking lot near the park that was across the street from the train station. Behind the park were the shops on Main Street. He had contemplated not coming to meet Rory. But the truth was he *had* to.

Whatever fantasy he'd entertained about her over the years had paled compared to what he felt when he'd held her. It was sexual, but more than that. He'd never allowed himself to think of the future or to really have a permanent relationship with anyone because he'd been so focused on vengeance. But one moment with Rory and now he was questioning it? Was it just the remembered childhood feelings of friendship or something more?

He couldn't deny he was excited just being with her. His phone pinged and he glanced down to see it was a text from his aunt Mal.

Mal was his father's sister. The two of them were all that was left of the family and they had been working together to restore their fortunes—which they had—even though Dash Gilbert hadn't left them much to rebuild with.

Did you find the sister?

Kit thumbs-upped her question. He wasn't sure what else to say. He really didn't have any news for her. And he certainly wasn't going to text Aunt Mal that he'd changed his mind about using Rory. He sucked in a breath. And was he even sure that he had?

Yes.

Kit and Aunt Mal had reformed the company using his middle name Palmer into Palmer Industries and they were thriving. It was only as Gilbert Corners was being revitalized and new industry was coming back to the town that he and his aunt had thought about what the Gilbert family had taken from them once again. They were interested in buying into the old factory that Declan had been meant to run before his death, and wanted to put in their own manufacturing plant there.

But they both knew that they were going to have to be careful about how they approached the deal. Hence him coming to town to figure out how to get some leverage with Dash Gilbert.

His aunt texted again.

Call me when you're leaving GC.

He replied: I might be a while. I'm having a look around town for potential investment properties.

The girl won't work?

Not sure yet.

Aunt Mal ended the conversation with Talk later. He pocketed his phone. Mal was his last living blood relative. Although he had distant cousins, he wasn't close to any of them. He and Mal had had each other's back for longer than Kit could remember. As much as he wanted to think that he could figure out something that would benefit both him and his aunt, while hurting the Gilbert family in the process, nothing in his past dealings with them had proven fruitful to that end.

He knew that part of his reluctance to involve Rory in his plans was that he didn't want to use Rory the way that the Gilbert family had used his brother. Yet wouldn't that be the perfect revenge?

Sitting in his car, waiting and watching the town that was somehow cheerier than he could remember from his childhood, just served to remind him of all that he had lost. Sure, Rory hadn't really been responsible for those actions, but she was a part of the family. She had, according to his father, led his brother on and then accused him of misreading her advances and had him thrown out of the party after Conrad had punched him.

Kit shook his head. When he'd seen her earlier, he'd been catapulted back to his childhood and the innocent girl Rory had been before she'd grown into a Gilbert woman. He had to remember that.

He saw her walking toward the coffee shop with her cane and got out of his car. His breath caught in his chest as her long blond hair, stirred by the wind, flew around her face and shoulders. She tipped her head back toward the breeze, a smile playing around her lips. As he glanced at the scoop-necked dress she wore and noticed the gentle curves of her breasts, he remembered how she'd felt in his arms.

Now that she wasn't in distress, he recalled how perfectly she'd fit against him. Her head on his chest and her arms wound tight around him. He remembered the floral scent of her hair and the way she'd exhaled softly, the warmth of her breath brushing against his neck and stirring him.

He wanted her.

She was his enemy's sister.

She was also his long-lost crush.

Kit shoved a hand through his hair and exhaled a frustrated breath. She was *complicated* and, honestly, he knew the smart thing to do would be to turn around and leave and let Aunt Mal come back and figure out a way to use her to get to Dash.

But she noticed him, lifted her hand and waved at him, and it was too late to resort to plan B. So instead, he found himself locking his car and heading across the green, well-manicured park toward her. As he got closer, he realized that everyone was watching her and then began noticing her watching him.

Rory had said she was trying to find her way back to living outside the mansion and he could see the struggle it would be for her. Again he wanted to help her. Wanted to be the hero that

she'd been to him when they'd been children.
But could he really be that for her, and was she
truly deserving of it?

He sighed. All he knew for sure was that he
had to come clean and tell her his name. He
didn't want to deceive her the way her family
had his brother. He needed to know that when
he and Aunt Mal were finally in a position of
power over the Gilbert family, they could be
satisfied that they had done it aboveboard.

Which meant no sneaking and deceiving the
way that Lance Gilbert had been with them.
And while he suspected that earlier he might
have been swayed by lust and nostalgia, he
couldn't afford to be now. It was time to remember who was responsible for all of the destruction that had happened the night of the
ball.

Kit smiled at her as he got closer. "If I knew
you were walking to town, I would have joined
you."

Yeah, so now she had to tell him she didn't
drive. But she could be vague as to the reason
why. She didn't have to say that she still freaked
out a bit every time she was in a car. That being
around people made her uneasy.

On the other hand, the ability to be outside and walk was something… *Magical* wasn't quite the right word because she'd worked damned hard at physical therapy to get to this point, but it did feel special to be able to walk.

She sort of smiled and then realized that Kit was awaiting her response.

"Oh, that's okay. I don't drive yet," she said.

"You don't?"

"Yeah, you know I was in a coma forever."

"I guess I'd forgotten that," he said with a sheepish look that was way too charming. In high school she would have flirted back but it had been ten years since she'd talked to a man who wasn't related to her or a medical professional, and she was so rusty.

"So outside or inside?" he asked.

"I'd prefer to be outside if you don't mind…"

"I don't. Why don't you grab a table and I'll go and get our drinks?" he suggested.

She asked him to get her an iced coffee of the day. And then went to find a table away from the others in the shade. As she sat down, her phone buzzed and she took it out. It was in her group chat with Indy and Rory. Indy had a good view of the coffee shop from her bookstore.

Indy: Who's the hottie?

Rory: Kit. He's my new neighbor.

Elle: I've got a patient in five. But I want all the details. Drinks at Indy's shop tonight?

Rory thumbs-upped the message and then put her phone away. She didn't have any good girl friends that she remembered from before the accident, and Indy and Elle had welcomed her as if she were their sister. The more her memories had returned, the more she realized that she hadn't had any friends in the town of Gilbert Corners. That her grandfather had deliberately kept her and Dash and Conrad apart from the townspeople.

She didn't like the fact that she'd been so easily led by his selfish desires. But she did remember that they had all been a little bit afraid of him.

"The coffee of the day was a strawberry white mocha," he said.

"Great. I haven't tried that before. But Lulu hired a new barista who has been experimenting and I haven't been disappointed yet."

He flashed a grin. "Good to hear. I followed your lead and got the same."

They both took a sip. Rory closed her eyes as the icy, sweet and fruity coffee slid over her tongue. She liked it. It was cold and delicious; she took another sip of it before opening her eyes to find Kit staring at her.

Oh.

The look in his eyes was intense and unlike anything she'd noticed before. His lips were parted and his pupils dilated, and there was a slight flush to his skin.

"Do you like it?"

"Mmm-hmm," he said. "So tell me about the person you thought I was."

"Yeah, about that. It turns out that the person canceled but I hadn't received the message. I'm sorry for putting you on the spot like that."

"I didn't mind," he said, taking another sip. "But you haven't said what you hired them for."

She turned the paper straw in her cup, staring down at her drink instead of at Kit. "I hired someone to help me get caught up on…um…life."

He leaned back in his chair and crossed his arms over his chest, drawing the fabric of his black button-down shirt taut across his chest. She stared at the muscles, which she could see for longer than she knew she should. "Like what?"

Kissing, she thought. She wanted to kiss him but she knew she'd be awkward at it and she guessed he probably wasn't going to be up for her fumbling around and figuring that out.

"Driving?" he asked when she didn't say anything.

"Yes and other things," she said. "Pretty much everything. I was eighteen when I went into the coma, so a lot of stuff that I should have picked up in the last ten years I didn't. I just don't want to wait for life to start. I need a jump start and I thought hiring someone to help would be the answer."

"But they backed out?"

"Yes. Or Dash found out and fired them," she said, her lips twitching. "He didn't think it was a good idea. That's why I said you were a friend."

"Well, if it helps, I did meet you when we were kids briefly."

"Did you?"

"Yes, at a summer party at Gilbert Manor."

"I can't recall too many details of the past, but I do remember the parties were always fun in the summer," she said. How dumb was that, right! She couldn't help feeling frustrated by the fact that she couldn't remember a party that her

family threw. Rory knew they'd had a bunch
of them and there were photo albums in the library that showed them, but she never looked
at them after she realized they weren't triggering any memories.

"They were," he said, reaching out and
brushing his finger against the back of her hand
where it lay curled on the table. "What else do
you need to learn?"

Fear was right there waiting to wrap itself
around her and make her retreat, but instead
she turned her hand under Kit's, slid her fingers through his and a shiver went through her
entire body. "Everything."

He leaned in closer. There was something
electric in the way their eyes met. God, he was
cute. She loved the dark stubble on his cheeks
and his thick eyelashes. The scent of his aftershave was subtle. She took a deep breath,
inhaling it all in. He rested his elbow on the
table as their eyes met and something that felt
almost magical seemed to pass between them.
"Everything?"

She nodded. "There is so much I've missed."

"What if I helped you out?"

"With driving?" she asked, because it was the
safest thing to suggest at this moment.

"And other things," he said, in a lower timbre. It sent a quiver throughout her entire body. Her lips felt dry and she licked them. His eyes tracked the movement of her tongue and his mouth sort of opened. Was he flirting with her?

"What kinds of other things?"

Ugh. The words just popped out and her tone…that was her flirting tone. Did she want him to flirt back with her?

"I have to be honest with you, I want you."

He *wanted* her.

She swallowed. So yes. He definitely wanted her to flirt with him, too. Her eyes widened and then she realized that she had no idea what to do next. "I… I…"

He squeezed her hand. "Do you want to spend more time with me, Rory?"

She nodded.

"Do I make you nervous?"

She shook her head. "You should. You're a stranger and a man… I am not sure why you don't."

"Well, I'm glad to hear that. What if we date? We can take things at your pace. I'll teach you to drive and whatever else you have on your list," he suggested. He spoke in that low, rumbly tone that resonated through her body and made her feel like she was back in his arms.

"Do you want to do that?" she whispered.

"One thing about me, I don't say things I don't mean."

Wow. Well, okay, then. That kind of honesty was what she was looking for. She was tired of people who were nice to her because of her condition and Kit was offering her a chance to have everything she'd been dreaming of with a real guy. Not the faceless lover who sometimes showed up in her dreams.

"Duly noted. Oh, and one thing about me? I'm trying to say yes to everything."

"So then we'll start dating, Rory Gilbert."

Dating. OMG. Was that still a thing? She didn't know, but apparently it was for her. A wave of giddiness swept through her. She was going to go out on *dates* with Kit and get to bask in his dreamy eyes, thick eyelashes and that kissable mouth of his.

"Yes, we will, Kit…" she said, then paused. "I don't know your last name."

THREE

WHAT *WAS* HIS last name? He had decided not to lie, and if he told her the truth there was a chance she wouldn't connect him with his brother. But then again, he wasn't sure. Something as small as a name could spark her memory. "Palmer. Kit Palmer," he said.

Liar.

But he still wasn't sure what part, if any, Rory had played in his brother's destruction that night.

"Palmer. I like it. So your family is from around here?" she asked.

He exhaled, releasing the tension that had been roiling through him. "We were for a bit. When the factory closed, we moved," he told her. "I was in college on the West Coast so didn't get to say goodbye."

"What did you study?"

"Business management."

She frowned.

"I'm a CEO, so it's served me well."

She shook her head and took a sip of her coffee. "It's just so *practical*."

She made it sound like it was the most boring job in the world. And honestly, she wasn't wrong. But he'd made the choice he had to in order to help his family survive. It wasn't exactly a dream job but he hadn't had her financial power to fall back on.

"Not all of us were born into the Gilbert family," he reminded her.

"Fair enough. I wasn't even thinking of that. I'm sorry," she said.

She sounded contrite and when she looked away from him, he realized he'd made her anxious again.

"What's worrying you?"

"Not trying to make excuses, but I haven't had a lot of conversations with anyone not related to me since I came out of the coma. Sorry to use that for my reason for everything but I truly didn't mean for that to come out—"

"Stop," he said, taking her hand in his and rubbing his thumb against the inside of her wrist. "It's okay. I think I'm a little bit sensitive when it comes to my past."

"You are? Why? You seem like someone who's got everything together."

"I have insecurities just like everyone else," he admitted.

She turned her hand in his, lacing her fingers through his, and a bolt of pure desire went through him. Their hands fit so well together, almost like he knew their bodies would. He wasn't sure what he expected Dash Gilbert's sister to be like but it certainly wasn't Rory. She was charming, shy and flirty but in an understated and almost innocent way. Made sense given she'd been in a coma for ten years.

A tendril had come free and curled against her cheek. There was something about this woman that stirred him to the core. And for a moment, he forgot she was a Gilbert and just enjoyed the thrill of being turned on. He shifted his legs as he started to get hard and looked instead into her eyes.

"Of course you do," she said. "One of the things my therapist told me was that just because I felt like I'm being held together with yarn doesn't mean everyone else has a solid foundation. Sorry again."

Kit lifted her hand and brought it to his mouth because he wanted to touch her and this might be the only time he could and not want more. Brushing his lips against the back of her hand, he rasped, "Apology accepted, and going forward you have nothing more to apologize for."

She shivered a little as his lips had grazed the back of her hand and then licked her lips and gave him that innocent smile of hers. The one he was sure she had no idea affected him as deeply as it did. But he knew he had to get his head back in the game. He had to stop looking at Rory and just seeing her as a woman he wanted. He had to—what? For the first time that he could remember, he wanted someone for himself.

Wrong woman, dumbass.

"You don't have to apologize either," she said.

Kit nodded. "So your list. I have about two hours free this afternoon. Is there something small we could tackle?"

She took another sip of her iced coffee, closing her eyes as she did so. "Hmm. This drink is so good," she said before pausing, as if this was the biggest question of her life. "Not really. Today was meant to be a get-to-know-each-other day. What do you suggest? Whatever you propose, I'm pretty sure I haven't done it."

"I haven't been back here for a while. Should we walk through the shops on Main Street?"

"No. I've done that. But what if instead of the shops, we go toward the path by the river?" Her eyes lit up. "I heard there are some wild blackberries growing down there. Maybe we can pick some and I'll make you a pie."

A pie? It was the last thing he expected of an heiress. But it suited Rory. It was almost too easy to picture her picking berries and making a pie. He had to admit that was another thing that made him want to kiss her.

"All right. Have you seen any?" he asked.

"No. I haven't had anyone willing to walk down the path with me. It's sort of steep and 'rough' according to Dash, but the truth is he thinks I should be carried everywhere."

He laughed at the way she'd put air quotes around *rough*. He couldn't say no to helping her with this goal of hers, especially since it would annoy her brother. But he knew they'd have to be careful.

They finished their coffees and headed toward the river. Today it was flowing steadily, looking serene and picturesque. Now that the train station and surrounding shops had been renovated and cleaned up, the town was starting to come to life again. He noticed that a camera crew was set up across the street.

He knew from his own research that they were from the Home Living TV network. Indy Belmont—Conrad Gilbert's fiancée—was filming a makeover show where she redid buildings in this town.

The paved road ended near the bridge and then a steep path led down to a dirt walkway that ran alongside the river. He looked at the trail and then back at Rory. The last thing he wanted was for her to hurt herself. "Someone should put a handrail in here."

"I'll mention it to Dash."

"Or you could go to the town council and tell them yourself," he suggested. She was too connected to Dash and if he was going to spend time with her, he wanted to see her standing on her own.

She nodded. "You're right. I'll do it."

Rory hadn't realized how much she needed someone like Kit until he pointed out that she could go to the town council herself. She had been thinking of the actual things Dash was forbidding her to do when she'd moved out. But she hadn't really contemplated taking a starring role in her own life.

She liked the idea of it but she knew that when it was time to show up and present her ideas, she was going to be nervous. But she didn't need to dwell on that just yet. For the moment she looked down at the slope and wondered how she was going to navigate it.

"Any suggestions for how I can do this?" she asked Kit. "My left leg is weaker than my right."

"Wait here while I see just how steep this is to walk down."

She watched with more than a little envy at the nimble way he went down the slope. He took his time, though, looking for rough patches and checking the sturdiness of the dirt path. When he got to the bottom, he took a few steps in both directions and then came back and returned to her side.

"Okay. The way down, I think you should put your hand on my shoulder and I'll lead the way. We will go slowly and you will be in charge of the pace. When we get to the bottom, the river path is level and has been edged with pavers, so it's clear someone has been maintaining that part. But getting back up might be harder."

Rory had already been thinking about that. She'd noticed the deep, almost lunge-like movement of Kit's legs as he'd come back up the path, and she wasn't sure she could do that. When she did lunges at her physical therapy sessions, she'd only managed two on each side and then her thighs started quivering.

"Do you cross that bridge when we get to it?"

"We can. But be prepared for me to do a lot more assisting. Is that something you're okay with?" he asked.

She had made so many strides in walking and getting around on her own, but she'd known from the beginning that when she tried more strenuous activities there would be times when she'd have to rely on someone else to help her.

It frustrated her because she wanted to be able to do things for herself. But she had no shame in asking for help. Conrad had been the one to make her feel normal about it. He told her that after his post-accident surgeries he'd had to ask for assistance with everything. With that one thought, her big, six-foot-five-inch, muscle-y cousin had made her realize that she was going to recover, too. But only if she asked for help and respected her limitations.

"Yes. Are *you* okay with it?" she asked. If he

wasn't, then no matter how hot he was she was going to have to end this before it really had a chance to get started.

He tucked a strand of her hair behind her ear and smiled at her. "I am. I like being your knight-errant."

She smiled at him. "Knight Kit. I like it, but I don't want to be a damsel in distress."

"You won't be. Ready?"

She took a deep breath. Then closed her eyes for just a second and looked up at the sky before glancing back at Kit. His dark brown gaze was steady and patient. He wasn't going to rush her. She also felt like he wouldn't judge her if she suddenly said no. But this was her year of *yes*.

She nodded.

"Okay, so something I have learned is that the first step is always the hardest," he said.

"Why do you think that is?"

"Because you don't know what it's going to be like."

She put her hand on his shoulder. He was strong, solid, and she felt the strength in him. He looked over his shoulder and winked at her. "You've got this."

She licked her lips and nodded. She did have this. And if she didn't, she'd come back tomorrow and try again. Hopefully with Kit, she couldn't help but think.

"Ready?

"Yes."

He moved slowly as he'd promised, and with her hand on his shoulder for balance, she found her footing without too much problem. In fact, it felt at times he was going too slow, but she knew that caution was needed. She realized about halfway down that she was holding her breath and reminded herself to breathe.

When they got to the bottom, she felt like she was going to cry. She blinked a bunch of times, keeping the tears in, but did take out her phone and snap a picture of the path she'd come down.

"Want me to take your picture next to it?" he asked.

"Yes, that would be nice." She handed him her phone. "I'm trying to document all my firsts so I can look back on it on the bad days."

"Good idea."

He watched her for a minute and then lifted the camera phone. She wondered what he saw through the viewfinder. Kit made her feel different, more like a woman than a sister or a patient. Which, let's face it, was totally a good thing.

But the butterflies in her stomach as he moved around trying to find the right angle… she wasn't sure what they meant. Of course, she liked him and he *had* said he wanted her…so now she couldn't help watching him and wanting him, too. Wanting to feel his arms around her and his mouth on hers.

He moved toward the river to get a good position of her and the trail, and she looked up at where she'd come from and felt like screaming for joy. But it came out as a little yelp as she turned and smiled at Kit.

He snapped her picture and then came over and put his arm around her shoulder, careful not to pull her off balance, and took a selfie of the two of them.

Then he turned his head and looked down at her. Their eyes met and something passed between them. Something electric.

She had no idea what she'd do if he lowered his head and kissed her. She knew she'd kissed boys before. Rory had never let being an heiress get in the way of living the life she wanted. But she had also been sexually attacked just before she went into her coma, which made her hesitate. All the thoughts she'd been having about his mouth and his body. Suddenly, she wasn't sure she was ready for a kiss.

What if she kissed like a high schooler instead of a woman? What if she totally sucked at it because it had been a long time since she'd locked lips with anyone? What if...and this was the scariest thought of them all, what if his kiss made her remember the man who attacked her and she freaked?

She chewed her lower lip...just watching him.

Waiting to see what would happened next. But then Kit cleared his throat and handed her phone back to her.

"Where are these blackberries I've heard so much about?"

"That way," she said, pointing toward the left.

She took her time putting her phone away, trying to calm the disappointment that was coursing through her. She wanted to kiss him. Had almost given in to the impulse but had stopped herself. One thing at a time.

But thinking about Kit and his firm mouth that was smiling at her as he waited for her to start walking toward the blackberries was a distraction. The best kind of distraction. Her body was alive in a way that it hadn't been despite all the months she'd been out of her coma. Those butterflies were back in her stomach and they made her feel warm and fuzzy all over.

It was like how she'd felt when she'd walked for the first time without the Zimmer frame or how it had felt when she'd eaten ice cream and realized how much she loved it.

But this time it was Kit giving her all the feels. Making her hum and vibe to something that she didn't really understand but she craved more of.

There was still so much that she hadn't realized she'd been missing until this moment.

Until Kit.

Nothing was going according to plan, and he knew that when he got home Aunt Mal was going to expect a report. But he realized he wasn't going to share this with her. This afternoon had made him feel like...well, in a way he hadn't in a very long time.

Kit was experiencing something with Rory that he hadn't with anyone else before.

He needed time to reassess and figure out how he was going forward...but not now. A small smile flickered on his lips as he watched

Rory. She'd taken a folded cloth bag from the crossbody she'd been carrying and they'd put the blackberries in it as they picked them. Then she brushed one on the skirt of her long dress before putting it in her mouth and closing her eyes.

"Perfect. Sweet but with just a tiny bit of tartness. Try one," she said, brushing another one on her skirt and holding it up to him.

Her fingers grazed his lips as she put the berry in his mouth. He stood stock-still, willing his body not to react to her closeness, but it took every ounce of his control and he didn't entirely succeed. He chewed the berry while looking at Rory and noticed her blush when he winked at her and said, "Tart and sweet just like you."

She turned away slowly and they continued picking berries. "I can't remember, but Dash and Con said we used to do this on our property when we were growing up."

"Is that why you wanted to do it again?"

"It is. But when I asked to go recently, Dash said no."

"Does he say no a lot?"

"He does. But the truth is it was just him alone for so long after the accident, and I don't think he's sure how to handle both myself and Con being healthy and functioning." Rory collected more berries, her silence filling in the blanks of Dash's and Conrad's lingering guilt.

"What happened to Con?" he asked. He had heard a brief report from his aunt that there were injuries, but Aunt Mal had only known that Rory was in a coma.

"He was thrown from the car because he wasn't wearing his seat belt and he broke every bone in his body and was covered in cuts from the glass. Apparently, it took multiple surgeries and then months of recovery."

Kit turned away. Slightly shocked to hear how badly injured Conrad had been. Why hadn't he ever been told about that? Kit had come back for Declan's funeral and then flown back to Berkeley to withdraw. By the time he'd returned, his father had started drinking heavily and had been living with Aunt Mal. Dash and his grandfather Lance had crushed all of his family's prospects.

"I never knew the Beast had gone through anything like that," Kit said, referring to Conrad by his celebrity chef name.

"He's better now. In fact he said I should pick

blackberries, but then he and Dash got into it and I dropped it," she said.

"Why?"

"Because I don't like to see them fight. We're all each other has. Plus I knew I was moving out and I'd eventually go on my own."

A shot of fear went through him at the thought of her trying to come down here on her own. "Promise me you won't come down here alone until there is a handrail."

"I won't. That's why I have you, Kit."

Hearing her say she had him made him feel... *fuck*. He wasn't sure he could do this. He was in some sort of muddy water here with her. Since the moment she'd looped her arm through his and said, "Pretend we're old friends," he'd been spinning out of control. He'd been pretending to make up some plan on the fly but he had to face facts right now that the was lying to himself.

He was totally at Rory's mercy. Hard as he tried to fight it, he was enchanted by her and he couldn't allow himself to fall for her. She couldn't be his weakness.

He had to get back on track.

"You mentioned making a pie. Have you made one before?"

"Maybe before the accident. But Conrad recently showed me how to make a crust that wasn't too complicated, but then Indy showed me a refrigerated one I could buy. So I have two in my fridge. I had been planning to pick blackberries this week."

"Why did you say you weren't sure when I asked at the coffee shop?"

She chewed her lower lip for a moment. "I thought you might not want to. But then when you said something so tame as walk down Main Street I realized that if I didn't start saying what I wanted I'd never get it."

"Yeah, took me a while to learn that one as well. But with me, Rory, you don't have to hedge. Whatever you want, if it's in my power to help you with doing it, I will."

She turned and put a handful of berries into the canvas bag and then tipped her head to the side, looking over at him. "Anything?"

"Anything." He was pretty sure that even at her wildest, there wasn't anything she'd request that he wouldn't want to do. "Well, nothing illegal."

She giggled at that but then got serious again. "What about dangerous?"

"More dangerous than coming down here?"

She nodded slowly.

"Definitely."

"Good. I want to see you push yourself," he said. "I love watching the joy on your face. It's like...well, you come alive when you try something new. I love that I get to experience that with you."

He expected her to ask him for this dangerous thing but she simply shook her head and turned back to her canvas bag. They finished picking the berries and went back to the path. He stood behind her this time, putting his hands lightly on her waist to steady her as she climbed up. She was moving slowly and her legs started shaking at one point, so he was tempted to offer to carry her.

But when he started to, she glared at him. "I want to do this on my own."

"No rush."

But he was still worried for her. She took about four steps and then had to rest. He was beginning to see Dash's side of things. Rory seemed to not want to acknowledge her limitations. But when they finally got to the top and she smiled at him, he realized it was worth it.

She hugged him, pulling him close and pressing her body against his. He held her in his arms, desperately wanting to claim a kiss, but knowing that he needed to figure out a few more things before he did that.

FOUR

THAT ALMOST KISS lingered in her mind for the next few days. She wasn't able to forget about it or how it had made her feel. What she felt around Kit was a sharp contrast to the feelings she could recall from that night ten years ago. She remembered flashes of moments from the night of the crash. When Declan—the man she'd been dancing with all night—had pushed for more than a few kisses in the upstairs hallway. She'd ripped her gown and he was in the process of clawing at her panties and trying to tear them off when she screamed.

Luckily for Rory, both Dash and Conrad had heard her. Conrad had gotten to them first. Rory wasn't sure of all the details of that moment. She'd heard Conrad yelling and punching her date. She'd sort of cowered there against the wall, trying to hold the bodice of her dress together over her breasts.

Dash had arrived and offered her his jacket and then things got fuzzy. The next thing she remembered was her grandfather admonishing her, Dash and Conrad to conduct themselves with more decorum and Conrad telling Grandfather to fuck off. Then they'd gotten in the car and...nothing.

Those memories were still so vague. She wished she couldn't remember her date's name or his face but she remembered it all. And as she stood in the kitchen waiting for her blackberry pie to bake, she wondered if the details she forgot, the details about why her date did what he did, were important. If unlocking that information would bring her closer to healing.

She knew there must be more to the story than she remembered, and if she was being completely honest with herself, she knew that she didn't want to linger in that memory. In a way she wished the events of that night had never come back to her.

It was sort of annoying to think that she had to relearn so many things but that one thing she wanted to forget wouldn't go away.

Her phone pinged. She still wasn't used to her cell phone. Everything was on there. Adjusting to technology was an entirely different challenge. She picked it up and saw she had a text from Dash asking for more details of her "friend." She sent him the angry face emoji as a response. Though she wasn't really angry.

She could appreciate that he loved her and worried about her. But her therapist had pointed out that unless she put some boundaries in place where Dash was concerned, Rory might never be able to stand on her own.

He texted back a thumbs-up.

She looked around the kitchen. Conrad had been over to look at it and recommended the appliances that Rory had purchased and installed before moving in. But the rest of it was in okay shape—dated and in need of work, but okay. The linoleum on the floors was faded and torn in a few places. The cabinets had been white originally but had faded to a dusty, dirty version of it.

The mansion she'd grown up in had been perfect. Everything was kept pristine by the housekeeping staff and the kitchens had been renovated every three years so they were always current and modern. But it had been the sort of perfection found in showrooms or magazines rather than a home, which was what she wanted her place to feel like.

Every room that she made over in her house was deliberate and she made choices that appealed to her, not because it was a room worthy of the Gilbert name.

Indy had helped Rory set up an inspiration board for the kitchen, and between Indy and Lulu they had indicated the projects that they thought someone with Rory's nonexistent DIY skills could master. Lulu and Indy were best friends and had a TV show they did together.

She decided to bake the pie before she started on the first project. Her legs still ached from the climb up the embankment after they'd picked blackberries. It had been raining for the last day and a half, so Rory had been inside.

Partially because of the weather and partially because there were times when the outside world felt too big and too much for her. Her phone pinged again and she glanced down, ready with the girl-with-her-hands-up emoji for Dash, but her heart skipped a beat when she saw the message was from Kit.

Sorry I had to run the other day. I'm back in town. What's next on your adventure agenda?

Glad you're back. I'm about to take the blackberry pie out of the oven. Next up is removing the doors from my kitchen cabinets. So adventurous…

For a slice of pie I'll be your helper.

She grinned as she typed, Done.

On my way, came his reply.

She couldn't help that giddy feeling in her stomach as she went to the hall mirror and checked to make sure her hair wasn't too messy. Rory sighed. She looked…well, like her. She hadn't been out in the sun, not that that would have made a difference since she'd always been extremely pale. She'd pulled her hair back into a ponytail when she'd been baking, because as Conrad had succinctly told her, no one liked hair in their food.

She wore a pair of skinny jeans and a Hello Kitty T-shirt as she went to open the door. All the design pictures she'd seen of these long, wooden-floored hallways had area rugs on them, but Rory wasn't ready for that yet. She had a hard time walking on surfaces as they changed so she'd kept the hardwood.

Her doorbell rang. She felt another swell of

excitement in her stomach as she undid the dead bolt and stepped back to open the door.

Kit stood there, his dark hair damp from the rain. He had on a leather jacket, black jeans and a tentative smile.

"I'm all wet. Sorry I should have grabbed an umbrella."

"That's okay," she said, gesturing for him to come inside.

"I don't want to ruin the wood," he protested.

"You won't. There are some towels in the powder room if you want to dry off and the kitchen is in the back. Join me when you're done," she said.

Rory linked her hands together and turned away to keep from touching him. She wished she'd stroked his face when they'd been so close the other day, but she hadn't. Now with the rainwater on his face, his thick eyelashes had stuck together and he looked starkly masculine with that water dripping off him. She'd wanted to put her hands on his face and kiss him.

Feel that strong mouth against hers.

But she wasn't sure what *he* wanted. Maybe that was why the memories of the past had been swirling around in her mind. She would never want to force herself on anyone.

After two days away from Rory he'd told himself he could come back, do the recon he and Aunt Mal needed and keep his perspective. When his brother was killed in the car accident, their family had lost everything. Lance Gilbert was no help and Dash was even worse, punishing their family while they were still grieving the loss of his brother.

Aunt Mal had been the one to keep them together as his father turned to drinking, and Kit, who had switched colleges and was still going to night school, tried to get up to speed on starting their own business. Returning from Berkeley had been a sort of wake-up call and he'd gone from frat boy to the one everyone relied on in what felt like a heartbeat.

The days away had sort of helped to clear his head. There was no way Rory could be as... enchanting as she'd seemed. And he knew that there wasn't another person on the planet that he'd describe that way.

But Rory had left him with that impression. He'd almost convinced himself that he'd been wrong until she'd opened the door to her cozy cottage on this cold, fall day. She'd smiled at him like she was happy to see him and invited him into her home that smelled of vanilla and blackberries.

She'd been so chill, not like women he'd dated in the past would have been after two days of total radio silence.

But of course he wasn't dating Rory. Was he? He'd come back for more Gilbert family secrets. That was all.

Except he knew that wasn't the truth. He hadn't been able to stop thinking about how she'd felt in his arms. Hadn't been able to talk himself into staying away from Rory Gilbert. Or Gilbert Corners. Hadn't been able to stop regretting that he hadn't just leaned down and kissed her after they'd picked those blackberries.

So here he was in her powder room, staring at himself in the mirror after having toweled off most of the water, trying to convince himself that he was cool with letting go of his need for revenge if it meant hurting her.

And the thing was, he didn't buy it.

Lying was such a slippery path. He could justify going after Gilbert International—after all Lance Gilbert had made promises to Declan that he'd reneged on when he'd sold the fac-

tory. He knew there had been a big fight at the
winter ball between his brother, Dash, Conrad
and Lance. But the details…well, no one on his
side of the family knew them. But Aunt Mal
and Kit assumed it had to do with the closing of the factory. Declan had been a hothead
and there was no doubt the loss of the factory
would have set him off. Had their brother tried
to stand up for the family? Or had anger dominated him that night, making him do something rash? They'd never been able to get any
answers and Kit feared they'd never know the
truth. It had died with his brother in the accident.

What a mess.

He opened the door to the powder room, left
his boots near the door and put his leather jacket
on a hook before heading toward the kitchen.
Stopping in the doorway, he realized that Rory
was singing along to "Helena" by My Chemical Romance.

When she tipped her head back and screamed,
"*What's the worst that I could say,*" he realized that
whatever lies he might have been trying to convince himself with were just that. He wanted
this woman. He wasn't here for any other reason than that she was enchanting him.

Kit shook his head and started to sing along with her. He had already decided he wouldn't do anything to harm Rory and he was going to have to trust himself not to. Because he couldn't walk away from her. And he wasn't going to pretend otherwise.

Her eyes flew open and she gave him a huge smile. "You know this song?"

"Love the band," he said, offering her his hand and pulling her into his arms.

She leaned into him for a second, and he felt her hands flutter against his chest as she looked up at him. Their eyes met and everything masculine in him went into overdrive. There wasn't a part of her that he didn't want to claim.

He skimmed his gaze down her face, over her pert nose to the pink of her cheeks to that sweet mouth that he had spent way too many hours thinking about. Kit started to lean down, not wanting her to feel pressured in anyway, and she came up on her tiptoes, her eyes closing. He felt the brush of her breath against his lips just as his brushed hers.

Suddenly, the kitchen alarm went off and she jumped, her feet slipping on the hardwood floor. He steadied her and stepped back as she muttered about the pie. She walked slowly to the oven, opening it.

The scent of freshly baked pie filled the kitchen, but honestly it was the scent of her perfume that lingered for him. He watched her as she bent over to retrieve the pie, then had to turn away after noticing how curvaceous her hips were.

"Done," she said.

"Looks good." Those were the only words he could force out as his mind was busy thinking of how he would love to have his hands on her waist and his body pressed up against her and this wasn't the time to indulge in such carnal thoughts.

But his needs had always been more savage than he wanted to admit. And with Rory he knew he needed to be more of a gentleman than he'd ever been before.

She just stood there in awkward silence after she'd placed the pie on a trivet, and he knew he should say something to make her feel at ease. But what? Forcing down the lust that was clawing at his self-control, he turned to the windows, saw the water dripping down from the rain. It had changed to a light, steady drizzle.

"It's been so long since I've been in the rain,"

she said, almost under her breath. "Before I used to like walking in it."

Just those words calmed the beast in him. *Before*. She was a woman recovering from something that took more strength than he'd ever understand.

"Would you like to walk in it with me now?"

Rory was mentally cursing herself for not staying in Kit's arms. She almost had that kiss she'd been aching for. But once the timer had gone off, she'd gotten nervous. Begun having second thoughts. She had wondered at first if he simply wasn't attracted to her, not enough to go at her pace. She knew that those feelings weren't always a two-way street. But now, after seeing the look in his eyes before she'd pulled away, she was pretty sure he was.

However, there was no denying that Kit was a hard man to read. It might be that she was simply out of practice because she hadn't been around people who weren't either related to her or hired to help with her medical needs. Also Kit treated her like she was...well just Rory. Not a Gilbert from Gilbert Corners or the tragic heiress. With him she was just herself. And even though he was indecipherable, she wanted to kiss him, so now she was second-guessing every-dang-thing she did with him.

"Rory?"

"Hmm?" She couldn't take her eyes off his mouth. His lips were full but not overly so; his mouth looked like it would be firm against hers, and from that one brief brush she'd had of his lips, it had been.

"Do you have shoes?" he asked.

She forced her gaze away from his mouth. "Yes, but...um... Okay, so the thing is, Dash is afraid I'll fall because the ground is slippery and I think I should mention that Hank, my PT guy, also said I should be cautious."

"What does that have to do with shoes?" he asked. "I know you have to take things slow. But we made it up and down that embankment. Do you trust me?"

She did.

It seemed to her that Kit might be the only man in the world to see her for who she was. Hank saw the muscles that had atrophied and needed exercise and routine to regain stamina. Dash and Conrad envisioned her as the broken girl who'd lain in a bed for ten years. But Kit... She wanted to believe he saw Rory. The woman whom she *wanted* to be.

"I do have shoes," she murmured, "but sometimes I'm steadier in bare feet."

"Let me take a look at the backyard and we can go stand out there if you like?"

"And walk?"

"Yes, walk. But not too far," he promised. "Your brother would definitely kill me if anything happened to you."

She laughed at that. "Are you afraid of him?"

"No. I'm sort of afraid for you. I don't want to see you get hurt even though I know you need to try new things."

"Ah, thank you. I was joking," she said, at his fierce denial. "I forget you're not really from around here. But everyone sort of holds my family in this odd way in town. Like the livelihood of the town is somehow tied to us. Anyway, that's what I meant. Plus there's the curse thing."

"What curse?"

Darn! Why had she brought the curse up? "Well, everyone thinks that the Gilberts have been cursed since Grandfather closed the factory. That was the night we were in the accident and then the economy in the town started to fail. But then Conrad came back and I woke up from my coma and Dash is living here again…"

"So the curse is broken?" he asked.

"I'm not sure there ever was one, but I was out of it for a while...and missing walking in the rain," she said.

"Let's fix that." He smiled gently. "Let me check the yard. I'll be back."

Kit toed off his socks and then opened the back door and stepped out onto the concrete pad that had recently been poured. She'd hired a crew that Indy had recommended to clean the debris from the backyard. The bushes and flowers were all overgrown but the grass had been recently mowed.

She watched as Kit took his time walking around the yard, checking the ground for stability before he turned back to her. The rain was soaking his T-shirt, making it cling to his shoulders and his chest. She felt that pulse go through her entire body, to her feminine core, and she stood there watching and wanting him.

Rory knew she was playing a dangerous game because she wasn't entirely sure if she could be brave enough to take what she wanted. To follow through on what she now realized she wasn't sure could walk away from.

"Ready?"

She hesitated as she stared at his hand held out toward her.

"It's up to you," he said.

It *was* up to her. She could stay in the kitchen, looking out at the world or she could take Kit's hand...

She did it, put her palm in his and he wrapped his fingers around her hand, holding it securely as she took a step out of the house. She stood there as the rain fell on her. It was colder than she remembered rain being. She tipped her face up and felt it falling on her cheeks and her hair.

Emotions roiled through her and she felt like she wanted to scream with them, but knew that wasn't okay so instead a grunt sort of erupted from her.

"You okay?"

She nodded and then looked over at Kit. "Better than okay."

"Ready to walk or are you good here?" he asked.

"Walk, please."

"The ground is pretty firm closest to the center of the yard. So we can walk out and then turn and come back."

She held his hand as they stepped off the concrete, and the first touch of the wet grass under her foot tickled a little. Spreading her toes out, she felt the sprigs between them. She stood there for a long minute, just happy that she could feel her toes and happy with her body.

The body that she'd been resenting more than a little because it was taking so long to recover and do what she wanted it to. But right now she was so glad to be standing in the rain with the grass under her feet and Kit at her side.

FIVE

"So when I decided to buy this property, Dash was—"

"Can we not talk about your brother?" he interrupted her. "Sorry if that sounded rude, but it seems he dominates your life. What about this property attracted you?"

He wished he had a plan to separate Rory from Dash in his mind. He didn't want her to have any part of his revenge for his brother. But he was realistic enough to know that might not be possible. Also, when he was with her, he wanted to throw off the heavy mantle of expectation that Aunt Mal had placed on him.

The rain was soft and a little cold, forcing him to be present, and he was enjoying their slow walk in her yard. Kit normally just put his head down in the rain and rushed to get out of it, but there could be no rushing with Rory. And if he were honest, he didn't want to.

She was enjoying this. Her steps on the grass were gentle and almost gliding. She tipped her head back repeatedly, her face turned up to the rain, and he had the feeling that this was something she had desperately missed.

"Sorry about that."

"You don't have to apologize," he assured her. "I like you more than your brother."

"I'm glad," she said, leaning toward him again.

He was struggling with that lip-lock they'd almost shared and really trying to keep some distance between them. Not because he'd changed his mind about wanting to kiss her, but she'd pulled back to get her pie from the oven. It could have waited. She'd chosen to move away. And he was going to respect that.

"So, about this place...? It's not exactly where I picture a Gilbert of Gilbert Corners living."

"Well, that's what I was going for. I wanted a place where I could figure out who I am," she confided. "I want to make it my own, so I talked to my financial advisor and he found this place."

"Is Dash your financial advisor?" he asked.

"No. My inheritance comes from my maternal side. So Dash oversaw it while I was in the coma but he didn't merge them."

"Why not?"

"He knew I'd wake up," she said. "At least that is what he told me."

He believed that Dash loved his sister, but Kit had always thought it was a guilty conscience that drove the other man. Now he was getting a glimpse that it might be more nuanced than all of that. "So you're happy here?"

"Yes, I am. My family wanted me to stay close and I agreed if they backed off. I have a home in northern California but haven't been there in years."

She started laughing after she said that. "I mean even before the accident."

They reached the point where he thought they should turn, and he halted for a second, looking around the overgrown brambles and flower bushes that lined the fence on the left and the right. This place also seemed special. Like it was hidden and, though neglected, it didn't have the abandoned feel that some of the other parts of Gilbert Corners had.

"I like it."

"Me, too," she said, then gave him a questioning look. "Why are we stopping?"

"This is as far as we go. Time to go back toward the house," he said.

"Can we stand here for a minute?"

"Of course," he said.

She moved so that they faced each other and their eyes met. His mind sort of stopped working as he watched a drop of rain roll down her forehead to her nose and then it hung there on the tip. He reached up to touch it and he felt the shiver go through her.

Every molecule of his body craved her. Kit wanted to feel her mouth under his as the rain was falling around them. He needed to know the taste of her on his tongue so he could understand her more fully.

He turned so that he wouldn't give in to his desire and his bare foot slipped on the wet grass. Acting on instinct, he tried to pull his arm from Rory so he didn't drag her down with him. But instead she put both of her arms around him, using her body to steady him.

She was pressed against him, her head tipped back and laughing and he shut off his mind to all the why-nots that he'd been dwelling on and kissed her.

Her laughter and joy flowed into him as their lips met. She opened her mouth under his and he felt the tentative brush of her tongue over his. He found his footing and made sure it was solid as he put his arm around her waist and lifted her more fully against him. Their wet clothing wasn't much of a barrier and he felt the fullness of her breasts against his chest.

His erection stirred. He wanted her with every fiber of his being, but he knew it had been ten years since she'd kissed anyone. His conscience demanded that he let her set the pace. Yet it was all he could do to keep his hand on the side of her face gentle. To just touch her with the lightest of caresses instead of pushing his fingers into her thick, rain-drenched hair and tilting her head so he could deepen the kiss the way his body demanded.

Then she sucked his tongue into her mouth and shifted against him. He felt the pebbled hardness of her nipples against his chest and savored the way her hips rubbed against his erection as she held tightly onto him.

He rubbed his tongue back over hers, tasting the sweetness that was Rory. This passion that was unfolding between the two of them felt like magic as he held her in the rain, taking his time with this first kiss and getting more turned on than he had been in a long time.

★ ★ ★

Kissing Kit was even better than walking in the rain. Another first for her. He tasted of coffee and mint. His tongue rubbed against hers, stirring to life feelings that she hadn't thought about in ages. He held her gently but solidly.

The joy she'd felt at being able to steady him had easily bled back into desire and this embrace was doing things to her that she hadn't anticipated. Her entire body was awash in sensation and her skin felt almost too sensitive. His hand against the side of her face was warm against the chill from the rain and she wanted to feel his big, strong palm moving down her body.

She couldn't remember ever having had a lover, but there was so much of that time before the crash and coma that she still couldn't remember.

He lifted his head, looking down at her with that fierce gaze of his. Her breath hitched because she wasn't exactly sure what she should say.

"I…"

"Rory? Where are you?" Dash called from inside the house.

"Out here."

"Out where?" her brother asked.

"I think we should start making our way back," Kit whispered in her ear.

"I suppose so. I'm getting cold but a part of me wants to stay here since I know it will tick Dash off."

She saw a smile tease the corners of his lips. "I can appreciate that but we don't want you to catch a cold, which will only prove he was right."

"True."

"Good God, Rory! What are you doing? And you, Kit, should know better than to—"

"Enough of that," Rory said sharply. "We are perfectly safe. Now either come join us in the rain or go sit in the kitchen and wait for us."

Kit didn't say anything but she felt the tension in his body as they walked slowly back toward the house. She was surprised when Dash stepped outside and stood there in the rain that was even lighter now, barely falling.

"Why are you doing this?"

"I haven't felt the rain in years."

Dash nodded and his face softened as he tipped his head to the side. "When you were little we used to dance in the rain, do you remember?"

He walked over to them and they all stopped.

She didn't recall that and couldn't imagine Dash ever doing that. "You're making that up."

"No. Mom loved it. Sometimes she'd even entice Dad to join us."

Rory turned to her brother and saw that usual mix of love and concern but also something else. Maybe a hint of sadness. She barely remembered her parents as she'd only been six when they died in a plane crash; but Dash had more memories. "I wish I could remember them."

"Me, too, ladybug," he said, then he looked past her to Kit. "Thank you for helping Rory with this."

"No problem," Kit said. "That's what I'm here for."

"Is it? I thought you were an old friend."

"He is. He meant that's what friends are for. He's helping me with all the things I can't remember doing and all the things I want to," Rory explained.

"Like what things?"

"All the things," she said again. She wasn't going to mention kissing because, to be fair, she wouldn't have kissed a life coach. Or would she? Her life was full of extraordinary surprises.

Maybe she would have kissed anyone who was attractive and spent this much time with her.

If Rory was honest, she was sure it was only Kit whom she wanted to kiss. But then again, she hadn't really been around a lot of other men that weren't related to her, since coming out of the coma. There was Hank, of course, but he was married and also was always forcing her to do exercises that hurt. She glanced back over at Kit.

Wanting something didn't mean she'd get it. She also had to be careful with her emotions. She had no real idea of the woman she'd been before but this woman she was today wanted connections. Wanted friends of her own, and after that kiss, a lover to call her own. She wanted it to be Kit, but was she just forming an attachment to him because he was the first hot guy she'd been around?

"Are you okay?" Kit asked.

"Yes," she said. "The pie should be cooled down enough for us to have some now."

"I'm looking forward to trying it," he said.

"It looks delicious. What kind is it?" Dash asked as they walked back to the cement pad outside her back door. She noticed he'd put a towel down on the floor when they came back in.

They all sat down in the doorway one at a time and dried their feet. Rory went first and once she was in the house went to the linen cabinet and grabbed bigger towels for Dash and Kit.

They took them and toweled off in the doorway. "I'm going to go and change quickly," she said. "Will you two be okay?"

"Of course. It will give us a chance to get to know one another," Dash said.

"Don't be..."

"What?" her brother asked.

"You," she responded with a grin. "Be nice."

"I can't be anyone other than myself," he told her.

She looked over at Kit and he just winked at her, which she assumed meant he'd be fine. She just didn't want Dash to say anything that would make Kit leave her. Then she realized how silly that was. Kit wasn't the kind of man to do anything he didn't want to do.

Kit hadn't been in the same room as Dash Gilbert since he'd been a boy, long before his family had started working their way up the corporate ladder at the factory and long before the night when his brother had died. In his mind he'd spent so many years hating Dash because he was the face of the company that was to blame for his family's hardships.

But this man didn't *look* evil.

"Thank you," he said as they both finished toweling off and moved into the kitchen. "I know that Rory needs this kind of activity but I can't get past my fear that she's going to fall and be back in the hospital."

There was no doubting Dash's sincerity. "She's capable of more than you realize."

"No doubt. Want some coffee?" Dash asked, deftly changing the subject.

"Sure," Kit said.

Dash moved around the kitchen, clearly familiar with the layout and where everything was, and started making coffee with the single-use pot that was on the counter. "So, what is it you do exactly?"

"I run my family's business," he replied. "You?"

Dash arched one eyebrow at him. "I run my family's business. Seems weird that we haven't met before. I know I'm not supposed to pry, but I don't remember you and Rory being friends."

"Fair enough. I think I'd have to say we were

more acquaintances than friends," Kit said. "But we always enjoyed each other's company."

"You did? Are you from GC?"

"I lived her for a while in elementary school and then we moved away when the factory closed," Kit told him.

Dash sighed. "So many families did. I'm not sure what my grandfather was thinking... Well, he was concerned with the financial bottom line, but the impact on the town was definitely worse than he had anticipated."

"It was."

Kit didn't want to talk about the closing of the factory with Dash. His time with Rory made him want to find a way to make peace with Dash but he wasn't prepared to be chill about it with the other man.

"Milk or sugar?"

"Milk," Kit said. It felt odd to feel this angry and have a mundane conversation about coffee at the same time.

"I hope your family wasn't too greatly impacted, though I guess you did okay since you are running your own business now," Dash said.

"We are. It wasn't easy at first but I think the move forced us to find something of our own," Kit said. He remembered finishing college remotely so he could save money and live with Aunt Mal while his father drank himself to death mourning his eldest son. Not good times at all. But they had shaped him into the man he was today.

Kit realized he needed this conversation with Dash to remind himself of why he'd come back to Gilbert Corners. It was one thing to say he was enchanted by Rory, but the truth was, he was a man who lived in the real world. And revenge through business was what had kept him going in the last ten years.

There was a big part of him that was afraid he was nothing without revenge. His entire adult life had been shaped by Declan's death and the fallout from it. The boy-man he'd been was a distant memory. He'd stopped dreaming of his future and focused only on taking down Dash Gilbert. Until he met Rory. She was the first one to make him lift his head up and see that there might be something other than getting back at the Gilberts.

"Glad to hear that things are going well for you. So where'd Rory get the blackberries, do you know? I'm hoping it was the grocery store."

"It wasn't," Kit replied. "I helped her down to the path by the river in town and we picked them."

Dash cursed under his breath. "Honestly, she's going to be the death of me. How'd she do?"

Kit looked over at the other man who leaned against the counter sipping his black coffee. "Good. It took a lot of effort to get back up the path and there were times I thought she might ask me to carry her but she didn't. She just gritted her teeth and kept on going."

"She's stubborn."

"Are you boys talking about me?" Rory asked as she came into the kitchen. Turning toward her, Kit noticed she was using her cane and she'd changed into a pair of leggings and long sweater. She'd braided her hair and it hung over one shoulder.

"We are," Kit confirmed.

"And?" Rory asked, giving Dash a pointed look.

"And nothing. I'm glad I didn't know you were climbing down to the river until *after* you were safely back in your house. Want some coffee?"

"Yes, please," she said.

She walked over to get down plates. Dash set her coffee on the table across from where Kit sat and then went back to get napkins and forks. It was interesting to watch them working together and Kit realized that he missed this—losing his brother had taken that one person whom he'd had so many shared memories with. The person who remembered the family they had been. And as Dash and Rory talked about pies of the past and their father's obsession with them, he realized this was one more thing that Dash had taken from him.

But this was tempered by the fact that he and Declan had never really been close. They might not have had this kind of close connection even if his brother had lived. In fact, Kit knew they wouldn't have, because Kit had planned to stay on the West Coast and live his life out there.

"What do you think?" Rory asked as he took a bite of the pie.

The taste of the warm, sweet blackberries with just a hint of tartness and the buttery crust was delicious. He opened his eyes, looking over at her, remembering the taste of her as he'd kissed her as well. "Delicious."

She blushed.

"I'm glad you like it."

"I think I might be addicted to it," he confessed.

"It's pretty good," Dash chimed in. "In fact, I think it might be better than Con's…but don't tell him I said so."

Rory glanced at her brother and then immediately back to Kit. It was as though she'd forgotten he was there.

"I am definitely going to tell him," she said with a wicked grin.

SIX

RORY SAT NEXT to Dash, enjoying her brother in a way that she hadn't in a really long time. Moving out had been scary—she wasn't going to pretend that sleeping at night was easy all alone in this shabby house—but she knew it was the right move.

"I'd better be heading off," Kit said.

She looked over at him, realizing that something had changed since their kiss and Dash arriving. Reaching for her cane, she stood when Kit did. "I'll walk you out."

Her leg was feeling the stress from being on her feet so much. But also she'd braced herself hard when she'd steadied Kit earlier. Something that Hank had taught her to do when she felt unsteady, but it always had repercussions.

"You don't have to," Kit protested.

"I do." She wanted to say goodbye to him in private, and also she knew if she sat with her leg like this it would just hurt more. Moving always made her feel better.

"Okay," he said. He put his mug and plate on the counter near the sink and she followed him to the front door, realizing as he sat on the floor to put his boots back on that she needed to get a bench.

"Sorry my brother arrived when he did," she told him candidly.

"Me, too. But I can see that his concern comes from a good place."

"Yeah, it does. Even though it feels suffocating sometimes. So…about the kiss…" she murmured as he stood back up and reached for his leather jacket.

He tipped his head to the side, watching her and waiting.

"I don't want to make assumptions and I'm not good at guessing what other people are feeling. So did you like it?"

Kit smiled at her and moved toward her, stopping when there was just a few inches between them. He leaned in closer, their eyes met and her heart started beating just a little bit faster with excitement.

"I did. I want to do it again. But your bro is here, so…"

"Good. I liked it, too," she said.

"I know," he said, brushing his mouth over hers. Then he lifted his head, winked at her and waved goodbye as he walked out the door.

She stood there, watching him leave. He didn't look back and his steps were sure and steady on the wet pavement. Something she knew he probably didn't have to worry about. But she worried for him.

Oh.

She was starting to care for him. There were butterflies in her stomach and her heart felt full when she thought about the kiss he'd just given her. It had been short and sweet and set off fires in her body. He waved once more as he drove by and she closed the door, carefully turning to walk back toward the kitchen.

Dash stood at the end of the hallway.

"You like this guy?"

"Kit. I like *Kit*."

"Yeah, Kit. Your old friend, except you don't have any old friends," he said.

"I'm sure I had friends, Dash, don't be a dick."

"I'm not being a dick," he said. "Or if I am... it's just because I'm concerned about you."

"Well, thanks, but I'm a big girl. I can handle myself."

"I know that, Rory, but it's hard for me to stop being your big brother." He sighed. "Honestly, there are times when I can't really believe that you are out of that hospital bed."

"Dash," she said, going over to her brother and hugging him with her free arm. "I'm okay now."

"Yeah."

But she knew that as hard as it was for her to make up for a decade that she'd lost, it must've been equally as hard for her brother to watch her missing out on life. He was the one who had to sit in a chair next to her bed and wonder if she'd ever wake up.

"You know I love you but I can't let you boss me around," she said at last.

"Life would be so much easier if everyone would just let me do that," he deadpanned.

"It's not just me?"

"No. Elle and Conrad are on that list, too," he admitted.

Of course they were. Dash wasn't ever going to stop watching over the people he loved. Even though she, Elle and Con didn't need his protection, Dash couldn't help himself. She linked her free arm through his and turned him back toward the kitchen. "You like independent people."

"I guess I do," he said. "So, about Kit..."

"No, we're not going to do this. I like him. I think he likes me. And I'm going to just see where it goes. You know my therapist said to try new things."

"She also told me to butt out of your life," Dash said gruffly.

"And you didn't fire her?"

"Ha. As if I could. You made it clear she worked for you," Dash reminded her. "Which I'm glad you did. Seeing you in the rain today was something special."

"I felt so alive." As she murmured the words, Rory realized that it wasn't just the rain that had made her feel that way, but also Kit's kiss.

"That's all I want for you," Dash confessed. Then he looked at his watch. "I didn't just come over to butt into your life. Conrad wants to start Sunday dinners at the Manor. You can bring a friend. Sunday at two."

"You had to come here to tell me?"

He shot her an unapologetic look. "Yes. I didn't want to just get a thumbs-up emoji. I wanted to see how you were doing."

She gave him a thumbs-up, which made him laugh. She started laughing, too.

Dash helped her take off the doors to the kitchen cabinets before he left and as she worked on cleaning and refinishing them that afternoon she realized that she was slowly figuring out who Rory Gilbert was.

Aunt Mal's house was in an older, established neighborhood on the suburbs of Boston. She'd bought it with the profits they'd made in their first big year. It was one of the McMansions that were all the rage back in the early 2000s and Aunt Mal had decorated it with her flair for midcentury design.

It was sleek and modern-looking in that sort of old-century way. Her housekeeper, Castor, opened the door when Kit arrived.

He hadn't planned on visiting his aunt today, but after seeing Rory and Dash together he had realized there were pieces to the Gilbert family puzzle that he didn't have. Something about them didn't add up the way he'd expected. And if anyone knew what had happened the night of the party, it would be his aunt.

"I wasn't expecting you today. Did you find something we can use?" Aunt Mal asked as he was shown into her sitting room. She was tall, thin and always wore her straight black hair pulled back into a tight bun at the back of her neck. She favored caftans in the summer but in the fall went all in on long, flowing skirts and sweaters with feathers on them. Today's outfit was a deep purple skirt with a black sweater.

She was seated on one of the tufted settees that she used in most of the rooms in this house. They were pretty small and when he sat on them he felt too big. The walls were lined with bookshelves and there was a mahogany desk that sat in front of the picture window overlooking the side yard.

"I'm not sure yet. I was able to spend time with both Rory and Dash today. And I have a few questions."

She arched a brow. "Like what? Did they say something about Declan or your father?"

"Nothing like that. It's just… Aunt Mal, what exactly happened the night of the ball?" he asked. "Some of the stuff they mentioned didn't really add up."

"Of course it didn't," she said, getting to her feet and walking over to him in a cloud of Estée Lauder perfume. "They are liars. We know this."

Liars. Except that Rory wasn't. In fact, if he had to place money on her being anything, it would be bluntly honest. Dash…well, he was a harder read. After a decade of watching his every move in the business world, Kit had thought he'd known the other man, but the truth was a bit more convoluted. There was so much to Dash that he hadn't known.

Ever since Conrad had returned to Gilbert Corners, he'd noticed a change in how Dash was running the company. And after Rory had woken from her coma there had been more changes. More focus on the communities and people. More giving back.

The man he'd met today had been sincere in a way that didn't surprise Kit that much, as Dash was known in the business world for being ruthless but fair. What had kind of thrown him was the humble love he had for his sister. It was painting a different picture of Dash in his personal relationships. Which was the type of relationship his brother and father would have had with Lance Gilbert.

So had they read Lance wrong or was Dash different? Though Kit remembered very clearly Aunt Mal calling him, crying as she informed him that Dash had been driving the car that had killed his brother.

"Do you know what happened at the party?" he repeated.

"I don't. Your father just said that the Gilbert heirs started a fight with Declan, and Lance was furious," Aunt Mal said. "Did they tell you more?"

"No. I didn't ask and I haven't told them I'm related to Declan." Kit was doing this for his brother and his intention had always been to avenge his death in the car crash. But it had been easier before he'd met Dash in person. They'd competed in some business deals and Kit had won a few, but this was different.

Dash was a loving and caring man with Rory. Which was more shocking than Kit had expected it to be. He remembered his father had been the same demanding man at work and at home. It was hard to reconcile Dash as two different men. But the Dash he'd met wasn't a cruel or vindictive man around his sister. He was loving.

"What's going on with you?" Aunt Mal asked suspiciously. "Is it the girl?"

"Nothing is going on with me. You know I like to have all the facts before I make a move. It feels like there is more to the incident between Declan and the Gilbert heirs than we know," Kit told her. "I need more information."

"I'll see what I can find," Aunt Mal said with a sincerity that Kit didn't doubt. The two of them had tried to piece together the truth. But his father…might have been an unreliable source of information since he'd been drunk most of the time. "Are you staying for dinner?"

"Actually, I'd love to take *you* out to dinner," he said.

She smiled. "That's my boy. Shall we say the Club at seven?"

"Perfect. I'm going to go back to the office until then. If you dig up anything else on that night, let me know."

"I will. But really I'm not sure what else we need." She shrugged. "We know that there was a fight at the Manor and that the cousins all piled into a car that crashed into your brother's car—killing him and injuring most of them. Except for Dash, who ruined your father and left us with nothing."

His Aunt Mal's summation wasn't wrong. All of that had happened that night, and Kit had been left picking up the pieces.

★ ★ ★

Rory had decided she wasn't going to worry about kissing Kit; she found herself sitting in her bed two nights later doing just that. She wondered if she should hire someone to teach her to kiss better. At the time it had felt sort of natural and she'd thought she was doing it right, but Kit hadn't called or texted since he'd left.

Of course, she knew *she* could text him.

Indy and Elle had wanted to know more about Kit but Rory hadn't really known what to say. Had she been the kind of woman who liked to talk about her feelings before? Who knew? She definitely wasn't that type of woman now.

But she did want to talk to Kit.

She was hesitating… The question was why. Why?

Then, after mulling it over, the truth finally dawned on her. She was *scared*. Fear had wormed its way into her mind and her heart. She was thinking of all the reasons why Kit hadn't reached out to her and she had to wonder if maybe he felt the same way.

Not about kissing her. He had been a really good kisser, so that wouldn't be a fear. Maybe he was afraid she didn't want to hear from him again.

She picked up her phone and saw the picture of the blackberry pie she'd taken and then the picture of her and Kit that he'd snapped when they'd picked the berries. Using her fingers, she zoomed in on the photo on Kit's face. She looked into his eyes and tried to see what he felt.

As if that had ever worked.

She was going to text him. She had heard via Indy that there was a Goth night coming up at the speakeasy next week. That sounded like fun and like something she hadn't done, so she was definitely going. She was going to text him before she lost her nerve.

Rory: Hey. You up?

Kit: Hey. I am.

Rory: So...there's a speakeasy in GC and they have a Goth Night coming up next week. Want to go with me?

Kit: Yes. But I don't want to wait until next week to see you. And I totally spaced on helping you with your cabinets. Can I stop by tomorrow?

Rory: That's cool. I refinished them and started

rehanging the doors. But could use your help with a ride to the hardware store.

Kit: I'll bring my truck.

Rory: You have a truck?

Kit: I do. I use it when I'm feeling macho.

Rory: laughing emoji

Kit: Uh-oh.

Rory: What?

Kit: You don't think I'm macho.

Rory: Is that important?

Kit: Nah. Was just being silly. So, what have you been up to?

Rory: Pt. Hank was impressed I'd made it up the embankment. And oh, I talked to the town council and they are adding ramps and railings to the pathway by the river.

Instead of texting back he video-called her. Rory answered the call, smiling when she noticed that Kit was sitting on a couch wearing a faded T-shirt and jeans. He had some scruff on his jaw, which made him look more devilishly handsome than she had expected.

"Hope you don't mind," he said. "I just wanted to see you. Sorry I was radio silent. I've been out of town on business."

"That's fine. I know you have a life," she told him. "What do you do?"

"I run a global conglomerate."

"Ah, corporate gibberish."

"Ha ha. It just means I oversee a company that owns lots of smaller ones. The global bit means we have companies all over the world."

Rory smiled, liking the deep timbre of his voice. She asked him more questions and he relaxed as he talked about what he did. Sighing, she sank deeper into the pillows on her bed. She hadn't thought that just hearing someone's voice could make her feel alive. Maybe because a voice was the one thing that had pulled her from her coma, but there was something about Kit's voice that made her feel tingly all over.

"But that part is boring," he said.

She hadn't been paying attention to his words so had no idea what he'd said. "Not it's not."

"Trust me, no one wants to hear about the

accounting department." Then he turned the conversation toward her. "Do you have a job?"

She shook her head. "I am intending to get one but I can't really stand for a long period."

She realized how lucky she was not to have to work or rely on anyone to support herself. "I'm also fixing up the house. Indy offered to have her crew film me but I'm not ready for that."

"I didn't mean to put you on the spot. I know you're a Gilbert."

"Yeah, right now I'm concentrating on getting healthy," she admitted. But at some point she hoped she'd be healthy enough to have a job. "I have no idea what I'd be good at when I do start looking for work. Maybe you should tell me about accounting."

He smiled. "It's working with numbers and spreadsheets all day."

She made a face. Numbers were always a jumble in her head, and having to go to an office every day made that seem even more like torture. She was still trying to figure out what she wanted to do but she knew it wasn't that.

"Exactly. I think you'd be good with people," he said.

"That's a thought. I guess I better add that to my list," she said.

"Speaking of that list, what's next?"

"Driving."

"Do you have your learner's permit?" he asked.

"Yes. I took the written test a few months ago. But Dash doesn't drive after his accident and Conrad...he said he doesn't have the patience to teach anyone."

"Are you just doing it because he said no?"

At first maybe that had been part of the reason she'd wanted to learn to drive, but the truth was more complicated. "I need to be able to do things for myself, you know?"

"I do. I'll give you your first lesson tomorrow," he said. "I should let you go. Good night, Rory."

"Good night, Kit," she said.

SEVEN

RORY PUSHED HER doubts about Kit aside as she got ready the next morning for her driving lessons. Elle had been busy at the hospital. She worked with long-term trauma patients, like Rory had been, but she was also the on-call brain trauma specialist. However, last night... Rory could have used a girlfriend to talk her off the worry ledge that she'd managed to find herself on.

Looking at herself in the mirror as she plaited her hair into one long braid that fell over her left shoulder, she tried to be objective. She looked like a woman, which always surprised her when she caught a glimpse of herself. She still felt like that eighteen-year-old girl she'd been when she went into the coma. It was odd to see that her face had matured into her mom's features.

Rory glanced at the photo of her parents that she'd stuck on the corner of her vanity. She had so few real memories of them because she'd only been six when they died. Dash had kept them alive for her by telling her stories. But their faces had faded. And when she thought of her parents it was simply in this pose from the picture.

It was odd to see her mother's face staring back at her from the mirror. She wished she'd somehow absorbed her mother's strength and confidence from back then, too. But she hadn't.

She wanted more with Kit physically than the arousing kisses they'd shared. But she wasn't sure how to tell him. And frankly, TV, movies and books weren't helping. It would be really great if there was an article about what to do when you went into a coma as a girl and woke up a woman. With tips on flirting and updates on what guys liked ten years later.

Which was part of the problem. Rory didn't want to change herself to make herself into something Kit wanted. And she knew, deep down, that he would not want that for her either. She put her head in her hands, smiling as she remembered the way he'd looked on his couch the night before. He'd been all relaxed and scruffy and cuddly but still undeniably sexy.

She'd wanted to be snuggled up beside him, making out.

Except she hadn't really ever made out with a man before. Well, there had been that one time the summer before the accident when she'd kissed one of Con's college friends on the deck of the yacht while the sun set. So romantic...until he'd told her he thought he'd had too much to drink and turned and vomited over the side of the boat.

Everything she'd done with Kit was way more romantic than that. But she still wasn't sure of herself as woman.

She went to the group text chat she had with Elle and Indy.

Rory: Help! I need to know more about sex.

Elle: Is Kit pressuring you?

Rory: I wish. I'm just so inexperienced and don't want to be.

Indy: I've got some books, come by the shop.

Her phone started ringing with a video call in the group. She answered and saw Elle sitting in her office at work and a moment later

Indy answered from behind the counter in her bookstore.

"Sorry, thought this would be easier," Elle said. "So what is it you're unsure about?"

Rory shrugged and took a deep breath and told them both about the kiss she'd had with Kit and how he'd semi-ghosted her after Dash had arrived.

"Sounds like Dash was being overprotective," Elle said. "I'll talk to him about that."

Rory laughed. "No, it was fine. He and I are figuring that part out. Last night Kit called and we talked. He said he'd been busy with work but I have to wonder if he knows I'm not very experienced and is turned off by that."

Indy shook her head. "You're never going to know that unless you ask him. But if he called and apologized, I think you can believe him."

"I do, too," Elle said. "He could have just never contacted you again."

"I hadn't thought of that." Even though Kit had bought the condo next door, it seemed he was away on business so frequently that it would be easy for him to ignore her. "So…" She trailed off. She wasn't sure how to put into words what she really wanted to know. Then she suddenly decided to just ask these two women who were her sisters of the heart. "Should I really tell him I don't have any experience?"

"I'd just see how it plays out," Indy suggested. "I had a date push me too far and really struggled with intimacy, and I was obviously not going to tell Con but it sort of just came out after we kissed. It felt natural and just…well, Con got it and he was great."

Rory smiled to herself. Her cousin Con had changed from the boy she'd known, and she really liked the man he'd become. She also thought he and Indy were perfect for each other, so hearing that they'd had some struggles helped her. "It's easy to look at y'all and think that you got together without any big issues."

"Everyone has issues," Elle said. "If Kit is the right guy, you'll know. Rory…"

"Yes?"

Elle hesitated. "Do you have any more memories of what happened the night of the ball?"

Though Rory recalled being attacked by her date that night, Elle had confirmed she hadn't been raped. Even though he hadn't gone further, knowing that someone had tried to hurt her and force her was still difficult to process.

"No. None. And it's totally different with Kit. I want him to want me."

"Good," Elle said. "I'm sure he does. Is he seeing you again?"

"He's coming by later to teach me how to drive."

"I think it's safe to assume he likes you. Teaching someone to drive isn't an easy thing," Indy remarked. "My mom used to yell at me every time I drove with her."

"That's nothing like Kit," Rory said.

"Good."

The doorbell rang and she smiled at the girls. "That's probably Kit. Talk later."

"Yes. If you need us, text," Indy said.

Rory disconnected the call and then stood. Looking at herself in the mirror, seeing not only her mom now, but also herself. She just had to get used to so much more than this body and she knew she was getting there one step at a time.

Kit wasn't any closer to figuring out what the hell he was going to do about Dash Gilbert. No matter how many times he reminded himself that Rory wasn't really part of the Gilbert family that he hated, he knew he didn't hate Dash anymore either. Meeting him the other day, talking to him had confused the issue even further.

A smart man would stay the fuck away from Gilbert Corners. And Kit had always been praised for his intelligence, which he knew would end the minute someone put the pieces together about his identity/past. He was back.

He couldn't stay away from her. There was a white-hot attraction between the two of them and his guy brain was saying just hook up and then that would go away and he could move on. Get back to just coming to Gilbert Corners to plot Dash's downfall.

But despite what he was currently doing, he was smarter than that. The draw to Rory wasn't just sex. If it was, Kit wouldn't be here ready to give her driving lessons. He was here because he couldn't stay away.

It didn't matter that he knew it would be smarter and easier to take down Dash Gilbert if Kit had nothing to do with Rory. But that wasn't happening.

It was a clear, cool, crisp autumn day. The leaves were changing and fell as he walked up toward Rory's house. She'd put two large terracotta planters blooming with mums on either side of the walkway that led to her front door.

The door had been painted since he'd last visited and had a large autumn-themed wreath on it with something hanging in the center. When he got closer he noticed that it was Jack and Sally from Tim Burton's *Nightmare Before Christmas.*

He rang the doorbell and stood there. Maybe this time when he saw her he'd be able to friend-zone her and let go of wanting to take her into his arms, kiss her and not stop until they were both naked and he was balls deep inside her.

He got hard just imagining that and shifted his legs, adjusting his erection before the door opened.

"Hi," she said.

His cock twitched and he had to look away from her to just try to get himself under control. But he couldn't get that warm, welcoming smile of hers out of his mind. The way her lips were curved, he knew what they felt like under his. He missed the taste of her.

How was he going to spend any time next to her in the close confines of the car and keep his hands to himself?

"Hi," he said back. He noticed she wore a black-and-white striped shirt tucked into a black flounced mini skirt, striped tights and a pair of flats. She looked cute and Halloweeny and he was trying to be chill.

But his chill was gone. He was completely swept away by the sight of her long, sexy legs in that fetching getup and then she smiled at him again and he was a goner.

There was no pretending that he didn't want more than a friendship with her. It didn't matter that she was the sister of his enemy.

"Want to come in for a minute?" she asked.

Yes. *Hell yes.* He wanted to come into her house, take her into his arms, ravish her until she became soft and pliant in his arms and then... "I'm not sure that's the best idea."

"Why not?" she asked, reaching for a leather jacket on the hook and shrugging into it.

The action pulled the fabric taut across her full breasts and Kit wasn't sure how much more his body could handle.

"Because I want you, Rory," he growled. "You invited me here as a friend and teacher, and I know you're not ready for horny me to be all over you."

"Oh! Well, I want you, too. I'm not sure, okay, well..." She was sort of rambling. "I've never had sex. I mean, I made out once and the night of the ball my date was...well, he was forceful and tore my dress but no actual—"

"Stop. You don't have to tell me all of that," he said. He ached for her as she was telling him this story. And it confused him. *A lot.* Because that wasn't any part of the story he'd heard about the ball from his aunt. But then his brother had died before any of them spoke to him. Had Dec attacked Rory?

He had no idea how his brother had been with women. Kit did know that his brother had been angry after learning the factory was being closed. Declan had often gotten physical with Kit when they'd been younger and arguing about something, but Kit had always thought that was just a sibling thing. He opened his eyes and looked at her, saw that she'd kind of shrunken into herself, and realized she needed to know that they were okay.

He opened his arms. "That doesn't matter. You and I will figure ourselves out."

She stepped into them and he hugged her close. He held her carefully as his mind was now spinning with questions that he was pretty sure he'd never get any satisfaction from, but he knew he had to find out what had actually happened the night that his brother died and Rory went into a coma.

She shifted back. "It's okay if—"

He put his fingers over her lips, not sure he could handle anything else she had to say right now. "No more talking for now. Let's go for a drive and just spend the day together. I'm not going to pressure you into anything."

"Oh, Kit, I know that. I just don't want you to be disappointed in me. In how I drive or how I kiss."

"Woman, your kisses are the best. Don't ever doubt that," he said.

Nodding, she locked her door and they headed to his car. He got behind the wheel and they drove out of Gilbert Corners together, over that bridge where the accident had happened, and once again he couldn't help wondering what had happened that night.

It had changed so many lives, even Kit's, and he hadn't been in town. But it had put him on a path toward this moment, driving him to questions that he knew he had to have answered.

They got on the interstate, which wasn't busy this time of the day. The leaves on the trees on both sides of the road were changing. Rory didn't remember particularly liking fall before, but now she did.

"Where are we going?"

"Oh, sorry, I went into autopilot and was heading back to Boston," he said.

"Was it me talking about sex…?"

"Yes. But please stop. I need a minute to think about something other than what you feel like in my arms," he said, his voice growing a bit husky on the last part.

"How about we get off at the next exit and find a spot that's not busy and you can help me drive?" she asked. "That's not sexy."

He signaled to exit the interstate. "Everything about you is."

She blushed, glad to hear him say that. "I was fishing."

"I know," he said, a wry grin flickering on his lips.

As he exited the interstate, she noticed there was a co-op off to the side advertising fresh cider, apples and doughnuts. Kit pulled into the parking lot and parked away from the other cars. He turned off the engine and put his arm along the back of her seat as he faced her. "I don't mind you fishing."

"That's one of many things I like about you,

Kit," she admitted. She couldn't remember dating before the coma. She had an idea that she'd probably been afraid to admit things back then. But having missed a decade of her life, she wasn't going to let fear keep her from the things she wanted.

And she wanted Kit.

"What else do you like?" he asked.

She undid her seat belt and reached over to put her hand on his thigh. She did envy him his healthy body but knew hers was getting there. She squeezed his leg. "That you keep showing up despite the fact that I coerced you into it."

"You didn't force me to do anything I didn't want to," he said, his hand idly playing with a strand of hair that had escaped her braid.

She and Kit noticed people coming out of the store. "We can try letting you drive here," he suggested. "Or we can go into the shop."

"Do you like apple cider?" she asked him.

"I do. You?"

"I'm not entirely sure. I think so. I know I've never tried apple cider doughnuts."

"Let's go," he said. "Afterward, I'll give you a chance to drive my car."

He came around to her side of the car and of-fered her his hand to get out. Which she took.

She left her walking stick in the car because her legs weren't tired and with Kit by her side… She stopped herself. She was supposed to be getting stronger on her own.

And she was.

But she also realized she didn't want to be on her own all the time. She craved this kind of interaction. Perhaps he did as well? And while she wasn't sure what he was struggling with, it was obvious he had some things going on, too. She wasn't so self-absorbed that she'd missed that.

"Do you mind if I have to hold your arm while we're walking around? Or I can bring my walking stick…"

"I don't mind," he said. "I'm sorry about earlier. I just feel bad that someone hurt you."

"It's not your fault," she assured him. "But I don't want to talk about it. I just wanted you to know what you were getting into with me. I hate lying."

Elle and Dash had faked being married to help Rory's recovery but when she'd found out the truth, she'd realized she couldn't tolerate lies. It wasn't that she thought they'd done it for a vicious reason, it was simply that she didn't want to have to look at the people closest to her and have to watch her back.

"I'm not a fan of liars either," he confided. "But sometimes white lies are necessary."

"I don't see how."

"To save hurt feelings or sometimes when it's not your secret to tell," Kit said.

He'd given this a lot of thought, she realized. Should that concern her? "If I asked you for the truth, would you be honest?"

He took a deep breath and then tipped his head as he looked down at her. "I would."

"Then that's all that matters," she said. Both Dash and Con had done things they regretted, so she knew how difficult it could be to revisit the past when Kit may have been a different man. But all that mattered was that she trusted him now.

He led the way into the shop, which smelled of fresh apples and cinnamon. They had a café in the back and Kit bought them apple cider doughnuts and hot apple cider. When they were done with their snack, he showed her how to drive and let her try driving around the parking lot.

Her legs didn't give her any trouble, and though she'd only gone twenty miles per hour, she couldn't help feeling triumphant when she parked the car and looked over at him.

"Knew you could do it!" he said.

Flushed with success, she leaned over, taking the kiss she'd wanted since she'd opened the door and seen him standing on her front porch. Whatever else she was unsure of in her life, Kit wasn't it.

EIGHT

Kit dropped Rory off at her place and she invited him in.

"Sure. Do you need help with any projects?"

"Always. How's your house coming along, by the way?"

"It's in pretty good shape. I hired a company to redo most of it before I moved in. Want to see it?" he asked.

The house hadn't ever been meant to be his permanent home. It was his base in Gilbert Corners so he could get the jump on Dash when it came to buying up property and figuring out what the Gilbert family was up to. Which right now made him feel slightly icky and his stomach to roil. The closer he got to Rory and her family, and the more he learned about his own, revenge seemed like overkill. He'd dedicated his life to avenging something that might have been a lie told by his father.

"I'd love to," she said. "I'm curious to know more about you."

"Like what?" he murmured as he parked in the driveway and turned toward her.

"Well, when we video-chatted, your couch looked so cozy. Gilbert Manor is always decorated for show and I want my place have a more homey feel, but I'm not sure how to create that. Maybe your place will give me some ideas."

"Ah, my place is sort of a bachelor pad. I don't think you're going to find any inspiration here," he said.

He got out and opened her door for her, offering her his hand as she got out of the car. "You never know..."

"Actually," he said as he led the way up to his front door, "I'm thinking about getting some of the flowerpots like you have. To pretty the place up."

His house had been completely brought up to code and modernized, like Rory's had on the outside, and it stood out among the other places that hadn't been redone yet. Kit had purchased three more on this street and was in the process of developing them with an eye toward offering affordable housing to his workers once he found a large enough property on which to build Palmer Industries' newest work hub.

His front door had been painted black and was a nice contrast to the brick stonework on the outside of the row house. The accents had originally been more Victorian but Kit favored wrought iron, which gave the place more of a contemporary feel.

He opened the door, gesturing for Rory to step inside. "There's a rug, so be careful."

"Thanks," she said with a smile. She stepped inside and then stopped after he followed her in and closed the door.

She shrugged out of her coat and handed it to him and then looked down at her booted feet. "Want me to take my shoes off?"

"It's up to you. I have a cleaning service and they are due to come in tomorrow."

He opened the coat closet and hung both of theirs up. Turning to find she'd sat down on the wooden bench to remove her flats, he sat down next to her with the intent of doing the same, but she put her hand on his thigh again and leaned into him.

Her breast brushed the side of his arm, sending a wave of want through him. He felt the warmth of her breath on his cheek, the smell of apple cider and then her silky soft hand against his jaw as she turned his face toward hers and kissed him.

He had told himself he needed more answers to the past before he let this thing with her go any further, but he was so tired of denying himself. He wanted her. More than he'd wanted anything in a long time, except revenge.

He slipped his arm around her waist and drew her close to him as the kiss deepened. She tilted her head to the side, her tongue sliding over his. God, she tasted so good.

Like everything he'd ever wanted.

Which jarred him because all he'd wanted for so long was to see Dash Gilbert fall. That once-clear dream was blurred. Now all he could see and think about was Rory, and this kiss sharpened the need in him that hadn't been far from the surface all day.

Stop thinking, he ordered himself.

He lifted her onto his lap, she wrapped both arms around his shoulders and he pushed his tongue deeper into her mouth as he slid his hand under the hem of her skirt, just lightly caressing the tops of her thighs. Her fingers were still on his jaw but her little finger was rubbing his neck right below his ear. Making him harden under her hip.

She shifted, her legs parting as he caressed her thighs. He lifted his head, looking down at her gorgeous face. Her eyes were half-closed, her lips parted and swollen from their kisses and there was a flush to her skin. He used his other hand to touch her lips and she kissed his finger before he drew it down her neck. She shivered delicately in his arms and shifted on his lap.

As she arched her back, his gaze fell to her breasts. He lifted one hand to touch her but knew if he did, this would go beyond a few heated kisses.

She took his hand, putting it on her breast.

"Don't stop now," she murmured.

Her words stirred something in him. He wanted her with a fierceness that he was fighting so hard to keep in check, not wanting to scare her. But when their lips met, he couldn't resist plunging his tongue deep into her mouth. Tasting her again, but also trying to tame her. Trying to find some way to overcome the need and want she was pulling so effortlessly from him.

He still had no idea what he was going to do

to resolve his own conflicted emotions about the entire Gilbert family. But as Rory writhed in his arms, making him crazy with desire, he realized she was becoming more important than the past.

Spending the afternoon with Kit had been fun but she knew she wanted more. Her life at times felt like she moved through it in a fog. Talking to Elle and Indy helped her to mold herself into the woman she was trying to become, but the truth was, she spent a lot of time dreaming about life instead of *living* it.

When Kit had sat down next to her on the bench in his front hallway, she'd started to think of what she wanted him to do and realized that she couldn't wait for that. She'd spent too long waiting. So she'd kissed him.

And it was...wow. Not at all what she'd expected but so much more. Her entire body felt alive in a way that she hadn't ever experienced before. She loved the feel of his jaw under her fingers. Loved the slight stubble under her skin and how it felt when she rubbed her finger against it.

The skin on his neck was soft and his lips

were firm and felt so good when she'd kissed him. And the way his tongue had rubbed against her made her wet and her breasts felt full and sort of achy.

When he'd stopped, she was sure that he was going to slow things down. She didn't know why, maybe he thought that was what she wanted. But she didn't. Her life was already going entirely too slowly. She wanted him, and unless he told her he didn't want her, too, she wasn't ready to get off his lap.

She felt the ridge of his erection under her hips and his hand on her thigh kept creeping higher and higher. She parted her legs as his tongue thrust into her mouth. She'd been binge-reading her favorite romance novels and she knew what she wanted to happen next: his hands on her naked skin.

But of course she had tights on, not that that seemed to stop Kit. His big hand glided over her thighs around to her butt and she felt his fingers flex as he cupped her and shifted her around on his lap.

She moved to straddle him and her thighs started shaking. They were still so weak at times. He lifted his head. His left hand still under her skirt, his other hand fondling her breast. "You okay? Still into this?"

"Yes. I just can't sit like this on you," she whispered.

"How's this?" he asked as he moved her back to the position she was in before. Sitting sideways on his lap.

It was better, but she briefly hated that weakness in her body. She looked down at her legs, feeling upset with the fact that she still wasn't strong, but there was no time to dwell on that. Kit's hand was back on her thigh, moving up again as his mouth was on hers again.

Winding her arms around his shoulders, she held on to him as his hands moved over her body. She felt like she was on fire and that momentary quivering from trying to use muscles that hadn't been used for too long was gone. In its place were a million little fires that were being started by Kit.

His hand under her shirt slowly moved around to her back, unhooking her bra and then rubbing between her shoulder blades as he brought her more fully into contact with him. He lifted his mouth from hers and she felt his kisses on her neck and then her shirt was up, the cool air in the foyer brushing over her heated skin.

She looked down at his hand on her ribs moving up toward her breast. Full and curvy, she liked the way it felt beneath his touch. Her nipple was hard and got harder as he swiped his finger over it. She wriggled on his lap, her hip rubbing against the ridge of his erection.

He lowered his mouth and licked her nipple, sending an arc of electricity through her body and a pulse of moisture between her legs. She shifted her legs against his hand. Feeling the roughness of his jeans beneath her and his fingers between her legs. Stroking her as his mouth feasted on her breast.

Surrounded by Kit, she had her hands in his hair, felt his hard-on beneath her as his fingers were rubbing against her, driving her higher and higher. Everything in her body was driving toward something, toward a mind-blowing climax, and then she was shuddering and shaking in his arms as it washed over her. Nearly delirious with desire, she pulled his mouth from her breast and began kissing him. Sucking his tongue into her mouth as her body kept spasming.

She felt wet between her legs but he kept

stroking her. His erection under her hip had gotten bigger, harder. She wanted more. The orgasm he'd given her had been out of this world but she wanted his cock inside her.

He lifted her into his arms and stood, carrying her down the hall and placing her on a large leather sofa. He stood there for a minute, and she could see the outline of his erection against the front of his jeans.

"Do you want more or do you want me to stop?" he rasped.

"More," she said, her voice sounding foreign to her own ears, filled with need and demand.

"Good. Are you on the pill?" he asked.

"I am not," she said. She'd recently come out of a coma after all. Birth control hadn't been the first thing on her mind.

"Let me get a condom. I'll be right back."

She lay there watching him go for a moment. Her shirt bunched up under her breasts and then she sat up and took it off, tossing it aside. She removed her tights and her skirt and her underwear. For a minute she worried about her body: it had scars from surgeries, but not too many, and she really didn't have muscle tone.

But then Kit walked back in, and she noticed he'd also taken off his shirt. He looked down at her as he undid his pants and took his dick in his hand, rolling on the condom. "You are the most gorgeous woman I've ever seen."

Seeing Rory naked on his leather couch was making it hard for him to think about anything but being inside her. Her blond braid fell over her shoulder to her full breasts. She had her legs slightly parted and as he let his gaze move over her body he couldn't help noticing the signs that were still present from her accident.

There were faded scars around her knees, and on her left hip there was a jagged one that looked like it must have been rough. He had also felt the scar at the back of her scalp when he kissed her.

Feeling her so alive in his arms a few moments ago made him so damn grateful that she was here now. These emotions weren't easy to process and his dick said, *forget about that for now.* She was naked on his couch, waiting for him.

She'd pretty much told him she was a virgin and he wasn't sure he'd ever been with one. He hadn't had sex until college and his girlfriend at the time had been five years older than him. She'd been the one with the experience. Was there something different he needed to do? He wanted this first time for her to be exciting and one she'd never forget.

But then she opened her arms to him and he realized he was overthinking it. He knew there were unresolved things he needed to deal with, but those could wait. Right now he wanted to feel her silky limbs wrapped around his body and forget about everything except Rory.

Her deep blue eyes, sweet smile and the sexy sounds she made as she came, *that* was all he wanted more of. Kit wedged his knee between her legs and then settled onto the couch, carefully putting his body over hers. He used his torso to caress her, feeling the moistness at her center against his stomach as he slid up her body.

Her nipples were tiny points against his chest and then he settled his cock right between her thighs. He kept his full weight from her with his knees and his arms, which he braced on either side of her head.

Her hands were on him as soon as he was close enough. He shuddered at the feel of her palms sweeping up and down his back and then cupping his butt and drawing him closer to her. And when she arched her back, parting her thighs and rubbing herself against the ridge of his erection, he groaned.

Needing to be inside her now.

He shifted his hips, put the tip of his cock against the entrance of her body and stayed there. She lifted her head and their eyes met.

"Will it hurt?"

"I don't know," he said gruffly. "I've never been anyone's first before."

She shivered a little under him. And rearranged her legs again, wrapping them around his waist. "I'm glad."

"Me, too."

Then he brought his mouth down on hers, using his hands to cage her head between them as her tongue rubbed over his. He took his time with the kiss, building the passion in her so that when he entered her it would be more pleasure than pain.

She started moving against him, her body undulating under his and he repositioned his hips, taking his time before he drove himself deep into her body. He heard her gasp and her tongue sucked his deeper into her mouth.

She used her feet against his butt to push him deeper into her body as she arched underneath him. He pulled back and drove into her again and she moaned in response. After that, thinking became impossible. Instead, it was just the feel of Rory's body under his as she writhed under him and made these cries in the back of her throat that drove him higher and higher until everything in him exploded and he came inside her. But he wasn't through with her yet. He kept driving into her and felt her pussy tightening around him, milking him as he kept thrusting until he was empty.

Afterward, he rested his forehead against hers as he caught his breath. Her hands swept up and down his back and her legs were still around him as they clung together, basking in the moment. He rolled to his side and pulled her into the curve of his body, holding her there and looking down at her.

"You okay?"

"More than okay," she admitted. "I had no idea my body could feel like that... I don't think you can understand how much I've been frustrated by how hard it's been to relearn everything. But today...helps me believe it's all been worth it."

He shook his head and kissed the tip of her

chin. "I'm glad. I love your body. You should be proud of the strength you've regained."

"I know," she said, wrinkling her nose. "But everyone else—"

"Isn't you. Which I'm very glad for," Kit insisted. "Be glad that you're not like everyone else."

She tipped her head to the side. "I hadn't thought of it that way. Just saw all the things I couldn't do or didn't know. But with you that doesn't seem to matter, Kit."

She put her hand on his jaw as she said that and the smile on her face went straight to that part of his soul that he thought had died the same night his brother had. It felt like caring and it scared him.

He had started something when he'd come here and thought about using her to get revenge against Dash. Begun something that was wicked—or maybe the real evil had started that night of the crash that had killed his brother and left Rory in a coma.

Kit had no idea what everything meant, but deep down in his gut he knew bringing down the Gilbert family was no longer the most important thing to him.

This woman was becoming that. But a Gilbert had cost his family once and he knew that if he was wrong about this, it would cost his family again.

NINE

RORY HAD A girls' night with Indy and Elle, the women who were engaged to Conrad and Dash, so Kit left her at Indy's bookstore. His mind was a mess. Normally focus was the one thing he fell back on, but not now. He drove back to Boston with one clear mission. He had to find out what exactly had happened the night of the ball.

Had his brother attacked Rory? Or had it been another man? He knew that Rory wasn't lying about what had happened to her. She had always been honest with him, and besides, lying wouldn't gain her anything since she didn't know he was related to Declan.

He didn't even allow himself to dwell on what had happened on his sofa or how much he wanted to keep her in his life. But the half-truths he'd told her when they'd been strangers loomed, and Kit knew he had to come clean. But he needed more facts before that happened.

He called his Aunt Mallory as he was driving. "Hello, Rory. What's up?"

"Do you know if Declan went to the winter ball with Rory Gilbert?" he asked her. His aunt had been living in Boston back then but she'd talked to his father and brother weekly.

"I believe he did. Why are you inquiring?"

"Well, she remembers her date..." God, why was it so uncomfortable to say this out loud and to his aunt? He wasn't the one who'd been attacked, Rory was, and *she'd* been able to just say it. "Her date assaulted her and almost raped her. Could that be Declan?"

There was just silence and then he heard his aunt's ragged exhale. "I hope not."

That wasn't a no.

"Was he violent around women?"

"Not to my knowledge," she said. "But he and your father were very angry about the factory closing... So much so that your dad decided not to go to the party and I invited him up here for the evening," she said. "But I have no idea if Declan was the one to attack the Gilbert girl. Your father never said anything to me about it either, but you know what he was like after the accident."

Which told him nothing. His brother and father had been angry because the Gilberts went back on their word. And Kit hadn't ever gone out with his brother, so he didn't know how he had treated women. Plus there was a part of Kit that knew his father would have lied to protect Declan. But even if his sibling had been a gentleman to every other woman he dated, it didn't change anything. Anyone could commit assault.

If only the person in question wasn't his dead brother.

"Are you going to be home tonight?" Kit asked his aunt. "I want to look through some of dad's old papers."

"I'm playing bridge with my friends but I'll tell the housekeeper to let you in," she said. "Kit? Do you think the Gilberts have made up this story about Declan to make themselves feel better about him dying in the car crash?"

Kit didn't know what to think. "I'm not sure. I just want to see if Dad has anything in his belongings that I missed."

"That makes sense. I hope...well I hope Declan didn't do that to the girl," Aunt Mallory said quietly.

"Me, too."

He ended the call after saying goodbye. He wasn't sure that he would ever really know what had happened that night. But he still needed more information.

Rory deserved the truth from him. He couldn't just say, "Oh, hey, that guy who attacked you was my brother and sorry I didn't say it before." He needed to make sure he knew what had happened so he didn't hurt Rory. Knowing her the way he did, he knew that she was going to be upset that he had...lied. *You lied, dude.* There were no two ways about it. But he wasn't going to be the one to traumatize her again.

He was beginning to think he was going to have to come clean with both Rory and Dash. Dash might be the only one who could provide the answers he needed.

He called his office and checked in and then went to work for the rest of the day, not leaving to head to his aunt's house until almost eight. When he got there the housekeeper let him in and Kit went to what Aunt Mal called "the library," where she kept all of his father's journals and records.

Kit grabbed a beer from the fridge before he sat down at the large writing desk in the corner and started opening the files that had been stored in an old, ornate-looking, leather-covered wooden chest. He pulled out some journals and notebooks as well as a bunch of business records.

Flipping through the pages, he found a few notes in Dec's handwriting. He ran his finger over the writing. There were so many questions he had for his brother. He remembered playing in Gilbert Corners at the factory on Saturdays while their dad was working. Running up and down the stairs that led from the floor to his father's office.

Smiling when he thought of his father draping his arms over their shoulders and telling them one day they'd run the factory. Those had been good times—before his mom had gotten sick and died, before Dec had left for college and his father had started drinking.

He rubbed the back of his neck, not really sure he wanted to keep digging. Then he saw the Gilbert International logo on a letter. He pulled it out of the stack and saw it was addressed to both his father and brother.

Dear Will and Declan:
I'm sorry to lead with bad news but the factory in Gilbert Corners in no longer viable. We've been losing money there for months and many of the local workers we relied on are leaving the town. The decision has been made to close the factory effective December 31.

The jobs offered to you both to buy a controlling share of the factory and take over running it is no longer an option. I'd like to offer you both new roles at our offices in Boston. Your salaries will have a fifteen percent increase and we will cover the relocation costs.

I know this isn't the news you'd hoped to hear, but I think this will be a good opportunity for both of you.

Looking forward to seeing you at the winter gala.

Sincerely,
Lance Gilbert

Kit let the paper fall from his hands, leaning back in his chair and locking his fingers behind his head as he stared up at the ceiling. *What the actual fuck?* Did Aunt Mal know about this? Kit figured she didn't, as she'd been the one encouraging him to make the Gilberts pay.

But his father had. Why hadn't the old man ever mentioned this?

He still wasn't sure that his brother had done anything wrong the night of the gala. But this clearly showed that his father and brother knew they weren't going to buy and run the factory. More than that, they still would have had jobs even when the factory closed—their family wouldn't have been ruined like he'd been led to believe.

What else had his father been hiding?

Rory was having fun drinking white zinfandel and sitting in the cozy corner of Indy's Treasures. Elle was getting ready for her wedding to Dash. So she had been showing them pictures of potential wedding dresses. She had her mother's veil, which she intended to wear.

"Though Dash has seen that," Elle said.

"He has? How exactly?" Indy asked, picking up a pretzel bite that her friend Lulu had made and popping it in her mouth.

"On our first date I had gone to pick up my

parents' stuff from my stepmom's house. It was in there and I put it on."

Rory had long gotten over her feelings of upset at Dash and Elle for lying to her about being married when she'd first gotten out of the coma. "I love this. So you guys were going on dates behind my back?"

Elle flushed. "Yes. I was trying to be professional and all and just help you get your memories back."

Rory shifted on the couch and hugged the other woman. "I know you were but there was something between the two of you. Something that I saw before you two did."

"Well, I'm glad you did," Elle said, hugging her back. "But enough about me. What's up with you and Kit?"

Rory tried not to flush when she thought about what it had been like to make love with him on his couch. She'd felt different since he'd left and she'd gone back home. Awake but in a different way than she'd been before.

"Wow. That good?" Indy asked with a soft smile. "I saw you two drive by the shop earlier today."

"He took me for a driving lesson," she said.

"Oh, is that all?" Indy teased. "I mean you're

blushing pretty hard for someone who just learned how to steer and brake."

"Not just driving," she said. "I think I'm falling for him."

"Really?" Elle asked, her eyes widening.

Rory thought she heard a note of concern in her friend's voice. "Why? Is it too soon?"

"There's no clock on emotions," Indy said. "I mean with Con... I think I fell the first time I saw him on the promo for his show. I mean I got hot all over when he looked into the camera and the voiceover guy asked, '*Who is willing to challenge the beast?*'"

"Hot and bothered isn't falling," Elle pointed out. "Is it lust, Rory? You're not on the pill—"

"Elle, be my sister, not my doctor," Rory said. "And yes, it's lust but it's also so much more. He just sees me. Not someone who's been in a coma for ten years like Dash, Con and you two do. Or that freaky Gilbert girl like the town does. And through his eyes, I'm starting to see who I want to be."

"Sorry, Rory, just looking out for you. I'm glad he sees you. Just make sure you keep being Rory and not Kit's version of Rory," Elle murmured.

Rory smiled at Elle, knowing the other

woman had her best interests at heart. "I will." She turned to Indy. "So how's Con...?"

Indy chewed her lower lip and then rolled her eyes. "A diva as always. Ever since we decided to share a studio and build it here in Gilbert Corners, I've been seeing another side to the man."

Rory let the conversation flow around her as the other women talked about the two men who'd always been so influential in her life. But she was only half listening. She knew that Elle was just being protective, sort of like Dash was, but the other woman had raised some concerns for her.

She knew she'd been struggling to find herself since she'd woken, and moving out on her own had been step one. If that escort/life coach she'd hired had shown up...would she even have met Kit? Had she poured herself into being what he wanted because she didn't want to be alone?

She hoped not. But how could she know for sure?

They chatted for a bit longer and then a push notification from the Gilbert Corners Chamber of Commerce came through announcing the clues for the speakeasy for that night. They were going Goth since Halloween was just around the corner and were having a My Chemical Romance tribute band.

They were one of her favorite bands, and after tonight's thoughts about being Rory or Kit's version of Rory, she wanted a chance to test herself. She messaged Kit to remind him about their upcoming date. He texted back that he couldn't wait.

Goth night sounded like just what he needed. All those angsty emotions he'd outgrown during his twenties were back swirling around inside. Kit pulled on his black jeans and old black biker boots, black tee and his favorite leather jacket. He put on kohl eyeliner that he'd picked up earlier and realized when he looked in the mirror that he missed this part of his life. Back before tragedy hit his family hard, leaving him with nothing but emptiness.

Aunt Mal tried, but his father and brother and he had been a tight threesome before Declan's death. She couldn't fill the gap that his drunk father and dead brother had left.

Pushing all of that back into the past, he locked his door and walked down to Rory's house. He was going to pretend he was just

Kit and she was just Rory. She was the woman he'd made love to that very afternoon and he hoped to do it again soon. He wanted more with her and that had nothing to do with her being a Gilbert.

He knocked on her door, and when she opened it, his heartbeat pounded in his ears. She had on dark eyeliner, too. Her lips were bright red and she'd twisted her blond hair into two ponytails that she'd colored the ends of black. His eyes drifted over her appreciatively. She wore a pair of tight leather pants and a black see-through blouse with a black bra underneath.

He got hard just looking at her. He loved it. Loved the fact that everything between them felt new and fresh. None of the past obligation or responsibility he had to his family could get in his way. The more they connected, the more Kit treasured getting to know who Rory was without the Gilbert name.

She cocked her head to the side. "I like this side of you," she said.

"Same. Are you ready to go?" he asked.

"In a rush?"

"Not really, but I can't help noticing you put a bench in your hallway and now I'm thinking about what we can do there," he said with a smirk.

She flushed. "Maybe later if you play your cards right."

"Oh, I intend to," he assured her. He helped her get her black leather jacket on and then noticed she reached for her cane.

"Everything okay?" he asked. She hadn't used it earlier.

"Yeah, my thighs got a bit of a workout earlier and feel weak," she said. "Does it mess with my look?"

"Did I hurt you when we had sex?" he asked hoarsely. Dammit, he should have been more careful with her.

"No. I just don't use my legs that way usually," she said with a tinkling laugh. "We can practice and get them stronger. That's what my physical therapist always says when I try something new."

"I don't mind practicing. So where are we going?" he asked to distract himself of the images in his head of her naked underneath him.

"The speakeasy."

"I don't know what that is," he admitted.

She told him that the Main Street businesses had all gotten together with the Chamber of

Commerce and helped fund and promote a pop-up bar that had been themed as a speakeasy. They sent out clues that took residents of Gilbert Corners around town, leading them to the bar.

"Sounds fun. GC didn't have anything like that when I lived here."

"No, they didn't. There's sort of a new energy to the town lately. Part of it is Indy and Lulu bringing their TV show here. For a while I think people were waiting for my family to come back and make things happen, but then decided they should just do it for themselves, sort of."

"Your family does have a lot of power here," he remarked. "But what do you mean *sort of*?"

"Well, Indy did break the curse when she got Conrad to come back and do his show, so it was like a combo of new ideas, new people and old superstitions."

He liked what she was saying and how she saw the town. Rory clearly loved it here despite the difficulties her family had faced over the years. He almost let himself get distracted and start thinking of business and how he could bring Palmer Industries into it. But he wanted tonight as a date. Not as an opportunity.

And until he figured out more of what had happened the night his brother died, he didn't want to push forward with anything involving either Rory or Dash.

"So the speakeasy is doing a Goth night?" he asked, not sure how it fit in with the previous theming.

"Yeah. I guess because it's October and Halloween is just around the corner. Or maybe they wanted to try something new," she said. "The tribute band is My Chemical Romance."

"You like them?"

"Loved them. I mean as soon as I saw their name, 'Helena' started playing in my head. I hadn't thought of them since I woke up but there the song was," she said.

Kit took her hand in his as they talked about music and followed the clues.

He knew that he was going to have to face the past and figure out what to do next, but for tonight it was enough to be with Rory, singing "I'm Not Okay" at the top of his lungs on a semi-crowded dance floor.

Her body brushed against his and he held her close when she stumbled. He knew that no matter what he wanted, sooner or later he was going to have ask her more questions about the accident and tell her about his brother, but not tonight. Tonight was about letting go. Tonight was for them.

TEN

THE GILBERT CORNERS Chili Cookoff wasn't something that Kit thought he'd find himself participating in. Especially not in a booth with the Gilberts. But he had to stop thinking of them as Gilberts. So instead he focused on being here with Rory and her family. A few weeks had passed since their night at the speakeasy.

Indy and Conrad were doing a special that would run on the network where they both had television shows. It was combining her town makeover idea and his quintessential cooking challenge. The differences in this show were that the challenge was just locals all cooking their favorite chili recipe—normally Con's show focused on a showdown between his professional persona "The Beast" and a solo challenger.

And then Indy and her makeover team, which included Lulu who ran the coffee shop, had undertaken the old Gilbert Civic Center space. Rory had worked with Indy's team on redoing the interior of the convention space and, after some thought, Kit and Palmer Industries had partnered with them as well. The civic center was one of the run-down properties that he'd purchased.

Rory had come to him about the needed updates so he'd immediately offered to make a donation through his company.

Aunt Mal hadn't been happy that he'd donated it back to the town but she'd liked the plaque on the side of the building that thanked them for the donation. She wanted more plaques around town that didn't have the Gilbert name on them.

The town wasn't beholden to the Gilbert family anymore. Which suited Kit. He still hadn't had a chance to talk to Dash and Con about the night of the accident and he hadn't brought up the man who'd attacked Rory. A part of him didn't want to know if it had been his brother.

Coward.

But the truth was, Declan had been the only positive male influence that Kit had had. His father's descent into alcoholism had soured the relationship between him and Kit. Something that Kit knew he'd never been able to forgive. His father should have stayed sober and helped Kit rebuild Orr Industries. Instead, at twenty-one, Kit felt like he had to start a new business, Palmer Industries, running a business in a field that had been dictated by ruthlessness and revenge. It had been what he'd believed was his dad's severance pay and Aunt Mal's savings that had given them the start they needed. And then…well, dumb luck. Aunt Mal said he had a head for business and maybe he did. They'd gone after smaller companies until they were established and then had targeted opportunities that Gilbert International showed interest in.

And slowly Kit had developed the skills and acumen needed to defeat Dash when it came to winning business deals and wooing clients. Not all the time, but often enough that he knew he could eventually bring the man down. But bringing him down was no longer the goal. Kit had come to realize that Dash wasn't a villain who'd taken away his family's opportunity. He was just a man. And he was Rory's brother.

"I have to talk on camera," Rory said, coming over to him. She had her long blond hair loose, hanging around her shoulders in a way that nicely framed her heart-shaped face. "What if I sound like an idiot?"

He took her hand in his and drew her away from the booth where Conrad's assistants were setting up the cooking area for their team. "You won't. You are too smart and you already rehearsed it for me this morning. You know what you're doing."

She chewed on her lower lip. "I know but it was easier talking to you."

"Do you want me to go and stand behind the cameraman? You can look at me when you're talking," he suggested. The more time he spent with Rory the harder it was to have any sense of perspective on any of the past. He was falling for her and it would be silly to pretend he wasn't. She'd also made him face the hard truth of his perceptions about the past with his father and brother.

Being around her made him feel alive for the first time since college. He wasn't constantly thinking about what the Gilberts had taken from him but instead felt like he was enjoying an unexpected gift.

She tipped her head to the side and gave him a soft smile that went straight to his groin and made him want to carry her from the hall and make passionate love to her.

"We are more." There was something flirty and sexy in the way she watched him.

He *knew* they were. And that made the secret he kept from her even worse. However, he didn't want to hurt her anymore than she'd already been hurt by his brother and the past. But was he just making excuses for himself? His greatest fear was that the longer he kept the truth from her the more betrayed she'd feel.

"We are. So I think even your therapist would say it's okay for me to be there for you when you speak on camera for the first time."

She nodded. "I can't believe I'm doing this."

"Why not?"

She shrugged and looked around the hall. The interior was modern and sleek and the walls were adorned with artwork and frescoes created by local artists and students from the high school. The civic center, which had previously held a large portrait of all of the Gilberts who'd served on the town council was now more of a town-focused place.

"It's just that until now most of my work has been quiet and small. I loved working on the interior of the building and doing the behind-the-scenes work. But this is me being in the spotlight." She stopped and then shook her head. "It's not like the people of Gilbert Corners haven't always talked about me, but I've always pretended I didn't know they were."

"This time you're controlling the narrative," he pointed out. "You're going to get up there and talk about the work you put into this space and how it's really part of the town and the people who live in Gilbert Corners. I think that's important and I also believe you're the only one who can do it."

"Oh, Kit, thank you," she said, throwing herself into his arms. He caught her and held her close, shutting his eyes and breathing in the scent and feel of her.

He wanted her. Not just right this moment but forever. He'd never thought of forever before. It scared him. He'd always known once he'd come to Gilbert Corners things would change but he hadn't realized how they would.

Rory was nervous and not just for the reasons she'd given Kit. This was her first project at the first paying job she'd had. She wanted the people of Gilbert Corners to like what she'd done to the civic center. Kit had asked her if she wanted to take her new renovating skills and apply them to the project.

She'd said yes as she had to everything new and risky since she'd moved out on her own. The work had been more fun than she'd realized. She could have done it for gratis but Kit had insisted. He'd have had to hire someone to oversee the project if she wasn't doing it. Which had made her even more determined to make sure the building exceeded his expectations.

She'd leaned heavily on Indy and Lulu at first, asking them for pointers when she'd run into things she'd never dealt with before. But as she stood next to Kit in the hall, watching not only the TV crew get set up but locals as well who were seeing it for the first time, she felt a sense of pride as she overheard comments about how good the renovation looked.

For once, people were talking about her not because she was one of those cursed Gilberts but because of the work she'd done. She turned to Kit.

"Thank you for giving me this chance."

"You're welcome. I knew you could do it," he said proudly.

But she hadn't shared his confidence.

That wasn't something she was sure she

would ever say to anyone but her therapist. But the truth was she'd had a massive anxiety attack after she'd signed the contract with Palmer Industries. She'd sat on her couch and listed all the reasons why she was going to fail and had to do box breathing to just calm herself down long enough to see.

But then she'd looked around her house at all the projects she'd done there and that had helped. And as Kit had said earlier today, she hadn't had to do it on her own.

Kit held her hand and stood next to her in his typical all black. Today he wore black jeans, a long-sleeved black button-down shirt and that thick leather belt that drew her eyes to his hips.

She felt a zing of sexual awareness go through her. Totally not what she should be thinking about at the moment. But when she was close to Kit it was hard not to.

The more time they spent together, the more she was starting to get used to him in her life.

Was that good?

He was the first boyfriend she'd had as an adult. Surely, she should date around before finding someone she wanted to spend the rest of her life with. And she *did* want a partner in life. She'd seen with Conrad and Dash how finding someone they loved and shared their life with had enhanced them. Made them seem more fulfilled.

She wanted that.

Was she just seeing in Kit what she wanted to see?

Her heartbeat sped up and a few doubts crept into the good endorphins that she always experienced when she was with him.

"What is it?" he asked, looking concerned. "You know, if you don't want to be on camera you don't have to do it."

She smiled and that knot in the pit of her stomach started to relax. Kit always thought of her first. She knew that was important. Or at least it was to her. "I know. I'll be okay. Thanks for coming over here with me."

"Rory, if it's possible, I'll always be here for you."

Oh! Why did he have to say things like that in the middle of a crowded room? She kissed him, long and deep, and then pulled back before it went too far. "Thank you."

He flashed a grin that made everything feminine in her melt into a puddle of want and need. She didn't know if she was going to be able to wait until the chili fest was over to be alone with him.

She flushed, thinking about making love in the back hallway of the civic center. She knew just the spot that would give them the privacy they needed.

"How much longer until you need me?" she asked the director.

"About ten minutes. You can go and I'll text you when we're ready."

"Great," she said before turning to Kit. "Come with me."

Rory took his hand and led him out of the main hall of the civic center and up the back stairs to the small room that had been used as a projection room back in the day. She'd remodeled it into a private meeting space.

She closed and locked the door behind them after she'd led him inside.

"Uh, Ms. Gilbert...what are you doing?"

She winked. "I was thinking there's one thing that I need."

"And that's...?"

Kit. She needed Kit. She was being flirty and playful with him but deep in her soul she knew she needed him.

It might not be wise to fall for the first man

she dated but she knew she was. She was totally vibing on Kit. Everything about him was ticking boxes and pushing buttons and in every way that mattered, he was just what she wanted.

She didn't know if she'd dreamed him up in her coma or how he'd dropped into her life… and she didn't care. She was just glad he was here now.

She pushed him back against the locked door, leaning into him and wrapping one thigh around his hip.

And from the look on his face he wanted her just as badly.

His eyes glinting with desire, he put his hands on her butt and drew her up into his body as his mouth came down on hers.

Kit was aware that Rory only had ten minutes until she had to be back downstairs. Hot and horny, all he wanted to was turn and bang her against the wall but he wasn't sure that would be satisfying for her. Though his mind was having a hard time staying in control.

Her mouth was on his neck, sucking at that one spot that seemed connected to his cock, which was only getting harder. She was rubbing herself against the ridge of his erection as her hands held his shoulders tightly.

"Rory…honey, we don't have time for this," he gritted out.

"I'm pretty sure we do. I mean last night you did it in five."

He groaned. He hadn't been able to resist her when she'd put on his T-shirt and danced around the living room, showing off her new strength. God, the more time he spent with her, the harder it was to keep from falling for her.

He looked into her pretty blue eyes and knew that it was time to stop pretending he thought he shouldn't fall for her. He'd already started. There was no going back and a part of him, deep down, knew he was looking for a way to have Rory and satisfy the need to even the odds with Dash Gilbert.

She put her hands around his neck and shifted so that her breasts brushed against his chest. He felt the hardness of her nipples through the silk blouse she wore. He lifted one hand, rubbing his finger over the tip.

Fuck.

He wanted her and she wanted him. Why was he hesitating?

The thought that he felt he didn't deserve

Rory danced through his mind and he shoved it away. Not now. He'd deal with that later.

Right now his woman was in his arms, undulating against him and making him so hard he might come in his pants. Which would be a waste. He kissed her neck and then lower, undoing the top two buttons of her shirt until he could see the fabric of her black, lace bra and the upper curve of her breasts.

He groaned, knowing there was no way he was leaving this room without satisfying his woman. He turned them so that her back was against the wall. Putting one hand on the wall next to her head, he reached between them, shoving his hand up under her skirt. She wore tights and he pulled them down far enough that he could get his hands on her skin.

Damn.

Her skin was soft and as he pushed his hand closer to her pussy he felt the warmth of her. He cupped her and she tipped her head back against the wall, her breath coming in short gasps as he fingered her. She was so hot and so ready. He reached between them and undid his jeans, freeing his erection.

She'd started taking the pill so they didn't have to use a condom when they had sex. His mind was conscious of that as he shifted his hips until the tip of his cock was nestled against the heat of her center. Her hands were on his butt, urging him forward as he slipped inside.

He brought his mouth down on hers, plunging his tongue deep into her mouth as he filled her. She was always so tight when he first entered her and her pussy tightened around him as he drove into her again and again.

She sucked on his tongue, her nails digging into his shoulders as he thrust faster, until she tore her mouth from his and moaned his name.

He drove into her harder until everything inside him tightened and he came in her in a long, heady rush.

Afterward, he braced his arm against the wall, holding himself up until he was empty. He rested his forehead against hers and she smiled up at him.

He shifted back from her, tucking his dick back into his pants and then doing up his jeans. "Why are you smiling like that?"

"Well, I had added *do it in a public place* to my list of things we should try," she replied. "But hadn't had a chance to mention it to you yet."

She pulled her tights up and rebuttoned her blouse and something deep inside him that had felt dead for too long sort of started to come back to life. His heart was racing and emotions that he didn't want to name swirled within him.

"*Do it?* Is that your sexy talk?" he teased, trying to keep things light when everything in him urged him to grab her and make her his. To take her away from Gilbert Corners and convince her that he was the only man for her. Now, before she learned who he really was.

She quirked a brow. "What do you call it?"

"Hooking up?"

"That's not really much better," she said.

Her phone pinged and she gave a nervous laugh. "I think I have to go."

"You're going to do great," he said again.

"Well, I'm not nervous about talking now."

"Are you still nervous in general?"

"Just hoping no one notices that hickey I gave you," she said with a wink as she unlocked the door.

Kit didn't mind if the entire world noticed. He was proud to be Rory's man. Grinning to himself, he followed her down the stairs. And as he predicted, despite what she feared when the cameras started rolling, she was a natural. She kept eye contact with him but her voice and attention were on the job she was doing.

His woman. He might not say the words out loud but his soul had claimed her and a part of him knew he was never letting her go.

ELEVEN

AFTER THAT NIGHT at the speakeasy, Rory stopped worrying about being strong enough or perfect enough and just started to find her footing. They were seeing more of each other—Kit was working from home in Gilbert Corners, and spending most nights at her house in her bed, making love to her all night long.

Kit was awakening dreams in her that she hadn't given a chance to bloom. A part of her was afraid to accept them but that part got quieter and quieter the more time the two of them spent together.

They were having lunch at Lulu's and sitting at one of the outside tables on Wednesday. It was the kind of crisp autumn day that wasn't too chilly in the sun. They'd ordered the special, which was vegetarian chili and jalapeno corn bread. Kit was at the counter waiting for their order and Rory couldn't help staring at him, feeling warm inside.

He was her man.

"Hey, cuz. Mind if we join you?"

She glanced up to see Conrad and Indy standing near the table. She stood up to hug them both. "Not at all. Kit's grabbing our lunch and should be back in a moment. Do you want to drag that table over?"

Con complied and then gave Indy a squeeze before he went into the shop.

"It's odd that you two are free at lunchtime," Rory said, knowing that the two of them had been working on the studio they were building near the old Gilbert International Factory.

"Yeah, well, your cousin saw the two of you together and wants to 'get to know' Kit better," Indy said.

Uh-oh.

"Like how?"

"Like the third degree. He used his Beast's Lair glare on me when I said we should let you two alone." Indy huffed out a breath. "You know how he can be."

Actually she did. Both Conrad and her brother were so overprotective of her that at times it was downright smothering.

"I think he'll find that Kit is a great guy," Rory said.

"I have no doubt that he is, but Con isn't going to see it that easily," Indy predicted. "If he gets out of hand, I'll kick him under the table."

Rory laughed at that. Her cousin's fiancée was about a foot shorter than Conrad, who was six-foot-five-inches tall. He looked fierce, with the scars on his face and the tattoos that covered his body. But Rory knew that underneath all that he was a softy. "I hope it doesn't come to that."

"Whatever happens, happens," Indy said.

"You guys okay?"

"Yeah, I just… I'm used to always being in charge and Con is, too. Working together is both the best and the worst," she said. "Also Halloween is coming up, and that's when I was attacked, so I'm edgy, which is making Con edgy, too."

Rory knew that, like herself, Indy had been forcibly attacked by her date, and though it had happened years before, the scars remained for Indy. In a way Rory thought it felt like a blessing that she'd been in a coma. The incident with Declan was still so hazy. The night of the gala felt like a scary dream instead of a real memory.

"I'm thinking of having a Halloween party. Maybe having a new good memory will help," Rory said.

"That might work," Indy replied. "Also, I relish the idea of seeing Con in a costume."

That could be fun. And it would give her brother and cousin a chance to get to know Kit on a deeper level. "I'm going to as well."

She pulled out her phone and set up a new group text chat with Dash, Elle, Conrad, Indy, Kit and herself. She titled it Halloween Party.

This Saturday. Costume party at my place. 8 p.m. No excuses. Be there.

Indy's phone pinged and she smiled at Rory. "I'll be there."

She glanced up inside Lulu's and saw Kit pull his phone out and turn away from Conrad, who was standing next to him. Kit was tall next to Rory but not compared to Conrad and she noticed her cousin wasn't slouching, as he sometimes did, but stood at his full height.

Kit came back to the table with their tray and smiled tightly as he sat down next to her.

"Hi, Kit. I'm Indy. It's nice to meet you," Indy said.

"Nice to meet you, too," he replied as he placed a chili bowl in front of Rory and then one in front of himself.

Rory took the tray and secured it under her seat and then, noticing her cousin walking toward them with his tray, leaned over and kissed Kit. She took her time with the kiss and after a moment Kit did, too. Putting his hand on the side of her neck as he deepened the kiss.

He lifted his head just as Conrad arrived at their table and set his tray down forcefully. She looked over at Conrad.

"I'm glad you met my boyfriend, Kit."

"Yeah, me, too," Con grumbled. "So you're having a party?"

Rory almost smiled at the way Conrad said it. As much as he might not be sure of Kit, one of the things she loved about her cousin was that he was never going to be difficult unless the situation called for it.

"We are. I can't wait to see your costume," she told him.

"We're going to go as Beauty and the Beast," Indy chimed in.

Conrad looked over at her and she smiled

at him and Rory saw her cousin's expression change into a look of pure love. Rory almost sighed. That was how she wanted Kit to look at her. Which floored her because she'd felt so flawed and like her life was still so much in flux that love wouldn't be right for her. But she knew that was what she wanted now.

"I guess I can wear my chef whites," Con murmured.

"Uh, no. A tux as you'll be the beauty and I'll be the beast," Indy said.

"Or we figure something else out," Conrad grumbled. "What about you two?"

Kit looked over at Rory. A couples' costume would be fun but he wasn't sure he had any good ideas. "Thoughts?"

Rory took a bite of her chili, he guessed to give herself time to think. She had her free hand on his leg and he was still turned on from the kiss she'd planted on him a few moments ago.

Working from Gilbert Corners had been a strategic move to give himself space from his aunt Mal and to try to piece together what had happened the night of winter gala.

But it had turned into something different. He'd practically given up his motive for revenge, spending more time with Rory with each passing day. It made him want to leave the past alone and start to think about a future.

The funny thing about revenge was that it never let you dream of anything other than someone else's downfall. It was a negative place to be for most of his adult life.

"Well, we could do classic monsters," Rory mused. "I've always liked Frankenstein and Bride of Frankenstein."

"Uh, not sure about that..."

"That's right, you don't like monster movies," she teased.

Kit didn't like being scared, so he'd been surprised when Rory had tried to get him to do a movie marathon of her favorite scary movies like *Halloween* and *Nightmare on Elm Street*.

"How about Rick and Evie from *The Mummy*?" Rory said.

He nodded. "You'll make a great Evie."

"And you a good Rick. Glad that's settled," Rory said.

"I think we should be Imhotep and Anck-su-namun," Indy murmured. "That would be fun and you'd be shirtless, which I always love."

"Not sure about that. We don't want Elle

and Dash to feel left out," Con said. "We'll do Beauty and the Beast."

Kit couldn't really square the guy sitting across from him being sweet and tender with his fiancée to the man who'd glared and tried to intimidate him in the coffee shop. "So how'd you two meet?"

He felt like the more that Conrad talked to and about Indy the more he relaxed, and it wouldn't hurt to get to know him better. Conrad had been at the party the night of the crash and it might be easier to talk to him about that than Dash.

"I challenged him on his cooking show," Indy said.

"Who won?"

"The Michelin-starred chef," Conrad stated drily.

"But I also won because I got Con back here to break the curse."

Kit wasn't too sure the curse had been lifted. There was still too much unresolved with his family. No matter that the Gilberts might have been the cause of the curse on the town, he knew his family had a part in it, too.

Conrad leaned over and whispered something in Indy's ear, which made her blush and kiss him. Kit looked over at Rory, who watched the other couple and then turned to him and smiled. "They are so cute."

"Yeah, cute," Kit muttered.

The conversation changed to Gilbert Corners and he was surprised to learn that Conrad and Indy were doing a lot of work around town. He had heard of her television show and knew she'd been filming but hadn't realized that she was redoing more than homes.

"My company is developing property as well," Kit said. "I'm interested in getting the old factory space renovated."

Once he'd started helping with the civic center with Rory he'd realized there were more places and projects around Gilbert Corners that could use his expertise. He might have wanted to be the CEO of a global conglomerate but he was damned good at it. And he wanted... *needed*...to put some good into Gilbert Corners. Not just for Rory but also for himself and his deceased brother and father.

"We are, too," Conrad said. "So far we have used part of the space as a film studio for our shows and I'm working on a test/teaching kitchen in another part of the space. What does you company do?"

"We develop run-down areas with an eye not toward gentrification but toward making spaces that serve the community already living and working there. I know that sounds vague but it really depends on what each town needs. I've been looking around GC and I think we need shared office spaces so that we can encourage people to stay here instead of moving away for work."

Conrad finished his chili and leaned back in his chair, crossing his arms over his chest. "I agree. We don't have to bring everything here, but with the new hybrid working environment we need to have structure in place to make it doable. Dash and I have been working with the town council to bring the fiber and broadband up so it's the best available."

"That's a good start," Kit said.

"Yeah. We're meeting next week to go over the details and could use some more local partners. Want to join us?" Conrad asked.

"Yes, that would be great," Kit said.

As he answered, his pulse started racing. He knew this plan to collaborate with the Gilberts would be hard to explain to his board and to Aunt Mal. He'd been focused on trying to take business from Gilbert International for so long, and if he suddenly partnered with them…well, it would take some explaining. But this was something he couldn't say no to. He wanted to get to know these Gilbert men better, not just to answer his own questions but also for Rory. He wanted to find a way where he could tell her who he was and keep her in his life, and right now, it seemed this was the only viable way to move forward.

"Great. I'll text you the details," Conrad offered.

They finished their meal and said goodbye. Walking Rory back to her place, he noticed that she was quiet. "You okay?"

"Yes. Are you?"

He nodded but inside he wasn't sure. He wouldn't be until he found a way to keep Rory in his life.

It was the Saturday before Halloween and Rory was excited about hosting the get-together for her family and friends. Well, she and Kit were hosting. She'd told him to invite his friends along, too, but he'd told her that he didn't have many outside of work. Rory's house was coming along and Kit had started spending most

evenings with her working on home improvement projects.

"Are you sure about this?" he asked, coming
out of her bedroom in the Rick costume that
went with her Evie getup. She loved the slim-
fitting shirt and the balloon-sleeve blouse she
was wearing.

Kit looked dashing with the suspenders on,
shirt open at the collar and his holster for his
fake gun.

"Yes. We look good, don't we?"

"We do," he said, coming up behind her and
putting his arms around her waist.

She looked at the two of them in the mirror
and her heart beat a little bit faster. It was getting harder to deny she was falling for him. Not
that she wanted to deny it. But she also wasn't
sure where this was going in his mind.

"We never talk about your family," she remarked.

"I only have my aunt left. My parents and
brother are dead," he said.

She turned in his arms, hugging him to her.
"I'm sorry about that. I'd love to meet your
aunt." She left it at that, knowing all too well
how difficult it was to talk about grief.

He squeezed her close for a second and then

dropped his arms and walked away to get the gun to go in his holster. "Yeah, we'll have to figure that out."

"Are you two close?" she asked because he sounded like he wasn't sure that he wanted them to meet.

"We are, actually," he said.

She almost let it go. But if she was going to let herself fall for him, then this wasn't the time to be timid. "So why don't you want me to meet her?"

He turned and the look on his face was... well, more complicated than Rory had imagined it should be. She was introducing him to the people who were important to her so why was he reluctant to reciprocate? True, both Con and Dash had been forcefully trying to get to know him...but still.

"It's not that exactly," he said.

For the first time since they'd met she wasn't sure she believed him. She took a deep breath.

"I know my family is about to show up and we have a party to host, but what's the deal? Are you embarrassed by me in some way? Am I good enough for Gilbert Corners but not for—"

"Don't be ridiculous. You're perfect and a Gilbert, so when have you ever not been enough?"

She didn't like the sound of that. "I'm not a Gilbert with you, Kit. I'm Rory. And I've not been enough a lot lately."

"You're all I need," he said roughly as he came over and took her into his arms. "And regarding my aunt… It's not you. It's me."

"You? If you're close she must love you and want you to be happy," Rory insisted, trying to understand what he meant.

"She does. But…as you said, we don't have time to get into the details. But the night my brother died changed my family forever. My aunt and I united in our grief, trying to get the people responsible to pay for their actions."

"Oh, Kit, that sounds horrible. Like you've been carrying this for a long time. Is there anything I can do to help?" she asked.

"No, Rory."

"So your aunt doesn't want you to date?" she asked, still confused. His refusal of her help sounded harsh. Like she was the last person he'd want help from. Or was *she* the one confusing things?

"She doesn't care about my personal life. She just cares about our agenda," he said, a thread of pain in his voice.

She put her hand on his shoulder as he was

about to turn away from her. "And what is her agenda?"

He took a deep breath and something in the air changed around them. She wondered what it was he was hiding. Because she suddenly realized he was.

"Revenge."

She shook her head. "That's not you, Kit. You're not someone who goes after people. I mean you helped me, a stranger, without even knowing my name."

There was no way she could reconcile in her mind what Kit was trying to say. Kit had been kind to her from the start. He'd been generous when she'd asked for his help in Gilbert Corners.

He was a man who didn't hesitate to offer aid. That was who he truly was. And hearing this...well, it filled in the gaps a little bit. The lonely man who seemed to carry the weight of the world on his shoulders would grapple with revenge.

"But I did know your name, Rory. I knew you from when we were children, remember?"

"Did you know it when I approached you?" she asked, having believed it was when she'd said her name that he'd connected it to who she was.

"I did."

"Oh. So…what are you trying to say?" she asked.

The doorbell rang. That was probably Dash and Elle. Her brother was always early.

"Go answer the door," he told her. "We can talk after everyone goes home."

She wasn't entirely sure she wanted to put this off, but she also didn't want to have this type of discussion while her brother waited outside.

"Okay. But I'm not going to let this go," she warned.

"I'm not either. It's time I told you everything," he said.

Everything? That sounded ominous to her. "Will we be okay after?"

He tried to smile but it felt sad to her. "I hope so."

But it didn't sound like he believed they would be. She went to answer the door, fake-smiling at her brother who was dressed as a patient and Elle who wore her surgery scrubs.

"We didn't have time to plan costumes so had to make do," Dash said sheepishly.

"You look great," she murmured, hugging

her brother close and realizing that she was happy he was here. She had wanted independence and thought she could make a new life for herself with Kit in it, but suddenly nothing seemed sure.

"You okay?" he asked as Elle and Kit were talking.

"Yeah, I'm fine. Just realizing that life doesn't always go according to plan," she said. Which, honestly, she should have realized long before this. But the coma had warped things and made the last ten years seem like a long dream.

Kit had changed her, helping her to wake up and live. She was only now realizing that living meant dealing with good times as well as bad.

TWELVE

KIT KNEW HE'D fucked up when he'd let the conversation drift toward Aunt Mal and his tragic family history. But it was past time to talk to Rory about what had happened the night of the ball, and he knew it. As usual, his timing sucked.

"Con tells me you have some ideas for business here in GC," Dash said as he came over to him.

Rory was in the living room with Elle and Indy, getting her in-home speaker to use the playlist she'd created for the party. And Con was in the kitchen whipping up something that smelled really good.

"I do," he answered, not sure how much to elaborate. "My company, Palmer Industries, has been buying properties around town with an eye to making Gilbert Corners a hub for people who want to live in a small town yet work for bigger companies."

"Palmer Industries... I think you and I have gone up for some of the same things recently."

"We have," Kit said. It seemed tonight was his time of reckoning. He was done hiding and pretending.

"Nothing wrong with some friendly competition, and if it helps GC I'm all for it," Dash confided. "And if it's okay with you, I'm interested in seeing your ideas. For so many years, it was just me trying to come up with things... Well, honestly, I think I was avoiding the town as much as I could."

Kit realized that Dash was treating him like a friend in a way. Like someone his sister was dating. He wanted to be chill and just see where this went. "Because of Rory?"

"Yeah, and Con and the accident. I don't know how much you've heard about that night but there was a huge car accident and another man died," Dash said. "It was the worst night of my life."

Kit heard the pain in his voice. "What happened?" he couldn't help but ask. To see if anything Dash had to say would help him get the clarity he needed.

Con came over with a tray of baked brie bites. "Try this." He gave Dash and Kit a curious look. "What are you two talking about?"

"The night of the crash," Dash replied, taking one and popping it in his mouth. "Fuck, it's hot."

"Let it cool down," Conrad admonished.

Kit took one and waited a moment before tasting it. But his mind wasn't on food right now. He noticed Rory watching him across the room, and while the last time he'd been sort of cornered by Conrad she'd been sympathetic toward him, this time...she looked like she didn't know who he was.

He knew that she didn't. That he'd been lying from the moment she'd introduced herself and he was sick and tired of it. He wanted to just demand to know what happened that night ten years ago. To figure out why his brother was dead, what caused his father to slowly drink himself to death. He wanted to know why his aunt had said one thing but the notes he'd found in that antique wooden chest had shown something else. He wanted...he wanted Rory to look at him like he was a hero and not some villain.

"Why do you want to know about the crash?" Conrad asked him.

"For Rory," Kit said. "She has mentioned a few things... I just want to know more and I don't want to push her into talking about anything that makes her uncomfortable."

"I don't remember much of the crash. Dash walked away without a scratch. Safe to say he remembers the most. We can discuss it next week when we aren't around Rory," Con told him before turning to address his cousin. "Dash, did you tell her about the co-op I mentioned?"

"Not yet," he said. "For years Con wanted nothing to do with the business and now he's sending me proposals left and right."

"You said to get involved," Conrad said, and turned to Kit. "He's a pain in the ass. But it was your idea, Kit, that got me thinking. We have a bunch of people with skills that are underutilized, like the Hammond sisters, who had run the kitchens at Gilbert Manor. They taught me to cook."

"I agree," Kit said, accepting the change of topic. "Can't wait to chat with you both more."

"Enough shop talk," Indy said, coming over to them. "It's time to get this party going. Give me those."

Indy grabbed the snack tray. "What do you have planned?"

Rory had set up a few games to play. Kit hadn't had a party like this before. It was so small and so intimate. While everyone was taking a seat and she handed out Post-it notes, he pulled her into the kitchen so they were alone.

"What's up?" she asked.

"I want this to be fun. There's just a lot of stuff in my life I haven't really ever talked about. But you are important to me," he blurted. He realized from her expression that it might not be what she was expecting from him, but still it had to be said. "I'm sorry for starting things before everyone got here. But the truth is… I'm nervous."

She looked up at him, then put her arms around him and hugged him close. "I'm nervous, too. Since you came into my life I've been just diving into things with you, trying to find someone to have in my life. I've been in a rush to know everything about you. And that's not fair to you."

He tipped her head back and looked down into her eyes, then kissed her long and slow. Everything felt better when she was in his arms. He needed to stop worrying and try to find the right words to say that would make her understand.

Because the truth was, there wasn't a way to explain what was between the two of them. He would do everything in his power to be the man she wanted.

"I think I want that, too," he confessed. "I'm not used to sharing things. I've always kept everything to myself."

She sighed. "And I'm trying to share it all."

"We're waiting, ladybug," Dash said, approaching them. "I'm glad you two are having a moment, but it's time for me to kick Con's ass."

"What exactly is this game?" Kit asked as Rory laughed at her brother.

"It's the Post-it note game. The category is favorite Disney villains." Rory explained the rules, which involved putting the name of a character on the Post-it and then putting it on the person to the left's forehead. A series of yes or no questions were allowed until someone guessed who they were.

Although Kit had never played it, he had a lot of fun, which wasn't surprising, but finding that Dash and Conrad were men that he probably wanted to be friends with was.

Somehow in his head it was okay for him

to fall for Rory but actually liking Dash and Con...that was going to take a lot more time to get used to.

Rory watched Kit more carefully than she had before. It was one thing to tell herself she wanted to take risks and feel completely alive, but the reality was that at times it was still scary.

Her world was so small after she awoke from the coma and she was proud of herself for expanding her horizons and really going all in with Kit. But there was a lot she still didn't know about him—stuff that hadn't seemed to matter before but now did.

"Hey, kid, you okay?" Con asked as he was eliminated from a round of the game and came to help her in the kitchen, refilling drinks.

"Yeah. It's just... I didn't know how this night was going to go," she said. Then realized that might have sounded dumb. "I mean you know how Dash is and you were all big and scary the last time you met Kit."

Con laughed. "I tried to be. But your man held his own."

"I'm not sure he is."

"Your man?" Con asked.

She shrugged. Why had she mentioned that

to him? It might be the rosé that she'd been drinking more of than usual tonight.

"What's up?"

"Nothing."

"Liar," he said gently. "I'm not going to pretend I have any advice for you but I will say this. Falling in love with Indy changed something inside me and I had no control over it. It was terrifying and I fought it with everything I had."

He grabbed three beers in one hand and Indy's glass of sauvignon blanc in the other.

"So everyone feels...out of control in relationships?" she asked her cousin.

"Just the ones that matter," he said with a wink. "Can you get those two?"

"Yes," she said, picking up her glass and Elle's. They rejoined everyone else and as she sat down on the couch next to Kit she looked over at him. He put his hand on her thigh and gave her a squeeze, then their eyes met and he lifted one eyebrow. She just smiled and nodded.

Con's blunt talk had been what she needed to hear. He was the biggest, baddest-looking dude she knew. And if even he had been scared of love...well, it reassured her somehow.

"You brat," Elle said, turning to Dash. "Woody is not a villain."

Dash just shrugged and smiled. "He does pretty much plot to get rid of Buzz. I mean that's not heroic."

"You know that's not what I was thinking," she pointed out.

"Sorry you couldn't guess it, babe," Dash said, pulling her into his arms and kissing her.

"I think we should stop now before things get more intense," Indy said. "What other games do you have?"

"Monopoly. I saw it on the shelf," Dash replied.

"I'm not playing that with you," Rory said, shaking her head. "You're a dick when we play that."

"How about Uno or karaoke then?" Kit suggested.

"Ugh, I suck at singing," Con said.

"You're not supposed to be good at it," Elle pointed out. "Yeah, let's do karaoke!"

Everyone agreed and Kit came to help her get the microphones set up with her TV screen.

"This night is more fun than I thought it would be." Kit's voice was soft, wistful.

"Good. Why didn't you think it would be fun?" she asked him.

"I'm used to parties at my aunt's house. Lots of small talk and circulating waiters… This is, well, more homey."

She turned closer to him, looking into his intense brown eyes, searching for something that would reassure her about whatever it was he had to talk to her about later. "Homey is what we do best."

He quirked one brow at her. "The big parties at Gilbert Manor don't seem homey."

She nodded at that. "They aren't. But that's for show. That's for the town and the company. Nights like this when it's just the three of us… and now our partners. Those are the best."

He pulled her into his arms, his hands around her waist. "Am I your partner?" he asked gruffly.

She put her hand on his jaw. "I think so. I mean until—"

He kissed her to stop her from talking, which concerned her. The kiss was nice but she knew he'd done it to hush her.

When he lifted his head, he gave her a contrite look. "Sorry. I can't explain anything now. Being here with your family tonight has given me a glimpse of something that I didn't know I was missing."

His admission struck a chord in her. What kind of upbringing did he have? He'd told her about the tragedy and the things that had torn his family apart. But his aunt had surely provided for him… Yet maybe she was a bit like Rory's own grandfather had been. More concerned about image than about them.

"I'm glad to hear that," she said softly. "I was sort of pushing you to talk but I get that we can't now."

"I'm willing to look away for a few minutes but if you two are going to be making out, I'm not sure I can handle it," Dash interjected.

Everyone laughed and Rory couldn't help but blush because she knew that his comment was directed toward her and Kit. But her embarrassment faded as the group brought the mics over and song choices were made. Rory sat on the couch next to Dash as Elle and Kit sang "Rock Your Body" by *NSYNC.

"You were right to move out, ladybug," Dash murmured. "I was worried this would be too much, but I can see now that you're becoming your own woman."

She tipped her head against the back of the

couch and looked over at her older brother. "Thanks. I know I was right."

"Brat."

"Seems to run in our family," she said with a laugh.

The party continued until almost midnight and Rory hadn't laughed that much in a long time. When everyone was gone and it was just her and Kit, she knew it was time for that talk she'd been thinking about all night.

But now that the time was here, she wasn't sure she was ready to face what was to come.

If finding the letter in his father's papers had started him questioning everything that his aunt and father had told him about Declan's accident, this evening had just muddled things even more.

Making it damn near impossible to keep the heat of hatred that he'd had for Dash Gilbert alive.

Because tonight, after watching him tease his fiancée, and duet with his sister and cousin, it was hard to keep that image of a man who was ruthless in his mind. Rory wasn't going to know what had happened during the car crash. Dash had said he didn't want to add to her trauma of that night, but next week when he spoke to Con and Dash, he'd learn more, hopefully.

But he was going to have to tell her who his brother was and try to find out more of what had happened at the winter gala, *before* the accident occurred.

"So...?" Rory was sitting in the big armchair catty-corner to the fireplace, with her legs curled up underneath her.

"I'm not sure where to start." That much was totally true. He'd made this into something bigger than he wanted it to be by his reactions earlier. And maybe if he'd been better prepared to let go of his vengeance he wouldn't have.

"Tell me about your family. I don't know anything about them," she said.

He moved to sit on the couch corner closest to her. Then glanced around the living room, seeing the work they'd done together to bring this room to life. This room could be a stepping stone to his future. If only he handled this right.

"You know my brother died, and then my dad turned to alcohol, which eventually led to his death." Starting with the easiest part of his past. Just facts. He tried to keep his emotions in check but it was hard.

"Yes, I do. I'm sorry about that. How old were you?"

"I was a freshman in college. I was on the West Coast when it happened. I flew back when my aunt called to let me know what happened," he said.

"I was a freshman, too, when everything happened to me," she told him. "It's funny that our lives were both changed at eighteen."

More like ironic. She didn't know it was the same accident that had shaped them. "Yeah."

That was all he could say to that. It was harder than he'd anticipated, going back to that time in his mind. The grief and anger and panic. All of those emotions had swamped him and it was only the fact that his father was always drunk that had kept Kit from turning to drink himself.

"So eventually it was just you and your aunt?" she probed carefully.

"Yes. I dropped out of Berkeley and moved back to Boston. Our family business was shattered and I took night classes at a community college while working to try to save it."

He looked over at her. She watched him with so much pure emotion on her face that it made his insides hurt. She shouldn't be looking at him with compassion and empathy. Not now.

Not when he'd taken what was left of his family company and reshaped it to go after hers.

He'd used those long days to form a plan with his aunt in their shared grief. One that would take everything from the Gilberts in return for what they'd lost.

"Kit, that's so..." She trailed off.

"What?"

"Sad. So sad." Turning toward him, she said softly, "You should have been enjoying college and making mistakes and finding yourself, and instead you had to come back and step into someone else's life."

Someone else's? "How do you figure?"

"Well, you didn't want to run your family company, did you? You had to because that's what your aunt and father needed you to do. You never had a chance to know if it was what you wanted."

He hadn't ever considered that before. At this point, ten years into running the company, he couldn't think of what else his life might have been. Until this moment, he'd just assumed that even if Dec had lived, he'd still be where he was.

But now he wasn't so sure.

"I guess so," he said.

"Did your aunt help you run it?" she asked.

"No. That's not her thing, really. She's good at socializing and finding the right connections. And I used those connections to build our business up from nothing," he explained.

"So you two are a team?"

"We are," he said. But he wasn't sure if they would continue to be. He knew there was no way Aunt Mal would accept Rory.

"So why haven't I met her?" she asked. "That's the thing I can't figure out. I know you're busy and that our relationship is new, but you and I...well, I think we have something real. Or am I just kidding myself?"

THIRTEEN

THAT WAS THE thing about Rory, she never pulled any punches. Sitting in that chair cross-legged, watching him with those wide eyes of hers so full of emotion. He wanted to step up. Be the man she needed him to be. And fear made it so hard for him to just let go of the past.

"This is real for me, too," he said gruffly, the words torn from somewhere deep inside him.

"Okay. Then we can take the rest slow," she murmured. "I just needed to know you were on the same pages as I am. It's okay if you're not."

"I am, Rory. It's just family is complicated and my life...well, it's been on one path until you."

"Mine, too," she said.

"What path was that?"

"One where I thought the only way I could prove I was independent was to do everything by myself," she said softly, tipping her head to the side.

"And now you don't?"

She got up and walked over to him. "It's that I don't have to. I know I can do it on my own, but it's nicer with you."

He thought about that as she sat down on his lap, putting her arms around his shoulders. Life was so much fucking better with her in it. That was a given. But there had never been a time in his life where he'd put anything other than family first.

He wanted to come clean but he had to ask himself if that was more for his peace of mind than anything else. Dash and Con had been clear that Rory could recall parts of the night of the gala. The night his brother attacked her.

Would confessing he was Declan's brother make things worse for her? He didn't know.

And if he were being totally honest, tonight was one of the few times in his life when he'd felt this kind of comfort and peace from another person. He cared a lot about Rory and there was a big part of him that just wanted more happy memories before he admitted he was related to her worst nightmare.

Just a few more days to enjoy this budding

relationship the two of them had stumbled into. A few more moments of being accepted for who he was, not what he could do for someone else.

He wrapped his arms around her waist, knowing he should follow her lead and let this conversation go. But a part of him, the part that knew he'd lied to her about key things, wasn't sure that was the right path.

But then she shifted on his lap, pulling that long skirt of hers to her waist before straddling him.

He leaned back and looked up at her. She rested her hands on the back of the couch as she sat down on him. Her mouth found his in one of those deep, tongue-tangling, soul-jarring kisses that made thought impossible. All he felt was Rory draped over him. He was hot and hard with the aching sweetness that came only from being aroused by her.

He wanted more. Resting his hands on her hips, he found that she wasn't wearing any underwear and a red haze went over him. So he just cupped her butt, running her finger along the furrowed crack between her cheeks.

She shivered delicately in his arms and ground her hips down, her center rubbing against the ridge of his cock through the fabric of his pants. He groaned. He wanted her now.

"Are you okay like this? I love you on top of me and in a minute, I'm not going to be thinking about anything but how good you feel on my cock. So if we need to shift around…"

She bit the lobe of his ear and then whispered directly into it, her hot breath sending a shaft of heat through him. "I've been working to strengthen my thighs, so…we should be good."

He could barely contain himself as she pushed the suspenders down his arms and undid the buttons of his shirt. Her fingers were on his chest, her nails digging into his muscles as he was fumbling between them to free his erection.

She smiled with sensual delight as he scooted around on the couch underneath her until he was comfortable. Then he put his hands on her waist and lifted her until she was positioned so the tip of his dick was at the entrance of her pussy.

Rory braced her hands on his shoulders, which put her breasts right in front of his face. The buttons on the blouse she wore were strained by her position and he let go of her hips to undo the button that looked like it was about to pop open and then undid the rest of them as she slowly lowered herself on to him.

But the position was wrong and she got frustrated, so he shifted himself underneath her and then put his hands on her waist again, bringing her down on him. She moaned as he slid into her, and when he was fully inside, their eyes met and he knew he wasn't letting her go.

He didn't care what happened the night of the accident or who her brother was. Rory was *his*. Not just for tonight but forever.

She rode him, throwing her shoulders back and moving on him slowly at first but then picking up speed. He undid her bra and fondled her breasts underneath it as she gained momentum and then swung toward him with each of her thrusts. She moved faster and harder on him and he found her nipple, sucking it deep into his mouth.

He felt his own climax building and knew he needed more. Taking her hips in his hands, he held her to him as he thrust up into her with frenzied strokes until she cried out his name and he felt her body pulsing on his cock. He drove into her a few more times until he came in a long, hard rush. Emptying himself and cradling her to him as she collapsed against him.

Her head on his shoulder, her breath brushing against his neck.

He held her to him, not letting anything but Rory into his mind at this moment.

Rory realized that she couldn't change what was going to happen between herself and Kit no matter how much worrying or planning she tried to do. The accident had been the kind of concrete proof that her life was on a path that she wasn't really choosing. But she could make the most of the journey.

Kit lifted her off his lap and sat her on the couch next to him about the time her thighs were beginning to shake. She looked down at her body, seeing the scars and the weakness but also feeling the strength. She'd changed in ways she'd never guessed she could and part of it was because of Kit.

He made her want to be whole—not perfect—just whole. That was a new way of thinking.

"Are you okay?" he asked tenderly.

"Yes. I think my thighs are going to feel it tomorrow," she said with a smile. Adjusting her skirt, she pulled it back down her legs, taking off her shirt and the unfastened the bra as well.

Kit stared at her breasts and then reached down to cup them. "You're so pretty."

She flushed. "Thank you. You are, too."

"Thanks. I don't know if anyone has said that before."

She laughed. No, she guessed they wouldn't have. Kit was pretty to her, but there was something rough and serious about him as well.

"I'm glad," she murmured as he lifted her into his arms and carried her into the bedroom. "Are you staying tonight?"

"Unless you don't want me to."

"I want you to."

He set her on her feet and she had to use him for balance when she took her skirt off. Her legs weren't as strong as they'd been earlier in the night and she was okay with that. For once the weakness had come from her actions. Not from the inaction of the coma.

In her mind that made a big difference. They got ready for bed not really talking. Her mind was buzzing with the excitement and affection that came from being in Kit's arms. She had no idea what he was thinking about.

But she felt she'd pushed him enough for the evening and let him be. When they were in bed and she was cuddled against his side, she felt his hands in her hair.

"I live in a big cookie-cutter mansion in a suburb of Boston. The house is the kind that I know my dad dreamed we'd live in before everything went to crap," he confided. "It's not very personal. I had an interior design firm decorate it for me, and when I'm there I pretty much just sleep and sometimes eat standing up in the kitchen."

She turned her head up so she could see his profile. "That house doesn't really sound like it suits you."

"It doesn't? I guess I figured it's where a CEO should live," he said as he wrapped a strand of her hair around his finger.

"Kind of like me and Gilbert Manor," she told him. "I should have fit in there but I don't. Not anymore."

"I'm glad. I really like this version of Rory," he said.

"Me, too." She'd been volunteering and figuring out what she wanted her life to look like. But Kit had a job and a house he didn't like. "What kind of home suits you? You said your place here isn't really you either."

He shrugged, which shifted her on his chest,

her nose going into the light dusting of hair on it where the scent of his cologne lingered on his skin. She took a deep breath.

"I'm not sure. I like your place and the stuff we've been doing around here to make it into a home. But I'm not really into the antiques like you are," he said.

"Why not?"

He didn't answer her for a long moment and she wondered why.

"Just feels too fancy for me."

"Too fancy?" she asked. "You just said you are a CEO. You can have whatever you want. You've worked hard and you deserve it."

He let his breath out in one long exhale and then moved around so that their eyes met. "I don't think that I do deserve it. I'm sort of on the path that I think my father wanted for my brother."

Her heart ached for Kit. She put her hands on either side of his face. "You've done them proud. It's time to start living for yourself."

"I'm not sure I know how," he admitted hoarsely.

There was a rawness to his tone that made her wanted to hug him tightly to her. "Well, as it turns out, I've got some experience in that. I can help you out."

"Would you do that?" he asked.

"Yes, I would. It's the least I could do for you, Kit, in return for all you've given me."

He kissed her then, pulling her fully under his body, and made love to her slowly and completely. She drifted to sleep afterward, and for once her sleep wasn't full of dreams of what she'd never had—they were dominated by Kit and their life in the future.

Kit left Rory sleeping and walked into town to Lulu's coffee shop to get some pastries and coffee for them both. He didn't let himself dwell too much on the fact that last night he'd made a decision for his future and he wasn't sure what his aunt was going to think of it.

But he *was* going to have to talk to her. And while he could use her busy social schedule as an excuse, the truth was that the moment he'd started sleeping with Rory, he should have let his aunt know that he wasn't as committed to their plan of ruining the Gilbert family as he'd been before.

There was a chill in the air as he walked back to Rory's place. It was early November and he couldn't help but feel that everything was coming together in his life. The accident that had taken his brother's life had been on December 12. Not too much longer until the eleven-year anniversary of his death. It was hard to think about a decade without Dec.

Last night was the first time he'd admitted to himself that he had been living the life that he thought that Dec would have wanted for himself. But they hadn't been close when Dec died, so Kit really had no idea what his brother had wanted.

Like Rory said, it was time to start living for himself.

He wasn't paying attention when he turned onto the street that he and Rory lived on but when he got to his house, he noticed his aunt's car in the drive. She got out when she saw him.

"Nephew," she said.

"Aunt Mal. I wasn't expecting you today," he said, going over and giving her a hug.

"I figured. You haven't been in Boston lately and you've been avoiding my texts. So I decided to come to you," she informed him.

"I'm glad. I'll let you into my house and then I have to go and give this coffee to my friend," he said.

"What friend?" she asked as he unlocked the door and motioned for her to go inside.

"Rory Gilbert."

Aunt Mal looked down her nose at him. "So you're still working that angle?"

"No. I'm not working her at all. I like her, Aunt Mal. Also, I have some questions about the Gilberts' involvement in our family's misfortune."

"Okay. Like what?" she asked.

"Well, for one thing, Dad and Dec were sent a letter telling them that the factory was closing and offering them work in Boston," Kit said. "That's different than what we were led to believe. Just makes me wonder what else we might have wrong."

She crossed her arms over her chest. "I see. Well, I guess we'll have to talk to the family."

"That's what I'm thinking. Get their side and see where there are discrepancies," he said.

"And you want to do all of this for the girl?"

He wasn't sure he liked the way his aunt referred to Rory. "She's a woman. And we've been dating. I like her, Aunt Mal. A lot."

His aunt stared at him for a long time before nodding slowly and then smiled. "It's about time you started dating seriously. I'd love to meet her."

Kit let out a breath he hadn't been aware he'd been holding. He'd been so afraid that Aunt Mal wouldn't want him to date Rory. But instead she was cool with it. How crazy was that? "I know she wants to meet you, too. Family is important to her."

"As it is to us," Aunt Mal reminded him. "We both only have each other. That poor woman was left in a coma and the cousin scarred. Seems to me that both of our families were impacted by that night and Dash's decisions."

They had been.

"Based on what we'd been told, I agree. It's why we started Palmer Industries," he said.

"It was. You were so determined to make things right."

The more Kit had gotten to know Dash the less he felt like the other man had made a rash decision to ruin his father, but then again he'd been in his early twenties that night. He might have done something out of temper instead of thinking it through.

"We were. I haven't told Rory that Dec was my brother or about our connection," he admitted to his aunt. He was anxious to go and get Rory so she could meet his aunt.

"Probably a smart decision for now," she said. "But what are you going to do? We can't pretend forever."

"No, we can't. I am planning to tell her everything soon. I have a meeting on Wednesday with Conrad and Dash and I'm going to ask them about the night of the ball. I told you that Rory was attacked by her date. I need to find out if it was Dec."

She narrowed her eyes. "Your brother was always honorable. I'm sure that the Gilbert men have it wrong."

He hoped so, but he didn't know either of them to lie. Not even old man Gilbert, who'd admittedly been arrogant and had closed the factory without much warning to the other townspeople, but still he hadn't lied.

The only lie that Kit knew of was the one his father had told him. And in truth he couldn't be certain his father hadn't been honest or if Kit had just interpreted what he'd said that way. There was a lot to sort out. But it was worth it if he meant he and Rory could be together.

He left his aunt at his house and walked down to Rory's place. She'd said she wanted to meet his family but he wasn't sure she'd be ready to do it this morning. Aunt Mal was a lot to take and he hadn't really done much to get Rory ready for her.

FOURTEEN

KIT'S AUNT MAL wasn't at all what Rory had been expecting. She was so sleek and sophisticated, and Rory couldn't help but feel she wasn't measuring up in Aunt Mal's eyes. In fact there was something about the woman that reminded her of her grandfather.

The older man had strict rules about everything to do with keeping up the Gilbert image in a way that made it easier to understand Aunt Mal. Just pretending she was like Grandfather was the simplest way.

She wanted Kit's only close relative to like her, so when Kit was called out of town on business, she invited Mallory over for brunch. Rory and Kit had been growing closer and closer, so much so that Rory had also extended an offer for him and his aunt to join her family for Thanksgiving dinner at Gilbert Manor.

Conrad had been working on the menu for

the last few weeks and Rory couldn't wait to see what her cousin came up with.

The doorbell rang and Rory walked to open it, realizing how far she'd come physically since she'd moved into the house. She still had to use her walking stick but not frequently and her physical therapist was moving her to a non-medical gym for light workouts as her strength returned.

She opened the door to see it was a cloudy day and some snow flurries swirled around Mallory. Kit's aunt wore a fake fur leopard-print coat and a smart-looking pillbox-style hat over her slicked-back, black hair. Rory noticed that Mallory had on pointy-toed stiletto-heeled boots and for a minute she was tempted to apologize that she was only wearing her best black jeans and a silk pussy-bow blouse.

"Hello, Mallory. I'm so glad you could make it today," Rory said as she stepped back and gestured for the other woman to enter.

"Of course, darling. I wouldn't have missed the chance to have a little girl time with you," she replied. She undid her coat and handed it to Rory, who hung it in the coat closet while Mallory put her hat on the table near the door. Soon they were seated at her kitchen table and chatting over the delicious quiche that Conrad had walked Rory through making, alongside a simple salad and mimosas. If ever there were an occasion when she needed some alcohol to keep the conversation going it was this one.

"Kit told me the two of you have been working on this place. It's quaint."

"Thanks," Rory said. "Kit's been a real help. He's really good at helping out but not taking over the job. It's been important for me to complete projects on my own as I regain my strength." Rory smiled at her guest, not bothered by the *quaint* label. She liked her house and when she looked around, she could see every part of it was filled with memories of her and Kit together.

"He is very good at that. When his brother was killed, Kit came home, determined to take over where Declan left off."

"*Declan?* I didn't realize that was his brother's name," Rory said. Declan Orr was the name of the man who'd been her date the night of the winter gala. The man who'd been drunk and angry and wouldn't stop when she had said she didn't want to have sex with him. She pushed her mimosa away and looked down at her plate. Rory hadn't expected that name to be triggering. But it was. She noticed her hands were shaking and brought them together in her lap and laced them together.

"Are you okay, my dear?" Mallory asked. "I thought you knew that Kit was Declan Orr's brother."

Shocked, Rory could only stare at the other woman. What was she saying? "How? I thought his last name was Palmer."

She was trying to piece this together and honestly it was difficult to even figure out what his aunt was saying.

"Your brother ruined Orr Industries after the crash," Mallory said. "Just bought up all the shares and then dismantled it. Kit had no choice but to use his mother's maiden name and start a new company. He built it from the ground up."

Rory felt almost sick to her stomach hearing this.

"Kit told me his father drank too much, leading to his death and the need for Kit to take over the company," she said, not sure why Mallory was telling her all this and if what she was saying was even true.

"He did. After your brother took everything from him," Mallory pointed out. "I guess everyone has been keeping you in the dark."

Had they been? Dash could be ruthless—that was a given, but would he have ruined Kit's father just because Declan had attacked her? She had no idea and would need to talk to him. It was somehow easier to think of confronting Dash than talking to Kit.

Dash had been hurt and angry after the crash. She was glad he'd been her protector and had defended her while she'd been in the coma. And she also understood how her brother's mind worked.

But then there was Kit.

The Kit she knew who had lied to her. There was no two ways about that. He'd never mentioned that he was related to the man who had caused the accident that put her in a coma. Not even when she'd mentioned that a car accident had set both of them on this path.

The same accident. It was hard on him, too; his life had changed that night as well. She knew that and wanted to be sympathetic, but she was hurt. Then she remembered how hard it was for him to talk about the loss of his father and brother. Was there more to this than the other woman was making out? Could she even believe her over Dash?

"I'm sorry, Mallory...but I'm not buying this," she said.

"That's up to you, but it is the truth, my dear. Maybe you should ask your brother."

"I will," Rory responded tightly. Taking out her phone, she texted Dash, asking if he had time to see her.

He texted back that he was at Gilbert Manor and could be at her place in a few minutes.

"My brother is on his way."

Rory put her phone down. She wanted to call Kit. To demand he tell her if his aunt was telling the truth. Had he come into her life just to use her? She didn't dwell on the fact that she wasn't sure if she'd given him any information he could use to hurt Dash.

Instead, she just sat there waiting for her brother to arrive, trying to hold herself together. She'd wanted to be alive and to feel all the emotions. But in her mind she'd seen only the good and the happy side of falling in love. She'd never let herself even consider that love could hurt. Not like this.

Kit got halfway to Boston before realizing that the meeting wasn't urgent and he could go and join Rory and his aunt for brunch after all.

His aunt had been...well, *off* since he'd introduced her to Rory. Normally Aunt Mal stayed out of the day-to-day running of the company but lately she'd been in the office all the time and on the phone to Kit daily. He was afraid she thought that he was going to abandon her, which he'd never do.

It had been the two of them for so long that he understood where she was coming from. But after his discussion with Dash and Conrad at Rory's Halloween party, he was confident that his family's version of events was far from the full truth. He'd hoped to talk to the Gilbert men and get more information on what had happened that night, but because of Aunt Mal being in the office so much Kit hadn't had time.

But today he was determined to get this sorted out. Last night when Rory had been sleeping in his arms, Kit had finally admitted to himself that he loved her. He hadn't been sure what love would feel like or if he'd ever experience it, but that was definitely the vibe he was getting around Rory.

He wanted to be with her all the time and when he wasn't, all he did was think about her. He had to get the past history between their

families settled so they could have a future together and that was all he was focused on.

Kit left the highway and drove toward Gilbert Corners. It was one of those cloudy autumn days that warned winter wasn't too far
away. A light dusting of snow fell and gathered on the side of the road, painting the town
in a soft white coat. Kit had so many complex
feelings toward this town. He remembered the
first time he'd met Rory when they were kids,
the good times with his family until his mom
got sick and died. Then the sadness when his
brother was killed and they'd had to leave.

He'd never thought he would drive through
Gilbert Corners and be thinking of it as his
home. But he did. And he knew that was because of Rory.

His original intent of buying up property
to keep Gilbert International from developing
them had been just a move to block Dash. But
now he saw those properties as an investment
in the future. In a town where if things went
well today, he and Rory would marry and raise
a family.

He stopped his car to the side of the road
as he approached the bridge where Dec had

been killed. He wished that he could talk to his brother and find out if he had been the man to attack Rory. But he couldn't. He was almost afraid to ask Conrad and Dash because if they confirmed it, he would be broken.

He'd spent the last decade trying to avenge his brother's death. To make up for the wrong that had been done to their family by the Gilberts. But if it turned out that Dec's actions had been responsible, that Dec had assaulted the woman he now loved...he wasn't sure how he'd go on. How could he ask Rory to be his wife if his brother had done such horrible things to her that had led to both of their families being torn apart?

He rubbed the back of his neck, putting his head against the steering wheel. To say he was conflicted was an understatement.

Sighing, he put the car back in gear and drove toward Rory's house. When he turned on their street he noticed Aunt Mal's car in her driveway but also Dash's. He parked his car in his own drive and hurried down the walk toward Rory's.

Why was Dash there? Had something happened to Rory? She'd decided to stop using her cane in the house. He knew she'd gotten much stronger, but the floors were hardwood and she had been wearing socks as the weather had turned cooler. Had she slipped?

He was in a panic as he raced up her drive and opened the door. Not even bothering to knock. But when he stepped into the hallway, he heard arguing and Rory's voice was the loudest of them all.

"I don't know what your brother told you, Mallory, but Declan was definitely the man who attacked me that night."

"And he paid with his life!" Mallory said. "Are you sure you weren't just overwrought with nerves? My nephew never had to force a girl—"

"Her dress was torn, exposing her breasts, and there were bruises and marks on her skin," Dash bit out the words coldly.

Kit raced down the hall and everyone turned toward him as he walked into the kitchen. Rory's eyes met his and he knew she was looking to see if he'd known these details. He hadn't. He was repulsed to hear the specifics of her brutal attack.

"Kit, I'm glad you're here. They are trying to make the death of your brother his own fault,"

Aunt Mallory said. "As if his death meant nothing or was okay."

"I'm sure they aren't saying that," Kit said. "There's a lot of confusion about that night."

"*Is* there?" Rory asked, her tone steeled and sharp. "There is also come confusion about who you are. Is it Kit Palmer or Kit Orr?"

The fact that Mallory didn't like Dash had been obvious since the moment he'd walked into the kitchen. Dash had come over to Mallory; and Rory had for one brief moment seen a side to her brother that she'd never glimpsed before.

"Mallory Orr...you're Kit's aunt?" he asked. It had taken a few minutes to clarify, while Rory stood there in shock. She half listened to the two of them and realized that Mallory and Dash had met before. But Kit hadn't ever met her brother before this year.

As unrealistic as it was, she had hoped he'd be shocked by everything. But he wasn't. He had known about all of these connections. She wanted to ask if he knew his brother had attacked her. If he'd made love to her knowing that the man who'd caused the drama that night, which had led to the car accident that had stolen ten years of her life, was Declan.

But she didn't.

She *couldn't*.

Rory wanted to be alone when they talked. She needed to look into his eyes and hear what he had to say. Listen for the truth amid all the stories he'd told her since the moment they'd met.

God, she'd played right into his hands, hadn't she?

"Kit? I asked who you are," she said in a strangled tone.

She was struggling to hold herself together. Oh, how she wished she could be smart and cool the way that both Dash and Mallory were in this moment. But that was impossible. Kit seemed at a loss and there was a hint of sadness… Was there? Or was she just looking at him and seeing something her heart desperately wanted to?

"I'm legally Kit Palmer but I was born Orr. I had to change my name after you and Gilbert International destroyed what was left of Orr Industries. I couldn't get a business loan nor would anyone even talk to me about working with them." Kit's voice was totally flat and emotionless. Simply stating facts.

"See," Mallory huffed out. "You want to blame Declan for everything that happened but *you* ruined us."

"Declan ruined you," Dash said. "He behaved horribly when he was told he'd be given a job in Boston. He and your father didn't want that. They wanted to run the factory here. But economically it wasn't feasible."

Her brother elaborated on the business dynamics, but Rory didn't understand it or care. She couldn't stop looking at Kit. She'd heard what he said but the truth was so much more. He might have had to use a different name in business, but once he'd slept with her he should have told her.

"Rory?" Kit asked.

"I don't care about the business stuff. I hate that you lied to me. That you didn't one time tell me who you really were. Even after I told you what I went through," she said to Kit. Not even looking at Dash or Mallory because they hadn't hurt her the way that Kit had.

"I didn't want to hurt you again," he gritted out. "How would it benefit you to know I was related to the man who'd hurt you so deeply?"

"It wouldn't have, but you should have told

me," she said. Dash came over and put his arm around her. "You should have been honest when you first got here."

"I couldn't. All my life I'd been told one version of the events of the night of the gala. The version we'd heard. Dash's actions I had seen firsthand, so that was the only part I knew for certain."

"What had you been told about the gala?" Dash asked.

"That my father and brother went there expecting to be announced as the new owners and head of the factory," Kit replied. "But instead your grandfather told them they were out and he was closing the factory."

Then he shoved his hand through his hair and shook his head. "But I now know that wasn't true. Going through my father's papers I found a letter from your grandfather with an offer for them to be transferred to the Boston offices and given generous salaries."

Kit turned toward his aunt. "At the time, I assumed you were not aware of the letter. But now I'm not so sure." He narrowed his eyes at Mallory. "*Did* you know about the offer?"

She shrugged. "It wasn't what had been

promised. They were meant to own the factory, not still work for Gilbert."

"Aunt Mal, we've made a similar offer to some of our workers in other situations," he reminded her, then turned back to Dash. "Given that, I wanted to ask you and Conrad about the gala itself and what had happened to Rory. I didn't know...we didn't know...that Dec had behaved that way."

"Are you sure he did what they are saying?" Mal asked Kit.

"Yes, Aunt Mal. Rory is telling the truth. Declan attacked her," he said.

"Then on behalf of our family, please accept our apology," Mallory said. She looked horrified as the details were being revealed.

Dash shoved his hands into his pockets, rocking back on his heels. "No one could have known about the assault but your brother. Your father had left earlier in the evening."

"What did happen? I have only snatches of clear memories," Rory said. "I don't mean just with Declan and me, but after that."

Mallory, Kit and Rory all turned toward Dash. Her brother took a deep breath. Rory wasn't entirely sure she was ready to hear about that night. Her memories of it were fragmented and Elle had suggested that it might be her mind's way of protecting her.

"Con got Dec first and yanked him off Rory. I arrived, pulling Con off him as Grandfather and a few other guests followed," Dash explained. "Grandfather was horrified at the spectacle and ordered us into the study. He demanded to know what happened. Dec suggested that Rory had led him on…and we had a fight. Grandfather wanted us to apologize and Rory and Declan to 'date' in public to make things look right. We refused and left."

Dash squeezed her tight as Rory was shaking and tears were rolling down her face. Images were jumbled together in her mind.

"Dec followed us, cursing the Gilberts. I'm not sure if he lost control of his car or rammed us, but he hit the back of my car as we were on the bridge. Both cars flipped and rolled. Con was thrown from ours as he wasn't wearing a seat belt. Rory was knocked unconscious. I got out as the emergency vehicles arrived. Your brother was mortally wounded."

Dash held her close as shudders wracked her

body. Mallory and Kit looked at each other, their faces pale. "I think you two should leave," Rory said.

FIFTEEN

KIT DIDN'T WANT to leave until he could talk to Rory, but the look on her face made it clear she wanted him gone. Aunt Mal turned on her heel, walking down the hall and out of Rory's house. Dash looked as cold and ruthless as Kit had always thought the other man to be.

Rory wouldn't meet his gaze, so Kit took a deep breath. "I'm sorry you had to find out this way."

"But not sorry you kept it from me?" Rory asked quietly.

"No. I didn't know you well. Or Dash, or anything about the Gilbert family except what Aunt Mal and I had been told and what I'd observed myself from being in the business world," Kit said, shoving his hands into the pockets of his pants and balling them into fists. "You were a stranger to me."

"I was," Rory admitted. "One who walked

up to you and asked you to pretend to be someone else. But we stopped pretending the moment you started sleeping with me. I think you
owed me the truth."

Dash's face tightened even more and Kit
knew that this was a conversation he didn't
want to have in front of Rory's brother. But he
wasn't going to back down from this. Not now.
"You're right. I went home and dug through
all of my father's old paperwork and found that
letter from your grandfather. It made me realize that not everything I took for fact was true.
And when I heard about my brother... I believed you. I still do. But accepting that someone I loved could assault someone..."

Dash rubbed the back of his neck. "This is
complicated and I don't think we're going to
resolve it—"

"We're not," Rory interrupted him.

"Just let me finish this and then I'll leave.
We hadn't been told any of that about what my
brother did to you. When you told me your
date—my brother—had attacked you... I had
no idea what to do next. I stopped thinking of
revenge and wanted answers. I knew I couldn't
have a future with you until everything was
cleared up. I wanted to know everything, to be

sure I could talk to you about it without hurting you all over again."

Cleared up was such a small way to frame what Rory had been put through. What his brother's actions had put both of their families through. But at this moment it was all he had. His mind was a whirlpool of jumbled thoughts and there was too much to process right now.

"I agree," Dash said. "You and I need to talk about the business side of things, but this stuff with my sister...you are going to have to make it right. It's all I can do not to kick your ass for lying to her and using her."

"I didn't use her. I've never used you, Rory. I might not have told you everything, but I never deceived you," he said. "You were the first person who I was wholly myself with. But I am deeply sorry for hurting you."

He knew that there was nothing else to say right now. He didn't want to sound defensive and there was no other way to frame this in his mind. He turned and walked down the hallway, seeing the hardwood floors that he'd helped Rory stain and seal. This house had felt like a beginning.

But he'd known even at the time that a solid foundation couldn't be built on half-truths. It was one thing for him to try to convince them that he hadn't lied, but in his heart he knew he had.

He'd been afraid to tell her everything, afraid that once she knew who he truly was, she'd see all the darkest parts of his soul and he wouldn't be good enough for her.

His aunt was sitting in her car. She got out when he approached.

"About time you got here," she said. "We need to talk."

"I agree." They went into his house, and when they were seated in the formal living room, he looked over at his aunt.

Some of the arrogance and pride that had always been so much a part of her was dimmed. She seemed smaller than she had earlier, which was exactly how he felt.

"I'm sorry I went behind your back. I was afraid you were forgetting our family and now... I know you weren't," Aunt Mal said. "That your brother would behave that way is unconscionable. I can never condone what Dash Gilbert did to us, but for the first time I think I can almost understand it."

"Thanks for apologizing. I could never forget you, Aunt Mal, never. You are the only one who has had my back for the last ten years. But you hurt Rory intentionally and that's going to take me time to forgive."

"I understand. I hope you can. You're all I have, too," she said brokenly.

For the first time, he saw her age. And that she was barely holding herself together.

"Did Dad know? I can't imagine that he did."

"I don't think so. He wasn't happy about the offer of jobs in Boston but he was preparing to move there and take the new job. When the job was rescinded, it destroyed him," Aunt Mal said. "It seemed like such a cruel move from the Gilberts after losing Dec."

Only knowing what the three of them had at the time, it had seemed that way. He was sad and angry about Declan. His father's drinking made so much more sense now.

"What's next?" Aunt Mal asked. "We've bought all this property in Gilbert Corners."

"I've been talking to local business owners. I think if we can work with the Gilberts, it might be the way forward. Take the tragedy of that night and turn it into a strength here for the town and our families."

"I'm sorry I betrayed you to Rory. If I'd

known what Declan had done——" Aunt Mal broke off on a sob.

He went to sit next to her, hugging her. He wished she hadn't as well, but it was past time to come clean with Rory and Kit knew he had been too afraid to risk losing her to do it.

"Is there anything I can do to make up for this?" she asked hopefully.

"I'm not sure what you *could* do to fix it," Kit admitted after a long moment. He saw that she was sincere and contrite, and while he still wasn't ready to forgive her, he realized that it had been a scared woman who had gone to Gilbert Corners.

"Honestly? Me either," his aunt said.

He released a deep breath. "All I know for sure is that I am going to do everything I can to win Rory back."

"I'll apologize to her again," Aunt Mal said.

"I think it's going to take more than an apology."

"Just tell me what you need and I'll be there," she promised.

Rory felt numb in a way she hadn't since she'd first realized that Dash and Elle had been lying to her. That had been months ago. She'd honestly thought there was nothing else from the past that could hurt her.

Oh, how wrong she'd been.

She'd had vague memories of what had happened the night of the gala but hearing Dash's abbreviated version had brought it all back. But now, despite the inner turmoil she was feeling, knowing she was safe and that her family had rallied around her, gave her strength. And the bad memories she had of Declan weren't as harsh as they might have been if she didn't have the distance of all the time she'd been in the coma.

Maybe her brain had been doing what it needed to in order to protect her.

"Are you okay?" Dash asked.

She looked up at her brother. "I have no idea. I'm not sure I really even know what okay feels like."

"What can I do?" he asked.

"Nothing. This is something I have to figure out on my own." She wanted to be angry with Kit and she was. He never should have lied to her about who he really was, but she could understand why he had at first. But the moment they'd talked about how car accidents had changed them… For the life of her she couldn't justify him staying silent.

"I hate this. I want to do something to fix this. I'm so sorry I had to bring up so much of what happened the night of the gala. Want me to call Elle or your therapist?" Dash asked.

Her big brother was doing his thing. Sweeping in to protect her. But she wasn't all right and doubted she was going to be for a while. She did need to talk to someone but right now she just wanted to sit here and cry. To think about how she'd gone from feeling like she'd figured out her life and her future to being like this again.

It was almost the same way she'd felt when she'd woken from the coma…

"I think Kit was the man who was with me when I woke up," she said.

Dash narrowed his eyes and then nodded. "I think you're right. What was he doing in your room?"

"That's something else I'll have to ask him," she said.

"I feel like part of it is my fault," Dash said. "If I hadn't destroyed Orr Industries, then Kit wouldn't have retaliated."

"How is this your fault?"

"I was the one who went after Orr Industries. That was all me. Then when they tried to move on, I crushed their business."

"Dash."

"Yeah, I know how that sounds. I was angry and you were in a coma, they didn't know if Con was going to live... I wanted the Orr family to be destroyed."

She put her hand on her brother's wrist and squeezed it. She didn't know what to say. She couldn't justify his actions any more than she could Kit's. They had both reacted in anger to a horrible catastrophe. It would be easy to just say it had all been Declan's fault but she knew it was more nuanced.

"I'm sorry, ladybug, for my part in this."

"I know you are. I've never doubted that everything you've done for me over the years is based on love."

"That's true, but I shouldn't have done what I did to Kit's family. I'm going to try to make that right," he said. "Are you okay with that?"

She wrapped her arms around herself. For a minute, she wanted to say no. To strike out at Kit because he'd hurt her. But she'd seen the pain on his face when he'd apologized. He'd never set out to hurt her. That didn't mean she forgave him, but she couldn't condemn him either.

"Of course."

He blew out a breath. "Are you going to…"

"What?" she asked.

"Take him back?"

"I'm not sure," Rory admitted. "I was just starting to feel like I'd found myself. And now I'm questioning things that I didn't before. Did I miss signs that Kit wasn't being truthful because I wanted to believe he was someone he wasn't?"

"I highly doubt that. He wasn't intentionally trying to fool any of us. We all like him. So aside from not telling us he was related to Declan, I can't fault him. He clearly had no idea his brother was capable of that shit. I kind of understand it."

She tipped her head back, closing her eyes. She could understand it, too. But he'd lied to her.

"That still doesn't make it right," Dash said. "But I get it."

"Me, too. I'm not sure where he and I will go from here."

"You'll figure it out. And if you decide you want that man, then you will make him yours," Dash said.

"I'm sorry, but do you mind leaving?" Rory said. "I think I just need to be alone and think things through."

Dash shook his head as he got to his feet. He leaned down and hugged her close. "I'm coming back for dinner and bringing everyone if that's okay."

"Sure. I guess you'll have to tell them what happened."

"No. That's up to you," he said. "I'll just say you need your family."

He wasn't wrong—she did need her family. After Dash left she looked around her house, the one that Kit had helped her renovate and make into her home. Rory saw him everywhere and in all the rooms. She sat on the couch where they'd made love after the Halloween party and felt tears burning her eyes.

She couldn't figure out what to do next, but in her heart she knew that without him even knowing what his brother had done to her, he'd helped heal that part of her.

The knock on his front door was loud, and when Kit walked down the hall to open it, he was not surprised to see Conrad Gilbert standing there. The other man stood on his doorstep in his chef whites, sleeves rolled back to expose his tattooed arms, glowering down at Kit.

Kit took a deep breath. "Are you here to talk or fight?"

"Talk," he said, but the word was bitten out from between his teeth.

"I guess you'd better come in, then," Kit replied, turning and walking down the hall to the kitchen, where he'd been sitting at the table, trying to make some kind of plan to fix the mess he'd made.

He heard the heavy sound of the other man's boots behind him. Conrad dragged out the chair across from Kit and sat down heavily. "So Dash said you're Declan Orr's brother."

"I am," Kit confirmed. "Did he tell you everything?"

"Yeah. That you guys didn't know what your brother had done to Rory and that Dash destroyed your father and your family financially," Conrad said. He rolled his head from side to side as if trying to relieve the tension. "Did he tell you I beat your brother pretty badly?"

"No. Just said you'd pulled him off Rory," Kit said, his own hands flexing. He had so much anger toward his brother and his despicable actions. There was no way to defend what Dec had done.

"Yeah, well, I probably would have killed him if Dash hadn't got us out of the mansion that night. I can't tell you what happened once we were in the car. But I wanted you to know my part."

"Thanks. If I'd been there, I would have done the same to my brother," Kit said. "I can't marry the image of his behavior with the brother I knew. He should never have done that."

"I agree," Conrad bit out. "Listen, I didn't know your brother at all before I pulled him off Rory. But you— I thought I had a handle on you since we'd met recently."

Kit didn't know what to say. Of course he hadn't been lying to them 24/7. "You do. The only thing I kept hidden was my family name."

"Yeah, see, that seems like a big thing. I get it, because I hated my grandfather and didn't want anything to do with him or my family name. He was a total dick. But you hurt Rory and I can't figure out why. What were you going to do, use her to hurt the Gilbert businesses?"

"No. It wasn't like that. I just needed to find

a way to get closer to Dash, see if I could exploit something he'd reveal."

Conrad almost cracked a smile. "You suck at the revenge business."

"I know. It's not really my thing. But I wanted Dash to be held accountable for what he'd done to my family."

Conrad leaned back in his chair. "I think he was, in a way that you didn't realize. Watching Rory in that coma was a constant source of pain for him. And it took years for me to regain my strength and then I ghosted him... So believe me, his life wasn't all that great."

Kit's head hurt from thinking through all the other ways he could have handled meeting Rory again. "From the outside I didn't see it that way."

"We never do," he said. "Fuck. I'm not sure what I was expecting when I came over here. It would be better if you were an asshole. Then I could punch you."

"Sorry."

"I'm not," Con said. "I texted Dash I was coming to see you, so he might show up, too. We never had a chance to talk about the business development in GC."

Kit had already talked to his board of directors and they were going to be doing some community outreach and using the property they owned toward that end. Aunt Mal planned to talk to the different charity boards she was on and get them involved, too. Dash did show up about thirty minutes later and Kit respected the fact that neither man said anything about Rory to him.

They talked about ways to make Gilbert Corners better, and after a few hours both men got up to leave. Dash lingered after Conrad had left.

"What are you going to do about Rory? I assume you're not walking away from her," Dash said.

"I'm not. I don't know if she can ever forgive me for lying to her, but I'm going to stay here and apologize as many times as I have to until she can believe me."

SIXTEEN

FOR THE FIRST few days after everything had happened with Kit, Rory sort of hid out at her house. She'd felt so exposed and raw. The fact that she'd allowed herself—as if her emotions had consulted with her!—to fall for him made her feel...dumb and sad and angry. She'd just sort of stopped going to physical therapy and sat on her couch.

Which worked until Indy and Elle showed up at her house. Rory hadn't showered and as she opened the door to find them standing there, she felt something snap to life inside her.

These two sisters of her heart took one look at her and both hugged her at the same time. And in that instant, the tears that she'd been fighting off and on for days finally fell. She cried as they held her, none of them saying a word. She didn't know how but suddenly the three of them were sitting on her large leather

couch, which she had been contemplating do-
nating since she couldn't stop thinking about
making love with Kit on it.

"I guess you guys know it all," Rory said.

Despite Dash's plans to come to her house the
night that she'd learned everything about Kit,
Rory had put him off. She just didn't want to
dissect everything. She needed time. But the
more time she'd spent alone in her living room,
the more she realized she had no idea how to
move past this kind of betrayal.

"We do," Indy said gently. "Do you need to
talk about it?"

Rory leaned back against the butter-soft
cushions with a sigh. "I don't know. I'm so...
God, I'm feeling too much. One person isn't
meant to have all of these emotions at one
time."

"Yes, you are. There's nothing wrong with
feeling that much," Elle said. "You can be mad
and still care about him. You can be hurt and
not hate him."

"Thanks for saying that. I am just so confused. How could I have spent all that time with
Kit and never once suspected he was lying?"

Indy shrugged, tipping her head to the side
as she considered this. "Part of me thinks it's

because Kit wasn't lying to you. Or he didn't think of it as lying."

Rory hadn't thought of that. "He definitely did at first. He knew I was Dash's sister…"

"So you think he's just a liar?" Elle asked. "Is it because he's Declan's brother you think he's like him?"

Rory chewed her lower lip between her teeth. "No. He's *nothing* like Declan was. Nothing. And I think he's been my white knight coming in the clutch when I needed him."

Elle leaned over to give her a one-armed hug. "So if Kit's not like his brother what does that mean?"

Rory looked down at her lap. She didn't know. All she knew for sure was that the man she'd fallen for hadn't used her. He'd been kind and almost selfless taking her to try things and helping her learn to live again. Was heartbreak the last lesson he had for her?

She realized she was struggling to believe that. And the white-hot anger and betrayal she'd felt when she'd learned who he was had started to cool. Now there was just hurt. And she knew it wasn't just hurt at his lie by omission, but hurt for *him*. Dash had behaved horribly to Kit's family, treating them like they were

responsible for Declan's crime. She could understand and forgive Dash for that. So it followed
she should be able to forgive Kit for harboring
his own animosity toward Dash.

"I just don't know what to do," she said at
last.

"Love is complicated… I'm assuming you
love him. Otherwise none of this would matter. You'd be able to get pissed, give him the
finger and move on."

"Yeah, I think it is. I mean, it's not like I always imagined love to be, because it's not perfect and it's messy. But I miss him. I'm still mad
at him and I really hate that he lied to me, but
I miss him."

"Love is like that," Elle said. "I understood
why Dash couldn't commit to me and it didn't
make me fall out of love with him."

"I remember that," Rory said. Watching
Dash work up the courage to open his heart
had shown her a new side to her brother.

"So, what do you want to do?" Indy asked.
"If you still love him, then how can we help?"

She smiled at the two of them. "You already
have. I was sitting her going over the last time
I saw him and feeling so stupid and betrayed.

But talking to you two has helped me figure out that it's okay to still love him."

"Of course it is," Elle said.

Rory released another sigh. While she honestly wasn't sure how she was going to move past this, she knew she was going to have to talk to Kit. She wanted to know why he'd been at her bedside in the hospital and then see where they could go from here.

After Indy and Elle left, Rory took a shower, and as she sat at her vanity doing her hair, she asked herself if she wanted Kit back because she loved him, or if she was simply afraid to be on her own.

She thought of the last few days when she'd had no trouble being on her own and knew she didn't need a man in her life. She wanted Kit. Just Kit. Life with him was sweeter than anything she could have imagined. But he was going to have to promise to never lie to her again and...she was going to have to figure out if she could believe in him again.

Making up his mind to try to talk to Rory was one thing; actually feeling like he had any idea what to say to her was something else. But Kit didn't want any more time to go by. He'd been sitting in his house up the street from hers, just sort of waiting. He had hoped he'd see her walking by or even at Lulu's, where he'd gotten a dirty look from Lulu when he'd gone in with his laptop and sat at a table in the back hoping to catch a glimpse of Rory.

But she hadn't come in and he'd found that he wasn't as thick-skinned as he'd always thought he was. He'd never meant for anyone—certainly not Rory—to get hurt. Which was how he found himself in Boston at the cemetery, where both Declan and his father were laid to rest. He didn't know what he'd hoped for when he visited their graves but his heart was heavy.

He stooped low next to his father's headstone. It was simple, with just his name and the dates of his birth and death. Aunt Mal had added *Beloved husband, father and brother.* But Kit had never really felt the "beloved father" part. His emotions toward his dad were so tied up in resentment and disappointment at the role that Kit had been forced into.

But knowing what he did now, he was sorry he'd let those last years with his father slip away. As much as Kit hadn't really wanted to take on a leadership role in the family business, being CEO had suited him as nothing else had.

Swallowing a lump in his throat, he put his hand on his father's headstone.

He wanted one more talk with his dad. But that wasn't possible. And really what would he say? *Sorry I was douchey at the end of your life?* Yeah, that wasn't much of a conversation starter. He just quietly apologized to his father, hoping his soul had moved on and maybe he knew that his son finally had let go of the bitterness that he'd been harboring all these years.

He finally stood up, putting his hands in his back pockets as he turned to the other headstone. This...he was dreading. He had so many complicated feelings toward Dec. His older brother. The guy who'd taught him to ride his bike, let him have his first underage sip of beer and had comforted him when their mother had died. No matter that he'd been killed in a car crash, Kit had still looked up to him.

But he couldn't...not anymore. Not after learning what he had done to Rory. He sighed, wanting to kick Dec's headstone but knew that would be useless. Instead, he crouched down and leaned in close as if somehow Dec's spirit was trapped in the headstone. "How could you do that? How could you be the kind of man who took your anger and disappointment out on a girl? That sweet, brave, remarkable girl. I don't pretend to understand any of your actions."

He shook his head as angry tears burned his eyes. "You were always my hero, Dec, not because you were perfect or anything like that. But because you were my brother and I thought you were better than what you became."

Kit stood up, realizing this wasn't going to bring him closure. He was going to have to talk to Rory and hopefully find a way to ask for her forgiveness for Dec's actions. And then he was going to have to let go of this familial bond that he'd used as his guide all these years.

He wiped his eyes with his gloved hand and heard the sound of footsteps behind him. He turned to see Aunt Mal standing there in her fake fur coat and those ridiculously high-heeled boots she loved to wear.

"Thought I'd find you here."

"I'm surprised to be here. I don't know why I came," he said gruffly. Honestly, he didn't. He knew they were both still dead and had been for years. But at the same time he needed to talk to them. Needed to find some understanding and some peace.

"You always thought your father let you

down and that if Dec had lived things would have been different," she said, coming up to him and looping her arm through his. "I think I did, too."

"I wish I'd been easier on Dad."

"I know you do," she said. "I feel the same. I hated that he was so weak and let addiction take control. I still sort of do. But Dec…"

"I can't forgive what he did," Kit blurted. "I'm not sure I'll ever be able to."

"I think we are both entitled to that," she said.

"I just always wanted to be like him," he said at last.

"You've never been like Declan or your father. You've always been the best parts of them. I know you think that they shaped the man you are today and in a way their deaths did, but you have always been a strong, honorable man."

"Except for our revenge plan," he added, but his aunt's words helped him more than he'd expected.

"We stink at revenge. Our big plan to buy up property, fix it up and then make sure that the town thrives so that the Gilberts know they aren't needed… I mean I'm pretty sure other people seeking vengeance would be embarrassed by us," she said ruefully.

He smiled and turned to hug her. "I love you, Aunt Mal."

"I love you, too, nephew."

Kit said goodbye to his aunt and headed back to Gilbert Corners, realizing that he'd done enough waiting. He needed to apologize and see if Rory could forgive him. He loved her and it was time to come clean about how he truly felt.

Kit texted to ask if he could come and see her. Rory responded yes. She had wanted to say more, but really in person would be better than text. She wanted to see his face when he answered her questions.

And she just wanted to see him.

Despite everything that happened between them, she'd finally admitted to herself she was in love with him. She wanted him to be in love with her, too, and she had already come up with too many different scenarios where he might say he cared for her when his feelings were motivated by guilt. He'd lied to her and she knew he felt bad about that. He'd apologized the last time she saw him.

But she hadn't spent ten years of life sleeping not to spend the rest of it wide-awake. So that meant taking risks. It was funny that she'd thought she'd been taking risks all this time, but until she'd admitted to loving Kit she knew she hadn't been.

She'd taken some chances but they'd always been with a safety net. And love was the biggest risk of all.

When the doorbell rang, her heart leaped into her throat, her pulse started racing and she shook her head. She had to calm down. This might be him just coming clean and clearing up the past. He might not be back here because he felt the same way about her as she did about him.

Ugh.

Rory stood at the front door, taking deep breaths and trying to rein in her emotions. She was so nervous and she hadn't been before. Well, other than that one day when she'd walked up to him and told him to pretend to be her friend. She'd been nervous then. The same man was making her feel that way again.

She couldn't help remembering how he'd

smiled and gone along with her. And how that smile had made her feel—

"Rory?"

"Yeah, just need a minute," she yelled through the closed door.

"Take as long as you need."

She turned and rested her back against the wall. That right there was why she knew she wanted to believe every word he said. He was always so calm and understanding. And finally something that she hadn't realized she'd been holding on to was set free.

In the pit of her stomach had been a knot of worry that Kit would be like Declan, now that she knew they were brothers. That stress and anger would make him react the way his brother had. Even though she'd always felt safe with him.

But this was the real Kit. This man who would stand on her doorstep all day waiting until she was ready. Until she was calm.

How could she *not* love this man?

She unlocked the door and opened it. A blast of cold air swept into her foyer and around her. Kit's hair was wet, making it curl around his face. His dark eyes seemed sadder and more serious than ever. He had stubble on his jaw, which just made her palms tingle from wanting to touch him.

Her arms ached to wrap around him and pull him close, but she didn't want to make a disastrous assumption. He might not be anything like his brother but that didn't mean he loved her.

Kit had come to Gilbert Corners and into her life for a very specific reason. She wasn't sure that falling in love with her had any part in his plans.

"Come in," she said after a minute, carefully stepping back and holding the door open for him. The need to touch him was so strong she wasn't sure she was going to be able to resist it. "Um, I guess we can go in the kitchen to talk…"

"Thank you." He shrugged out of his jacket but carried it with him down the short hallway to the table in her kitchen.

Rory hesitated as she saw him there, remembering the last time he'd been in her kitchen and how everything in her life had changed. She wasn't sure she was ready for another upheaval. As much as she wanted him in her life, she knew that she wanted him on her terms.

And she wasn't going to back down from them. She wanted Kit but he had to be honest. He had to be the man she thought he was.

Rory took another deep breath and realized that the panic she'd felt before she opened the door was gone. She was oddly calm. Squaring her shoulders, she sat down at the table, gesturing for him to sit across from her. "I know you have something to say but would you mind if I asked you something first?"

He shook his head. "Not at all."

"Were you in my room the day I woke from my coma?"

"Yes."

"Why?" she asked.

He leaned back in his chair and crossed his arms over his chest and then let them drop to his sides. "I came to talk to you. When I heard you were in a coma all these years and learned about the curse, I thought my actions were going to make a change. I told you that I was going to break the hold the Gilberts had on GC. But mostly I just talked to you about that first summer we met and how your kindness was the reason I wanted GC to be prosperous again. Your kindness had helped me all those years ago, and I wanted to pay it forward."

SEVENTEEN

KIT WAS GLAD that he could finally tell Rory about being in her room the day she woke from her coma. He hadn't planned to stop by to see her but in a way he'd felt that she'd been another victim of Dash's. And he'd wanted her to know he was taking care of her brother for her.

He now knew different.

"Why didn't you say something sooner?" she asked after a few minutes.

It was hard for him to defend why he'd kept silent. Probably because his main focus had been on the big lie he was keeping. That he didn't trust her brother. That he wasn't sure how he could move forward with his plan and keep her safe. That once he realized the man who hurt her was his brother, he didn't want to make things worse.

"How could I? I had planned to keep my distance from you, but—"

"I came up to you and said just go along with me," she said. She put her arms on the table and leaned forward.

He couldn't help but remember his surprise in that moment. He still didn't know if it had been fate or luck or what. But whatever it had been was what he'd needed. It was almost as if everything had happened the way it had for a reason.

So he could find out the truth about their families' complex history and find a way to bring some closure to both of them.

He laced his hands together in his lap to keep from reaching out and touching her. He couldn't help it. It felt like it had been a lifetime since he'd held her. He missed her. So damn much. And seeing her now, she seemed tired but she also looked strong and healthy. He was proud of how much she'd changed since she'd moved into her home here.

"Yes. And then everything I had planned went out the window," he admitted a bit sheepishly.

"What was your plan exactly?" she asked.

"Well, funny you should ask. It was sort of a make Gilbert Corners awesome and then say 'see, Dash Gilbert, we don't need you.'"

She shook her head and smiled. He felt a *zing* all the way to his groin. She had the best smile.

"Great revenge plan, *not*," she deadpanned. "I can understand why you wanted to get back at Dash and Gilbert International, so of course you couldn't tell me who you really were. But I'm struggling to be okay with the fact that you lied to me."

He reached for her hands then, taking them in his. "I'm sorry I did. I didn't know how to tell you who I was, and that was before I knew that Dec had hurt you. I can't forgive him for that. I don't know how you could ever accept me into your life knowing he's my brother."

She turned her hands under his and pulled them back, and the hope that had been growing in his heart stuttered to a stop. But of course he'd respect her wishes. He might have to spend the rest of his life in unrequited love with her but he wasn't going to be the second Orr man to take something from her that she didn't want to give.

"When I look at you, Kit, I see a man who is so different from Declan. That night is such a foggy memory that it doesn't have the power to hurt me. You are more real to me. I've never felt threatened by you. I've always felt safe," she admitted.

"I'm so glad to hear that. Can you ever forgive me for lying?" he asked.

She just looked over at him with her eyes wide and serious. He didn't know if words would be enough to convince her to believe him.

Kit got up and came around to her side of the table, dropping down on his knees next to her chair and taking her hands into his. He had always been afraid to admit how he felt, afraid to be vulnerable in a way that emotions always made him feel.

"I love you, Rory Gilbert, with my entire being. I know that it's going to take time for you to learn to trust me again. But I will do whatever I need to in order to make that happen."

She turned toward him but he stayed where he was. He needed her to hear this. He needed to tell her everything that was on his heart and mind.

"You might have asked me to help you take risks and learn to live again. But the truth is you were the one who taught me about living.

You made me let go of the past and start to see myself—and the world— in a new light."

"Kit..."

She put her hands on his face and brought her mouth down to his. Her kiss was soft and tentative at first and he let her set the tone, but she tasted so good and he wanted her. With every cell in his body. He wanted her love, her happiness and her forgiveness.

He wanted this woman in his arms and in his life.

When she lifted her head, he waited for the rush of lust to pass so he could talk.

"I don't know if you can love me, but I am willing to wait as long as it takes until you do."

Kit stood up and looked down at her. He remembered the first time he'd taken her for a walk in the rain around her backyard. The first time he'd kissed her. His life had changed in that moment. He hadn't realized it then, because he had been too focused on trying to figure out how to keep Rory safe while bringing down Dash.

He should have known that there was no way he could hurt anyone she cared about. No way he could tear apart anything that mattered to her. She was the only thing that mattered to him. Her love and her happiness. He had to find a way to convince her of that.

She licked her lips and then stood up next to him. His heart was beating so loudly it was a pounding in his ears.

There was no doubting Kit's sincerity. She just had to trust herself to accept him. To say yes to this. And it felt riskier than anything else she'd ever done. He loved her. That almost made her more afraid.

He loved her.

She had to repeat it to herself because it was so hard to believe that he'd said the words. And how they made her feel. She stopped thinking about all of the bad energy that had been surrounding her family, and Kit's, since the night of the winter gala and the accident.

She stopped thinking about the fact that everyone thought there was a curse on her family and this town; and that the last person who anyone would have expected to break it were outsiders. But they had. Indy, Elle and now Kit had all done their part to bring love back into the lives of herself, Conrad and Dash. She knew that without love there could be no change.

Not for herself and not for Kit.

He'd dedicated his life to avenging his brother and father and when he'd realized he had the wrong idea, he'd changed. He'd started to question those long-held beliefs and he'd fallen in love with her.

But he was watching her and she remembered how she'd felt when she'd first learned he'd lied about who he was and why he'd come into her life. And as much as she'd wanted to lean into being angry and hurt and let that dominate her, she couldn't. Because she loved this man more than she'd known she could love another person.

"Rory?"

"Kit."

"Woman, you're *killing* me here. Did what I said mean anything to you?"

She put her hands on his face. She just liked touching him and holding him. "It meant everything."

She took a deep breath and leaned her forehead against his. "I love you, too."

The words, once they were said, weren't as scary as she'd thought they would be. "I'm not sure how we move forward from here. But I want to."

Kit lifted her off her feet and spun her around

in his arms. She wrapped her legs around his waist, holding him tightly but letting her head fall back as she laughed. Love was flowing through her body, joy washing over her and making it impossible not to smile and laugh.

"We can figure it all out. As long as we love each other."

He set her down carefully. "When I came to Gilbert Corners... I'm not going to lie—I had a lot of hate in my heart for your family and this town."

"I get it," she said. "Dash won't admit it but I think he felt the same way. Con definitely hated GC and he avoided it as much as he could."

"What about you?" he asked softly. "I never really asked how you feel about the town and everyone thinking your family was cursed."

"I was sleeping, wasn't I? So I didn't really know about the curse or the town. I think because I missed all of that and am here now, experiencing the rebirth of Gilbert Corners and my new family... Well, I like it here," she said. "I think that's because of you."

"Me?"

"Yes, from my first day here on my own, you were there with a smile and stories and a helping hand, even though I was a stranger."

"But you weren't," he said. "You were that sweet girl who smiled at me that long-ago summer day."

He put his arms around her, holding her close to him. This felt so good. So right. She leaned her head on his shoulder and found tears burning the backs of her eyes. She hadn't been sure she'd ever be in his arms again. And loving him the way she did, it hurt to think that she might have missed out on Kit.

"I missed you," she said quietly.

"I missed you, too," he admitted. "I thought about all the reasons you wouldn't want me back—and there were a lot. I thought about how I had used Dash's actions to rationalize trying to take him down. You'd be justified to do the same."

"I don't know if I'd agree to *justified*," she said, looking up at him and smiling.

"Well, I would. I treated you poorly—"

She put her fingers over his lips. "You never treated me poorly. I have spent a lot of time thinking about our relationship to date and I realized that other than not telling me you were Declan's brother, you were honest about everything else."

"I tried," he said. "Legally I did change my name, so that wasn't a lie."

"I'm glad. No more lies."

"No more lies," he agreed.

He lifted her into his arms once again, carrying her to the bedroom where he made love to her. Then he held her in his arms as they cuddled close and made plans for their future. And Rory realized that, like herself, Kit had been trapped for the last ten years in an almost choking vine of brambles. His life had been pushed down a path he hadn't chosen. But he'd made that path his own.

He'd woken her with a kiss in the hospital, but… "I rescued you."

"You did?"

"Yes. You were trapped behind the walls of half-truths and bitterness and you were doing your best to live your life. But then I came along and shook those walls and they started to crumble and made you look at the Gilberts and Gilbert Corners differently."

He rolled her underneath him, his mouth on hers, kissing her so deeply she almost forgot what she was saying. She was consumed by the feel of Kit's body against her. And she had to be grateful for her own body. The limbs that had been so weak not that long ago were now strong enough to wrap around him and hold him to her.

"You did rescue me by falling in love with me," he said. "I love you, Rory."

"I love you, too, Kit."

★ ★ ★ ★ ★

Mills & Boon says farewell to Desire...

Thank you, dear readers, for coming back to Desire month after month. Sadly, November 2023 will see the final release of Desire titles.

There are still many great reads released by Mills & Boon each month!

If you're after sinfully seductive heroes and exotic locations, check out the **Modern** series.

Or for heart-racing suspense, adventure and romance, **Romantic Suspense** is for you.

Medical will transport you to the world of medical professionals, where emotions run high and passion and love are the best medicine.

There's something for everyone!
Details of all Mills & Boon series can be found on **millsandboon.com.au**.

MODERN   INTRIGUE

Romantic Suspense   MEDICAL

HISTORICAL   WESTERN

Keep reading for an excerpt of a new title
from the Modern series,
THE CONVENIENT COSENTINO WIFE by Jane Porter

PROLOGUE

THE FUNERAL WAS held the same weekend the wedding had been supposed to take place, although Rocco scheduled the private burial service for the day after the wedding, so as not to draw too many comparisons.

The funeral was very small as Rocco Cosentino wasn't interested in a drama-filled service for Marius, his younger brother, and only member of his family. Marius had been everything. His world, his responsibility, his hopes, his dreams. But then daring, fun-loving, big-hearted Marius died after being thrown from a horse, doing what Marius loved—and knew—best. Polo had been Marius's passion, and so Rocco grieved, but it was his private grief, and he refused to have others there to witness his pain and loss. He'd raised his brother since Marius was six, and now Marius was gone.

Unfathomable. The aristocratic Cosentino

bloodline ended with Rocco then, as Rocco would never marry, not again.

Rocco had politely, but firmly, told all that it was a private funeral, only family would be in attendance. But Rocco couldn't refuse Clare Redmond's attendance as the twenty-four-year-old American had been Marius's fiancée.

If Marius hadn't broken his neck, Clare would have been Marius's wife by now.

One could say, if only Marius hadn't played that final match on Wednesday, Clare would have been his sister-in-law, but it was too late for that. Accidents happened, and a most tragic accident had happened, and Marius, the little boy who'd become a brilliant, generous man, was forever gone.

Rocco stood next to the young American woman who'd arrived for the service shrouded in black, head to toe, wearing even a veil as if she'd stepped from a Gothic novel. He couldn't see her face, but he didn't need to—he could hear her weeping during the brief service, making Rocco wish the service was over.

It was said that funerals were for the living, not the dead, but Rocco had attended far too many in his life, and never once had he been glad to be there. Never once, had he thought ah, thank goodness for this archaic service filled with prayers and scripture that mean nothing to me. He'd never found comfort in the priest's words, not when he'd stood in the family plot for his father's funeral, his mother's funeral, his young bride's funeral, and now his brother's funeral.

The fact that he was the last of the Cosentino line meant nothing to him. He viewed his family as cursed, which in of itself was problematic, so perhaps it was a good thing there were no more of them. He was the last, and he would remain the last, and there would be no more to grieve. No more funerals to attend. No more good people to be missed. No more guilt for being the sole survivor.

Once today was over, he'd shut the Cosentino ancestral home, sell off Marius's Argentinean estates and move to one of his smaller estates, far from Rome. Far from everyone. He was done with death, done with grief, done with caring for anyone.

Clare had cried so much the past few days she didn't think she could shed another tear, but somehow during the service, listening to the lovely eulogy for her beloved Marius, the tears started again. Tears because Marius was truly one of the best people she'd ever known— strong, kind, honest, loving. She never knew how he'd grown up to be just so loving when he'd been raised by his stern older brother, who she found nothing short of cold and disapproving, but Marius always defended Rocco, saying Rocco might not appear affectionate, but he was fiercely proud and protective of him, and would die for him if need be.

Those words, *die for him*, came to her now, and Clare cried fresh tears because it would have been better if Rocco had died and not Marius. Marius was so full of light and love whereas Rocco barely interacted with the world, living like a hermit in his monstrously big house, a house he'd inherited as a sixteen-year-old when his parents died just weeks apart from an infectious disease they'd picked up on their travels. Clare hated visiting the big dark house, but Marius would drag her there every six months for either Christmas or New Year's, and then again late July for big brother Rocco's birthday.

Rocco was never friendly on those occasions, barely speaking two words to her. When Marius proposed, her first thought was yes, yes, because she loved him desperately, but later, when she'd gone to bed that night, her new ring so wonderful and strange on her finger, it crossed her mind that now Rocco would be her family, too.

And that thought hadn't been pleasant.

In fact, that thought had kept her awake far too late.

Now she stood next to the man who'd never be her brother waiting for the service to conclude. She would be leaving as soon as they returned to the house. She had a car already arranged to pick her up and take her back to the airport. No point remaining in Rome longer than necessary. It's not as if she was wanted or needed here. Rocco didn't need comforting, at least not from her. Marius didn't have a will. The estate in Spain was all in his name. There was nothing else to be done but for her to return home and figure out how to continue without her heart, as that had been buried with Marius.

From where Rocco stood in the drawing room he could see outside to the manicured circular drive where a big black Mercedes waited for Clare.

He admired the young woman's foresight, appreciating her desire to not prolong today's events. Any mourning Rocco would do, he'd do in private. He suspected Clare felt the same.

"I see your car has arrived," he said, hands clasped behind his back.

She still wore that heavy black lace veil, but he could see the haunting lavender blue of her eyes as she looked at him. "Yes." She hadn't sat down, either. The two of them were standing still in the formal room. "I hate to leave you like this—"

"But you don't," he said, cutting her short, raw pain in his deep, gravelly voice. "We're not close. We have no desire to grieve together."

She lifted her head, and again he could see that lavender of her eyes beneath the lace. "Will you grieve for him?"

"He is all I had left." The moment the words left his mouth, Rocco felt foolish. Exposed. It was easier if others believed he didn't care or feel. Easier to let strangers believe he was as hard as he appeared. He gestured toward the tall ornate doors. "I have no wish to keep you. You mustn't miss your flight."

Her head inclined, once, and then she folded the lace veil back, exposing her golden hair and her pale face with the deep violet shadows beneath her unusual lavender eyes. "I probably won't see you again," she said, "but maybe it will help for you to know just how much Marius loved you. He said you were the best brother, father and mother a boy could have." Then she dropped the veil and giving him another faint nod, walked out of the house to the car.

That should have been the last time Rocco saw her. In any other situation it would have been, because he had no desire to be reminded of Marius, or the others he'd lost, but when the envelope finally reached him, catching up to him in Argentina where he was supervising a harvest on his late brother's estate in Mendoza, Rocco had set it aside, and then it had been covered by other papers and mail, and when he went to open it, the envelope had gone missing. He'd searched everywhere and then feared it had been thrown out. Instead it had simply been misplaced, gathered with an expense report and filed for end of the year taxes.

When he'd finally discovered the envelope amongst his tax paperwork, eleven months had passed. Opening the envelope Rocco discovered he wasn't the last of his family.

Beautiful American Clare Redmond had delivered a healthy baby boy two years ago.

Subscribe and fall in love with a Mills & Boon series today!

You'll be among the first to read stories delivered to your door monthly and enjoy great savings.

WE SIMPLY LOVE ROMANCE